THE CITY

C000231489

"*The City Revealed* is an a
imagined world. A lovin
characters struggle both personally and politically with the
consequences of their own and others' actions, and strive
for cooperation without sacrificing principles. A
thoroughly satisfying read."

Una McCormack
New York Times bestselling science fiction author

"Eminently satisfying epic fantasy where the personal, the
political and the magical are multilayered and interlocked."
Juliet E. McKenna
Author of the *Green Man* series and the *Tales of Einarinn* series

THE
CITY
REVEALED

BOOK 4 OF THE MAREK SERIES

ALSO BY JULIET KEMP

☺ ☺

THE DEEP AND SHINING DARK
"A rich and memorable tale of political ambition, family and
magic, set in an imagined city that feels as vibrant as the
characters inhabiting it."   **Aliette de Bodard**
Nebula-award winning author of
The Tea Master and the Detective

"Juliet Kemp's *The Deep And Shining Dark* (Elsewhen) was one of
the best debuts of the year, set in a chewy and thought-provoking
secondary world that one hopes to see more of."   **Graham Sleight**
Locus

"*The Deep and Shining Dark* is a fast, fun romp of a book, diverse,
queer, and deeply entertaining. I'm looking forward to Kemp's
next work already."   **Liz Bourke**
Tor.com

SHADOW AND STORM
"*Shadow and Storm* is an absolute delight to read, the literary
equivalent of sinking into the embrace of a dear friend. Warm and
cosy but never short on adventure and intrigue, Kemp's second
entry into this series won't disappoint. The characters are real, full
of depth, and richly drawn, and you'll wish you had even more
time with them by book's end. A fantastic read!"   **Rivers Solomon**
author of *An Unkindness of Ghosts,*
Lambda, Tiptree and Locus finalist

THE RISING FLOOD
"Fantasy politics with real nuance and believable uncertainty,
characters whose richness and depth has developed over three
books, and a growing threat that starts pulling together threads
across the series make *The Rising Flood* a fantastic read, while
Marek is a textured place that is a joy to return to."   **Malka Older**
author of the *Centenal Cycle* trilogy
Hugo Award finalist

JULIET KEMP

THE
CITY
REVEALED

BOOK 4 OF THE MAREK SERIES

Elsewhen Press

The City Revealed
First published in Great Britain by Elsewhen Press, 2023
An imprint of Alnpete Limited

Elsewhen Press, PO Box 757, Dartford, Kent DA2 7TQ
www.elsewhen.press

British Library Cataloguing in Publication Data.
A catalogue record for this book is available from the British Library.

ISBN 978-1-915304-21-6 Print edition
ISBN 978-1-915304-31-5 eBook edition

Designed and formatted by Elsewhen Press

For my parents

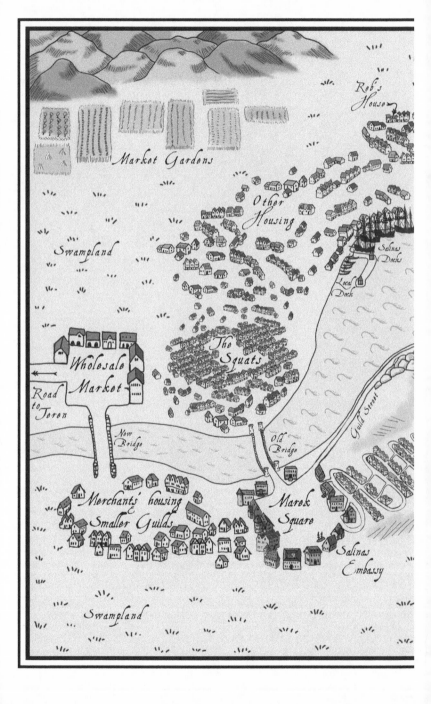

Housing
e Shops

Swamp
Fishers'
Village

Tanneries

Old
Market

Oval
Sea

Ferry

Cliff

Cliff path

Statues of
Beckett & Marek

The
Council
Chamber

Marekhill

Goat
Herders' Village

Marek

© Juliet Kemp and Alison Buck, 2018

ONE

This was, Marcia was glumly certain, a horrible idea; but it was necessary. Or at least, she couldn't think of any less-horrible ideas, and she couldn't just not do anything, so...

She'd put it off more than long enough already. It was a good couple of weeks since she'd been acquitted and she and Reb had got back together. It was the start of Dein now – the sun outside the window had broken briefly through the clouds that had been raining over the city all day, but it was winter-low, and she was grateful for the big ceramic stove in the corner of the room – and the baby would be here in another two months. It was definitely time.

Reb, at the other end of the couch, was shifting awkwardly, glancing around House Fereno's smaller reception room and running a thumb over the grey-on-blue embroidery on the upholstery. Reb had visited more than once in the last couple of weeks, now their relationship could be more public, but she still wasn't entirely comfortable here.

She looked over at Marcia, eyebrows pulled together, and Marcia made herself smile at her girlfriend. "It'll be fine," Reb said, leaning in to grasp Marcia's arm reassuringly, although her tone wasn't entirely convincing. Or, perhaps, entirely convinced. "You like him, so I'm sure I'll like him, and in any case, we're both reasonable adults who can be polite to one another."

Which would be plenty good enough, between Marcia's girlfriend and her friend-and-occasional-lover – not that *that* had happened lately between her and Andreas – if it weren't for the fact that in the near future Andreas and she would be co-parents. Reb wouldn't be parenting that baby, but she was going to be *around* –

Marcia most strenuously hoped – for a while, and Marcia didn't want Reb to be in her life but never allowed around the baby. Which, by the child-contract she'd signed, meant Andreas had to agree. It wasn't that he was unreasonable, not at all. But Reb was a sorcerer.

And they couldn't even avoid that topic today, because the other purpose of this meeting was for Andreas to get a clearer idea of Marek sorcery, in pursuit of Marcia's plan to reduce the distance between Council and sorcerers. A plan which Andreas was…only halfway on board with, at most. And if she'd got moving a little faster with introducing Reb and Andreas, maybe they wouldn't have to be doing everything at once, but there was no point wishing after time gone in the river.

The door opened, and a footman ushered Andreas in. He crossed the room, smiling, towards Reb and Marcia. He wore a half-formal House tunic over loose trousers, his short dark curls neatly oiled, and Marcia allowed herself a moment of aesthetic appreciation. She'd been somewhat annoyed with him immediately after her trial and the whole business of Marek's independence – in part that he hadn't told her what he and Daril were planning, in part that the timing undercut what she'd been trying to do about the Council and magic – but she was mostly over it now. And he *had* agreed to come along today.

"Don't stand up, Marcia, you're fine there," he said, then turned to Reb, already on her feet. He offered her a formal bow, which Reb returned after a visibly startled pause. She'd dressed semi-formally for the occasion too, in a dark grey over-tunic and leggings. She glanced over to Marcia, and Marcia's heart twinged as she met Reb's dark eyes and saw the swift affectionate crinkles around them.

"This is the sorcerer Ser Reb, of the Marek Group," Marcia said, entirely unnecessarily, but she ought to go through the formal motions, oughtn't she? She wished she'd stood after all; looking up at the two of them felt awkward. Though they'd both overtop her even if she were standing; Reb was nearly as tall as Andreas. "Reb, this is Andreas, Tigero-Head."

"A pleasure," Andreas said.

"Likewise."

Andreas was doing a better job of looking genuinely pleased with the situation than Reb was – he was, after all, Head of a Marek House – but his slightly too-frequent blinks and the way his gaze darted towards Marcia suggested he wasn't as sure as he looked. He and Reb both sat – Reb on the couch by Marcia, Andreas in the chair at right-angles to them – and there was an awkward moment of silence.

"Infusion? Spicecake?" Marcia offered, to break it, and the flurry of cups and plates that followed did help.

"I hope the weather wasn't too unpleasant for you, coming over here," Andreas said to Reb, once he was settled with cup and plate.

"Oh, it's been worse," she said, with a shrug. "Has it come off again, then? You look dry."

"Ah, well, I took a litter," Andreas said comfortably. "Unlike Marcia here I don't think it's bad for the moral fibre or whatever."

"It's not that," Marcia protested. "I just…prefer to be under my own power." She pulled a comical face. "Despite Mother's best efforts to convince me otherwise."

"I am ever impressed by your abilities to stand against your mother," Andreas said with sincerity. "She scares the life out of me."

"Must be awkward, being a Head alongside her," Reb observed. Though Andreas was far from the only Head who was unnerved by Madeleine on the rampage.

"Well, yes, quite," Andreas said, and hesitated. "I wasn't supposed to be Head," he said, almost apologetically. "There was – well, it's a long story, but my sister wasn't cowed at all by Fereno-Head, let's put it that way."

Marcia remembered Andreas' older sister being tough as nails. "You're not so bothered any more, though," she said. "I mean, I accept you're alarmed by her – aren't we all – but you wouldn't know it from the way I've seen you tackle her in Council." Something which hadn't happened lately, because Madeleine was *still* in Teren, and Marcia was beginning to get nervous about it. Her decision to visit the Archion's court in Ameten had sounded like a terrible idea to Marcia even before Marek declared independence, but by the time Marcia'd heard about it, it had been too late to stop her. Madeleine had sent a brief note announcing her arrival in Ameten and giving her direction for correspondence – she was staying with her friend Grainne – and Marcia had replied to let her know about the independence vote. It was probably too soon to expect to have heard back. Marcia resisted the urge to count courier-days on her fingers again.

"Well, if I'm doing this after all, I would hope I'm getting better at it," Andreas said, and Marcia pulled her attention back to the room. There was no point in worrying about Madeleine. Madeleine would do exactly what she wanted. And worrying about what Madeleine would think of this particular discussion – or of Marcia's now-public relationship with Reb – could wait too. She'd missed that out of her message; though she had a nasty feeling more than one of Madeleine's other correspondents would have been only too keen to update her. Madeleine had promised to be back before the baby's birth; soon enough to discuss it all (argue about it) with her then.

"The only sensible attitude." Reb nodded approvingly at Andreas. Well, that was positive.

There was another pause. "Since we're talking of the Council and the responsibilities of a Head," Marcia said into the silence, "– did you want to hear about magic, Andreas?" Hardly the smoothest transition, but it *was* part of why they were here.

Andreas twitched, visibly nervous again, then nodded with determination. "Yes. Ser Reb, I would be honoured if you would help inform my ignorance."

Marcia listened quietly, sipping her infusion, as Reb

explained about Beckett, the cityangel, who made Marek's magic different from anywhere else; the Group which ran Marek's magic, although Marcia noticed that she was cagey about the exact number of sorcerers (two, plus apprentices, and the other full sorcerer Marcia's infamous brother Cato); and the covenant between the sorcerers and the cityangel.

"So Beckett *cannot*, by their covenant, intervene in politics," Reb concluded.

"Not directly," Andreas said, eyes narrowed. "But there are a number of ways of affecting *people* by magic which might not fall under that interdict, no?"

"True," Reb agreed.

True indeed, and Marcia had caught Dyesha Pedeli-Heir at it not three weeks ago – breaching the Council's rules, if not Beckett's agreement – but she'd made a deal to keep that quiet.

"Your brother, Marcia? Is he part of this Group?" Andreas looked over at her.

"At present," Marcia said. "It's not entirely his kind of thing," a gross understatement, "so I'm not sure how long he'll last." Exactly until one of the apprentices could take his place, was her guess, and possibly not that long if he and Reb seriously fell out again.

Andreas was scratching thoughtfully at his jaw. "Thank you," he said. "I see your point, Marcia, about having a perspective that's missing from the Council, but –"

"We don't want to be part of the Council," Reb said, right on his heels. "Even if it were permissable within the covenant –"

"Which I don't see why it wouldn't be as long as you weren't doing magic actually in Council meetings," Marcia interjected.

"*Even if*," Reb repeated, giving her a look that was perilously close to a glare, "we still don't want it. Too unbalanced."

"But you could advise," Marcia said.

"Perhaps," Reb allowed. "We'd have to discuss it."

"Seems you're more enthusiastic about this than the

sorcerers are, Marcia." Marcia couldn't quite read Andreas' tone, or his glance between her and Reb.

"I want the Council to think more about people other than the ones sitting in that room or related to them," Marcia said. She could hear the tartness in her voice. "And surely *now*, while we are still discovering what our independence will look like, is the time to look at what the Council can and should be." Another reason she hadn't wanted to put this conversation off any longer. Getting Reb to talk to Andreas privately was a necessary first step before getting Reb to talk to the Council more formally.

"You don't need me standing there in your Chamber to get the sorcerers' perspective," Reb said. She sat back and folded her arms. They'd had this conversation before. "We can write you a letter. Or *you* can listen to me, and then tell your Council about it."

"I'm not all that keen to be the Council's go-to person for magic," Marcia said. "I've gone far enough down that road already for my reputation. And I can't answer the questions you can."

"It would give rise to still more questions if you could," Andreas said, with a half-smile. "But Marcia, Ser Reb is right – there is no need for her to be there in person, if she does not wish to be. And that surely has less risk of breaching the agreement with the, uh, cityangel, too."

"*Thank* you." Reb nodded to Andreas.

"But the idea of a liaison is a good one," he went on. "A link between your Group, Ser Reb, and the Council."

"Just Reb is fine," Reb said, waving a hand, and Marcia cheered up; even if Reb wasn't going to budge – yet – on speaking to the Council, at least she and Andreas seemed to be getting on. "What do you have in mind, then, as a link? Marcia's right, it shouldn't only be her."

"And it is perhaps unwise just myself and her, as well, given the connection between our Houses. But Daril – Leandra-Head," he added in an aside to Reb, "is open to magic, as well."

Reb's mouth tightened – she knew perfectly well who

Daril was – but Marcia didn't think Andreas noticed. Daril's previous history with magic was something else she'd made a deal not to publicise. And Andreas was right, Daril was a good choice in other ways.

"Given the known tension between Fereno and Leandra, it would avoid any accusations of one-sidedness," she agreed. Andreas liked Daril, for reasons which escaped her. He could act as buffer.

"If Ser Reb is willing?" Andreas asked. Maybe he had noticed Reb's reaction after all.

"A small group, acting as informal liaison between the sorcerers and the Council, as necessary." Reb sat back. "I suppose that could work. And I am willing to work with Leandra, yes." *If I must*, her tone said. Well, Reb could cope, if Marcia could – and with a bit of luck, perhaps facing Reb might make Daril uncomfortable too. Though sadly she feared it would not; Daril was hard to discomfit.

"It won't hit the spot for everyone, of course," Andreas admitted. "There's a couple that wouldn't believe magic exists even if they had a spirit stood in front of them."

Andreas himself had only just accepted it, but it would be impolite, not to mention impolitic, to mention that. "The ones who don't think it's true in Teren, who don't think sea-spirits are real," Marcia agreed. "But most people reluctantly accept the other plane exists, and even that spirits enter this plane sometimes. They just don't think that it happens here."

"That's not very coherent," Reb rolled her eyes.

"No. Indeed not. And yet that's how they think." Marcia shrugged. "Can't be helped. I think the Council as a whole will – well, be willing to listen, at least. All I want is to start to bridge the gap. We needn't do everything at once."

"Which is just as well," Andreas said, "because I suspect it'll take a fair while." He shrugged. "And at that, if you're worried about the Council hearing from people not inside the Chamber, I'm not sure it's the sorcerers that are the most urgent. Daril says…"

"Daril's gone all radical," Marcia said. And didn't she want to know what he thought he was playing at? "Didn't think you were following him."

Andreas tipped his head slowly from side to side. "Well. I'll accept that the pair of you are right – there's a huge part of the city we don't hear from."

Listen to, more like it. "If the Council can swallow sorcerers, they'll cope a lot easier with unGuilded messengers and all," Marcia said.

"Or they'll balk at the sorcerers and not cope with anything," Andreas said, then stopped himself and turned to Reb. "Forgive me, Ser Reb. I'm sure this part of the argument is of little interest to you."

"I'm not particularly in touch with politics," Reb said, which wasn't entirely true, though Marcia knew she wished it were.

"Very wise," Andreas said with a laugh. He took a breath. "Well. A discussion for another occasion. I did want, while we're all here," he gestured around the three of them, "to talk about the baby, and the parenting-contract."

"Right." Reb eyed him cautiously.

"Go on," Marcia said, stomach lurching. This conversation had to happen, but that didn't mean she actually, well, wanted to have it.

Andreas put his cup down with a clink against its saucer. "I'm sure you know, Ser Reb, that Marcia and I have spoken a little about this already."

They had, immediately after Reb and Marcia had got back together. Andreas had leant forwards and said to her, '*Our friendship, and the parenting relationship that we're about to enter into, those are the important things. We said that at the start, and its still true. You don't owe me anything'.* It was a good memory, a warm one. They'd agreed to leave the matter of their own physical relationship until after the baby arrived – and this meeting hadn't only been Marcia's idea, though Andreas had left it to her to arrange; Andreas had wanted to meet Reb.

"I wouldn't dream of standing in the way of your relationship," Andreas went on, with evident sincerity. Marcia's heart warmed, looking at his earnest face, eyes on Reb. He was a good person. "And I understand the limitations of parenting a small baby, and I understand, Marcia," he turned to her, "that you don't want to keep secret an important person in your life."

"The baby might not notice," Marcia said. "An older child will."

"My only concern isn't Ser Reb, or your relationship. It's –" a pause, "– the magic."

"Reb's not going to do magic in front of a child," Marcia scoffed.

"Not a Marekhill child, no," Reb agreed, with a note of irony.

"Well," Andreas said, "that's all I would like to stipulate. Not that the child not *know* Ser Reb to be a sorcerer – after all, I assume that your brother will also be known to the child, and known as a sorcerer – but that magic not happen in front of them."

"That's it?" Marcia said.

Andreas shrugged. "That's it. Well. I wish no offence to you, Ser Reb, but I would not be willing to write you into the parenting contract. But as I understand it you have no wish to be so written in."

"No," Reb agreed promptly. "I've no desire to parent. Never have had."

"But you don't mind being around a child?" Marcia asked, again. Another conversation they'd had already.

"No. As long as I'm not responsible for their wellbeing, I've nothing against children."

"I'm glad we're all so easily agreed," Andreas said. "Ser Reb. I look forward to further making your acquaintance, over time." He was on his feet, bowing himself out – it seemed abrupt, but then again, they'd done all they meant to, hadn't they?

"Well," Reb said, once the door had shut behind him. "That went well, I thought?"

"Thank you," Marcia breathed, and fell into her arms. It

9

had indeed gone well. Much better than she'd feared.

"About magic, in front of your child, though," Reb said, sounding hesitant. Marcia could feel Reb's warm breath on the side of her neck.

"Yes?" Surely Reb had meant what she'd said?

"In the birth. I know, I offered before, and you said no. But there are things, that I would do for anyone in labour. Charms, for comfort and safety, and…"

"No," Marcia said, firmly. Though not without an internal pang of regret. It wasn't a phase of this whole thing she was looking forward to. "I won't risk it. If anyone thought my child was born around magic, they could lose their birthright."

"It could be very subtle. Hidden," Reb said. She looked, when Marcia twisted backwards slightly to see her face properly, even more uncomfortable. "It sits badly with me, not helping when I could."

"And it's absurd for Marekhill births to be riskier than lower city ones?"

"Not that the cityangel's help is always enough," Reb said, soberly.

Marcia pressed Reb's hand, then leant upwards to brush a kiss over her lips. "I understand. And thank you. But no. I can't risk it. Even something hidden. I need to be able to swear honestly that I am not benefitting from magic."

Maybe by the time she was bearing the second child of her contract, it might be different. But for now, much though she would have *liked* to accept Reb's assistance, she couldn't.

☺ ☺

Alyssa sat on the edge of a table in the Bucket, stick propped against her leg, and unclenched her teeth for the third time. The room was full, more than full, warm with crowded bodies, and the meeting had been due to start some time ago. Delays always aggravated her – couldn't people just get *on* with it – but tonight even more than usual. Her neighbour, Thea, could only mind Jina for a couple of hours, and Alyssa *needed* to be here tonight.

The Council weren't listening to the lower city; they weren't running Marek for everyone's benefit, but for their own. That at least was something everyone here agreed on: that things had to change. *How* they should change, and how to achieve that; well, that was what all the arguing was about. The Petitioners were too weak, asking for too little, and Alyssa was fully prepared to keep pointing that out for as long as it took to persuade them that creating their own Parliament of Marek, ignoring the Council altogether, was the correct way forwards.

Except. Except that the declaration of independence, a few weeks back now, changed things. This was a moment of change, of shift, throughout the city. They had to grasp it *now*. They couldn't just let it slip through their fingers, the way it would if they kept on with the arguing and debating that had been going on even more fiercely than before over the last weeks. Petitioners, Parliamentarians, anyone in the middle, they had to find some kind of unity, so that they could act together to put their demands to the Council as the Council rebuilt Marek. Before that rebuilding was settled as 'exactly what we had before but without the pretence that Teren had anything to do with it'.

That was the purpose of this meeting, which had made it especially aggravating when Alyssa had arrived to discover that Tey, one of the only meeting facilitators acceptable to everyone, had broken his wretched leg this afternoon and was laid up at home. At this point, even a facilitator who half the room perceived to be biased would be better than *no* facilitator; but no one else wanted to give up the opportunity to speak today. Not even Jeres, de facto leader of the Petitioners. Alyssa disagreed with her on a great number of things, but Jeres was almost always ready to pitch in wherever it was needed to make things happen. Not today.

Mind you, Alyssa herself was equally unwilling to

11

facilitate on this occasion. She had *plenty* of things to say.

Jeres, up at the front of the room, was speaking to Radec, one of the other prominent Petitioners. His mouth was crimped at the edges as he listened to her, and after a moment he made an irritated gesture, and stepped forward.

"In the absence of Tey," he called out, and the clamour dropped a little, "how about I facilitate?"

"Well, it's not like we're getting anywhere without," Alyssa said loudly, and there was a murmur of assent.

"Right. Settle down, settle down." He waited until the room was as close to settled as it was going to get. "So. The point we can all agree on – have all agreed on – is that this moment – this declaration of independence, while things are changing – is a great opportunity to put our case to the upper city."

"Whose case?" Simeon, sitting next to Dyson, called out.

Radec rolled his eyes slightly. Tey wouldn't have done that. "Indeed, Simeon. The aim of this meeting, our sole agenda item, is to discuss, between *all* of us, how we are to act together in order to best take advantage of this moment. What we are to do, and what we are to demand."

Together was exactly the problem. The Petition – which broadly speaking just asked politely for the Council to think a bit more about the lower city, as if *that* would magically fix things – didn't go anything like far enough for the Parliamentarians to settle for it; and Alyssa couldn't see that the Petitioners would be willing to support any actions that her own Parliamentarian group – or groups; the Parliamentarians were not exactly a cohesive entity, which was in Alyssa's own view one of their strengths – wanted to take. But. It was worth a try. Perhaps they could at least agree not to step on one another's toes.

Jeres raised her hand and Radec (of course) acknowledged her. "It's unfortunate that this is happening before I was able to fully put our arguments to the Guilds.

I still think we might be better to consider deferring any more dramatic actions until we have more support for the Petition."

"And how long will that take?" Alyssa demanded. Jeres glared at her. "You've been *talking* to the Guilds for months!"

The Petition was weak anyway, but even if it wasn't quite so toothless, she didn't share Jeres' belief that the Guilds would provide enough support to get it through the Council. Not to mention that the issue of unGuilded workers was one of the points on the Petition, and if the Guilds cared about unGuilded workers they'd have fixed the issues already. She didn't see how Jeres could truly believe that if she only found the right moment to 'fully' present it to them, that they would. Even if some of them did, the Guilds won against the Houses only if they voted as a block and there was no way that the more traditionalist Guildwarden Council members (Warden Hagadath most obviously) would ever go along with the Petition, however persuasive Jeres considered herself.

"We can't defer this!" someone across the room called out. Radec glared them to silence.

"But I accept this is a key moment," Jeres went on. "I propose that we plan for the New Year Council meeting. Between now and then, we further attempt to strengthen our case, and then present the Petition to the Council on that day. That is the meeting where they intend to discuss the changes to Marek's Statutes, to reflect our new independence. Clearly, that will be the most powerful moment to lay our requests before them."

Requests. That was Jeres' problem, right there, thinking in terms of *polite requests* from those who quite evidently weren't interested in this half – more than half – of the city.

"What the fuck makes you think they'll listen?" Simeon called out, voice disgusted. Simeon was even further along the Parliamentarian side than Alyssa, and she wasn't exactly moderate herself.

"That's exactly why I want us to gather support." Jeres

said. "That's why I think – why I still think – we should wait until the Guilds are behind us. To make it less likely they'll just ignore us. Push us aside."

"Then why *bother*," Alyssa muttered.

"But," Jeres spread her hands, "events have overtaken us. Those of you saying we must make our voices heard now are right too. I know many of you here feel the Petition doesn't go far enough. But we can all agree that it would be *better* than the present situation. Absent support from the Guilds, our strength is in a united front." She gestured around the room. "All of us, acting together. I will do my best to make sure there is someone to speak for us on the Council at New Year, but to make the most of this moment, we must be *united*."

Alyssa sucked at her teeth. Jeres wasn't wrong, at that. It just wasn't the Petition they should be uniting behind.

Across the room, a man with a dark beard who'd been sitting with Simeon, perhaps another of the radical writers Simeon printed, stood up as Radec nodded at him. "Your Petition is toothless. Pointless," he began angrily. "Even if the Council agreed to the whole thing, it provides only a handful of weak sops, to support the Council's unfair rule. The acceptance of the Petition – unlikely though it is in any case – would undermine any real progress. The only option, the option we *must* take, is to do away with the Council altogether. The Council ignores us; very well, let them sit across the river, talking away to themselves. While *we* ignore them, create our own meeting, run Marek ourselves. Jeres is right. This moment *is* crucial, and we need unity. This is indeed the perfect instant to create our own power. Let us seize Marek's new independence for ourselves – rather than rolling over and allowing it to be merely a matter of whether or not Teren has a hold over the privileged idiots over there."

Alyssa, broadly speaking, agreed with him, and some of the Council certainly were idiots; but she'd been forced recently to acknowledge that not all of them were. Marcia Fereno-Heir was ignorant, for certain, but not stupid. But there was no reason why they should be allowed to run the place without reference to the people they were running it over. As she'd explained herself to Marcia, and forcefully enough.

"Indeed, Jeres is right," she said, standing up herself at Radec's nod. Jeres made a comically shocked face, and laughter rippled round the room. "This is the moment for any formal changes to be made in the way Marek is set up. But as my friend over there says – why stop at the Petition? Why not demand more? Why not the People's Parliament?"

"Why bother to demand anything from the Council? Why beg for scraps when we can *take* our own power?" That was the bearded man again. She'd have to ask Simeon for his name.

"But what use is your People's Parliament if no one who has power pays it any mind?" That was one of the Petitioners, in tones of frustration.

"We seize the power! It belongs to us!" Simeon shouted.

From a magical perspective, as Alyssa now knew, there was a very real sense in which that was true. Beckett's power arose from everyone in Marek, via the compact they'd made with the city's founders, and one could argue that – whether or not the Council recognised it – Beckett was the real source of Marek's power as a city. But now wasn't the right time to have that discussion, that was for certain. And whilst Alyssa felt that fact *should* be usable for the revolution, she hadn't yet worked out *how*.

"Even if that is true, is this really the correct moment to go that far?" one of the Petitioners asked in excessively reasonable tones. "As Jeres says – we lack support. Yes, the Council is discussing Marek's underpinnings later this week, but we all know that in practice, very little of what Teren has been doing has affected the running of Marek in a great many years. Yes, we should put our views, ask for a place at the table. But why rush at this now, with talk of *seizing* and insisting, when we could do better if we go more softly, a step at a time?"

This was not, judging by the mutterings from around the room, a popular view.

Alyssa rolled her eyes. "If what you're saying is that the Council is unlikely to do anything, I couldn't agree more, which is why we would be much better off missing out the Petition and moving directly to a new form of government."

"As if you can just snap your fingers and bring that about," the Petitioner scoffed.

"As if your carefully-engraved pile of paper is going to bring anything about save the enrichment of the printers," Alyssa retorted.

"Hush!" Radec bawled. "I see a proposal in the corner."

Francis, a diffident person with strong ties to neither Parliamentarians nor Petitioners, stood up. "It seems to me," they began quietly, "that we can agree on our overall aim of reforming Marek – hence having these shared meetings. We disagree on the extent of the reform, yes. Just like today, we agree, most of us, on the value of this moment. But disagree on what to do with it. Need we decide? Why should we not, as separate groups, do both? The Petitioners present their petition, while a People's Parliament is conducted in the square. Does that not increase the pressure on the Council to institute change?" There were murmurs of approving agreement around the room.

"You want to use us to implement your penny-ante sniping around the edges," the bearded man said with dislike.

"Francis makes a good point," Alyssa said with force. It was better than just the Petition, and she wasn't about to let *good* wait on *best*, not if there was support for this solution. "And yes, the existence of the People's Parliament will increase pressure for the Council to do something about the Petition. But the reverse is just as true. When the Council does nothing about the Petition, it will give us more force behind the People's Parliament. I would – genuinely, as you all know – be delighted if the Council implemented the Petition. I just wouldn't stop there."

"Implement the Petition and no one will push for more," the bearded man grumbled.

"Then perhaps more would not be needed, if we truly then found we could not convince anyone of it," Alyssa said. "Isn't that the whole point? To do what the city wants? Alternatively, once the Petition is in place and not enough changes..." she spread her hands. "Maybe the good Jeres will be there in the square with us." Over the hubbub from that, she raised her own voice. "We have shared goals, all of us in this room. The Petition is good, just not enough. We should have, should *demand*, more. But if we've not yet convinced the Petitioners of that, very well. Let us all do what we can, rather than lose this moment in arguing. We're not one another's enemies. We're pulling in the same direction – so if we can't quite row in the same boat, we can use our separate boats to tow in the same direction."

The ensuing half-hour of debate only made the same points again in different words and in different voices; in the end, Francis' proposal was adopted, and Radec closed the meeting with a sigh of relief. Just in time for Alyssa to get home before Jina's bedtime. She nodded at people as she made her way through the room and out into the street, but didn't stop to talk; Jina would want a bedtime story. Alyssa had saved up for a new child-story from a stall in Printers Street for her New Year gift, but Jina loved best the stories out of Alyssa's head.

It wasn't *enough* – it was never *enough* – but it would at least mean that all the energies were put into reform, whatever 'reform' meant to each person and group, rather than into sniping at one another and putting the others down. It was a compromise, and much though Alyssa chafed at compromise, it would do.

For now.

☺ ☺

Andreas had fought hard to get the role of diplomatic negotiator with the Crescent Cities. It was past time that

17

he made a better name for himself than the dismissive 'the youngest Head'. Or, worse, 'a weathercock drifting with the wind'. Though that hadn't been entirely unfair for a while after he first became Head. He'd never expected to run the House; it was his sister Lani who'd been trained up for that, and Andreas had never envied her. He'd had other plans. When she died, he'd have fought harder against becoming Heir if his father hadn't been so distraught. Time enough to sort it out later, Andreas had thought, and then a bare few months after that his father died, and Andreas was thrown into the role of Head; barely trained, newly grieving his father and still missing Lani every time he turned around. He'd found it difficult to make decisions. He'd constantly second-guessed his own judgement, knowing all too sharply how little preparation or knowledge he had. His father had, after all, not scrupled to tell him as much during those few months. Andreas hadn't been the only one constantly missing Lani. His father had tried to hide it, but…well. Andreas could hardly blame him.

But he was settling in, now; had begun to stand up for himself and to have his own opinions, this last year or so. It was paying off. He was earning respect from the other Heads and Heirs. The alliance with Fereno had, overall, been good for both him and his House, despite Marcia's somewhat erratic reputation. (And he was very fond of Marcia; he couldn't regret the contract, or her friendship.) And now he'd been at Daril's right hand while they brought Marek out into the world on its own, out from under Teren's oppressive 'protection'. He was becoming a power in the Council. And powers in the Council got to take responsibility for important matters such as liaising with the ambassadors to renegotiate their treaties to recognise Marek's new independence.

"The critical point is," Daril told him, sipping an infusion in Andreas' study on the morning of Andreas' meeting with Berdian of the Crescent Cities, "to get them to recognise us as soon as possible. Without giving too much away, of course. Having Exuria and the Crescent on our side will undermine any Teren efforts to reclaim us."

"They can't, can they?" Andreas asked, startled, turning from the mirror where he was putting the final touches on his formal face paint.

Daril shrugged. "Depends if you think Selene is back home rounding up demons, like she halfway threatened."

"Surely not," Andreas scoffed. "She was… under pressure, in the Chamber. She was very polite in her parting speeches, you remember? Ongoing relationship and so on."

"And *that* can certainly cover a multitude of sins," Daril pointed out, leaning back in the armchair by the window, where Andreas did his reading. He propped one foot across his knee, showing off new boots of bright red tooled leather, matching the thong he'd plaited through his dark hair; Daril still got a fierce satisfaction from wearing things that would have irritated his recently-dead father.

Andreas bit at the inside of his lip. "But surely…I mean. It's one thing using them on, you know, protestors and the like." He nearly added, *if that's even true*. But as it happened he did believe the reports from Teren, more or less, and he knew Daril did too. Still. "It's rather another to… to bring them along the river and set them on a whole city."

"And the cityangel, too," Daril said.

Andreas looked sideways at him.

Daril shrugged, but his casual manner didn't hide the tension in his shoulders, or his thumb flicking against his knee. "Oh, the cityangel's real enough. Real, and powerful." Something flickered across his face, there and gone again. "Believe me, I know."

"Of course I wouldn't deny that magic and spirits are real," Andreas protested.

"Well, no, you are involved with Marcia, aren't you?" Daril smirked at him. "Have you met the sorcerer lover? Or ex-lover, rather."

"Yes," Andreas said stiffly. He considered, and discarded, the idea of updating Daril's beliefs about Marcia's current relationships. It was really none of

Daril's business. "We had an afternoon infusion together last week, at House Fereno."

"An afternoon infusion, eh?" Daril was still smirking, which was more than a little annoying, especially given that Andreas wasn't quite sure what was, in fact, between himself and Marcia these days.

He ignored Daril's expression and moved instead to tidy the stacks of papers on his desk. "I found her very pleasant." That wasn't strictly true, or at least, not the whole truth. Reb had seemed like...someone Andreas could respect. That was more accurate. *Pleasant* wasn't exactly the word – though evidently Marcia saw her differently.

"Myself, I wouldn't want to mess with her any more than with the cityangel," Daril said. He sounded unusually fervent, as though he knew Reb better than Andreas had thought. Andreas tucked that away to mull over later – or to try to get more out of Daril about over a drink one evening.

"Nor I," he said with honesty. It was a very accurate description of Reb.

"Anyway," Daril said. "The Crescent. We need their recognition, but we need it as cheaply as possible."

Which was quite the tall order. Not that Andreas didn't have experience of bargaining – with Salinas captains, with merchants from all over who came to Marek to deal directly – and not that he hadn't overseen the deals made by Tigero factors in cities around the Oval Sea. But...well. Maybe this was a little bigger than anything he'd done before, but he would manage it.

The Crescent Cities had an embassy on Guildstreet, facing the river, directly opposite the docks. It was, Andreas reflected as the litter travelled down the Hill – it was too chilly this morning for walking – a helpful location if you wanted to keep abreast of trade. If the ambassador, Berdian, didn't himself watch all the cargos that went in and out of the port, doubtless his people did.

Andreas was shown immediately up to Berdian's office. The floor underfoot was tiled with Crescentimport tiles, and a Crescent-make glass decanter and small rose-pink glasses sat on a side table.

"Tigero-Head," Berdian said affably, nodding at him over a vast mahogany desk, perpendicular to the large window, offering an excellent view over the river. Berdian obviously didn't leave all the watching to his people. "Congratulations on Marek's new status. We, the Crescent Cities, are delighted to have the chance to support you."

It had taken longer than Andreas would have liked to arrange the meeting; Berdian had deferred, possibly in order to report home and get instructions. The Crescent had a complicated web of city and bank relationships; even if Berdian had written home, they might not yet have reached, still less sent him back, any conclusion.

Berdian didn't get up, merely gestured to a comfortable leather-padded chair across the desk from him. The jewelled rings on his fingers caught the sunlight through the window; it was a clear bright day, if chilly. Andreas realised, too late, that he should have called the ambassador to House Tigero, rather than visiting him in the embassy. Still. He could play it off as…good manners. There was no need to act as if he was aware he was on foreign soil, and accepting a disadvantage.

"I'm glad to hear it. I've taken the liberty of drawing up a draft of a new treaty – using your existing treaty with Teren as a basis." He slid the papers across the desk.

"Oh, indeed, indeed," the ambassador murmured. He didn't look down, just steepled his fingers and gazed at Andreas. "Of course, though, Marek is a very different place from Teren, with very different things to offer." He leant back in his own comfortable leather chair. "I hear, too, that the lower city have opinions on this matter?"

Andreas cursed inwardly. There had been some kind of rally in Marek Square yesterday, with some of the, well, less-radical-radicals publicly discussing their requests to the Council. Independence should mean an opportunity for change, that sort of thing. Something they intended to present to the Council? Daril had said something about it while waiting for their infusions to arrive that morning, but none of the rest of the Council had had the slightest intention of noticing it. Andreas himself hadn't paid any attention at all, too busy thinking about these negotiations. He hadn't thought it would come up.

"There was some business in Marek Square yesterday, yes," he agreed, with a careless shrug. "But I don't think it has much bearing on our discussions today?" He bit his tongue, without letting it show in his smile. That shouldn't have been a question.

The ambassador wore a concerned expression. "Civil unrest, you see. It *concerns* me, both that trade might be disrupted, and that the city as a whole is perhaps unhappy about the current situation. How can I make an agreement with a Marek that is as yet so uncertain of itself?"

Andreas stared back at him and scrabbled for an answer. This was not going quite as planned.

An hour later, he was feeling hot, harassed, and thirsty. He had, however managed to convince the ambassador that Marek was not about to erupt into civil war, partly by leaning heavily on comparison with the situation in Teren – no one, after all, was fleeing Marek with their families and belongings, while Teren refugees were still arriving, though he gathered somewhat more slowly now. The lower city, he'd pointed out, merely wanted to share their thoughts with the Council. A different matter altogether. (He slid over the part where the Council, as far as Andreas could tell, had no intention whatsoever of listening to them.) He'd successfully cut off the ambassador's attempt to link in matters of Crescent banking, which Piath had strongly warned him *had* to remain separate from any trade deals. And he'd – repeatedly – avoided the matter of a reduction in taxes on trades with Crescent merchants. Partly by reminding himself that if he gave discounts here, Exuria would be certain to hear of them, and then the whole thing would become a race to the bottom of the river with both of Marek's major trading partners acting the insulted party to the limit of their bent.

Berdian, on his part, had steadfastly and repeatedly refused to sign anything.

In response to Andreas' latest attempt to suggest that they might have reached a tentative agreement, he shook his head yet again. "There are some arrangements, some contracts, I would feel able to sign immediately, yes. Safe in the knowledge that my principals at home, in all of the Cities, would support my choice."

Andreas translated this as 'if you offered a deal that was exceptionally good for us and bad for you, I would sign it before you realised how much of a mistake you were making'.

"As it is –"

"But this is a perfectly functional deal for both of us," Andreas said, for the hundredth time. "On a very similar basis to your existing treaty with Teren. I'm willing to offer you a tenth of a point, to counter your argument that Marek is less able to support the Crescent than Teren is. Certainly, we are small. But our goods are popular around the Oval Sea, and we are not asking for an extension of credit. And Teren goods are still flowing downriver, as I am sure you are aware, and will continue to come through us." Landlocked, mountain-surrounded Teren hardly had any other option, as both of them were aware, though Berdian had tried to claim concern on that point.

"Indeed, indeed." The ambassador nodded. "But I'm afraid, reasonable though this offer is, I simply cannot sign it without confirming it with my principals. I will of course send word on the next ship to depart for the Crescent." He nodded some more, and looked sorrowful. "Of course, there are *several* cities that will have to agree, you understand. It all takes time." Annoyingly, Andreas knew that both this was true – several cities and several banking conglomerates, indeed – and that Berdian could cut through the lot if he was so minded.

They *needed* these agreements – but Andreas couldn't sell Marek out to sea just to get something in writing, could he? Whatever they agreed now they'd have to live with for a long while yet. He bit his tongue, again, and gave up.

"Very well," he said, standing up. "I will look forward to you receiving your authorisation, and I thank you deeply for your time. In the meantime, of course, we will continue to collect taxes on Crescent trades at the current rate, based on the Teren treaty, without the new rate. Since it is not yet authorised." It was a petty blow, but satisfying.

"Indeed," Berdian said affably, which rather took the satisfaction out of it.

Andreas left in a foul mood. At least he was fairly certain that Daril was wrong, and this wasn't going to matter as far as Teren were concerned. Selene wouldn't be so foolish.

TWO·

Jonas tipped himself backwards on Cato's stool as he thought, balancing against the wall behind him. Cato was over in the chair by the window, waiting patiently – for once – for Jonas to speak. Outside, a sleety slush was falling; at least Cato's room was warm, the blocky stove in the corner radiating heat. All the rooms in the squats had stoves; not everyone could always afford to run them. Jonas' friend Tam had been talking about that lately, about fairness and all that.

Which wasn't what he was supposed to be thinking about just now.

"The thing is," he said. He stared at a spiderweb in a corner of the ceiling to avoid meeting Cato's eyes. "I know now that using magic often – not always, but often – means I get a flicker. And that often – not always, but often – it's associated with the magic I've just done. What I don't know is whether I can use that deliberately."

He was *more* comfortable, now, talking to Cato about flickers, but it still made his insides feel weird. It had been such a deep secret for so long. It still seemed strange that Cato was just curious, not horrified; that no one he'd told in Marek had reacted like his mother had always told him Salinas folk would.

"How do you mean, exactly?" Cato asked, voice calm but interested.

"Well. If I want to know about something, can I do magic about that, and initiate a flicker?"

The bare idea, never mind voicing it aloud, gave him the shivers. For so long he'd *avoided* flickers. They'd been a shameful thing, to be hidden, the thing that meant he might never be able to sail with his people as an adult. To his own self as little as a couple of years ago, the idea of *deliberately* bringing a flicker about would have been a horrifying absurdity.

But he was in Marek now, and he was a sorcerer – or at least an apprentice – and that in itself was likely enough to keep him off Salinas ships. Though he refused to accept that that was true forever. He'd find a way around it yet. What he had discovered in Marek, though, what he'd finally been forced to admit and to accept, was that he couldn't just ignore it all. He had to work out what his magic looked like, and how his flickers worked. The weird thing was that – it was *fun*. Well. Fun, and also annoying.

"It's frustrating that it's so unreliable." He screwed his nose up, dragging his gaze back down from the ceiling to look at Cato. "Mostly this, or sometimes that."

"'Not always, but often' is kind of the rule with magic," Cato said, shrugging apologetically. "Beckett is pretty reliable, and I'm teaching you stuff like it's mathematics or baking, do this and you'll get that, but…"

"You've never baked, have you?" Jonas rolled his eyes.

"What? Bakers produce bread every day! It must be predictable!"

Jonas grinned at him. "Go talk to a baker. Yeast is finicky stuff."

"*Anyway*," Cato went on loftily, flicking his red-brown hair off his forehead. "My point is, magic doesn't always do what you want it to, when you want it to, and it certainly doesn't work exactly the same way every time."

Jonas, interested now, chewed thoughtfully at a rough patch on his thumb. "It always seems to for you."

"That's because I'm good at –" Cato paused, thinking about it. He was far more honest with Jonas, these days, about magic. And other things, come to that. "Improvising, I suppose. I can feel how things are going today, and what I'll need to do. And it's partly about state of mind. The more you practise, the better you get at the state of mind you need. I've been doing this a fair old while, you know."

Jonas switched to the other thumbnail. "Maybe that's

part of the thing with the flickers. The state of mind I'm in."

"More or less focussed?" Cato suggested.

Jonas shook his head. "Not as simple as that. But I'll think about it."

"Anyway. We've moved somewhat away from the problem you brought up. Being able to produce a flicker on demand, about a specific subject."

"It feels wrong, though, doing magic about a thing just in order to see its future."

"Wrong in what way? Nothing wrong with magic. Nothing particularly *special* about it, either. It's just a way of doing things." Cato, by way of illustration, snapped his fingers, and the candle on the dresser lit. "Blow that out, would you? Don't care to waste it."

"Blow it out yourself. I don't want to get up any more than you do."

"Don't *get up*," Cato said, impatiently. "I lit it with magic. Blow it out with magic."

Jonas frowned at him. "I don't know how."

"Haven't we just finished saying it's about state of mind? Partly about state of mind," he amended. "The herbs and snippets of this and that help focus the mind, especially for anything larger, and with a client, you need to create a show or they won't believe you. But this is easy. You can blow it out from there." He folded his arms and waited.

Jonas reached for that place in his head where magic lived, felt for his internal sense of Beckett, and gestured at the candle, envisaging it out again. To his amazement, it worked; and at the same time, he saw *the candlestick falling sideways* and then blinked and the candlestick was upright again.

"Well done," Cato said.

"It was knackering," Jonas said. His hand was shaking; it often was after he did magic.

"Oh, absolutely, almost always easier to do it by hand, as it were. But what's the point of being a sorcerer if not to spray magic around the place to save your legs?" Cato lounged pointedly backwards in his chair and put his feet up on the edge of his unmade bed.

"And I got a flicker."

"Aha! Tell me more?"

Cato leant forwards over his knees, and knocked into the dresser. The candlestick wobbled, and began to fall. Jonas automatically lunged forwards to catch it, sending the stool flying; caught it; and jarred his knee painfully against the dresser.

"Ow." He set the candlestick back on the dresser, righted the stool, and sat back down. He rubbed at his knee. "That was it. The candlestick fell."

"Except it didn't."

"Except it didn't. And I hit my knee instead."

"The price of changing the future." Cato's eyes were bright.

"I could wish that the price of changing the future was less often me getting injured," Jonas said irritably. His arm had mended fine, weeks ago now, after he broke it saving Tam – he twitched, remembering that and what would have happened if he hadn't – but it had hardly been an enjoyable experience.

"Well, that's something to experiment with as well," Cato said comfortably. "It's not like you've tried all that often, have you?" He considered the matter. "When we stopped that wretched demon, you weren't *hurt* then, were you? A bit, uh, generally wiped out, maybe, but not *hurt* per se."

Jonas grimaced. His recollections of that event were less positive than Cato's, but perhaps Cato was right; he hadn't been physically injured. 'Wiped out' didn't begin to cover it though.

"I suppose that doesn't really count as deliberately doing magic to try to get a flicker," Cato carried on. "Still. Good practice. And let's think of something you *can* do magic on to deliberately get a flicker."

"Not today," Jonas said firmly. He was exhausted, more now than immediately after the candle, and still uncomfortable too. The flicker, even that tiny little one, had shaken him. Maybe they always would.

"Oh, fine. Off you go, then. Tait's due over soon anyway. Shoo."

It was good to have someone to talk properly to about his flickers. Maybe, even, he considered as he went down the stairs, being comfortable talking to Cato about them would translate, sometime soon, into feeling properly comfortable about the flickers themselves? That would be nice. It was, after all, better now than it ever had been.

At the bottom of the stairs, quite unexpectedly, it happened again.

...the deck of a ship, a proper ship, the wind in his air, the salt smell, nothing but sea and sky ahead of him, the joy of it filling him from the inside, toes to the top of his head, and he turned to speak to the person beside him and it was Asa...

He caught himself on the doorframe as he staggered. For a moment he could swear he could still smell the salt, could still feel the deck lifting under his feet. Could feel that swell of joy. A ship. A real, proper, Salinas ship, out at sea – and Asa there with him? He couldn't envisage how that could possibly happen – but it most certainly wasn't anything he'd want to try and prevent. Rather the opposite. A *ship*. A proper ship.

Tears prickled for a betraying moment at the corners of his eyes. He liked Marek. He liked – mostly – finding out about his magic, and his flickers. Understanding himself. But he did his utmost to forget how desperately he missed the sea. He'd nearly given up hope that he might make it back, one day – his people were so vehemently against magic. But if he'd seen it...maybe...

Well. He'd just have to wait, wouldn't he? And hope that he didn't accidentally do the thing that would prevent it.

Marcia, with a heavy sigh, sat down in the small reception-room, and took advantage of the fact that she was finally alone to put her head back and scream, gently and quietly, through her closed teeth. The baby kicked, apparently in response, and she shifted awkwardly, then put both hands up to rub at her temples.

Well. That had been an utter screaming disaster, hadn't it? It was just as well that Reb hadn't been there herself, in the end. The idea had been to prepare the ground for Reb being there another time – ha. Marcia grimly contemplated the excessive optimism of that former self. *Another time.* Right.

It wasn't, to be fair, that *all* of the Council were wholly unwilling to listen, or to entertain the idea of some of their number talking to the sorcerers. It was more that those who were unwilling were so very loud and self-righteous about it. Athitol-Head in the lead, of course, as one might expect, but others alongside her. Like Kilzan-Head, for example; and Nisha, sitting next to her Head, had winced ever so slightly but failed to overtly disagree. Nisha couldn't, she supposed, not in open Council, but…

Even bloody Daril hadn't said much, and according to Andreas he was in favour of this. But Daril always did have an excellent sense of how the wind was blowing.

And now where was she to go from here? It was just *wasteful*, having the city splintered like this: Council, sorcerers, lower city…and that was a problem to consider as well, wasn't it? From the posters she'd seen the last time she walked to Reb's, and from the reports of that public meeting the other day, a problem that was growing more urgent. Her head hurt.

A gentle tap sounded at the door, and an apologetic-looking footman appeared. "Kilzan-Heir is here to see you, Ser. Are you at home?"

Nisha. What could she be after? Marcia couldn't turn her away, though; Nisha knew she was at home, polite fiction or no, and she'd take dismissal as admission that Marcia was annoyed with her. Which…maybe she was, even if it was unfair to expect Nisha to stand against her Head, but it wouldn't do to give her the silent treatment, either way. "I am. Show her in. And send for an infusion-tray, please."

Nisha, shown in, hurried towards Marcia, face apologetic, and took her hands. "Marcia. I'm so sorry. That was all deeply unreasonable, and after you tried so hard to be reasonable about it."

"Yes," Marcia agreed, biting back 'and you just sat there and accepted it'.

"And I just sat there quietly," Nisha agreed, and for an alarming moment Marcia wondered if she'd spoken aloud. "I *know*, darling, I know. That's why I'm here." She sat down on the armchair that half-faced Marcia's, leaning forward. "I want to help."

"What? Why?" That was too blunt to be politically astute, but Marcia was tired, and this was Nisha who she'd known forever, and – well, she was taken aback, to put it mildly.

The infusion-tray was brought in, with pots of greenmint, chamomile and lemon, and bitterwort with a jar of honey (the cook thought it was good for late pregnancy, and Marcia didn't have the heart to stop her sending it up, even if she couldn't bring herself to drink the stuff), together with a tray of barley-cakes. There was a pause while Marcia poured chamomile for Nisha and greenmint for herself.

"You're right, is the thing," Nisha said, once the footman had gone and she had taken the first polite sip from her cup. "Everything you were saying so eloquently in there. The city's fractured. Look at all this business with the lower city, going round writing pamphlets and all that."

"You've been reading pamphlets too?"

"If you recall, darling, I was doing that before you were. I just rather let it go when I became Heir." She shrugged. "More important things to do. But I'm still *aware* that it's happening. I keep drip-feeding little pieces to my Head, in the hope that he'll become a little more aware himself, but it's slow work."

"And you don't want to antagonise him." Marcia couldn't resist pointing that out.

"Of course I don't, darling. After all, he's got rid of one

31

Heir already." Nisha shrugged an elegant shoulder. She'd been the one who handed Kilzan-Head the evidence he needed to disinherit his previous Heir for defrauding the House, and she'd become Heir – not exactly *in exchange*, but it hadn't hurt.

"You're not committing fraud." One could refuse to confirm an Heir for whatever reason one liked – Daril had had that issue with his late father – but once confirmed, it was difficult to get rid of them without proof of real wrongdoing.

"If he wanted to, I'm sure he could find something."

It would, Marcia felt, look far worse to disown a second Heir, but Nisha looked uncomfortable, and there was no point arguing further; Marcia wasn't going to talk Nisha into security.

"I freely admit that I'm not keen to push the boundaries," Nisha continued. "I'd say, what influence can I have if that happens, and it's even true enough, but we both know that primarily I just want to stay Heir, and Head in due course."

"So you're here because I'm right," Marcia said. She sat back and looked sceptically at Nisha. "Really?"

"Really, darling. I'm not bothered either way about magic, myself. But many people are, or at least accept it as a regular part of their lives, and obviously we care about it – like you said back at that very tedious trial Athitol forced you into – because we have all these rules about it, and it's all very inconsistent. I don't like inconsistent."

"You're *always* inconsistent!"

"Then I'm inconsistently inconsistent." Nisha beamed at her and took another barley-cake. "It's an unnecessary divide, is the point. And from everything you've said – well, it's more like, what you've *not* said, darling, but I have been paying attention – it's more important than Marekhill as a whole would like to think. I do wonder what exactly happened with Selene, back in the summer." Her eyes were sharp on Marcia's face. Marcia wondered when, exactly, she'd forgotten just how on the ball Nisha could be, despite the casual air and the way she behaved at parties.

"Do you," she said, neutrally.

"I shan't make you tell me, don't worry. But what we *should* be worrying about, given the reports coming out of Teren, is what happens if Selene comes back, and the Council is still busy pretending magic doesn't exist."

Marcia felt her mouth fall open. "Yes," she managed. "Yes, that's exactly it."

"And yet," Nisha said, "you're going to point out that I was just sitting there quietly next to Fredere and letting Athitol and Co harrumph you and Andreas right out of the room." Not that Andreas had done much beyond nod supportively; Marcia had taken the real risk.

"You were," Marcia agreed. There wasn't much to do now but to roll along as Nisha drove this conversation.

"Because me standing up and contradicting my Head right there in the Council would achieve something?"

It was a solid point. Marcia had known it at the time. And it wasn't like she hadn't had her own experience of that, albeit the other way around, when Madeleine had contradicted her – voted against her, broken her agreements – right there in public.

"So," Nisha said, sitting back and crossing one leg over the other. "What you need, is someone on the *other side*, who can have some nice thoughtful private words, just a little at a time, with the holdouts."

"You are never going to convince Athitol." Marcia shook her head.

"No, of course not, but I can undermine her. It's all about the alliances, as well you know. If I can slide Fredere over to the side of – well, I can't say I expect him to get enthusiastically on board with the idea of entertaining sorcerers for a lovely afternoon infusion, but at root he's a very practical person. I can get him to realise that *informal liaison* – of the sort you proposed this afternoon, darling, not the sort you get up to in your spare time – would be a benefit to us all. And to House Kilzan, more specifically. Haran as well, he's persuadable, and he's over all the time lately. Just give me a little space to work on him. Then Athitol stands alone, just like with independence, and she can't do anything from there." Nisha shrugged.

"And you're doing this because..." Marcia folded her arms. She *wanted* to trust Nisha, but...

"Because it's the right thing to do," Nisha said impatiently. "Haven't you been listening? Marek needs to be stronger, if we're to be independent. We must stand together, and we must look to our strengths. Clearly our magic is one of those strengths. And if Selene does come back, with a collection of sorcerers – what is the group noun for sorcerers, I wonder? – we'll need ours, won't we. So. I want Marek independent, and strong, and united." She hesitated. "And I want to prove to Fredere that I'm clearsighted and can see where our best interest lies."

"You really are worried about that?" Marcia asked. She'd assumed Nisha was just nervous, not that she had reason to be.

Nisha's nose wrinkled slightly. "He's antsy. Made a bad decision with one Heir, already, didn't he? And it took him forever to find an acceptable reason to get rid of her once he realised. *Which* was stupid of her, because if she'd just sat tight and been useless but not actively illegal, he'd have been stuck. So he very badly wants to be right this time, but he's worried he's not. I want it to be *extremely* clear that he can relax and stop fretting. I think this can help me do that." She pulled a face. "You'll find this whole business with the lower city rather tougher, I fear, and I'm certainly not willing to antagonise the Guilds, that wouldn't impress Fredere at *all*. But perhaps options will appear, if you insist on worrying about them. Right." She beamed sunnily at Marcia. "Now that's out of the way, let us get onto the portion of the discussion where we exchange the *interesting* information. And you tell me how the whole baby thing is coming along."

None of this was what Marcia had expected when Nisha walked in the door; for now, she put it all away to think over carefully later, and let Nisha move onto the social gossip she was so good at. And which, now Marcia came to think of it, so ably underpinned her political movements. Nisha was a deeply useful ally, as well as a friend, and she shouldn't be surprised, should she, that Nisha was keen to play both sides to her own advantages. It was convenient that that was – at least for now – to Marek's, and Marcia's, advantage as well.

Tait dropped their hands, sank down onto the floor of Reb's small, bare workroom, and let their head fall backwards against the wall with a thunk. Worse than the bone-deep exhaustion that dragged them down into the floor was the frustration knotting their insides that this wasn't *working*.

"I can do it with blood magic," they muttered, staring up at the cracks in the planks of Reb's ceiling. "Why can't I do it this way?"

Reb made a considering noise. "Habit?"

"I've been here nearly a year." Tait could hear the whine in their own voice.

"And you were at the Academy for three. Mostly, from what you've said, using blood magic." Reb's tone was bracing. Reb wasn't the sort for gentle reassurances; which fit well with Tait's current mood. Right now they felt more like biting someone than being reassured.

Reb was right about the magic they'd done at the Academy. They hadn't liked demon-magic, had avoided it as far as they possibly could, sticking with their own blood long past when their peers had moved onto sacrifice-blood and then to demons. When they'd finally been forced to use demon-magic, for real – that was when they'd run. And maybe, they thought, guts churning in self-loathing, if they'd had the nerve to run sooner they wouldn't be stuck like this. Maybe, maybe. That and tuppence would get them a haircut.

Think of something else. There had to be a different

approach. There had to be *something* would break them through this. "Maybe translocation would work?" They tipped their head forward again, braid falling over their shoulder, and squinted hopefully at Reb.

"You can't *move* the thing," Reb gestured at the small ceramic dish squatting innocently in the middle of the room, "and you want to try translocating it?"

"I never tried moving things with blood magic. Only translocating them."

"If it's habit, surely that'll make it harder?" Reb frowned doubtfully at them.

"Maybe it's not habit," Tait argued. "Maybe it's…I don't know." They'd shifted a dragon-bear across a ravine, once, with blood magic, and pulled a person out of a river at full flood. They *knew* they had enough power for this. It just – wasn't working the Marek way. "If I could move Bracken…"

"Yes, well," Reb said tartly. "You certainly don't want to make a habit of that sort of thing. Can I remind you that blood magic is *illegal* in Marek. Even for good reasons." Tait still wasn't entirely sure why Reb had let them get away with it when they'd rescued Bracken; though 'feeling bad to punish someone for saving someone's life' might be it. Reb was softer than she let on. Like Cato, albeit in very different ways.

Reb sighed. "But feel free to try it if you really want to. Maybe you're right, and knowing what you're about will help." Tait could hear the forced cheerfulness in her voice; this must be almost as frustrating for Reb, trying to teach them, as it was for Tait themself. "Come on then. On your feet."

Tait stood back up, and looked doubtfully at the ingredients Reb had laid out on the small table against the workroom wall. "Would it be the same ingredients, for translocation, as for moving something?"

Reb sucked air through her teeth. "Hm. Well, it's a similar idea, but…" She picked up the dish, shook the snippets of things from Tait's last effort into the box in the corner of the room, put the dish back down, and went to the shelves that lined the rear wall where a window ought to be. Reb thought a window in a workroom was dangerous. Cato thought she worried too much. "Here. Try salt with the periwinkle, and leave out the crushed willow. It's all mostly as an aid to concentration, anyway, so if that feels right to you."

None of it felt right, or not right, to Tait; none of it felt like anything much at all. But saying that wouldn't help. They had to keep trying, and surely eventually it would click. They nodded politely, took a pinch of each of the pots Reb offered them, and mixed them together in a cupped hand. They sprinkled a little of the mixture onto the dish, and then onto a spot on the other side of the room. The rest stayed in their hand, and they touched it gently with the fingers of their other hand, and tried to, as Reb had told them, focus their intention, reach out towards the idea of Beckett...

...but it felt so *different* from when they did blood magic. At so much more of a remove, like – trying to move the dish with tongs at arms-length while looking in a mirror. Tait ground their teeth, pushed that thought away, and tried again to focus.

No. Nothing.

They opened their eyes and scowled at Reb, who wore her best sympathetic expression. It didn't sit all that well on Reb's face, but Tait appreciated the effort.

"It just isn't *there*," Tait said.

"Do a light again," Reb suggested.

That, at least, Tait could do. They turned their empty hand up and summoned the little dancing witch-light. It restored their spirits, a little.

"Right. Think about *that* when you try the move."

It felt, this time, like Tait might – maybe – be slightly closer; but still the dish remained stubbornly where it ought to be.

"I don't understand it," Reb said, frankly. "It's the same power, you're just asking Beckett to make the connection, rather than using your blood. I don't see why it shouldn't work." She hunched a shoulder slightly.

"Worked fine for me. When I moved here." Reb didn't like talking about her Teren past, but she'd said one or two things to Tait about it, in the course of lessons. "And Beckett likes you fine, and you can do it for *some* things. It doesn't make sense."

"Small ones," Tait said, with a sigh. "I can do small things. It feels – muddy, or something. Fuzzy. Awkward. Far away," they tried to explain.

Reb scratched at her nose. "It always felt so much easier, to me, right from the start."

They'd tried, several times lately, Tait piggybacking on Reb's power when she did something, but though that had helped Alyssa a great deal, it didn't seem to make much difference to Tait. Tait could feel what Reb was doing, and the difference between that and the blood magic they were used to, and they could copy it to the extent of a witch-light or a minor finding-spell, but beyond that, the feeling seemed to slip straight through their mental fingers.

"Maybe if you tried with Cato instead?"

Reb had suggested that before, and Tait had demurred. This time, they sighed, and told her honestly, "Cato's shown me one or two things. Wards, I can do that. A warming-spell."

"Well, that's good!" Reb said encouragingly. "Those are harder than the witch-light."

"But we tried moving something, the other day, after I couldn't do it here last time, and I couldn't get it with him either." Tait could hear the frustration in their own voice, and saw Reb's face fall, though she tried to disguise it.

"You'll get it," she said, encouragingly. "You're a strong sorcerer, you just need to…readjust. It just takes time."

Walking home through the cold, winter-afternoon-dim streets, Tait reflected on the idea of readjustment. They were a strong sorcerer, they knew that – with blood. But did that mean that they would be strong when working with Beckett? Reb obviously thought it ought to work that way – the same power, accessed different ways. But surely you might as well say that a flautist should be able to play the lute? For certain, a flautist seeking to learn the lute might have advantages in their existing knowledge of music, but you wouldn't *expect* them to be as good at one as the other. Smiths worked in different ways, some specialising in large things, some doing detailed work; a smith who made swords would doubtless do a better job than, say, Tait would, making a tiny coat-hook, but not as good as a smith who specialised in the small work. All the professions Tait could think of had their specialities. Why shouldn't magic be the same? Tait was a sorcerer, so they could do *something* with Marek magic, but maybe they never would be as good with that as with blood magic.

Frustration surged at the idea. They remembered with a pang of loss, of absence, that sense of power, of being able to do things, of bone-deep knowing what they were about. That sense that they just didn't have with Marek magic. Blood magic, too, had its limits – especially when working with your own blood – but Tait had always been able to do more with it than others in the Academy, and they'd put a lot of effort into honing that ability, driven by the desire to avoid the other ways the Academy wanted its sorcerers to work.

What if they never could be a Marek sorcerer the same way they'd been a blood-sorcerer? What if this, or something like it, was it?

They'd rather be in Marek with little magic than in Teren with lots, that was a certainty. For a great many reasons, starting with the absence of the Academy and demons, and moving onto their relationship with Cato; and they just liked Marek, more than they ever had liked Ameten, or even the village they were born in. If the trade-off for being here was no magic, or not very much magic – well, fine, yes, they would take that.

Tait kicked at a stone in the gutter. They didn't *want* to, though. They didn't want that to be the trade-off. They wanted Marek and magic both. And fine, they understood why blood magic was banned in Marek – there were so very many ways that a blood-sorcerer could go to the bad – but. But.

Maybe Reb would be right, after all. Maybe it was just habit, and sometime soon Tait would try Marek magic, and it would work, and all of this would be behind them. Maybe it was just around the corner. They clenched their jaw until their teeth creaked against each other, and hoped.

THREE

Jeres had persuaded Alyssa to be here today – the first day the Council returned to session after New Year, the day chosen for the presentation of the Petition – not so much against her own better judgement as against her strong preference. She didn't think the Petition would achieve anything, and she didn't think that the amount of pomp and circumstance surrounding the presentation of the wretched thing would influence that – in either direction – in the slightest.

But she did, as Jeres had somewhat forcefully pointed out to her, believe in solidarity and all that. She'd signed the Petition herself, in the end, because it would be better than what they had now; and after some thought and quite a lot of argument, she'd concluded that she didn't buy the arguments of some of the more extreme Parliamentarians that improvements would reduce the pressure to do better still. Improving things now mattered, even if those improvements weren't as much as you wanted. It wasn't worth making things worse now to make hypothetical future changes more likely – and she wasn't even sure she believed that they would be more likely. Miserable people, people who'd tried and failed, gave up, didn't they? People who'd tried and won *something*, even if it wasn't everything – maybe they kept pushing for the next thing.

And, yes, fine, Jeres was right that the more people willing to walk up the Hill with the thing, the more obvious the pressure was. And the more protected everyone was, that too, not that the Petition was likely to attract much overt trouble.

Also, Simeon had tried to argue her out of going, and she was irritated with him just at the moment.

Alyssa rested on the edge of the fountain in the centre

of the square – no point in being on her feet until she had to be – and propped her stick against her knee. The Square was full of people milling around. At least it was dry today; the sun had even come out, though there was little warmth in it yet, right at the start of the year, and Alyssa was glad of her sturdy cloak and shawl. To one side were a knot of people in ink-spattered printers' aprons (clearly worn deliberately as a badge of their trade rather than because they lacked anything smarter), while other folk around them wore best outfits or winter flowers in their hair. The Broderers Guild had brought their banner – a predictably beautiful piece of work in red and gold with flowers surrounding their crest – and the Horologists were there as well, with a clock mounted on a carrying-pole in place of a banner. That was, as far as Alyssa could see, the only Guild presence. So much for Jeres' claims that she could talk the Guilds around given more time. Not even her own Guild, the Vintners, were visible, other than in Jeres herself and a handful of people with her that Alyssa happened to know were also vintners. There were a fair few folk she recognised from the Bucket, and a collection of people in Teren-style longer skirts, some of whom she thought she'd seen come through the refugee reception tent at some point in the last few months.

Over the other side of the square, Alyssa saw Cedric leaning against the front railing of the Salinas Embassy, chatting to a couple of people she didn't know. He looked over and caught her eye, and she gave him a nod. He was one of those who'd undertaken to move the People's Parliament in once the parade had moved out. Jeres knew that was happening – it couldn't be much of a secret if they wanted anyone to come along, despite the risks of publicising it – but they'd agreed to keep the two things separate, to avoid the Petition getting linked in with the Parliamentarians. Shared pressure, but separate; that had been the eventual agreement. Alyssa and Sara, going up with the Petitioners – she hadn't seen Sara yet, but she'd be around somewhere – were hoping to bring at least some of them back down again after the presentation happened.

The piles of paper – the signed sheets of Petition, and they really were lucky it wasn't bloody raining – on their fancy bed were moving out, half-a-dozen people on either side holding poles to support it. Time to go.

She'd forgotten how long it was, walking all the way up the Hill. Long time since she'd last been up here, even up the side path to reach the park up top. Her hip was complaining by the time she reached the top. The rest of her had also become ever more annoyed as they walked past the increasingly fancy – and commensurately expensive – shops. And in particular the last two streets that wound up the Hill, occupied by the Thirteen Houses. One house per family, when you could house tens of families in there, easy. Why should they get all the good stuff?

The procession fetched up in the courtyard outside the Council Chamber, close to the top of Marekhill. The very top of the hill was taken up with Marek Park. She'd brought Jina here once, for the view, but this wasn't her side of the city, and right now she truly felt that.

Radec was on the steps, declaiming aloud the points of the Petition. His voice carried well, not that Alyssa didn't know it all by heart already. Making access to the Guilds easier, by allowing potential journeymen to be tested without a formal apprenticeship history. Protection for unGuilded workers – limits on the hours that could be required of them, same as for those employed under a Guild-stamped warden; and equal access with the Guilds to the better-quality raw materials. Removal of the censorship laws – that seemed particularly optimistic, given that it was only a few months back the censorship laws had been brought in. And – most unlikely of all for the Council to touch with the proverbial bargepole – an elected Committee of the City to represent anyone not part of a Guild or House. As if the Council would just meekly share power on request. Alyssa suppressed a snort. She wasn't here to antagonise people, even if she wished some of them might see a little clearer.

43

Radec finished, and Jeres, at the front of the crowd, climbed up onto the steps beside him. She waded into a speech about how she was convinced that the Council would listen, that they were representing Marek, she knew they all wanted what was best for the city now in this glorious moment of independence, all that sort of thing. Alyssa didn't pay attention. Wasn't like she hadn't heard Jeres on this subject before. The front doors of the Chamber were shut, though the guards standing outside them, one to each side, didn't look particularly concerned about guarding the place. What was Jeres' plan? Were they going to knock politely on the door? Storm the place? (Unlikely, sadly. Not Jeres' kind of deal.)

The doors shifted slightly, and Alyssa's attention sharpened. Jeres was coming to the end of her speech, Alyssa reckoned, and whoever was behind those doors was listening for that. She'd planned *something*. Or, perhaps more likely, someone in there had.

"And the Council will have to heed us!" Jeres concluded, with ludicrous optimism.

The doors, more or less on cue, opened, and the crowd made a sort of enthusiastic ooh. Fools. Alyssa would bet every coin in her pocket that they were about to be *managed*.

For once, Alyssa slightly regretted her stubborn refusal to recognise any of the Heads or Heirs of the Houses – well, fine, except for Marcia, who she'd met often enough now that it would be more work not to remember her. But it was clearly one of them – not Marcia – standing there, not a flunky. Fancy robe and all the rest.

"Greetings, Marek citizens. I am Daril, Head of House Leandra."

Oh, though; this one she knew of. He'd been in the lead with all the business of independence, for starters, to hear the news-sheets tell it; but as well as that, this was the one that had got himself involved with magic, wasn't it, and then got himself uninvolved with it and somehow gotten away with it, despite all the official line about Marekhill and magic. Marcia couldn't stand him, Alyssa

44

knew that much, even despite the fact that she and Marcia generally avoided talking about politics or anything related to it.

She didn't necessarily rate Marcia's judgement of someone – she was Marekhill just as much as this Daril was, after all – but, well, if someone warned you about a snake, you'd best at least hold it in mind. And by Marcia's telling of it – and Reb's, and Alyssa rated *her* judgement rather more – Daril had both eyes *firmly* on his own best interests, whatever words he surrounded it with. That sort were good to watch out for.

And now she squinted across at him a little harder, she realised that she did recognise him. Not from being up here, though. From the Bucket, more than once. Dressed down, not like this with the robes, of course, but not even fancy day-to-day Marekhill wear. He'd not spoken publicly, not that she'd seen – plenty of people did, in the Bucket, it was like that – but she'd seen him there. Talking to people. Listening, too. Huh.

He was, apparently, pleased to see the Petitioners, and the Petition. "I feel confident that my colleagues in the Council will be just as interested as I am in what you have to say." Yeah, right – and if you believed that, Alyssa had a bridge to sell. The Council were going to be the opposite of thrilled with this whole thing, whatever Daril Leandra's position might be. And she wasn't at all sure that she trusted his presence in the Bucket any more than she trusted what he was saying here and now. "I will take this document, and show it to them. I will put your arguments – your very strong arguments – as cogently as I may. I am keen to support you."

Was Jeres actually going to let him get away with this? Taking the whole thing over from those as owned it? Classic Marekhill right there. Alyssa rolled her eyes. She was; she was nodding, allowing Daril to take the stacks of pages – well, to signal to the guards to take them inside. Jeres ought to be insisting that they follow him in there, that they *speak* to the Council themselves, not get some House fool to do it for them, even if Jeres knew him from meetings, and Alyssa was far from sure about that. But no; there he went, with a mouthful more puffery on the way, and the doors closed again.

Idiots.

Someone else was up on the steps now, about to begin another speech, by the looks of it. Alyssa had had enough.

"Alyssa?" Sara came up, nodded to her. "Are we gonna bring them down to the Square?"

Alyssa pursed her lips. "Don't let's tread on anyone's toes right now. Interrupting speechifying will only upset the ones waiting to get their chance to stand up there." And for plenty of folk that really mattered, for good reasons as well as for bad ones. "I'm going to head down to the Square to warn 'em this lot will be back down the Hill shortly, depending on how many people are keen to hear the sounds of their own voices."

"As if we aren't about to do just that," Sara pointed out, mouth wry.

"Ah, but we've a purpose to achieve. This is just self-congratulation, and for what? They delivered a bunch of paper that's doubtless been fed straight into the furnace the moment that Marekhill fucker got it inside." Alyssa snorted. "In any case. How about you go stand by the road on the way back down the Hill, and if people start trickling away, tell 'em that a *real* Council is meeting right now in Marek Square. Then get Henry to hop up on the stage once the speeching's done, tell 'em all the same before they leave. That'll do."

"Right. See you soon." They clasped hands as farewell, and Alyssa began to make her way down the hill, leaning heavily on her stick. It was going to be a long, long day.

It was quicker going back downhill than it had been uphill; or perhaps Alyssa was just more keen to get down to Marek Square and see how things were progressing there than she had been to follow a pile of wasted paper up to the bloody Council Chamber. Her knee was grumbling now to go along with the spike of pain in her hip, but she ignored both of them with the ease of long practice. A handful of people had followed her as she'd left the square outside the Chamber; hopefully Sara would bring a few more and, once they got started properly, with luck more of the Petitioners would stop when they came back through the square to listen.

She rounded the last corner into Marek Square and cast an eye over the group by the fountain. Looked like they were still in the process of 'setting things up'. A big word for what came down to the fifty-odd who'd agreed, when they were planning, to go with Cedric – it looked like most of them had showed up, even, which you could never count on – marching into Marek Square with a couple of banners, and laying claim to an area close to the fountain. It seemed to be going as planned; no point in starting too soon if they were to rope in the returning Petitioners.

Tey – broken leg now recovered to the point that he was moving around on crutches – hadn't wanted to facilitate the first meeting of the People's Council. And usually Alyssa would have respected that, except that Tey was the best they had, and this had to go well. If it dissolved into chaos they'd be destroying their own arguments. So she'd spent much of the previous two days talking (bullying) him into it. He eventually agreed, but only on the condition that he'd stay away until they'd taken the space, and set things up.

"I'm not sure it's a good idea," he said, bluntly. "Or that you won't all get yourselves arrested by the guard."

"Too many of us," Alyssa argued.

"Yeah, well, I'd rather not rely on that. Especially not given that I can't exactly move fast at the moment." He'd glanced down at her stick, and flushed slightly, but hadn't retracted what he'd said. Instead, he continued, "But. Once you're there, and it's really happening, no trouble in sight. I'll do it then." She'd had to settle for that.

Simeon was busy putting boards across a corner of the fountain for Tey to facilitate from, given that his injury meant he couldn't just stand on the edge of it. The advantage of being better able to see people, he'd insisted, was worth the slight risk of falling in.

Alyssa stumped over towards where Cedric's group were scattered around the edge of the fountain, spreading out to claim the space, and the people who'd followed her down from the Hill came with her. Starting to bulk up the numbers, good. An infusion-seller and a pastry-seller were making the most of the situation, standing at the edges of what you couldn't quite yet call a 'crowd'; which, Alyssa noted happily, was encouraging more people over in that direction to get a drink or a pastry. The more people heard the discussion, the better. Around the square, Cedric and a few others were giving out quarter-sheet notices to passers-by – cheap paper, cheap ink, the best they could afford. Keren the printer had been up all night churning them out, and there she was over by the Old Bridge, with dark circles under her eyes and a headscarf over her ink-grubby hair, pressing sheets on people with a smile.

Some folk were stopping to read the sheets. Some of those were even wandering over towards the fountain.

"All well?" she asked Simeon, who'd finished with his platform-building and was standing on it looking round while he stamped his feet to test it.

"Not bad," he said, jumping down. "There was only one guard hanging around when we got here, and she was flirting with one of the infusion-sellers. Didn't react quickly enough when she finally spotted us."

"No reinforcements?" That had been Alyssa's main concern; that they'd be cleared out while there was still only a few of them.

Simeon gestured at where a couple of guards were standing over the other side of the fountain. "Officer in charge showed up, rolled their eyes a bit. I reckon they've been told just to leave us be, for now."

Alyssa made a non-committal noise. Fifty – a hundred, now, but most of those would probably disappear if the guard started shouting – was enough that it would take a lot of force to remove them. The guard could do it if they wanted, or if they had instructions, but it would be a nasty situation; and if they weren't doing anything violent, it would look bad. She hoped. And it wasn't as if they were technically doing anything illegal, not that that would necessarily prevent them being dispersed if the guard thought they could get away with it. The guard had let the meeting the other week go ahead but – as a lot of the Teren refugees had been very keen to point out – you never knew when they'd change tactics. At least there were no demons here, and no chance of Beckett or any of the sorcerers getting involved.

The chances of someone – several someones – being arrested later on, when people were dispersing, were rather higher. They'd doubtless be able to think of something to do them for. Two printers had been arrested at the last meeting, for 'seditious material', and no Marcia to get *them* out of jail, the way she'd rescued Alyssa that time; she scowled, remembering it.

Anyway. There were people here now, and nothing happening, and they wouldn't stay all that much longer. She should find Tey. They needed to start as soon as Sara's group showed up.

Tey, to her lack of surprise, was lurking on the corner between the Square and his street, despite having told her to come and find him at home once they were ready. She'd guessed he wouldn't really be able to stay away, whatever he'd said.

"Well," he said, pushing himself off from the wall he was leaning against. "Might as well get started, I suppose?" Alyssa glanced round – there was Sara now, and another good few folk with her, including the Broderers with their banner. *That* was good, and unexpected. She nodded at Tey in agreement and led the way to the fountain.

It was, Alyssa estimated as Simeon assisted Tey to climb up onto his makeshift platform, mostly the usual suspects – plus those Broderers – but there were a few she didn't recognise, and some more lurking in the vicinity, at a deniable distance but close enough it suggested they were interested.

"Welcome!" Tey called, and the conversations of the crowd hushed. He went into his usual introductory patter, explaining how he'd be calling on people if they had things to say, encouraging them to listen to each other and to indicate their approval or disapproval. Encouraging everyone to join in. It usually didn't work on the new folk initially, but it was good to establish how things were supposed to go. That this was for *everyone*, not just a select few.

There were enough people who weren't new to start things off, anyway. Unguilded workers was the first thing mentioned – everyone was bothered about that over this side of the river, Petitioners and Parliamentarians both – and there was a rumble of approval from some of the unknowns around the edges; good. Squats maintenance; plenty over here were bothered about the way the Council had been letting that slide. Rising prices, too, that even got some people Alyssa didn't recognise joining in.

"And what about the barges?" someone asked, after a while.

"The barges?" a prosperous-looking printer asked.

"Teren barges. Not been coming in like usual, have they? Oh, there's one or two. But where're the rest? Where's our grain? Eh? Was the only thing I could still afford." The speaker, a middle-aged woman in a neat but patched gown, sounded bitter.

Alyssa hadn't noticed that. She felt like an idiot; she of all people ought to be aware that Teren might be reacting to Marek's declaration of independence – and perhaps to the magical implications – and not necessarily in ways that were immediately obvious.

"Independence is all very well," someone else chimed in, "but not if they're going to stop shipping us food. Not like we can *be* independent that way, is it?"

"There's still Exuria, and the Crescent," someone else objected.

"Yes, but," the first speaker started authoritatively, and

went on to explain trade numbers in a knowledgeable way that, Alyssa suspected, anyone in the Council would be deeply surprised by given her accent.

"We should take this to the Council!" a person towards the back shouted, and there was a rumble of approval from, at a quick glance, the newer folk.

"Never mind the Council," Simeon said. He'd been standing near the back with his arms folded. "We should deal with these things ourselves. Why should we go cap in hand to the Council, begging for their help?"

"How?" the trade-knowledgeable woman demanded. "What do you propose we do? You going to go talk to Teren about their exports yourself, are you?"

Argument broke out, but Tey seemed to be managing it well.

It was all going about as well as Alyssa could possibly have expected. And yet – somehow, she still felt faintly dissatisfied. She wasn't even sure why; there wasn't anything she could put her finger on.

But...what difference would any of this make, in the end? Was anyone who wasn't right here in this place listening? And what could they do if – when, she suspected – the Council just ignored them?

It was the right thing to be doing, she still thought that. Still knew that. It just...wasn't the only thing. Couldn't be. Not if they wanted to get anywhere. And what clawed at her as she listened was that she couldn't think of what else might work.

FOUR

The warmth in the Council Chamber was almost stifling, the furnace fired up for the winter weather. Even only in half-formal Council robes it was, for Marcia's money, far too hot. She shifted uncomfortably as her belly twinged, and wished for a glass of water. At least the bringing in of the Petition had also brought a welcome blast of cool outdoor air.

Pirran, Pedeli-Head, was on her feet. "Where did this come from?" she demanded, gesturing towards the stacks of paper sitting to one side of the Chamber, now in the care of the Reader's Clerk. "Out of *nowhere*, all of a sudden, this nonsense."

Marcia rose to her own feet, narrowly avoiding a roll of her eyes. "With all due respect, Pedeli-Head, some of the lower city have been discussing this for months. Longer, really. The Petitioners have been having meetings, and printing pamphlets, and so on. It's only now that they are bringing it directly to the Council, certainly, but…"

"Opportunism," Pirran huffed not-very-under her breath.

"They wish," Marcia said more loudly, "to be part of Marek's new independence. In that sense, yes, they are taking the opportunity they see to be part of Marek's recreating itself."

"There is no need to *recreate* anything simply because we are formalising a separation from Teren that in all truth has existed for decades, centuries, already," Tabriol-Head said crisply. "Marek can continue to operate exactly as it always has."

Indeed, it could; that didn't mean everyone wanted it to. Especially the 'everyone' that didn't gain from the existing setup. Marcia, sitting down again, wasn't quite sure how to put that in words that might achieve anything in the Council. Andreas, sitting half-sideways a couple of rows in front of her, caught her eye and pulled a face that suggested he was having much the same thought.

Pirran was a friend of Madeleine's. What would Madeleine think of all this? It was a distracting thought for reasons other than its content; the last she'd heard from Madeleine had been a brief message sent a couple of weeks ago that she was nearly ready to leave Ameten. Nothing since. And at that, she'd been unusually reticent about what she'd been up to in Ameten. Marcia refused to *worry* about Madeleine, who was more than capable of taking care of herself, but...

She'd be back soon. Marcia made herself focus on the discussion.

"This," Warden Amanth, of the Haberdashers, was saying sourly, "is why we put limits on what can be printed. If these pamphlets hadn't been circulating..."

"There's nothing in the Petitioner pamphlets, or in their demands, that is banned by law," Andreas pointed out.

"And those radicals down in Marek Square, making out like they're having a Council of their own?" Athitol-Head demanded. "Listen to one lot," she gestured again at the piles of petition sheets, "and you just encourage the worse."

"Or," Gil Jythri-Head said mildly, "listening to the more moderate voices undermines the power of the extremists, because the moderates are achieving something."

"We're not Teren," Cerit-Head said, without bothering to get up. The Reader frowned at him, but William rarely paid much attention to the Reader. "We're not Teren, as we've all firmly agreed now, and *we* here in Marek permit disagreement. Civil disagreement. This lot, with their petition, they're perfectly polite, we just don't agree with them. Not wanting to do what they ask don't mean they shouldn't ask it. Even the lot down in the square, nothing *wrong* with what they're doing. Free to speak their minds and all that. Don't mean we have to listen to them, mind." He shrugged.

There was a sort of mutter around the room. Marcia couldn't quite tell who was agreeing – or disagreeing – with which part. Daril, despite having gone out to accept the Petition, was staying quiet now. Playing both sides, as bloody usual.

"But what are we going to *do* about it," Athitol-Head said, querulously.

There were a few blank looks.

"Do we have to *do* anything?" Warden Tialla, of the Accountants, asked. "These petitioners, they have presented us with their – requests, let us say, as Cerit-Head suggests. We have accepted the presentation, and we are discussing it. Does that not end the matter? And as for the rabble in the square, surely they are best ignored."

"We cannot just *ignore* them," Warden Hagadath said. "This petition is bad enough but this *meeting* now going on in the square, that goes too far. Too far indeed. They claim they will run the city? That, surely, is treason. *We* run the city, for the good of the city. Not some grubby squat-dwellers." Athitol-Head was nodding approvingly.

Andreas, in front of Marcia, was acknowledged by the Reader. "They're really just holding public discussions," he said. "Some of them have more extreme views, perhaps, but what they are *doing* right now is talking about their concerns. Some of them, I gather, even wanted to come and represent themselves to us. Could we not see this as a way to get a clear idea of what the people of Marek really want?" Sensibly, he ignored the 'dirty squat-dwellers' part.

"They're dangerous rioters who should be put down by force," Athitol-Head announced. "Send in the guard and be done with it."

Well, at least she'd won her bet with Andreas as to whether it was Hagadath or Athitol-Head who would first suggest the use of force. To her relief, there was a murmur of disapproval around the Chamber.

"There is no sign at all of any unrest," Gil said firmly. "Overreacting would be the quickest way to *create* unrest. And the guard might struggle."

"There would be no further unrest if they were all dead or in jail," Athitol-Head said, jaw set. "If the guard cannot cope," her tone made her disdain for this clear, "the mercenaries can join them."

Marcia wasn't at all sure that would be enough, either, depending on how many people there were down there. Marek wasn't set up for the use of force, against its own citizens – an unpleasant idea anyway – or anyone else. Something she'd been thinking of, from time to time, since Selene's last threat. Even if Andreas, when she'd mentioned it to him immediately afterwards, had been dismissive, certain Selene had just been blowing hot air. Marcia wasn't nearly so sure. In this instance, anyway, even if the guards and the mercenaries together *could* make that many arrests, it would be exceptionally messy. Thankfully, the mutter of disapproval was louder and more insistent this time.

"They're Marek citizens who are discussing their views," Tabriol-Head said, shaking her head. "If those views begin to sound dangerous, we can react then. *Proportionately.* I am choosing to assume that your words are hyperbole, Athitol-Head." She frowned across the Chamber. "Unless and until there is a real, evident danger to the rest of the city, let us leave them to it. They'll go away of their own accord eventually."

"Perhaps so, but we cannot – contrary to Tigero-Head – afford to listen to them," Athitol-Head said stubbornly. "We cannot *encourage* this nonsense. At least the Petitioners," her voice held disdain, "came to us."

"Came begging at the door, you mean?" Daril asked, his voice more of a drawl than usual. "With *due deference.*"

Marcia gazed thoughtfully across the chamber at Daril. Was he becoming annoyed with the tenor of this debate, as well? After all, historically he'd supported this sort of thing, before he became Heir. He wasn't exactly expressing an *opinion* though, was he?

He was doubtless planning something. Daril usually was.

"Yes, Leandra," Dintra-Heir said crisply. "With due deference to the government of this city."

"What," Gil enquired pensively, "is the difference between a request to consider involving others in the city's government, made by citizens, and our own decision to govern ourselves in the absence of Teren?"

No one spoke for a moment. Everyone respected Gil, and no one was willing to shout them down, but equally obviously, no one wished to accept what they'd said.

"Oh, come now, Jyrthi," Cerit-Head said. "I've a lot of time for you, and I do see your point, but obviously it's not the same thing at all! We already are the rightful governors of the city, we just want Teren to leave us to it. That lot aren't, that's all there is to it."

"The only thing to do," Pedeli-Head said, "is to ignore it. Ignore them and they'll go away." She nodded decisively.

"Perhaps," Piath suggested, "we should take the two matters separately. It seems to me that the feel of the Council is to ignore the discussion in Marek Square. As Pedeli-Head and Athitol-Head say, we should not give them legitimacy. The Petitioners, however, have correctly come to us – the rightful governors of the city, indeed, as Cerit-Head says. We owe it to them to consider what they say. And, as Jyrthi-Head says, by doing so we encourage correct behaviour."

There was a slightly reluctant murmur of agreement.

"I would recommend," Gil said, rising to their feet, "that we consider the petition point by point, in order to think more clearly about it. Perhaps, indeed, there are *aspects* of what is being said that we could usefully take some input on. Obviously, everyone wants Marek, and Marekers, to be happy, and it is true that this moment of independence is a reasonable one at which to think about structures we might otherwise take for granted, no?" Trust Gil to put things as reasonably as possible.

"Preposterous," Athitol-Head said.

"Well, indeed," Gil said, "if you disagree then of course you are free to do so. But I would be more comfortable to be able honestly to say that we have considered the matter. Reader," they turned towards the centre of the room, "that is a formal proposal to discuss in parts."

It passed, more easily than Marcia had expected.

"So," the Reader said. "The points, to remind you. Firstly, access to the Guilds for all, with the option for anyone who pays a reasonable sum to be tested as a journeyman, with or without a formal apprenticeship history. Secondly, protection for unGuilded workers, with the institution of work-hours limits as with Guilded workers, and equal access with the Guilds to better quality raw materials. Thirdly, removal of the censorship laws. Fourthly, representation for those parts of the city which are neither Guilded nor House-aligned, via an elected Committee of the City, to be involved in city-wide decisions which are not House- or Guild-specific."

"The Guilds are not willing to discuss the matter of journeyman testing," Warden Amanth said, jumping up immediately. "This is a matter for the Guilds, not for the Council, to be dealt with in the Guildhall."

"Perhaps," Daril suggested, "the Council might wish to record its desire for the Guilds to consider the matter."

"When the Council as a whole interferes in House-only matters, Leandra-Head, I am sure we will be happy to bring Guild matters to the Council." Warden Amanth folded his arms.

Daril scowled. The Council as a whole indicated its unwillingness to go further on that particular point, and the Reader moved on.

"Protection," they intoned, "for unGuilded workers."

"Just as with journeymen," Warden Amanth was on his feet again immediately, "protection for unGuilded workers is not Council business, affecting as it does the business of the Guilds..."

"Oh, come now, come now," William scoffed. "That most certainly is a matter for the Council. It touches upon the whole of the city, not just your own internal affairs. No, indeed."

"One might, however," Piath suggested, "argue that it is not a matter of *governance* but one of legislation. As such, we can agree to discuss it once our immediate issues of establishing our new independent structure are managed."

That suggestion passed with a sigh of relief all round. Marcia wasn't *surprised* to find the Council keen to pole the boat further down the river, but she hadn't expected quite this level of alacrity. The issue of censorship was dealt with in the same way.

The Committee of the City, of course, couldn't be tackled with that argument. It was, entirely unsurprisingly, largely unpopular, despite the efforts of Marcia, Gil, and Andreas to make points about joint governance; though Cerit-Head was keener than Marcia had expected. Warden Ilana spoke up on their side, too, despite visible disapproval from other Guildwardens. Daril said nothing, on either side.

"Perhaps," Gil suggested eventually, "some kind of consultation, rather than a direct involvement? A group which could formally represent the views of the lower city to us? We cannot argue that the views of all in Marek are unimportant, even if we argue that the current mechanism is the best for making decisions."

There was a rumble of agreement, but the Reader was checking the clock, and stood, banging their stave on the floor. "Time, all. Time, I fear. We must discuss this further tomorrow."

Well, and wouldn't that be fun. Still; perhaps this evening would provide opportunities to talk some people around. Marcia stood, narrowly missing slamming her bump into the edge of the pew in front, and made her way over to Gil. They might have some ideas.

☉ ☉

As part of the ongoing negotiations around the business of the Group (or: Cato taking some kind of responsibility over Marek's magic and not just leaving it all in Reb's perfectly capable hands), Cato had reluctantly agreed to meet up once a month or so in order to discuss the current status of their respective apprentices, in exchange for otherwise leaving one another alone about it. At the time, this had seemed like a reasonable deal; now, sitting in the front room of Reb's small house near the Old Market, he wondered if he should have gone for two months, or even quarterly. Still. Here he was: bit late to renegotiate.

And Reb was being relatively welcoming, for her. She'd offered him an armchair, and provided a couple of infusions from the seller that had come past the door. Cato would have preferred wine, or possibly, for this time of the afternoon, ale, but you couldn't have everything, and his cinnamon and rose infusion was perfectly pleasant. The heat from the corner stove was welcome, too; it had been chilly and damp, walking over.

"Jonas is doing well," he reported, leaning back in the battered, much-patched armchair and crossing his ankle over his knee. "Strong. Beckett likes him, that's most of it, I think, but he can concentrate when he wants to."

"No more going off on his own?" Reb pushed her dark hair back from her forehead and frowned questioningly at him.

Cato shook his head. "I really do think he learnt his lesson on that one. He's – I don't know. Grown up a little, I suppose. Working with me rather than in spite of me."

"Any more on the flickers?" Reb asked. She already knew they'd established that Jonas *could* prevent a flicker, sometimes, and that if he did, there might be consequences. Well; all actions had consequences, didn't they? That wasn't saying much. Once again, Cato wished he could convince Jonas to do a bit more deliberate research; he hated the feeling of not knowing, of an unsolved problem niggling at the edges of his mind. Not much he could do about it, though; it was already more than clear that pushing harder didn't help at all with Jonas.

"The other day he tried to bring one on," Cato reported,

"and succeeded – just a little one, but the link between that and his use of magic is interesting. Evidently there *is* a link, but it's far from clear, or reliably reproducible. He's willing to talk to me about it now, so that's an improvement." He shrugged. "I mean, perhaps it never will be clear. Magic isn't always predictable, however much we try to make it so, and Jonas' flickers are something else again. They're not Beckett's doing, we know that."

"That there is any link between his magic and his flickers suggests to me that they're something to do," Reb gestured, "with the two planes, or the space between them."

"Mm, me too," Cato agreed, "but in what *way* I have no idea." His toes twitched irritably at the admission.

"You're the one knows more about the space in-between," Reb said, with a slight edge. She might have backed him against Beckett in that particular disagreement, but Cato knew well enough that she still didn't like it.

"Indeed," he said, choosing not to rise to her tone. "Perhaps I should ask Yorick, at that, although I'm not sure Jonas would go for it." Jonas hadn't seemed all that comfortable with Cato's demonstration of how he used the space-between to allow other spirits to act within Marek – without, crucially, ever *being*, technically, in Marek, which was why Reb had backed him against Beckett. To Cato's grateful surprise.

"Well," Reb said, clearly keen to move on. "Let me know if you and Jonas find out anything more about it. In the meantime, it sounds like you've no concerns about his progress as an apprentice."

Cato gestured assent with his infusion-cup.

"So. Alyssa is doing well enough, I suppose, but I'm certain she would be better with more time and focus allocated to magic." She grimaced dissatisfaction.

"Yes, well, she's busy leading an insurrection, right?" Cato said, grinning over the cup at Reb. He'd been quite impressed by the Parliament Alyssa's lot had conducted in Marek Square the previous week.

Reb's dissatisfaction morphed into irritation, vertical lines appearing in her forehead. "We don't talk about that."

Cato sucked at his teeth thoughtfully. "You don't, perhaps. But should you? Shouldn't we be involved, in Alyssa's – insurrection is unfair, so far at least. Attempted revolution, perhaps?" He was asking mostly from mischief – this was definitely going to wind Reb up – but partly because, when it came down to it, he more or less approved of what Alyssa was doing, even if he couldn't *really* be bothered being involved himself.

"No. We should not," Reb said crisply and predictably. "No magic in politics, remember?"

"Eh, I dunno. Isn't that the cityangel, not us?"

"Our power is from the cityangel, or had you forgotten?"

"Not to mention that my mere existence arguably has political impact."

Reb scowled at him. "Hasn't mattered much the last ten years or so."

"That was before my sister began her little campaign." Cato raised an eyebrow pointedly. "Didn't Marcia have you up on the Hill explaining magic? Just a few weeks back?"

Reb shifted in her armchair, looking away from him and over to the window. "She wanted to. Wanted me talking to the whole Council, no less. I said, she should try the ground first, and apparently it was as well I did that." After a grudging moment she added, "I did talk to that Andreas, though, and he listened, even if he wasn't sure what to think. If he's her co-parent, does that make him your brother-in-law, then?"

A transparent attempt to distract. "It does not," Cato said. As well Reb knew. And if she pursued that line, one could argue that Reb was almost Cato's sister-in-law, which was a thought he really wished he hadn't had and was going to move on from immediately. "And does it matter whether it's one or many? It's on the Hill, talking to Marekhill types."

"We *both* talk to a Marekhill type already," Reb said impatiently. "We just don't do magic for her."

A fair point, which Cato ignored. "You've been up on the Hill chatting to Council-members, Alyssa's rabble-rousing...Maybe I should go lend a hand?" He found himself, somewhat alarmingly, sounding more sincere than he'd intended.

"Alyssa is not doing that as a sorcerer. Trust me, we have discussed it."

"We're part of this city too. Why shouldn't we have a say?"

"You can have a say as a citizen. Not as a sorcerer." Her tone was uncompromising.

"Are you going to stop me?" He managed to keep the question just on the edge of polite. He didn't like being dictated to.

Reb sighed, and slumped back into her chair, rubbing at the crease in her forehead. "No. Of course I'm not going to *stop* you. But I thought we were trying to work together. So I am very strongly asking you, as a fellow member of the Group, not to do such a demon-fool thing. Because I am worried about how it might impact on sorcery as a whole. And because I truly cannot see how it will help anyone to wave magic around with the radical types. What if the Council notice? What if they make that their excuse to wade in with the crossbows and pikes and all, the next time that lot get together somewhere?"

"Screw the Council," Cato said automatically, then sighed in turn. "But I take your point. Very well. I will not intervene against your will. Not officially, anyway. I presume the honoured Ser does not object to my observing incognito?" He couldn't believe he was agreeing to this but...well, Reb was right. He'd agreed to work together. And Beckett would be pissed off if he didn't stick to that; and in any case, Cato only broke his agreements under *certain* circumstances and this wasn't important enough to be one of them. He wasn't going to insist *just* in order to upset Reb.

Yet.

"Incognito my arse," Reb said, cracking a half-smile. "I don't believe you're going to be reliably unrecognisable. But that's up to you. I don't care where you go, Cato. I just care about whether you're being a sorcerer there. And you know exactly what I mean by that."

"All right. I won't." He drained his cup, and put it down with a click on the table between them. "So. Alyssa's mediocre and not concentrating hard enough. Tait?"

Reb sighed, and Cato's internal warnings prickled. "I don't know. They're a strong sorcerer outside the city, seems to me. That business with the dragon-bear, for one. And with the bridge during the floods."

"That was inside the city."

"But not Marek magic. Blood magic. As I'm sure you remember. They're good with that, no question. It's Marek magic they struggle with." She scowled. "I've no real idea why, either. They're trying hard enough. The power's the same, surely, however you get to it – doesn't make sense to me that they can do it one way and not the other. I thought, perhaps, habit…"

Cato chewed at his lip. "Maybe. We all do things different ways, don't we? You use more ingredients than I do."

"And you're better off-the-cuff," Reb agreed.

"That's because you don't use magic enough, or informally enough, because you've got these silly ideas about keeping it for best," Cato said, "but we've been over that before. The point is – maybe blood just is the way they access it."

Reb scowled. "Ingredients and gesture, though, they're both ways of focussing the power you get through Beckett. Blood cuts Beckett out altogether. Didn't that ought to be different entirely?"

"You've done blood magic before," Cato said, treading on dangerous ground. "I wouldn't know."

Reb glared at him, and he raised his hands defensively. "Not a criticism! Just that I only have experience of one way of doing things. This seems more like your area.

Even if it was a while back."

"But you know Tait better," Reb pointed out. Evading, Cato noted, the matter of blood magic. "And, like I said, I'm stuck. If you do have any thoughts, even tentative ones, I'd be happy to hear them."

"We don't talk about it much," Cato said with perfect truth. Although now he came to think of it, maybe Tait had been more evasive than usual about magic just lately. He just wasn't sure whether or not it would be wise to push. "Tait's your apprentice. I don't want to step on any toes. Ethically, either."

"Indeed," Reb said. "Which would hold more water if I didn't already know you'd taught them ward-holding, for example."

"Yes, well, that was *necessary*," Cato said with great dignity.

"Did you notice anything, though?" Reb pressed.

Cato thought about it, and slowly shook his head. "Don't think so. It was early on, though. I wouldn't have expected much."

Reb sighed. "Well. If anything occurs to you, I'm open to ideas. Now. Before you go, now that we're done with the formal stuff, I was going to offer you a glass of wine…"

Cato beamed happily at her. "Reb! I didn't know you cared."

"Shut up," she said, and poured him a glass of what turned out to be an only moderately terrible white. Cato preferred red, but for once, he didn't say anything.

"So," he asked chattily. "How're things going between Marek's newest power couple? Has my sister got you doing the rounds of the salons and parties yet?"

Reb's look of horror was priceless. "*No*," she said firmly. "And she won't. Thanks all the same."

"Eh," Cato said. "You're public now. I would brace myself, if I were you. This week it's Tigero-Head in a private room over infusion and crackers. Next week it'll be posh robes and parading round House Whatever with a glass of Exurian fizzy wine in hand." He gestured with one hand. "Invited, the Sorcerer Reb…"

Reb rolled her eyes. "Not my scene."

It had been Cato's, once, sort of, although he'd only been old enough to attend one or two before everything had *happened* and he'd been off Marekhill and over here. Which was not exactly a sore point, but… He grinned at Reb and moved the conversation on.

It was surprisingly pleasant, actually, spending twenty minutes drinking wine and making small talk – and, fine, exchanging gossip – with Reb. A fellow sorcerer to actually be on pleasant terms with? Well, wasn't that a turn-up for the proverbial.

He just wished he knew what was going on with Tait.

FIVE

Marcia was shown to Ilana's workroom, not their office, when she arrived at the Jewellers' Guild; and Ilana was in their work attire, long grey braids wrapped in a red flowered cloth at the back of their head, not formally robed. Marcia took this as a good sign for their working relations. This was, after all, an informal meeting; she'd dressed down herself.

"I hope all is well with the baby," Ilana said, gesturing Marcia to take a seat by the fire, in one of the worn armchairs. The large table by the window at the other side of the room was crowded with tools and pieces of jewellery in various states, and there was a faint smell of metal in the air. "May I pour for you? I have rose here, or I can find an apprentice to fetch something else."

"All is going along perfectly as far as I can tell," Marcia said, "and yes, an infusion would be delightful. I do like rose."

They talked of inconsequentialities for a few minutes, sipping their infusions, before Marcia brought the conversation round to her true reason for being here.

"I have been wondering," she said, keeping her voice light, "what the Guilds' position is on the matter of these radicals that have been petitioning the Council."

Ilana looked at her silently for a moment over the rim of their cup. "I assume," they said, one eyebrow lifting, "that you are not referring to the publicly expressed positions in the Chamber. Given that you were there for that."

Marcia shrugged. "Obviously you must speak as you see fit, but," she coughed slightly stagily, "I do consider this a private conversation."

The corner of Ilana's mouth quirked; both of them knew that a 'private conversation' wasn't an entirely reliable concept in politics. Marcia was engaging not to give the name of her sources, rather than not to repeat any information Ilana gave her. "Well," they said, after another pause, "you say 'the Guilds' position' as if that is a single thing."

Marcia gestured for them to go on.

Ilana sat back and continued. "There are some, of course, who are very keen to maintain and defend the Guilds', ah, political position." They didn't mention Warden Hagadath; they didn't need to. "A valid, or at least understandable, point, in that the Guilds have more power now than we have had for a long time."

"Would the radicals' demands reduce that?" Marcia asked.

"Well, now, there you have put your finger on one aspect of the debate. One side maintains that to hold a share of a concentrated power is, well, at the least, not something to be idly given up. The other argues that to be part of spreading power more widely would, in itself, be a source of power. And, of course, yet another side argues on purely moral grounds that all should have an equal say in governance, or at the very least be heard." Ilana pursed their lips. "The Guilds I think hold very few Parliamentarians. Petitioners, though, those we have, a fair few. They argue that all should be heard, and considered properly in the government of Marek, whether on moral or on practical grounds."

"So this debate is going on within the Guilds as well as in the streets and in the Council?"

"You say that as if there *is* any real debate going on in the Council," Ilana said, their voice tart. "But, yes, this debate has been active within the Guilds for some time. Jeres Arianden, of the Vintners – you may recall that she has been involved with helping the Teren refugees, and reported to the Council on the matter – has been the main driving force. I understand her to be deeply involved with the Petitioners. She is very persuasive; she's convinced many, especially of the younger members of the Guilds."

Including Ilana, Marcia wondered? Not that they were a

younger member of their Guild; Ilana was only a little younger than Madeleine. But they didn't sound disapproving. She remembered Arianden speaking to the Council about refugees, some months before. In the last couple of weeks, the number of refugees coming into Marek had been much lower; Marcia hadn't yet found out why, and the rest of the Council seemed mostly relieved that they weren't having to find housing for them.

Ilana put their cup down on the low table, and drummed their fingers thoughtfully on their leg. "Several of the Guilds – including my own – have their own elections for Guildwarden coming up soon. This is – a salient debate in that."

Marcia nodded slowly, and cursed herself for not knowing that already. Of course if Ilana was facing election, that would affect how they were approaching this. Not to mention the fact that if Ilana *lost* their election, they'd also lose their Council seat.

"And your position, Fereno-Heir?"

She couldn't avoid giving information in return, could she? She chose her words with care. "I see the – natural justice, I suppose, in the Petitioners' arguments. Even in those of the Parliamentarians, though I cannot see how we could possibly move so rapidly from where we are now, to what they would wish to see, even if I wholly agreed with them. In any case, as you will doubtless not be surprised to hear after the discussions in Council, I would very much like to see the Council – the Houses, in particular, in all honesty – actively listening to more of the city." She sighed. "Very few of the Heads go down to the south-west, still less set foot over the river. They don't know or understand what goes on there. I cannot see that that is a good recipe for successful governance."

"And yet, one might argue that it has *been* successful for several centuries now." Ilana was watching Marcia narrowly.

"True," Marcia allowed. "And yet, times change. And success depends in part on the happiness of the city as a whole. For better or for worse, if the lower city wants

JULIET KEMP

change, surely that in itself indicates that the 'success' of the Council is – well, at the least, no longer overwhelming? A great many other things are changing just now. Perhaps they're right, and this is the moment for change."

"An interesting argument," Ilana said non-committally. "So. Are you here to ask something of me?"

"I honestly don't know," Marcia said, spreading her hands. "I suppose I am here to find out more of the thoughts of all the groups involved in this situation, in the hope that there is a way forward everyone can agree on. Exploring, rather than requesting."

"There's no way forward that the lower city radicals and Hagadath or Athitol can agree on," Ilana said bluntly, "but, yes, perhaps there is a middle road that you, and I, and the Petitioners, can find." They looked at Marcia over the edge of their cup. "I mentioned Jeres Arianden? She's niece to Warden Zeril of the Woodworkers."

"Really."

"Not a connection either of them make much of publicly, but, well. As I said, she's been talking to younger Guildmembers, and in the Vintners I gather she's been convincing the higher-up folk as well. The Broderers and the Clockmakers were both represented – formally represented, with their banners – in that procession up the Hill. And I get the impression Jeres has been speaking to her uncle. I could be wrong, but it seems to me he's been moving away from Hagadath's side of things."

Hagadath's side of things. And elections coming up for several of the Guilds.

"May I ask, who is standing against you in your election?" Marcia asked.

Ilana inclined their head. "Indeed you may. I face opposition from both sides, as it happens."

"Traditionalist and radical?"

"We have had a recent influx of younger journeymen and wardens," Ilana said. "It would be oversimplifying the matter to say that the young are always more radical –

70

some of them rather the opposite – but the radical campaigning against me is *very* young, and would struggle to obtain votes from Guildmembers of longer standing. I believe I am well-trusted by the older Guildmembers, and that my own position – of gradual change, listening to the city as a whole – is supported across the Guild."

Marcia translated that with ease: the radical would attract primarily other radicals, and Ilana, with a slightly progressive approach and a long and competent history, could poach any votes that weren't already radically committed. And the traditionalists knew and liked Ilana, and would stick with them so as long as Ilana didn't stray too far into radical territory.

"I'm glad to hear you feel positive about your chances," Marcia said.

"Thank you. So. Let me talk more to my connections, and investigate the situation with the other elections. I will send you word, when it's convenient to speak again."

Ilana obviously thought they were done; and Marcia hadn't brought up the other matter she'd wanted to speak of.

"While we're discussing the political future of Marek," she said, quickly, "what about the sorcerers?"

Ilana sighed. "Marcia. Don't you feel that dealing with lower city radicals *and* sorcery, all at once, might be biting off a little more than you can chew? The radicals are important, right now. Leave the sorcery for another time."

Which was all very well, if you weren't worrying that Selene was going to show up with a cartload of demons on the doorstep and make magic a very salient point indeed. But Marcia had learnt her lesson on that one; if even Andreas wouldn't take the threat seriously, she wasn't going to convince Ilana here and now.

"May I be blunt?" Ilana continued. Marcia inclined her head in acquiescence. "You shouldn't have tried to introduce the sorcerer so soon. I fear you've only antagonised some who might have been your allies."

They shrugged. "I, obviously, do not share the prejudices of the Houses about this. But sorcerers shouldn't be involved with politics."

"That wasn't my intention…"

"No. And yet it is easy to portray it that way. Leave it for now. Let us resolve these matters of the lower city first. There is plenty of time to think about how – *if* – the Council needs to speak more to the sorcerers." Ilana smiled, and Marcia tried not to see it as patronising. "Patience, yes? Marek wasn't founded in a day."

Which was true, as far as it went. Marcia just hoped *patience* was going to be possible.

☺ ☺

"Well it's not *had* any effect," Simeon said loudly across the mutterings in the room, from his usual position at the back, leaning against the wall which was covered with a layering of tatty posters. His arms were folded, his shoulders set aggressively; he was, in Alyssa's estimation, spoiling for a fight. As usual.

The Bucket was fuller than normal, with both Petitioners and Parliamentarians, and the atmosphere was febrile. Alyssa, grateful that she'd arrived early enough to snag a chair that didn't aggravate her hip too much, leant back against its battered and slightly inadequate padding and chewed at the inside of her lip as she listened to the debate.

"It's not had any *immediate* effect," Finn countered. Finn ran an apothecary-shop of sorts down in the south-west, unGuilded and working in a variety of recreational substances as well as cheap medicines for those that couldn't afford a Guilded apothecary. "Surely none of us were expecting that we would present our demands and hold our discussions and the Council would immediately throw the doors open?" He made a scoffing noise, and Simeon scowled. Served Simeon right; he was usually the one making scoffing noises at people.

Finn was right, of course; it was never going to be an

immediate change. But even Alyssa, who hadn't expected that – she was, she acknowledged, too cynical these days to expect anything much – was frustrated by the absence of any meaningful reaction at all.

"At least they didn't send the guards in against us," Tey pointed out. He was always one for looking on the bright side, to a degree that Alyssa sometimes found more than a little annoying, though it made him a good facilitator. Sara was facilitating tonight, though so far the discussion had been rolling along fine by itself.

"Maybe better if they had," Simeon countered. There was a rumble of confusion at his comment from most of the room, although the couple of people leaning against the wall next to him were nodding along. "Might have stirred people up a bit," he clarified, raising his voice over the murmuring. "Seeing the Council strike us down for daring to speak our thoughts. Rather than this – nothing." She'd heard Simeon on this tack before – he'd printed a whole anonymous pamphlet about it, if she remembered right, though it hadn't been popular.

"I don't feel I can be *sorry* that no one was hurt or arrested," Tey said, sounding shocked.

"I would have been more than happy to be arrested for the cause," Simeon announced, and his supporters nodded vehemently again, like puppets on a busker's string. Which was fine and all – Alyssa had prepared for that as well, would have been foolish not to – but getting into a row about it here and now wouldn't help anyone. And not everyone did feel that way, for better or for worse.

"Rather than arguing about what just happened," Alyssa called out, drawing attention away from Simeon and Tey glaring at one another, "we need to decide what to do next."

"We need to put more pressure on the Council to consider the Petition," Jeres said, to an angry murmur from the more radical elements of the crowd. "As Finn says, we could hardly expect an immediate response. The Guilds are considering it, and…"

"The Guilds are sitting on their hands!" someone called out. They weren't wrong.

"There are elections coming up in the Guilds," Jeres said, more loudly. "We need to put our efforts into winning those elections, in order to put more pressure on the Council. If there are more Guildwardens on our side…"

"Guildwardens are one thing. Guildwardens on the Council are rather another. How do you propose to ensure that your hypothetical sympathetic Guildwardens *attend* the Council?" Alyssa demanded. There were only thirteen Guild seats on the Council, and there were more Guilds than that; the Guildwardens were selected in a separate election, and that wasn't due for another year.

"We can unseat Hagadath, for a start," Jeres said, "and then there will be a by-election for their Guild seat, and…"

"So we sit around with our thumbs up our arses while you chase election after election, and nothing changes in the meantime?" Alyssa shook her head. "While the Council sit on high and solidify the arrangements of this new independent Marek? No. Too slow by far. We will miss our moment."

"The increase in the Guild seats only last year shows that the Council *can* change at any time," Jeres pointed out, arms crossed defensively.

"Indeed, in theory, except that in practice, those extra seats just make the Guilds more determined to hold jealously onto their power instead of expanding it." Alyssa shook her head. "I don't see the Guilds pushing for the squats to be better maintained, do you? The Masons didn't lift a finger to stop those incompetents out in the south-west until the floods came in, and then it was the *Houses* had them hopping, from all I heard, not the rest of the Guilds."

"We need real action!" one of Simeon's friends shouted.

"What does that mean?" Jeres challenged. "Are we to march on the Council Chamber waving torches like in a melodrama?" Her voice was scathing, but as Alyssa looked round the room, more than one person seemed like they were seriously considering the matter.

Which – much though Alyssa would quite like to see it too – would not in fact serve. At least, not here and now. Jeres had a point; Simeon and friends were good at having big ideas, and generally not so good at the implementation.

"We must not waste our energy – or even, perhaps, our lives – without due consideration," Alyssa said, slightly reluctantly. "Marching on the Chamber all unprepared is unlikely to see success."

"So let us prepare!" that same enthusiastic person called. "Let us gather swords and pikes!"

Almost instantly, the room erupted into hubbub, those who liked the idea of violent revolution arguing hotly with those who preferred other solutions. There were far fewer of the first, though they were louder; Alyssa could already see it wouldn't pass. She scowled. She wasn't much for marching on the Chamber with weapons, but nor did she fancy waiting for Jeres' slow reforms via – maybe, perhaps, one day – winning elections. She only wished she could think of an alternative.

No decision was going to be made here, tonight, at any rate. She could predict that with certainty right now. But she'd still have to sit here and wait it out; she couldn't just up and leave halfway. She found herself wishing that this was one of the evenings when she could duck out early using Jina as an excuse, but Jina was sleeping at a friend's tonight. She sighed, and pushed herself up to make her way to the bar. She definitely needed another beer.

SIX

Marcia was at breakfast in her room when she was finally proven right.

Griya had brought her a mint infusion and some fresh rolls, and she was sitting in the window, looking out over Marek. One hand rested idly on her stomach, feeling the baby wriggle inside – it was often active in the mornings.

"This is your city," she said softly to the baby. She thought of introducing her child to everything she loved about Marek – the beauties and bustle of Marek Square at a festival; the Old Market first thing in the morning; the view from their very own windows out over the river – and her heart warmed.

It was mid-Ein, and spring was just beginning to show its face. Marcia had seen the first crocuses coming through around the trees in Marek Park, walking there with Andreas earlier in the week. And today the sun was bright and promising. It was the sort of day when the city looked its best from up here, that welcome sunlight glittering off glass windows and metal lamp-holders and all the rest. Marcia looked out to her right, east to the sea with its small fisher-boat dots; then let her gaze travel back westwards upstream along the river, through the city towards the barge-yard. There was the small pale rectangle of the tent where the Teren refugees went for information – she really should follow up on what was happening there, and whether the numbers really had dropped or it was just temporary – and even further, the dots of a few barges coming in…

More than a few barges. A lot of barges. Marcia squinted, straining the limits of her eyesight. Unless it was debris from upstream, that looked like a great many barges, and all coming down the river at once, in a mass. That wasn't usual, was it? They normally trailed one after the other, with a decent gap between them for safety. Never in that sort of clump. And so many of them. Could something be wrong? Some kind of accident meaning they'd needed to group themselves together?

Except... she couldn't see properly, it was too far away, but she could swear the sunlight was throwing tiny glints of something from them, and her mind shouted *breastplate, armour* at her.

Her skin prickled, the rolls souring in her stomach.

That was impossible. Wasn't it?

Was there commotion in the barge-yard? She couldn't *see* properly, it was too *far*, but there was something about the way things looked, about the shadows and shapes moving there...

She was imagining things. Surely, she was imagining things. Fanciful, like one of Cousin Cara's more irritating friends had claimed pregnant people got. She clenched her teeth until her jaw hurt.

It would be ridiculous to get properly dressed and go down to the barge-yard herself. It certainly wasn't the sort of place for Heir-Fereno to be, and whilst Marcia did go exploring the rest of the city far more often than most of the Heads or Heirs, or indeed anyone else from Marekhill, the barge-yard was a step too far. Especially given how much her hips ached at the moment, with the baby. She hadn't even finished her breakfast yet.

And she was, surely, imagining things.

The barges, if that was what they were, in their pushed together mass, had reached the bargeyard, and stopped there.

About halfway down.

Approximately where Beckett's dominion over the city began.

Carefully, Marcia put down her half-eaten roll. Trying not to hurry, she put on tunic and trousers, not outdoor wear, just house wear, but enough to be seen in, unlike her night attire, and went down to the hallway to ask one of the footmen to find a messenger.

The messenger looked surprised to be asked to go out

to the barge-yard just "to see what was happening there", as well she might. But her shrug as she pocketed the coins made it clear that she was happy to humour the strange ideas of some Marekhill type if it meant getting paid for it.

Marcia was imagining things. She told herself, all the interminable time she was pacing up and down the reception room, unable to settle to anything as she waited for a response, that she was just overreacting, seeing what wasn't there. *Fanciful*.

But she wasn't, when it came to it, surprised when the messenger came back, face white, and blurted out, "It's Teren, Ser! Teren come with soldiers and demons to take us back!"

It wasn't, strictly, a *siege*. Marek was, after all, quite a difficult city to besiege. There was nothing preventing anyone from entering or leaving the city at the side that gave into the sea; indeed, a Salinas ship with fresh Exurian produce and Crescent rice had come in just that morning. There was nothing, come to that, preventing anyone from crossing the swamps and going up into the mountains, except for the swamps themselves. (Which weren't so much impassable, technically – at least for a small unburdened group – as they were unpleasant and difficult to pass through; and then assuming you didn't want to wander round Teren, which seemed a bad idea just now, you'd have to climb the mountains after that – the nearest pass was some way away and even that was hard to navigate – and on the other side you'd be in Exuria, and what would you do there?)

Also, arguably, for it to be a siege, there would need to be some kind of city gate or wall, and Marek had never had one of those. Had never needed one.

But whatever you called it, there were a couple of battalions of Teren soldiers at the Teren-ward side of the city, and the only reason they weren't all the way into the city was that the sorcerers they had with them all had demons under their command, and Beckett, Marek's cityangel, would not let the demons into the city.

The previous day had involved a lot of running around, some shouting, and a largely useless Council meeting. Now it was breakfast time, and time for Marcia to do some proper planning.

So far, the demons hadn't pushed all that hard, according to a note from Reb, who had consulted with Beckett. (Beckett was, apparently and unsurprisingly, very irritable.) So far, for whatever reason, the soldiers hadn't tried to enter without the sorcerers. So far, they were – Selene was – just squatting there, blocking traffic both downriver and upriver; and making demands.

Making demands; and passing on *information*. Including, perhaps most importantly for Marcia, the information that Madeleine was with them. Which Marcia would have doubted, absent anyone seeing Madeleine in person – which no one had, yet, or if they had, it hadn't been brought to Marcia's attention. Except that there was a note from Madeleine, in her own writing, which had been conveyed privately to Marcia along with the more general notes from Selene to the Council as a whole. And the note had their House code in the middle.

> *I am, unfortunately and somewhat against my preference, the temporary guest of the former Teren Lieutenant,*

the plain-text ran, and then, underneath, encoded,

> *Truth. Ignore demands. Consider future, not past.*

Which was what Marcia would have expected of Madeleine, who wasn't the sort to give in to demands; and she didn't think it was something Selene would have written if she had got her hands on the code and was faking the message. It rather undercut the other implications of Madeleine being – Marcia's gut clenched at the word – Selene's hostage.

The trouble was, Selene hadn't *made* any demands of her, specifically, yet. Hadn't tried to leverage Madeleine's situation. Hadn't even mentioned, in her general public announcement demanding Marek's return to the Teren fold, that she had Madeleine; it was only Marcia who'd been told that. And no one else had brought it up to her; so either no one else knew, or someone was plotting already. She was hoping Selene wasn't quite that competent.

"I don't understand why no one's seen her though," Marcia said, fretfully.

She and Andreas were in House Fereno's small reception room, at the back of the house. It was more private; and you couldn't see out to the river from there, which meant that Marcia wasn't constantly trying to see down towards the barge-yard. Not that she'd get any useful information from that anyway. Too far to see anything in detail, but that didn't seem to stop her looking. They were awaiting Reb, although Marcia hadn't told Andreas that quite yet. He did know about Madeleine; always best to keep your allies informed, and in any case, she didn't want to handle this alone.

"Selene's holding her in reserve," Andreas said, shrugging. "She's implied the threat, and she's hoping you'll jump straight away and start making things happen behind the scenes."

"And that I'll have less leverage if everyone knows why I've changed my mind about Teren?"

"That would be my guess."

Marcia rubbed fretfully at her belly, which was aching again. "Well, I'll bring it up myself at the Council meeting later." Making it public pulled Selene's teeth. Not that that helped Madeleine; it wasn't like the rest of the Council were going to rate her safety above the safety of the city as a whole, even if Madeleine had asked them to.

"Another couple of downriver barges left this morning,

I'm told," Andreas said. He was picking at a thumbnail. "Turned around when they couldn't get down to the yard, went back upriver."

"Left? Not conscripted?"

"I was told, left. The blockade's no bigger. What I don't know for certain is what happened to their cargoes. If I were Selene, I wouldn't be turning away free provisions. And I can't see the bargees wanting to pull their cargoes back upriver, either. If they could sell them upriver they wouldn't bring them here."

Marcia hummed. "Well. It's more that, if they could sell them for the same price upriver, they wouldn't sell them here. They might prefer to take them back than have them requisitioned."

"They might not have had a choice."

"Wouldn't Captain Anna have seen them loading off from the barges?"

"Not if they did it at night," Andreas said. "Her report said, she couldn't be sure either way." He glanced over at her as she made an irritable noise. "I'm sure you'll get a copy through soon."

Captain Anna and her troop were in the barge-yard, on the Marek side, under strict instructions not to do anything other than observe. They'd also been busy putting up a barricade across the middle of the barge-yard – roughly on the line where Beckett's influence ended, from what Marcia gathered, though she didn't know if any of the sorcerers had helped identify that line – out of all the junk that had been lying around and some more robust bits they'd requisitioned from the warehouses. Marcia hadn't yet seen it, due to the fact that no one, in particular Captain Anna, was terribly keen for any of the Heads of the Marek Houses to go down and hang around somewhere where there were a bunch of soldiers also hanging around. Even if none of them had apparently *done* anything yet.

Pirran-Head had taken charge of receiving and circulating Captain Anna's reports, which was faintly annoying, but so far Marcia had *received* all of the reports – just a bit late, occasionally.

A knock on the door, and a footman showed Reb in. Andreas swung round, looked startled, and then did his best to hide it. Maybe Marcia should have warned him, after all. Reb, who could read a room, cast a swift glare at her and crossed the room to greet Andreas.

"Delighted to see you, Ser Reb," Andreas said, with every appearance of sincerity, standing to give her a formal bow. He had been making efforts to manage his wary feelings around A Sorcerer, and in an ideal world, Marcia would have stuck with intermittent low-tension social meetings for rather longer.

In an ideal world, they wouldn't have Selene and a bunch of soldiers and sorcerers camped on their doorstep.

"I asked Reb here," Marcia said, "because along with the soldiers, there are sorcerers out there. And we need to be able to talk to the Council about them, this afternoon." She looked at Andreas. "I need your help."

Andreas pulled a face. "Well, that's going to go down like a cup of cold sick, isn't it?"

Reb choked back a laugh.

"You're not wrong," Marcia agreed. "But we can't just ignore it, and we can't let the Council just ignore it. So." She looked over at Reb. "Any joy on the whole demons thing?"

"Hold up," Andreas said. "Demons? There are demons out there?

"With the Teren sorcerers," Marcia said, confused. "Yes, of course."

"You mean – each of those sorcerers has a demon in tow?" He sounded genuinely shocked.

"Yes," Reb said, not sugar-coating her tone. "What did you think?"

"You don't have a demon."

"No, because Marek magic uses the cityangel. Teren magic is demons. Or blood."

Marcia had *thought* Andreas understood that already, but apparently… This was going to be even harder in Council than she'd supposed, if even Andreas needed remedial instruction.

"Right." Andreas swallowed. "Right. I didn't – I mean. I knew Teren had demons. I've listened to the refugees. But I didn't realise...I didn't think Selene..." His face creased. "I thought the sorcerers were just a threat. That there *could* be demons. Not..."

"That would be possible," Reb allowed, "except that it's not what Beckett says. Beckett can feel other spirits against the, hm, the *skin* of their magic, I suppose, over the city. If they say there's demons there, it's true."

"Right," Andreas said again, horror plain on his face. "But you're hoping to – do something? About that?"

Reb grimaced. "That's – well, that's what we need to do, yes. But if you're meaning, 'do we know how', no." She spread her hands. "Cato's working on it. I spoke to him this morning. And for now, of course, they can't enter the city – Beckett prevents that – and Beckett says they're not really trying, not yet. They're shoving a little, sort of, but mostly they're waiting."

"What *for*?" Marcia demanded, but neither of the others answered. Fair enough; she didn't know either. For Selene's political efforts to pay off, maybe? Surely she'd rather keep the demons as threat, and use them only if she had to.

"You say Cato's working on it?" Andreas asked. He glanced over at Marcia, then back at Reb. "What is he working on, exactly?"

Reb sighed. "So. The spirits out there – it's not really fair to call them demons, given what we know about current Teren binding practices – are bound to their sorcerers. We've broken one such binding, in the past, but it took an enormous amount of effort."

"We?" Andreas asked.

"Marek sorcerers, with Beckett," Reb said, repressively. And Marcia herself, but it wasn't like she'd been doing *magic*, exactly, herself, owing as how she couldn't. She'd just been helping Beckett use their link to the city. Not that the Council – or, perhaps, Andreas himself – would necessarily see it that way. She wasn't about to make the trial unless she really had to.

"You can't just do that again." It wasn't exactly a question; Andreas wasn't stupid.

"Like I said. Enormous amount of effort, just for one single demon. There's a whole lot out there right now. And the other thing is, I don't work with spirits myself, beyond Beckett themself which is different. So I'm not sure where to go next. Cato does, sometimes. He's trying to work out if there's another way."

"A sneakier way," Marcia murmured.

"Well, exactly," Reb said. "This being one of those occasions where your brother's natural inclinations might actually be useful."

"We have to get you into the Council," Andreas said, abruptly, as if he'd been having a different conversation in his head. "We can't just explain all this ourselves. As soon as anyone asks questions, we'll be screwed."

Marcia might be able to answer more questions than Andreas could, but then she would be screwed in a different way, because people were going to start asking questions, again, about her own involvement with magic. She'd weathered that once; it had left her on very thin ice.

"I'm sure they'll love that," Reb said. She looked alarmed, if resigned; Marcia didn't expect that Reb was any more enthusiastic to go talk to the Council than she was to take her. Especially given that she knew how things had gone the last time Marcia had suggested it. Mind you; the situation had rather *changed*, now.

The Council's single emergency meeting had involved a vote on whether to welcome in Selene and her army and give up their newly-announced independence; a near-unanimous 'No' – even, to Marcia's surprise, from Athitol-Head, who might be perfectly happy to work with Teren but who didn't like being threatened. Then they'd spent the rest of the time arguing about what to do instead and failing to get anywhere. The discussions were to resume this afternoon. Marcia wasn't looking forward to it.

Andreas was picking at his thumb again. "They won't

like it at all, but they need to deal with it." He pulled a face. "I don't exactly like it either – no offence, Ser Reb."

"None taken," Reb said politely. She hesitated. "And truly, Reb is fine."

Andreas nodded, appreciating the gesture. "And I'm Andreas. So. Yes. I don't like it. But you're telling me there's a whole raft of demons out there, or spirits or whatever you care to call them – they're a threat, is the point – and neither I nor the Council have any idea what to do with them. They didn't even *mention* demons or sorcerers yesterday." It had been a glaring lack, and Marcia hadn't brought it up either; she wanted to speak to Reb first and find out if there was anything Marek's sorcerers could *do*. She would have far rather Reb were able to present a coherent proposal.

But they couldn't keep waiting. They had to get the Council on board sooner rather than later. Because one way or another, the demons had to be dealt with. Beckett might be able to keep them out now, when they weren't – for whatever reason – really trying. Marcia wasn't foolish enough to think Beckett could do so indefinitely or against a concerted push. They'd nearly fallen against only the one. No point in explaining that any more clearly now, to Andreas. It wasn't like just leaving Selene and Co out there indefinitely would be a good idea even if they *couldn't* get in.

"I'm going to have to introduce her this afternoon, aren't I?" Marcia said. "I'm the only one that has the slightest idea what I'm talking about, and therefore any chance of talking them into listening."

"I could do it," Andreas said, doubtfully.

"No point you getting yourself any deeper into the mess I'm already in regarding magic," Marcia said, slightly reluctantly; she would have been quite glad not to be on her own. But Andreas would be more useful with a tiny bit more distance. He couldn't be all that distanced from Marcia, given the whole child situation, but every little helped. They were allies – independent allies – and they could lean on that. "And I know more," she added, accurately. She sighed. "We can't have the Council and the Group working independently on this. It's absurd. If we want Selene to go away, we must get rid of the demons as well as the soldiers."

"More than the soldiers," Andreas amended.

"Well, we're not exactly well-equipped to deal with them either, but I take your point. There's not that many of them." Captain Anna could handle the soldiers, at a push, supported by the guard, but it would be costly. In lives, not money.

Of course the other problem, that none of them were talking about right now but Marcia couldn't believe she was the only one to think of, was that even if the demons were 'dealt with', and the soldiers too, there was a whole country full of sorcerers or soldiers available to come down the river to push their way into Marek. If they got rid of Selene this time, all they did was buy time. They needed more than that to defend their independence in the longer run.

But. One thing at a time. Buying time would do, for now. They couldn't work on *more* or *better* if they'd lost already. And that was without getting into what would be the likely outcome for Marcia herself if Selene returned to Marek.

"Very well," Reb said. "I see your point. I don't much like it either." She glanced over to Andreas, and Marcia saw them both share an expression of resigned agreement. Well. At least perhaps this disaster might bring them closer together.

"So," Marcia said briskly, "I need you ready to explain the basics of spirits to the Council this afternoon, and I need you to at least *pretend* that you have some kind of plan."

"That Cato has some kind of plan," Reb said gloomily. They both knew there was no way Cato would set foot in the Council Chamber. She stood up with a sigh. "In that case, I'll go nag Cato – I'm sure that will help – and I'll see you at the Council Chamber. When?"

"Three," Marcia said.

"Three. Marcia. Andreas." She nodded to both of them, hesitated, then came towards Marcia to give her a gentle kiss on the forehead.

It warmed Marcia more than it ought, as she and Andreas settled to strategising about the Council.

Neither of them mentioned Madeleine again, but the knowledge of where she was lodged like a cold stone in Marcia's heart.

SEVEN

The pounding on the door intensified. Cato groaned and burrowed his head under the blankets. It was too early in the morning – that was to say, it was still the morning, albeit from the brightness of the sun around the curtains only just – for anyone to be knocking on Cato's door. Especially given how late he'd been up the night before. Working on this business with bloody Teren and their equally bloody demons, rather than being out or drinking or anything remotely enjoyable; he'd eventually crashed into bed after burning his fingers with two experiments in a row because he'd lost concentration. It was woefully unfair that *working* felt nearly as bad the next morning as carousing did.

But given his wards, there was only a limited number of people it could be, and he was at least in theory pleased to see all of them.

Well, not necessarily *pleased*, not *all* of them – Reb sprang to mind – but at least probably willing to open the door.

"Cato! Open the door!"

Marcia. Pleased, or not pleased, to see? Could be either. Early, and unannounced. Not entirely promising. He wasn't going to turn her away, though, was he.

"Coming," he called, reluctantly extracting himself from the blankets and wincing at the sudden spike in his head. Possibly he should drink some water. Another way the morning-after feelings were similar. For now, he grabbed a grubby tunic off the pile on the floor, pulled it over his head, and gestured the door open.

"Morning." His sister, stepping over the threshold, looked about as tired as he felt; and she had her hand on her bump as if it were paining her.

"How's the baby?" he asked. "Uh, sit down..." He

looked around, failing to see anywhere obvious to sit.

Marcia rolled her eyes, swept a collection of bits and pieces off the stool and sat down.

"Some of that might have been important!" Cato protested.

"Then you should have put it away properly."

"Is this my room or yours?"

"Yours, most certainly," Marcia said, looking around with a wrinkled nose. "I thought Tait was trying to inculcate better habits in you."

Cato shrugged. "I've been busy." He rubbed at his forehead. "Shit, I feel rough."

Marcia raised her eyebrows.

"Fuck you. *Not* from drinking." Well, he'd only had the one, to help him focus.

Marcia's mouth compressed sideways. "Getting anywhere?"

"Sort of."

"You'll be able to get rid of them?"

Cato scowled down at the floor. He badly wanted to say yes. "Wouldn't quite say that yet. I've got…a better idea of what I don't know, is about it so far. The problem I'm running into is that I don't know enough about what Teren magic looks like." And he was loathe to consult his obvious resource on the matter – Tait – because of how Tait felt about Teren magic. Except, in the excessively bright light of day, he had to accept he'd reached enough of a dead end now that he would *have* to. Wasn't like Tait was any keener than anyone else to let Selene and her tame magicians into Marek.

"Right." Marcia shifted awkwardly on the stool. Her hand got halfway to her mouth before she visibly remembered she didn't bite her nails any more. Cato got a cold feeling in his stomach.

"Did you know that Mother – that Madeleine is out there?"

"With that Selene woman and all the sorcerers? Yes, as a matter of fact, I did. One of the news-sheets got hold of it." And hadn't that been a shock to the system he could have done without, seeing Madeleine's name in print letters the size of his thumb sprawled across a news-sheet on one of the Purple Heart's tables yesterday evening when he'd gone in for something to eat and a mug of wine.

Marcia's jaw clenched. "Didn't bloody take them long. I only told the Council yesterday afternoon. Selene seemed to want it secret."

"Yes, well, newshounds in this city are obviously coming on," Cato said flippantly. "Tough luck Selene, no secrets here."

"She's a hostage."

"Yes, I suppose she is." He gritted his teeth. The cold feeling was spreading. Marcia didn't bring things up just for fun, did she? What did she want? What had she come all the way over here for, unannounced...

"I want to get her out," Marcia said.

She couldn't mean what he thought she meant. He wasn't...he was misjudging her. Surely. She couldn't be about to do this.

"Good luck," he said, voice clipped. Last opportunity for her to back out, to show she didn't...

He saw her swallow. "I...you're the only one who can do it."

He was on his feet before he knew he was moving. "No."

"Cato..."

"*No.*"

"She's...if Selene thinks she's losing, I don't know what she'll do to her. She – Mother's in danger of her life."

"I don't care." He felt sick to his stomach. How could she. How *could* she?

"Cato..."

Cato set his teeth, churning nausea giving way to a rising red fury he welcomed. "She *threw me out*, Marcia. Do you remember? She threw me out, without anywhere to go, and she didn't care."

"She..."

"If you try to tell me that she did care, so help me, I will never speak to you again."

Marcia shut her mouth.

"I'm very, very close to that right now anyway. I was *sixteen*. I had nowhere to go, and nothing to pay my way with. You don't even *know*...yes, I made it through, that's not the fucking point. She didn't know what I would do, and she didn't care. She didn't even bloody watch me leave, did she? And you. You let it happen."

Marcia flinched.

Cato had never said that before. He'd always...Marcia had been sixteen, too, and she hadn't known what to do. She'd run after him, she'd tried to stay in touch, she'd even smuggled him money from her own allowance, until Madeleine realised and stopped letting her have it for a couple of years. But she hadn't...

She'd stayed. And Cato had spent a long time being *understanding* about that, but in the name of the angel, he wasn't about to do that any longer. Fine, Marcia had been sixteen. But so had he.

"You sat there, in that house, and you did what she said."

"I have *never* just done what she said!"

"Really? That's not what I've seen." Unfair, and he knew it, but he no longer cared.

"When you were ill..."

"Yes. When I was ill, you looked after me. *You* did. *She* just left me to rot. She knew, didn't she? She knew what was happening, she knew sorcerers were dropping dead across Marek. She knew where you were off to every day." And Marcia had been frantic with worry while she nursed him. He'd seen that, despite how ill he'd been and despite her trying to hide it; Madeleine must have known too. "She didn't lift a sodding finger. Why, exactly, should I lift a finger to save her now?"

"Because it will help Marek," Marcia said, voice rising. "If Selene doesn't have a hostage..."

"Oh, come *on*. You're telling me that anyone else in the Council gives the smallest of shits about what happens to her? You're here, the House continues, why do they care."

Marcia bit her lip, and Cato knew, stomach lurching again as that last tiny excuse wisped away, that he was right. He'd known anyway. He might not be involved in House politics any more, but he'd always had better instincts than Marcia. She spent too much time caring about the detail, unable to see the mountain for the rocks. The crucial point about the Houses was that they cared primarily for themselves, second for the Council, and third for Marek. Losing Madeleine – well, her friends might sorrow on their own behalf, but they wouldn't risk anything for her.

"You might care," he went on. "The Council doesn't. So don't try and give me that goatshit. It's not about *saving Marek*. When it comes to *saving Marek*, I have spent every waking moment of the last twenty-four hours trying to work out what to do about those fucking demons out there. This isn't about that. It's about you wanting to rescue her. And I *don't care*."

"Cato. Please. She's our mother."

For a horrible, heart-pulsing moment, the flare of fury was such that it genuinely felt like the top of his head might blow off. "That doesn't matter to her any more, so it sure as fuck doesn't matter to me."

"She's – the baby, your niece or nephew," Marcia put her hand on her stomach again, almost performative, "she's their grandmother…"

"*Fuck. Off.* Do not bring your *baby* into this. They'll be a person, their own person, in their own right. Not your final card. You're going to use them in your games *now*, before they're even out in the world? You'll end up just as bloody bad as *her*."

Marcia flinched again, putting both arms around herself protectively, and Cato felt a fierce satisfaction. He was right. He *was*. But Marcia didn't have to to – she'd grabbed at that idea, but she hadn't committed to it yet. He might yet be able to stop her from going that way.

And if he claimed, even just to himself, that was why

he'd said it, he'd be almost as bad. He was right; but he hadn't said that for the sake of the baby. He'd said it to hurt Marcia, and it had, and he was glad. He was *glad*.

"You are going to leave now." He gestured to the door, and it flew open. "I am going to let this go, just this once, because for some unfathomable fucking reason you still care about that wretched woman. Despite everything she's done to me. Despite everything she's done to you, come to that." He bared his teeth. "At least, if Selene has her ripped apart by demons out there, she won't be able to get her claws into the baby. Silver lining."

Tears were standing in Marcia's eyes. Cato kept going. "If you ever. Ever. Do this again. I will never speak to you again. Do you understand?"

Slowly, Marcia nodded.

Cato stood, arms folded, until she left. Then he sat down on the bed and cried.

☻ ☻

Tait was reading when they heard the commotion on the stairs, and someone banging on Cato's door. They looked up from their book, wondering if they should intervene, then heard Marcia's voice and relaxed. They'd been up a while now, had had their own breakfast, sitting by the window for the sake of the spring sunshine, window cracked to let the breeze in even if it did mean they needed to wrap themself in the blanket. Maybe once Marcia left they could go check on Cato. He'd still been working on the demon problem when they'd left him the previous evening. Tait could fetch him some breakfast, or something. Maybe drag him down to the bathhouse. The skies knew, solving this was urgent, and important, but sometimes you needed to give your mind a break more than you needed to just keep hammering away.

Cato's door slammed, and feet hurried down the stairs. Marcia must be interested in the demons too, though Tait would have assumed Reb was keeping her updated so she needn't come bother Cato.

Tait finished their chapter, then threw on a robe and padded next door, tapping cautiously on the door.

"Fuck off," came from inside. Tait paused, surprised.

"Uh," they called, "it's me. Tait."

"I'd still fuck off, if I were you," Cato said. He sounded slurred. But even Cato couldn't be *drunk* before noon, could he? Especially if Marcia had just been here. Had something gone wrong? Was he hurt? But then...

"Are you all right?"

Cato, inside, laughed. It sounded almost hysterical. Tait, cautiously, put their fingers to the door. They couldn't tell any difference in the wards, and the normal wards let Tait through, so...

"I'm coming in," they called, waited for a warning, then opened the door.

The wards tingled against their skin, but let them through without harm. Tait pushed the door shut behind them, and turned to Cato. He lay full-length on the bed, clutching a bottle of wine. There wasn't much left in it. Was that the one he'd brought back from the Purple Heart yesterday? Tait couldn't see another bottle around.

"Tait! Told you you should fuck off. Leave me to it."

Tait frowned. "Leave you to what?" Tentatively, they crossed the room and sat down next to him. At least he didn't properly stink of alcohol...so he'd only just started drinking? Had Marcia said something?

"Drowning my fucking sorrows, is what."

"Has something...gone wrong?"

Cato overindulged. Tait was fully aware of that, and Cato knew that Tait didn't entirely approve, and in recent months he'd been cutting back, if less than Tait would have preferred. They'd never seen him like this before, though they'd understood from other people that it wasn't that unusual. But – it wasn't even noon yet. Even Cato at his worst hadn't been the type – or hadn't yet become the type – to start in this early. And this wasn't just booze. Cato couldn't be even a bottle in, and Marcia had just been here, wouldn't she have – done something, if he'd been drunk already?

Unless...Tait's spine ran cold. Unless something had gone wrong. Badly wrong. With the demons? Was Marek going to be overrun after all? But Tait could still feel, when they reached out, that sense of Beckett's presence, tense like it had been since the Terens arrived the previous morning, but not...

Beckett was still there, still strong.

"What's happened? Has something gone wrong with the demons?"

"Ohhhhh, fuck the demons. The demons're going to get rid of my mother for me, finally, aren't they? She'll fit right in with them, won't she, before she doesn't fit anywhere any more." Cato's voice was high, strained; but Tait was certain now that his incoherence wasn't just drunk-sloppy, it was more than that.

"Your mother...?"

Cato buried his head in Tait's thigh, his shoulders heaving, and after a moment, Tait realised he was crying. They'd never seen Cato cry before. They put an arm round his shoulder, a little awkwardly given the angle, and waited.

Eventually, Cato explained: Marcia's visit. Marcia's request.

"I thought she'd just come to – I don't know. To see how I was getting on, maybe, to offer to help." Cato's voice cracked. "Not to...because she wanted *that*."

There were a lot of things Tait could say, but none of them that would help even a little bit. They thought of their own mother, back in Teren, and their heart seized; but their mother wasn't Cato's, and they didn't know any of the history of this beyond that Cato had been disowned, all those years ago. Cato had never said much about it, and Tait hadn't wanted to ask.

They found out more than they had before, over the next few minutes. What Cato's mother had said when he left; that she'd stopped Marcia's allowance when she realised it was going to Cato.

"Course, plenty of sixteen-year-olds quite competent," Cato mumbled into their thigh. "Not Marekhill types though. Marcia and me, we weren't brought up to look after ourselves. Bit of a failure really. But it was her raised us that way. She knew I wouldn't be able to cope."

"You did cope," Tait said, stroking his shoulder.

"Skin of my teeth," Cato said. "No thanks to her. She didn't know what would happen and she didn't care. Marcia cared. But she didn't care enough not to stay, did she? Didn't care enough not to – *fuck* her, fuck her, how could she?"

Tait had known that Cato had been here in the squats at sixteen. They hadn't realised just how precarious everything had been for him, because Cato had always played the matter down, laughed it off, when it had come up before.

And then, the plague. Tait had known about that, too, known why there were so few Marek sorcerers now. They hadn't known that Cato had only barely survived it. Nor that Marcia had been here nursing him through it. And Madeleine had still never said a word. Not when Cato and Marcia both thought he was dying; not when he survived.

Right now, Tait too could quite happily have kicked Madeleine out of any available window. And yet, still, to leave her to the demons…Tait knew, bone-deep, about demons. Cato didn't. Not really. You couldn't, if you'd never been out of Marek.

Slowly, the storm subsided. Tait, eventually, managed to take the wine bottle away, and replace it with a cup of water, despite Cato growling at them.

"It won't help," they pointed out firmly. "Not like you haven't already had plenty. Save it for a bit."

"Doesn't need saving. More where that came from. Still haven't run out the tab at the Purple Heart."

"Even so," Tait said, giving Cato's shoulder a soothing rub, and hid the bottle under the bed.

Cato sat up, took a swig of the water and grimaced, then scrubbed his spare hand through his hair. "Expect you think I should save her. Like Marcia said. Blood bond and all that."

Tait shook their head. "It's not my decision. You don't…I can say, if it was my mother, of course I would." They couldn't bear to think about it. Not even at the edges. But… "But my mother hasn't hurt me like that. You don't have to forgive someone who's done that to you. Even if they're family."

"Marcia thinks I should." Cato drained the rest of the water.

"Then she's wrong." Tait felt very certain of that. "If you wanted to forgive her, that would be up to you. But – you were a child, and she let you down. She forfeited those…blood claims, already. Just because someone shares blood with you, just because they bore you, it doesn't mean you owe them something. She brought you into the world. She owed *you* something, and she betrayed that."

"I betrayed the whole of Marekhill," Cato said. "Magic."

"More fool Marekhill," Tait said. "And even then…look, I don't understand your politics here at all, but even if she couldn't, if you couldn't stay in the House, if you couldn't stay part of your whole Council thing…"

"Was going to be me was Heir," Cato said. He was picking fiercely at the nubs of wool on the blanket. "Not Marcia. We both knew it. Better instincts. Before the magic."

"So you couldn't do that and magic as well, maybe that part was true." It seemed nonsense to Tait; they hadn't been understating how much they didn't get Marek politics. "But she didn't have to…she could have supported you. Helped you. She didn't have to just throw you out."

"She wanted me to break," Cato said. He looked up into Tait's eyes. "She thought, if I didn't have anything else, I'd have to choose the House."

Tait snorted. "Well, she obviously didn't know you all that well, then." Cato was the most stubborn person they'd ever met.

"Ha."

"She made those decisions. They had consequences. How you decide to act now is one of those consequences."

"Oh, fuck. Tait. I didn't know how much I needed to hear that." Cato's face was open, for once, shorn of all his usual defences. "I love you, you know that?"

Tait's heart jumped. They'd not said that before, either of them. Tait had been holding off, waiting, not wanting to scare Cato off. But Cato was drunk, and emotional, and maybe he wouldn't mean it, when he sobered up.

He might, or he might not. Tait did, and they weren't going to leave Cato hanging, not here and now. "I love you, as well."

"Really? I wouldn't. Don't think I'm a good bet."

Tait shrugged. "I guess that's up to me to decide."

"Fuck, I'm drunk." Cato turned his face back into the bedclothes, then suddenly sat up again. "You think I'm drunk."

"You are drunk," Tait said, cautiously, not sure where Cato was going.

"You think I don't mean it. Fuck, can't even say that I do definitely mean it, because 'm drunk. Not that drunk." He grimaced. "Shouldn't be that drunk. Empty stomach. Ugh. But I do. I promise. I do mean it."

"All right." Tait put his arm around Cato again, and Cato slumped into their shoulder.

"Don't deserve you," Cato muttered.

"Probably not," Tait agreed. "And yet, here I am. How about you lie down and sleep for a bit, and then we'll go to the baths and sweat it out?"

"Stay with me? Please?" Cato's face turned up to them, and Tait's heart stuttered again.

"Of course," they said, and hugged Cato, as hard as they could. "Come on. Let's get some rest. We can sort everything out after that."

They lay down next to Cato and held him, listened to him fall into sleep, and let their heart hurt for him.

EIGHT

The back room of the Bucket was full to overheating despite there being no logs in the stove. Alyssa sipped at her beer, and wondered how long it would take until that ran out. The owner of the Bucket brewed out in the yard behind the pub, but you made beer with barley, and that came in from Teren by barge. How much was there kicking around in storehouses? How far in advance did the Bucket brew? And in any case, if barley was short it should be eaten, not brewed. Best appreciate this while she could, she supposed.

And at the same time she felt almost ridiculous to be thinking like that. Teren only arrived outside the city two days ago. The Salinas ships were still coming in. But – Marek was a big city, and a lot of staples came in from Teren, because the closest farms were just a little upstream, where the swampland surrounding Marek gave way to rich, fertile soil. You couldn't grow much in Marek itself, even with squeezing kitchen gardens and herb-boxes into every corner the way most folk in the lower city did to save a demmer or two on food. You couldn't grow anything in the swamps. Barges came in daily from Teren and now they weren't. Walking over to the Bucket in the late morning for this emergency meeting, Alyssa had seen that already the grocers had less that was really fresh, though the milk churn was full (so the goats the far side of Marekhill were still fine) and the fishmonger had a good fresh catch. Not starvation, no, this wasn't a siege, but...

She should concentrate. She dragged her attention back to the room.

"We must be able to *use* it," Simeon argued. He looked like he wanted to be up and pacing – he always did like to be on the move – but there was no room today. Plenty of people keen to discuss what this meant for them; keen enough to run over here during their lunch, even. Almost entirely Parliamentarians. "The Council need us – the whole city – to pull together, to get through this. Right? We can *use* that to put pressure on them"

"So what, you're suggesting you offer to invite the Terens in instead?" Patrice demanded, leaping to his feet. "If they don't do what you say? Invite the *demons* in?" His voice was biting, but Alyssa could hear the fear underneath it. Patrice had run from Ameten, a couple of months back, after his sorcerer brother died. Apparently because he'd lost control of his demon, but Patrice was certain the Academy of the Court had done it to silence him.

"No one is inviting anyone in," Alyssa spoke up, voice as firm as possible. Best put a stop to that argument before it began. "I don't believe for a second Simeon meant to imply that."

She glared at Simeon, who muttered, "No," then rallied. "But even if we wouldn't actually *do* it…"

"Never make a threat you're not willing to follow through on," Alyssa said, and sat back.

"Fine," Simeon said irritably. "We don't say that, then. But still. Surely, surely this changes the situation. Surely it must mean there's something we can do, some pressure we can bring to bear. The Council need to keep us, the people, with them! That gives us something."

"Persuasive power, you mean?" Tey, on the other side of the room, frowned, scratching at his neck. "We agree that it's important that the city be united, and ask that they demonstrate that by actually, well, *uniting*."

"It's all too vague." Keren shook her head. "I mean, we could put some posters up, arguing that the reward – no, that's not the right word, but something like that – for the city uniting against the common enemy should be a real unity thereafter. There's wording that will sound good. I'll find it." Keren was a printer, and a writer – more the latter than the former, but she had opinions about the way her words were typeset which had led her to learning to work a press. "But either way…"

"Either way, we haven't the leverage to make them do anything. It's moral suasion only," Alyssa agreed. She folded her arms. "Which is infuriating."

"Warehouses," Francis said quietly from the corner.

Everyone turned to look at them. Francis flushed – they didn't like attention – but carried on. "The barges have stopped coming. We've all seen the empty boxes at the wholesale market. Empty shelves at the grocers."

"Ships are still coming in," someone objected.

"But prices are up. And the ships might stop too, soon, if there's nothing here for them to pick up," Francis went on doggedly. "We're all going to be short on food, pretty soon. There's always fish, I suppose…"

"Won't last long," Patrice said. "The demons will come in, or they won't – probably they will – and then it'll all be over. We won't have time to get hungry." His voice was bleak.

"Francis is right," Alyssa said. Something had suddenly clicked, something that had been niggling her earlier when she'd been thinking about food. "Who owns the warehouses?

Most of the room looked blank.

"Varies," Francis said. "The Houses have some, for trade mostly. The Guilds have some. But then there's littler ones all over, people who buy from the Grocers and so on and keep things in hand against the prices changing, and those as supply the smaller shops." They grimaced. "Not that there's more'n a few days in hand, mostly, not for the whole city, but…"

Alyssa tapped her fingers together. "There can't be much in the smaller ones. You're telling me it's the Houses and the Guilds have most of the stocks?"

Francis shrugged. "Well now. *Have* them, you say. What'd'ye mean by that, then. Have the keys to the door? Well, I've an axe, too. Ah, you say, but there's guards to the doors'll stop you."

"Not *the* guard, though," Simeon put in. He was chewing thoughtfully at his lip. "They're away at the barge-yard, with the mercenaries."

"There's folks on the doors, still," Francis said thoughtfully. "But perhaps we can have a word…"

"When you say, have a word," Alyssa began.

There was a sharp rap on the door, and she stopped speaking. They all stared at the door. Whoever it was knocked again.

"If it was the guard, they'd not knock," Alyssa said, more for her own benefit than for the others. "Come in!"

It was Jeres who walked through the door. They all stared some more.

"Afternoon," she said, shut the door behind her, and stood by it, hands in pockets.

"Afternoon," Alyssa said. "Wasn't expecting you."

"No," Jeres agreed.

"What do you want?" Simeon demanded. Simeon didn't like Jeres at all. Simeon was even less good at words like 'compromise' than Alyssa herself, and she knew well enough it wasn't her own strongest point.

Compromising never was a strong point. It was weakness. It led you away from your aims, it left you vulnerable. Just…once in a while, Alyssa knew, it was necessary; inevitable. Once in a while, it got you where you wanted to go.

Jeres didn't seem to be taking offence. Jeres wasn't prone to taking offence or she wouldn't be where she was. "Thing is," she said. "They're not shifting on what we want." She didn't need to specify that 'they' was the Council. "We wondered, what're your plans. In the current situation. Can we revisit the matter of… solidarity."

Simeon opened his mouth, but Alyssa got in first. "What, you want us to support you?"

Jeres shook her head. "No. We want to support you. Well." She grimaced slightly. "I've been sent to negotiate. I admit, if they're not shifting on our stuff, I can't see them shifting on your stuff, either. Not without violence." She looked intently at Alyssa.

"There's people who share my political views," Alyssa said carefully, "who advocate violence. But they're not…that's not what we're doing. Here and now."

"No one's letting the demons in," Patrice said. His voice was still tight. There was a shadow of a question in it.

"No one is letting the demons in," Alyssa said, again, and was rewarded with a tiny relaxation of Patrice's shoulders.

"Right. Glad to hear it. Demons aren't the only ones can hurt folk, is the thing," Jeres said.

"We, as a group, do not intend to hurt anyone right now," Alyssa said.

"Right, well, that'll do," Jeres said, and chopped her hand down swiftly. "I'll take your word. You'll tell me if that changes. So. Given that. I still don't think you'll get everything you want. Not sure you would if you took swords in either, as it happens. And then, too, it always spills over, doesn't it? It's always the same people who suffer the most, and it isn't those up on the Hill."

"You're up on the Hill," Simeon muttered, inaccurately. Jeres might be Guild, but she wasn't the sort of Guild that was doing their best to creep up Marekhill – as if those born up top would ever accept the Guildfolk anyway.

Jeres ignored him. "But. They're not shifting on our stuff. They're not going to shift on your stuff either. But if we're all pushing at your end, maybe we'll get something we all want. I mean, honestly, if there was a Committee of the City, wouldn't you welcome it?"

"It's not *enough*," Simeon said.

"Fine," Jeres said. "But would you actively refuse to accept it."

Simeon scowled.

"I wouldn't," Alyssa said. "I don't think any of us would. We'd just...not stop. Because it wouldn't be enough."

"Right. But it's better than what you have now, right? So. We support you. And then maybe we'll get some of what we want."

"And then you'll stop supporting us and accept that?"

Jeres shrugged. "Yeah. I imagine we will. Who knows,

though, maybe in the meantime you'll have convinced some people."

"Which is all very well," Alyssa said, "talking of *support* and that, but what leverage do you think you have? Against the Council?" Maybe Jeres had a better idea than theirs.

"Well. We don't want Teren getting in," Jeres began, "so that limits us."

"No one wants that." Alyssa shrugged. "I'm a sorcerer, remember." There was a murmur around the room; people *knew*, in theory, but it wasn't something she generally drew attention to. "I have personal feelings about this, never mind anything else."

"So we can't say we'll refuse to resist. It's not true, and it'll scare people."

"Indeed," Alyssa agreed. The whole room was listening hard.

"We're under siege, as of yesterday. What's everyone going to be after."

"Food," Alyssa said. "But the Guilds, and the Houses, they've got the warehouses. The grain. That's what we were just discussing." Had Jeres reached the same conclusions?

Jeres grinned, sharklike. "The Guilds have the warehouses, you say? Well now. Turns out that I'm not the only one who's Guilded and pissed off."

Alyssa's eyebrows rose slowly.

"The Victuallers are looking after their own warehouses now. I know a fair few Victualler journeymen. Do you know, I don't think the Guilds have as much control over their supplies as they think they do."

"Well now," Alyssa said. "I didn't think you had it in you. I admit, we'd begun to think along those lines, but we didn't know how we were going to convince those looking after the doors."

"Good thing we're working together then, hey?" Jeres said. "We need to do it carefully, mind. We're trying to open discussion, to make them consider us, not to take control ourselves."

"Speak for yourself," Simeon said.

"He makes a good point," Alyssa agreed. "But yes, I take your point, that now is not," yet, "time for showing our full hand."

"We've got links with the Guilds, and we can do that, maybe, nice and gentle-like. The House warehouses, those might be trickier."

"Well then," Alyssa said. "Sounds like it might finally be time to put the thumbscrews on them up on the Hill."

The last thing Marcia wanted to do after she left the squats was to prepare for a Council meeting; but it wasn't like she had much choice. Her gut churned with a swirling nauseating mix of guilt and anger as she hurried, as best she could at this stage of pregnancy, back across the river, to pick up a litter at Marek Square. How could Cato just *leave* their mother out there at Selene's mercy? Out there with *demons*? Surely despite everything he still had some sense of feeling for – for a fellow human being, if nothing else!

How dare you.

You'll end up as bad as her.

She flinched, sitting within the litter, arms wrapping automatically around her belly. No. She was right; she had to be right. She *owed* it to Madeleine to try any ways she could to rescue her, given that accepting Selene's demands was impossible. Cato was just – being dramatic. She hadn't done anything wrong.

She managed, back at House Fereno, to get a small amount of lunch down her, enough to get past Cousin Cara's worried clucking. It sat lump-like in her belly as she dressed for Council and took another litter up the road to the Chamber. It wasn't far, but she was so *weary*. Outside the Chamber, Reb, obviously, asked what was wrong, and Marcia dissembled – though she wasn't sure Reb truly bought it, from her continuing frowns. But she absolutely couldn't handle having this discussion right now.

And then she was walking into the Council Chamber, deliberately keeping her hand off her belly no matter how it ached. Never show weakness. Madeleine had taught her that. *In more ways than one*, the back of her brain supplied.

Everyone looked irritable as they settled down. Marcia hadn't stopped in the foyer, but she'd noticed on her way through that the usual trading of information (or votes) was absent, replaced with hushed gossip and rumours. Exactly why she hadn't stopped; she didn't want to talk about Madeleine and she didn't want to think too hard about the fact that she was about to bring Reb in here. She settled into her seat. Over half a year since Madeleine had taken the empty seat beside her, and she'd *enjoyed* having that freedom, hadn't exactly been looking forward to going back to being only Heir again, and yet now she was suddenly, rawly aware of that gap. She nodded across the room at Gil, and at Andreas in the row in front, just arrived. His face had been creased with a frown as he came across the room, but he'd turned around once he'd sat down to smile at her.

The baby was squirming again. Surreptitiously, now she couldn't be seen below the railing, she put a hand on her stomach, obscurely comforted by her awareness of their presence. Her future. Marek's future. That was why she was doing this. All of it.

The Reader banged their staff on the floor, and the room quietened far faster than usual. "The only order of business for today is the discussion of the Teren situation."

Tabriol-Head popped up immediately. "I move to introduce Captain Anna Barcola, of the soldiers quartered in the barracks, and one of her troop, to give us their report."

A murmur of agreement, and the Reader gestured to their clerk, sitting by the door in her long grey robes, to bring in Captain Anna. She came into the chamber slightly hesitantly, but straight-backed; Marcia could see the lines of strained concern on her face. The soldier following her was a short man with broad shoulders, wearing a leather vest and thick canvas trousers in a grubby-looking grey-brown. He was glancing around at the assembled Heads and Heirs, eyes a little wide. The two of them reached the middle of the central stage, and Captain Anna took a formal stance, feet slightly spread and hands behind her back. The other soldier, after a sideways look at her, copied her neatly. The mercenary troop weren't generally hot on strict military discipline. They were good at what they did – looking after trade expeditions, like the trading trip over the mountains Marcia had sent them on a while back; providing ceremonial guards from those of the troop who cleaned up sufficiently well; going out into the swamps or up to the foot of the mountains to deal with the occasional troublesome wild animal or bandit operation; reinforcing the city guard when needed. They'd never been needed for anything like this before.

The Reader nodded at Captain Anna.

"Heads. Heirs," Captain Anna started. "You asked me for an assessment of the situation out at the barge-yard. I have taken the liberty of bringing with me Bracken, from my troop." She paused.

"Sers," Bracken said, after a moment, touching his forehead.

Captain Anna went on. "He's spent time as a Teren soldier, before." Ah, now Marcia understood. "I thought you'd like to hear his assessment first-hand. Given that, to be wholly honest, Sers, he has more actual combat experience of this type than most of us." She didn't pull a face, but it looked like it took an effort. Several of the assembled Council members did grimace. Well, it was true enough, and they all knew it.

"Carry on, Captain," the Reader put in, when Captain Anna seemed like she'd run aground.

The Captain took a deep breath. "Sers. I would like your permission for myself and Bracken to be blunt. I think. Uh. I think perhaps it is better not to nibble politely around the edges here."

"Absolutely," Athitol-Head said bossily, but the rest of the Chamber nodded agreement. "We would rather hear uncomfortable truths now than be surprised by them."

Dintra-Head was looking a little green around the edges, Marcia saw. Well, she wasn't feeling all that comfortable herself. But Dintra-Head's *mother* wasn't out there.

"Bracken." Captain Anna stepped backwards, yielding the floor to Bracken.

"Well then, Sers," Bracken said, back straight, staring at the back of the room. "So the first thing is, there ain't really that many soldiers out there. Not if they wanted to come through the city forcibly, hand to hand, kind of thing. That's hard, that is, which I'll be coming to later, begging your pardons. If it were just soldiers, I'd say, t'ain't a serious proposition. Just trying to scare us." He scratched at his chin. "Trouble is, ain't just soldiers out there. There's at least as many sorcerers, far as we can see."

There was an intake of breath. Marcia didn't know why they were surprised. Hadn't that been clear already? Or was the shock at Bracken mentioning *magic* in the Chamber?

"Excuse me," Athitol-Head put in. "How long were you in the Teren army?"

"'Bout ten years," Bracken said. "And that were maybe seven years ago. Don't look like they've changed much though." He paused. "We only had the one sorcerer at a time then, mind."

"So you did work with – sorcerers?" Athitol-Head demanded. She sounded like she was handling the word with tongs.

"Didn't have that much to do with 'em. Just the odd one, sometimes. Purified the water for us, that were useful, and rounded up animals for the pot when the farmers was bein' troublesome. And then we sent 'em out sometimes beforehand if we had an actual fight, and they'd do a bit of damage before sorcerer called the demon back and we went in."

"One moment," Marcia interrupted. "Where were you fighting, in the Teren army?"

Bracken shrugged. "Towns that was misbehaving, mostly. I didn't pay much attention. I went where they pointed us, and stayed in the barracks when we didn't get pointed. Minding my own business."

Marcia frowned. "But you were sent against Teren cities and towns?"

Bracken shrugged. "Yeah. Din't take much to get them to surrender, mostly. Having a sorcerer at the front to do a bit of dramatic tearing people apart, that definitely helped. I think they used the demon after, too, once they'd surrendered, but that weren't my problem neither." He wrinkled his nose. "Eventually I got so's I'd had enough of it all, see, and that's when I came down here. Didn't never expect to be on the other side of the demons, mind." His tone was light, but there was something dark underlying it.

"Right," Marcia said. "And that was – you just had one sorcerer at a time?"

"Yeah. Which were plenty enough, y'see. But the Captain and me, we went to look, and there's a lot more here. They let those demons loose, won't need the soldiers. That's the problem." He sighed. "Sers, fighting inside a city, it's a right b– uh. It's very troublesome, is what I'm saying. Bad news for everyone. But anything like even numbers – soldiers I mean, not counting the regular folks – the city's got the advantage. The attackers don't know the place, they can be ambushed, all that stuff. Some of the regular folks can help. Like I said, the soldiers they've got out there, wouldn't stand a chance against us and the guard and some of them as'd help. I'd say, if it were just that, bite our thumbs at them and tell 'em to go – uh, to go off home."

"But you're telling us that it's not just that," Gil said. They were watching Bracken intently.

"It's the demons, Ser. Sers. We counted twelve of 'em. Twelve, Sers. I've seen what *one* can do. They'll send the demons in, scare the – scare everyone, hurt people bad,

Sers. Could take us and the guard right out, whatever we tried. Then everyone left, they'll hide in their houses and let the soldiers march right through, and they'd be right to do it. Can't stand against that."

"So you're telling us there's no hope?" Tabriol-Heir's voice was high, and shaking.

Bracken was pulling a face, but before the Chamber could react, Marcia cut in. "What if we could get rid of the demons?"

"If you could do that, Ser, we'd be in fine shape." Bracken's voice was level, but Marcia didn't think he sounded hopeful.

"The other point," Captain Anna said, stepping forward, "is that everyone – as I imagine you are aware, Sers – knows what the Lieutenant – ah, the former Lieutenant – is offering. Owing as how she sends someone out in a white tabard to shout it on the regular, as well as the notes she's been sending all formal. To me to send to you, Sers, and I've done that, but also there's no way of keeping that private, not when she's sending things unsealed. And there's posters she'd put up too, on her side, all nice and big to read from a distance. Can't stop people knowing, Sers, is my point, even if you wanted to. They're saying, nothing much needs to change, they'll be gentle as lambs if we just let 'em in."

"What do the soldiers think? Or the people who live out near there?" Gil asked.

Fine lines appeared around Captain Anna's eyes, and the corner of her mouth crooked down. "Well, on the one hand, they think Teren can get lost, and they don't like a bunch of sorcerers sitting on their doorstep, and they don't like it even more when the demons come out to sniff around the boundary. Which is very unsettling, Sers, I can tell you that, even with the barricade up. On the other hand, they think, at least some of 'em, that the cityangel'll keep 'em safe. But I won't say that people aren't tempted. There's some of 'em reckon, saving your presence, Sers, what odds does it make to them who's sitting up in the Council? But then there's others think that…" She ground to a halt, looking awkwardly around the room.

"Please, Captain," Gil said kindly. "The Council is aware that there is unrest in parts of the city. We would appreciate your honest opinion."

"Well, Ser. There's others think that, what Teren's been doing to its own people, we don't want that. There's a lot of radicals handing out pamphlets, down in the city. They don't want Teren, and they don't want demons, and there's some hair-raising stories in some of those pamphlets, about Teren demons. But they don't like, uh…The Houses. Either. Saving your presence, Sers."

"Do you think they would resist the Teren soldiers?" Gil pressed.

Captain Anna grimaced. "Honestly, Ser, I'm not sure how some folk'll jump. There's a lot of disagreement, and people with demons looking at them across the yard, they get antsy, they do. If you're wondering, would the city stand firm if they were to try and push through – I wouldn't want to count on it one way or the other, Ser, honestly I wouldn't. Some will, for certain. We will, of course." She nodded firmly. "But – you've heard what Bracken's said about demons, and I can tell you, he's not the sort to exaggerate. If they send the demons against us, we haven't a chance, and that's the truth."

"Demons," Athitol-Head scoffed. "Haven't we heard quite enough of this nonsense by now? A 'sorcerer' going in ahead of troops to scare people, that may work in Teren, but Marekers are of stronger stuff. And in any case, if there's *demons* out there, why haven't they marched in already? Stories and myths and theatre-tricks, that's all that's out there."

"The cityangel," Marcia said, clearly. "They can't get in because of the cityangel."

Athitol-Head scoffed again, but Piath, to Marcia's surprise, cut in. "Whilst I understand your doubt, Athitol-Head, I fear that we must, at this time, step away from our previous position on this matter. We cannot reasonably doubt the existence of demons; and far too many of those fleeing Teren in recent months have described events there for it to be a trick." Marcia remembered Piath saying something similar during her trial over involvement with magic. "Teren has brought them here, now," Piath continued. "I would not doubt the word of the good Bracken. And clearly they *are not* coming into Marek. Something must be stopping them, although perhaps it is only that Selene would rather we came quietly." They shrugged. "I am sure that the Archion would prefer we remain fat and profitable, after all."

"Before any further discussion," the Reader cut in, "are there any further questions for Captain Anna and Bracken?"

A few more small queries about the disposition of the troops, which Captain Anna answered, and then they were dismissed with thanks.

Andreas turned around to widen his eyes at Marcia; he was right. This was the correct moment.

"Given that we need to discuss demons and the cityangel," Marcia said, standing up. "I would like to introduce the sorcerer Reb, of Marek's Group, those who look after magic in the city."

There was a lot more kerfuffle around the Chamber this time, but the Reader cut in to demand a vote, and a bare majority agreed to let her in without further debate.

The clerk led Reb in. Her face was set sternly, her cheeks a little dark with nerves, but she looked composed as she took her place in the centre of the room.

Unfortunately, and despite Marcia's best efforts, things went downhill from there.

☉ ☉

Reb was halfway across the paved yard in front of the Council Chamber by the time Marcia caught up with her, storming past the litter-bearers – the self-employed waiting on spec, and the House ones – who were congregated over to one side drinking infusions and playing dice while they waited.

"Reb…" Marcia put on another burst of speed and then slowed to fall into step with her.

"I'm not going back in," Reb said, without stopping.

"No, of course not." Marcia said soothingly. *Not right at this moment*, anyway, she added mentally.

Reb stopped and swung round to face Marcia, who scrabbled to a halt beside her. "They're not listening," Reb said, her voice rising. Marcia had rarely seen Reb this agitated. She wasn't looking at Marcia; she was staring back at the Chamber. "They don't want to hear it, so they just don't."

"Yes," Marcia agreed, trying to catch Reb's eye, keeping her own voice level. Trying to calm her. "That is quite common. Unfortunately. But it isn't everyone. Some people are paying attention. Some of them are capable of letting themselves rethink. It just…you have to give them time, some of them." Time which they didn't really have, right now.

"Athitol!" Reb burst out. "How does that one – how is that House not a raging disaster?" Athitol-Head had been flat out rude. Though she was clearly not the only one doubting Reb.

"Athitol-Head used to be quite an acute trader," Marcia sighed, and nearly rubbed at her cheek before remembering her face paint. "Believe it or not. It's only in recent years that she's lost it altogether. The House is suffering for it, too, though they won't admit it. I happen to know that the Heir is tearing his hair out, privately, but Athitol-Head already disinherited the previous Heir for arguing with her, so he feels limited in what he can do."

"You can do that?" Reb asked, briefly derailed. "Disinherit someone once they've been confirmed, just because you fell out with them?"

"Generally not," Marcia said. "They need to have done something serious, criminal or at least approaching it, and it needs to go through the Council. It's a long story. Athitol-Head – pulled some strings, let's say." She grimaced. "It was messy, that's for sure, but she's been around for long enough that she knows where quite a few bodies are buried. Metaphorically," she added hastily. "I'm not sure she could get away with it a second time, mind, but...Anyway. My point is. There's no point in letting Athitol-Head wind you up. Fools will be foolish, right?"

"It's a waste of time," Reb said. She was visibly still angry, but at least she looked marginally less likely to turn round and set something on fire. Which, somewhat alarmingly, Marcia was aware Reb could actually do if she chose. "They'd all be much happier – and life would be easier for everyone, come to that – if they just pretended the demons didn't exist at all, let Cato and me deal with them, and then dealt with all the political stuff afterwards. And the soldiers and that. It'd likely be just as effective, even. Just – let things be how they've always been before."

"But things *aren't* how they've always been before. They need to realise there's more to Marek than they've been willing to see. More to the world. Fine, you're right, for a long time, the Marekhill attitude to magic hasn't really mattered. But now there's a bunch of Teren sorcerers – and their demons – sitting on our doorstep. That's the real threat, not Selene's pathetic handful of soldiers. And they know that, in there. When Captain Anna was in, before you. She talked about demons, and Athitol-Head was still arguing, but the rest just sat there. They accepted what she – Captain Anna – was saying."

Reb folded her arms. "Just sitting there isn't good enough."

"I know."

"And they didn't accept what *I* was saying."

"They didn't *not* accept it," Marcia argued. "Apart from Athitol, fine. The rest, they weren't denying it. They're just uncomfortable. Listening to you."

"Never mind listening to me. They won't even *look* at me."

"I know! And they have to look. This has to change."

Reb set her jaw, clearly pissed off. "I'm not here for

your political crusade, Marcia. I'm here because there is one specific problem to be fixed."

"That's what I mean! We need you, and Cato," his name made her wince, made her remember she hadn't told Reb about that row, and she probably needed to, but now definitely wasn't the time, "because otherwise Selene is going to walk straight in here. We need Beckett."

"Beckett," Reb said, "is the thing they *really* can't accept."

"I know, but…"

Reb looked at her for a long moment. "You know, Marcia. It doesn't really matter what these people think of magic. I know you all think, up here, that you *are* Marek somehow, that you're the most important of all. That what you think matters in some intrinsic way to the city. But you're not, and it doesn't. Oh, certainly, the decisions made up here can affect a lot of people. But what Marek is, is all over the city. This, here, is only a tiny part of it."

"Yes," Marcia agreed, trying not to be hurt by 'you people'. "But that's part of what I want to solve…"

Reb shook her head. "That's up to you. It's not my problem, though. I'm done here, trying to explain reality to folk that won't listen. Cato and I will find a way of getting rid of those demons, and we'll do it without bowing and scraping to be listened to. I'm not going to stand here and be patronised by a roomful of people with an inflated opinion of themselves. I don't need them, and Marek doesn't need them."

"Reb…" Marcia began, but Reb was already marching off again, and Marcia couldn't just leave, not while the session was still ongoing. It was bad enough she'd left the room and come out here.

"I'll send word," Reb called back over her shoulder. "Whatever we do, we'll likely need the soldiers, after, and your lot might actually be useful for that. In the meantime, I have work to do."

Well, shit.

117

And she still didn't know about – well, maybe the row with Cato didn't matter after all. Marcia turned back, debating whether to go back into the Chamber, only to see the doors opening and people moving around in the foyer. The session was done, then. Athitol-Head marched out first, past Marcia without so much as looking at her. Athitol-Heir trailing behind her, gave Marcia a pained grimace.

Marcia paused irresolutely. Should she try to speak to Andreas, at least, before going back home? In another situation, she'd let things settle before she tried again, but they didn't have *time*. The decision was made for her when Andreas, striding briskly out from the doors, waved to her.

"Marcia! A moment." He reached her, and lowered his voice. "Daril has invited Gil and myself to House Leandra, to discuss our next moves. Come with us. The Council can't *afford* to waste time arguing about this."

"I couldn't agree more," Marcia said, fervently. But. Daril. House Leandra. She hesitated, unsure how to ask, *is this your invitation or Daril's,* or perhaps, *are you sure I'm welcome at House Leandra*; then heard Daril's lazy drawl.

"Andreas inviting you to join our merry band? By all means. Plenty of room, though you'll have to excuse my late father's execrable taste in furniture."

"Thank you," Marcia said politely, and only slightly through her teeth. This was more important than her and Daril's petty disagreements. Even if she still didn't trust him for a second. And it was Daril and Andreas, with Gil's quiet backing, who had driven the Council into declaring Marek's independence; if they were going to defend that, it was the four of them who needed to work out how.

"Shall we?" Daril moved towards the gates to the road, Gil with them. "Hardly far enough for a litter, I feel." House Leandra was only two houses down the road from the Council Chamber.

"If that is all right for Marcia?" Gil glanced over at her, eyebrows raised.

"Of course," Marcia said. She was pregnant, not ill, and even if a litter might have been nice, she wasn't about to betray weakness in front of Daril. It was downhill, as well.

"The baby will be soon?" Gil asked politely as they set off.

"Within a few weeks," Marcia said. And wasn't *that* wonderful timing.

"I keep offering to introduce you to the master woodworker I've been frequenting," Andreas said cheerfully to Daril. "I'm beginning to think you prefer complaining about the stuff."

"Ah, well, it reminds me of my father," Daril said. "Keeps me motivated to do as many things as possible that he'd disapprove of."

Andreas laughed as if Daril had made a joke. Marcia suspected it was more or less the truth.

House Leandra's reception room did still have the dark, weighty furniture that Marcia remembered, but at least Daril kept the drapes open.

"Everyone will know we're having this discussion, you realise," Marcia pointed out as a servant took her wraps. She sat with a sigh of relief on one of the big armchairs. More servants were already appearing with infusions; someone must have been watching from the upper windows for the end of the session.

"We've hardly time to skulk around," Andreas said.

"Might focus their minds, watching us walk off," Daril agreed, shrugging a shoulder. "So. Help yourselves to whatever refreshments you wish. What do we intend to do?"

"What does *Selene* intend to do?" Gil asked. "This Bracken thinks there's enough – sorcerers," Marcia could hear their doubt about the word, and sighed internally, "to win if they come in, but she hasn't moved yet."

"What would she do once she was here?" Daril looked irritable. "March in here and take the Council by force? How do they intend to govern once they've taken us out?"

"Because the Council is well-known for its bravery in standing up to armed individuals," Andreas said drily. "I mean, if you're claiming that you'll still refuse to do what Selene says even with a sword at your throat, have at it, but I'm not ashamed to admit that I'm not sure I would, and I certainly don't think it would take long to find enough other Council members that would fold like a parat player holding the Flying Fish."

"I am not particularly physically brave myself," Gil agreed.

"What, you're not willing to defend Marek's independence?" Daril's jaw was set.

"I'm not convinced that Marek's independence would be benefitted by me getting my throat slit," Gil said.

Andreas nodded fervently. "And in any case, I imagine Selene would be quite happy to rule all alone."

"Does it matter?" Marcia demanded. "If we keep her out, then it doesn't matter what her plan is when she gets in here. And I don't know about you, but I'd prefer that."

"My question is, why haven't they come in already?" Gil said. "That's one of the things that causes me to doubt this business of demons. There aren't enough soldiers to take the city. She has a hostage, so that might explain why she tried it, but it must be clear by now that won't work – my apologies, Marcia."

Marcia waved a hand. No point in discussing that.

"So. It's not exactly that I doubt what the Captain and her soldier said, nor do I suggest that they are lying. However, it seems to me that the whole business is quite adequately explained if the 'sorcerers' are merely a sham, intended to scare us, or more likely, the lower city, into letting her in without her having to fight. In which case, surely our move must be to go out there and take the fight to her. We can't let her squat on the river – preventing the barges from coming in or out – indefinitely."

"The problem with that," Daril said, "is that the sorcerers, and the demons, are real enough."

Gil frowned. If even they were still doubting…

"We've all heard the reports out of Teren about

120

demons," Marcia agreed. "I've *seen* a demon." Not something she was keen to admit in full Council. Here – well, Daril knew, Andreas wouldn't be surprised, and she trusted Gil. Whose expressive eyebrows went up, very slowly. "They're real enough."

"Let me rephrase," Gil said. "Demons exist, very well. But does Selene truly *have* any? If she does, why aren't they already coming straight through? Unless you're suggesting that Selene is still hoping for a peaceful settlement, without having to hold knives to anyone's throats. I could understand that, I suppose; easier in the long term to govern a city you haven't damaged. And Teren does need our trade."

Marcia's personal feeling was that Selene would be utterly delighted to hold some knives to some throats, but she wasn't about to go there.

"The cityangel," she said instead. "The cityangel won't tolerate other spirits in Marek." She was going to use the words until she made people comfortable with them.

Gil was frowning again. "Marcia. Demons are one thing – Piath is right, one cannot doubt that they *exist* in Teren and are being used in roughly the ways described. My doubt, as I said, concerns whether Selene has truly brought them here and why, if they are as powerful as is claimed, why she is delaying. But the cityangel…"

The cityangel *explained* precisely that problem, but before Marcia could open her mouth and say that, possibly in slightly intemperate tones, there was a knock on the door, and a footman opened it. "Excuse me, please, Sers –"

Someone was already barging past him.

"Marcia! Here you are."

"*Nisha?*"

Nisha thrust her wrap at the footman and came cheerfully towards them. "I've already been down to Fereno and back, before someone said you'd all been seen coming in here. Daril, Andreas, how lovely to see you both. And Jyrithi-Head too, charmed I'm sure."

"Gil, please," Gil said courteously, sitting back and

regarding Nisha. "And what can we do for you, Kilzan-Heir? Or are you here purely for Marcia?"

"Nisha, by all means." She sat down at the other end of the couch from Marcia. "No, I'm not here for Marcia. I'm here because the Council is ridiculous, my Head is worse, and we need to do something *now* about that wretched woman and whoever else it is she's got out there making unpleasant threats." She wrinkled her nose. "Having said which, I'd rather my Head wasn't *fully* appraised of my presence here, if you don't mind."

"Delighted to have you," Daril said. "I'd say, take a seat, but you already have." His tone was slightly barbed.

Nisha beamed at him. "No point in wasting time, is there? So. Where are we?"

"Wondering what's keeping Selene from marching straight in," Marcia said.

"Well, the cityangel, obviously," Nisha said, then, looking round at them, "What? You *must* know that the Council – Marekhill, indeed – is wholly ridiculous about this. Did you never see what it is you make your oaths on every year?"

Marcia grinned. Daril laughed out loud. Gil blinked.

"In any case," Nisha carried on, "perhaps that hardly matters. Selene *isn't* coming in just yet. Which means we have time. She's using – threatening, anyway – magic. We need magic. Marcia, why isn't your girlfriend here? Or your brother, come to that?"

Marcia's grin collapsed. "Cato won't come up here. You know that."

"Then go to *him*," Nisha said impatiently. "He's the expert. Well, him and your girlfriend who just stormed out of Council, and who can blame her, really."

"Cato and I have fallen out," Marcia said, stiffly.

Nisha eyed her, and visibly decided not to say anything. Marcia didn't look at the others.

"We do of course have Reb as a link to the Group. She has gone to – do research. In the absence of anyone willing to listen to her in Council."

"I think, in fact," Daril said thoughtfully, "the details of the magic, at this point, are irrelevant. Our role must be to get the Council to do what is needed for the sorcerers to defend the city."

"Which is what?" Andreas demanded.

"An excellent question. But as I understand it, the sorcerers don't know that yet. So I'm reluctant to disturb them while they're thinking. My question is, in the meantime, how do we move the Council? And that, I think, we can work on immediately, even in the absence of further detail."

"The most pressing matter," Marcia said, "is the ongoing reluctance to accept that there really are – well, such things as demons in the first place, and then that there's some on our doorstep."

"I take your point," Gil said, dryly.

"Well," Andreas said. "Whilst I'm uncomfortable with this too – if you can tell us what would convince *you*, Gil, perhaps we can apply that to the rest of the Council."

"I am convinced that they exist," Gil said mildly. "My questions are about the reality of this particular situation, and the best way to deal with it."

"There's a couple of the Heads," Nisha said, "wouldn't believe magic exists even if they had a spirit stood in front of them. Those, I suppose, we just need to work around."

"I think they're a minority," Gil said.

"Yes," Marcia agreed. "Most reluctantly accept that the other plane exists, and even that spirits enter this plane sometimes. They just don't think that it happens here."

"Hardly coherent," Daril said. "Unless you accept the cityangel, and then that's a different incoherence."

"Ouch," Gil murmured.

Daril raised an eyebrow. "By all means, explain the coherence to me."

Gil rubbed at their lips. "No. No. I take the point. Ugh. I do dislike having to *rethink* things." They half-smiled. "So, I need to convince myself to be more coherent, and then I have to reproduce that with the rest of the Council?"

"It's a start," Nisha said. "And then there's the Guilds."

"Who ought to be a bit more reasonable," Marcia put in.

"Except Hagadath," Daril contradicted her. "And their gang of cronies."

"Yes, well, some people just have to be left to their own devices," Andreas said, wrinkling his nose. "Marcia. You're on good terms with Warden Ilana, aren't you?"

Marcia nodded. "They might well be open to discussion."

"I could talk to Aden," Nisha said thoughtfully. "I'm not sure offhand where the Broderers stand, but that in itself means they can't be strong in either direction, so likely persuadable."

"Aden? The one from House Tigero who joined the Broderers as an apprentice after the new seats were agreed?" Gil said, brows drawing together. "I suppose, if he has insight into the way the Guild is thinking, but surely, as an apprentice..."

"He joined as a journeyman," Marcia corrected.

"Absent an apprenticeship? Wasn't that one of the things the Petitioners were demanding?"

Gil was right. Marcia hadn't even thought about that, when Aden had told her about it at some party or other, somewhere around when she was getting involved with Andreas.

"Turns out," Daril murmured, "that House influence can put a certain amount of pressure on a Guild. All sorts of things can happen by virtue of a special vote. Quite wondrous, you might call it."

"He's coming up to his mastery exams soon, even," Nisha said. "He's progressed very fast; turns out he wasn't wasting all that time spent sitting around not allowed into the Guild. He is very good indeed."

"And he has useful connections," Daril added.

Nisha frowned at him. "*Which* – the progression, not the connections – has not made him popular with some of the more old-fashioned Guildmembers. They can't deny he's good, or that he's worthy of a mastership if he can pass the exams, but, well, he's been complaining a lot about Guild politics."

"Aden? But he's never been remotely politically inclined." Marcia objected. She felt stirrings of guilt about the fact that she hadn't seen him herself for a while.

"Indeed no, but it sounds like he's been forced to get involved with the more modern side of the Guild out of self-protection."

"Least likely to feel he simply shouldn't be there?" Daril asked. He was sitting back in his chair, rubbing thoughtfully at his chin.

"Precisely. So. I'll talk to him. We can get information, and maybe put a bit of pressure on if I tackle him the right way. Any other useful Guild links?"

"I can speak to the Vintners," Gil offered.

"Smiths won't be much good," Daril said. Marcia suppressed a grimace; Daril's links with the Smiths were courtesy of the deal he'd cut her out of the year before, and she would be lying if she said she wasn't still sore about it. "But I can try the Cordwainers."

"And I go drinking sometimes with Warden Amanth," Andreas said. "I'll contact him."

"It's a start," Nisha said. "But still leaves us, I can't help feeling, with a certain amount of work to do." She sat back, and smiled round at them all. "So. Let's talk *manipulation*."

NINE

Tait knocked tentatively at Cato's door; then, hearing no response, traced their fingers lightly over the red C that marked it. The wards shivered and let them through, which suggested that Cato – probably – wasn't in the middle of anything dangerous.

Inside, the curtains were mostly shut, the last of the spring afternoon sunlight peeking through the tiny chink between them. A bird sang furiously from somewhere nearby, probably the roof gutters, high and repetitive. Cato was slumped on the floor, leaning back against the bedframe, head tilted back and eyes shut. "Hello," he said, without opening his eyes.

"Hey," Tait said. They looked doubtfully at the floor – Cato didn't sweep often – and sat instead on the bed. Cato tilted his head towards them, resting it against Tait's knee, and Tait carded gentle fingers through the close-cropped red-brown hair.

"How're things going?" Tait asked.

Cato made a dissatisfied noise. "Terribly, since you ask. I can't work out how to weaken the bonds so they can break them from within, and even if I could do that, I can't work out how to bind them not to turn around and attack me immediately afterwards just for shits and giggles."

"You'll have freed them?"

"And if Reb's right, and some of them are what we might otherwise call angels, maybe they'll take that into consideration. But as we both know, not all spirits are nice or kind or have any interest in human morality, and some spirits who might otherwise be reasonable are going to be *really pissed off* and quite rightly so. The fact that *I* wasn't responsible for it doesn't mean they won't lash out. And it isn't just me either – if they want to push against Beckett on their own behalf, if they're pissed off enough to do that...We'll just be in the same position but with unbound spirits doing what they feel like, not bound ones doing what Selene tells them."

Tait scratched at their wrist. "But – spirits can't just come through here of their own accord? Can they?"

"Well now," Cato said. "That's a long-argued point, as it happens. Elementals do it. Why only them? Do other spirits just *not* – in which case why not, and why never any exceptions – or is it that they can't – in which case, why is it that elementals can? But either way – these spirits *have* been brought through, at least partway, by the binding. Breaking the binding would send them back, of course, but usually that's the binding sorcerer does that. If it's an external force instead – I really don't know how *that's* going to go down. Ugh." He banged his head once, lightly, against the bedframe.

"You'll work it out," Tait said, with all the conviction they could muster. Cato got like this, occasionally. He gave the strong and deliberate impression of never exerting himself more than he absolutely had to. But he was genuinely passionate about magic, though he did his best to hide it; he was extremely and justifiably confident about his own ability, and he absolutely hated not being able to solve a problem.

Tait was genuinely touched that Cato let them see that; they were fairly confident that no one else saw that side of him. His sister might know, maybe; the little Tait knew of Cato's history strongly suggested that he'd been equally stubborn as a child. Otherwise, wouldn't he just have shrugged his shoulders and let magic be, rather than walk out of his family home with his mother's banishment floating after him? In fact, though Tait didn't know Marcia well, they suspected she was about the same.

"Oh, for *fuck's* sake," Cato said explosively. He looked as if he was admitting something that pained him a great deal. "I've been hoping to be able to get further than this with theory, but no, I'm just producing more questions.

Which I suppose is a start, but I'm going to have to go out to the wretched barge-yard, and *look* at what's going on."

"I'll come with you," Tait said,

"You bloody well will not. I don't want any of that lot recognising you. In any case. This is my problem to fix. I'm the sorcerer – as in, not an apprentice – I'm the one knows about spirits, to the extent that any of us do. I already told Jonas I didn't need his help. Bloody grumpy he was about it too."

"Not like Selene doesn't already know I'm here," Tait pointed out. "Also, you're not the only one knows about spirits, are you?" Not that Tait had ever done much with demons – spirits – in Ameten, due to both being bad at it, and hating it; they'd stuck with blood magic for as long as they could. "And you don't know what a Teren sorcerer looks like."

"I'm guessing they're going to look a bit like the people with the demons hanging around them."

Tait pursed their lips. "The demons might not be right there."

"Hang on, hang on." Cato scrambled up onto his knees. "What do you mean? I thought they were bound?"

"Well, they are, but that doesn't mean they stay on this plane all the time."

"That one that sorcerer – what was his name? Hira? Selene's sorcerer, that came after you."

Not a memory Tait liked. They shuddered involuntarily; fortunately Cato was looking the other way. Hira was still in Marek, even, wasn't he? Not that he could raise any demons here, thankfully. Selene had wanted him to testify against Marcia, and he'd been persuaded out of it then stayed in the city afterwards, presumably to avoid Selene.

"The one he had," Cato continued, snapping his fingers irritably, and Tait pushed the memories aside. "That one was right here. We could see it."

"Only because he – Hira – told it to be," Tait said. "It's like what you do. You invite them here, for a bit, and then you bind them to a thing, and they go away again 'til they're called. Right?"

"Yes – well, sort of, they don't *go away* exactly – but I'm not binding them like your Academy people –"

"*Not* my Academy people."

Cato's eyes scrunched in tacit apology. "Not your Academy people. *The* Academy people. They're binding them properly. Not like what I do, which is more of a gentlemen's agreement."

Tait shrugged. "Doesn't mean they have to stay here all the time."

"Huh," Cato breathed. "Right, well, in that case I definitely have to get close enough to see what's going on. And you're definitely not coming with me."

Tait could be just as stubborn as Cato when they wanted; it was just that they didn't want all that often. Fifteen minutes later they were both making their way to the barge-yard, and Cato was stomping ahead, refusing to talk. Tait didn't care. There was no way they were about to let Cato go off out there on his own.

At least Cato was happy to be extremely cautious. "I don't want *either* of us to be seen, if we can possibly avoid it," he said, once he'd walked off enough of his snit to speak to Tait again. "For a great many reasons. But if one of us has to be, it'll be me."

As it happened, that made perfect sense to Tait. Cato didn't look like anyone in particular; he was a scruffy bastard, and was at his scruffiest today – grubby trousers, tattered coat, dark circles under his eyes, red-brown hair a mess. No one was going to look at him and think he was one of Marek's strongest sorcerers. (Was Cato stronger than Reb? Or just differently strong? Tait wasn't going to ask, because Cato himself definitely knew, and if Reb *was* stronger, Cato had made his peace with it and Tait wouldn't risk upsetting that equilibrium.)

In any case. Cato wasn't obvious. He could fit right in with the guards who were sitting out in the barge-yard behind their barricades, except for his lack of breast-plate. Put a red armband on him and he would certainly fit in with the occasional visiting messenger. Tait, on the other hand, might well be recognised if they got close enough for one of the Teren sorcerers to see their face. They hated the idea that there might be someone out there they knew from the Academy, but that didn't stop it from being true. And whilst Selene already knew they were in Marek, it might still be a warning that someone was scouting magic.

...Hang on. A messenger. That would work.

"Could you put an armband on and pretend to be a messenger? To get a bit closer?" Tait asked.

Cato, to Tait's bafflement, looked wholly scandalised. "Pretend to be a messenger? What, next you're going to be asking me to pretend to be a medic?"

"What? No, of course not."

Cato spread his hands in exasperated not-explanation.

"You lot are very peculiar about messengers," Tait complained.

"Before I worry about getting closer, I'm going to see what I can from here."

They ended up loitering at the end of an alleyway which cut in a quarter-square between the main road out of the barge-yard and the yard itself. The alleyway ran behind one of the inns on the yard, and smelt quite strongly of old beer and piss; plus Tait had just seen a rat scurry into the pile of refuse behind them. Still, it gave them some cover.

They both looked out towards the barricade, and beyond. Tait shuddered.

"Well," Cato said cheerfully. "There are definitely some demons there."

There were a handful of shadowy shapes, in different colours and sizes – purples and reds and dark browns, some half a person's size, others towering over them. Most of them looked vaguely humanoid; they tended to, though Tait's tutors had never been clear on whether that was related to how they looked in their own plane, how a being of that plane intruded into this plane, or the binding process. Beckett looked really very human, but Cato reckoned that was mostly due to their brief time as a (sort of) human.

"You want sorcerers, though." Tait looked around. "Over there," they said. "The one in the green tunic, in among the soldiers wearing blue." Mostly the sorcerers and the soldiers were keeping away from one another, but this one looked to be playing dice with a couple of soldiers. Tait remembered her: her name was Jenny, and she played a very good game of dice, if by 'very good' you mean 'cheated like mad and won a lot'.

Cato would probably like her.

Tait had liked her, too; but she was here, raising demons against people, so maybe they wouldn't like her any more. Or maybe they shouldn't judge. They'd only just got away. Most people didn't, and all the Academy sorcerers knew that.

Cato squinted where Tait was pointing. "Right, I get that she's not a soldier, but she hasn't got a demon, so what makes you so sure she's a sorcerer?"

"She's got a demon," Tait corrected. "The demon's just not there."

Cato was scowling, still staring at Jenny. "How can you tell?"

"Well," Tait admitted. "Mostly I can tell because I know she's a sorcerer, and why else would she be here?"

Cato turned to look at them. "You mean, you know her?"

Tait nodded, and Cato laid a hand on their shoulder, absently comforting. For a horrible moment they felt tears prick at their eyes, and they blinked them back fiercely. Now wasn't the time to have a breakdown over the past, was it?

"So you only know her demon's there because she's a sorcerer. Well that's no bloody use, is it?" Cato's tone was grumbling, rather than critical.

"No, but, once you know to look for it, there's something…" Tait stared over at Jenny, trying to find a way to describe what they knew they could see. "It's not an aura, exactly. It's not like when I look at you, or Reb."

Other Marek sorcerers had a sort of glow about them, although it wasn't visible in the usual sense. It was a pale imitation of the way Beckett looked when they were here. Teren sorcerers didn't look like that, it was more… "It's a bit like some of her is leaking away. It's like an anti-aura, I suppose. Like she's partly anchored somewhere else."

"Because she is," Cato said absently. "Oh. Yes. Yes. I see what you mean. She's kind of…faint. Ugh. I'm not sure I could spot it if I didn't have other clues, though."

"Right," Tait said. "But right now we just want to see if you can get at the binding, right? So let's worry about the other part of it later. Can you follow the way that she's fading?"

Cato was frowning, concentrating hard. At times like this Tait almost felt they loved Cato more; when he dropped his casual attitude and revealed the fact that, underneath, he was a driven fucker with a deep desire to understand and to achieve. Although, that wasn't quite right; the casual attitude was true as well. Just not the whole truth.

"I need to get closer," Cato said, finally.

"Without getting shot," Tait said.

"Obviously." Cato sucked at his teeth. "If I just make a run for the barricade, fast enough…"

"Alternatively," Tait suggested, rolling their eyes, "we could ask for the assistance of the guards who are sitting around and who might have better understanding of the situation? And also who won't then get angry with us for charging around close to their barricade?"

"Oh, fine," Cato said. "*Be* sensible then."

The inn by their alleyway was evidently the centre of operations. Cato marched straight in the back door, Tait trailing behind him.

"I am the sorcerer Cato, and I need to speak to the captain," he announced, throwing open the door of the taproom. Scruffy clothes or not, he exuded an air that got an immediate reaction from the guards sitting around there.

Unfortunately, one of the immediate reactions was less than ideal. "Sorcerer..." one guard said, in ominous tones, rising from her seat.

"Sit down, you idiot," another one said, shoving her shoulder. "He's Marek. One of ours."

The first guard subsided, but she still looked mistrustful. Cato didn't bother to respond to any of it, just stood there with his arms folded looking aristocratic.

The second guard touched his fingers to his forehead. "I'll take you through to Captain Anna, Ser."

Behind them, as he led the way out, Tait heard a flurry of whispers. "That's the one lives in the squats!"

"They say as how you don't want to mess with him. Dark stuff."

"Used to be Marekhill," someone else said authoritatively.

"If he's on our side, dark stuff is what we bloody want right now, with that lot out there," someone else said, to a general mutter of agreement.

Captain Anna was sitting behind a desk writing messages, while a teenager with a red armband stood by the door, shifting from foot to foot.

"Sorcerer to see you, captain," their guide said, rapping on the open door. "Marek sorcerer, I mean."

"Yes, well, I sincerely hope the Terens wouldn't have managed to send one of theirs over the sodding barricade without one of you coming to tell me first," the captain said tartly, without looking up. "Thank you, Erdie." She glanced up at Cato and Tait. "If you'll excuse me for just a moment, Sers, this really must go immediately."

"Certainly," Cato said grandly, and stood with his chin up, waiting.

Once the messenger was sent away, Captain Anna gestured them to seats, which Cato ignored.

"I have come to examine the Teren sorcerers," he said. "We – the sorcerers of Marek – believe we may be able to disable them."

Which was a *gross* overstatement of the current situation, but Tait could see that 'we are really hoping

134

we'll find a weakness if we look hard enough' wouldn't sound so good. From Captain Anna's expression, she read the latter in the former anyway.

"That would be extremely helpful," she said, cautiously. "How can I assist you?"

"I need to get closer," Cato said.

"We need to get closer," Tait put in.

Cato glared at him. "*I* need to get closer, and my colleague here needs to stay put."

"Cato…"

"They'll recognise you, and you know it. No."

Captain Anna looked between the two of them. "One is easy," she said. "Two might be harder."

"Fine," Tait muttered, subsiding.

"So you can get me out there?"

"Stick you in a uniform tabard," she looked Cato up and down, "and you need canvas trousers, those ones stand out too much, and we'll march you out with the others at shift-change. Which is in a few minutes, as it happens."

"How dangerous is it?" Tait asked. Cato glared at them.

"They've got a sniper, but so have we now, so basically neither of us does anything any more. Tit for tat kind of deal. *But* if they think you're a sorcerer I imagine they'd go for it anyway. We tried their sorcerers, right at the start, of course, but they're all protected."

"So it's a good thing I'll look like a guard," Cato said.

"Can't you…" Tait began.

Cato cut in before they'd finished. "No, I can't use a protection-spell, because any sorcerer who's actually talking to their demon will see it." Which Tait should have realised, of course. They flushed.

"Come through to the guardroom and we'll sort you out," Captain Anna said briskly. "And Ser," she nodded to Tait, "if you come through as well, there's a window you can keep watch out of. *Carefully*."

It was better than nothing. Tait followed Captain Anna and Cato out, and tried to ignore their racing, panicked, heartbeat.

☺ ☺

Cato's feet seemed to ring very loudly on the cobbles, in his borrowed, ill-fitting, extremely ugly boots, as he walked between someone called Bracken and someone else called, inexplicably, Pill. The equally ill-fitting helmet was already making his head hurt, and the rim cut across the top of his vision in a way he absolutely hated. His hand itched to push it up out of the way. This was, self-evidently, a very bad idea, in the very real sense that if something went wrong, he could get himself *shot*. And fine, whilst he had never been anywhere near a gun in his life, he'd met a few folk who had, and he was aware from all the complaints and boasts that most of them weren't worth shit in the aiming. But it sounded like this lot did have someone who was a decent shot and had a decent gun – or at least one they'd worked out how to compensate for.

His back was crawling. He tried not to look over at the Terens beyond the barricade. Bracken and Pill weren't looking, after all.

The sensible thing to do would be to turn round, march swiftly – or as swiftly as he could in this wretched footwear – back to the inn, grab Tait, go back to the squats, and stay there until someone else had solved this problem. The sensible thing to do would be never to have been here in the first place.

Except that it was altogether probable that no one else currently in Marek *could* solve this problem. Reb was a good sorcerer – an excellent sorcerer, if he was being honest – but this wasn't her area of expertise. Beckett wouldn't be able to hold the Teren sorcerers and their demons – spirits, he corrected himself – off for ever, however dramatically they'd proclaimed their devotion to Marek when Reb asked. Devotion wasn't the point. Beckett had limits; even Beckett's power, drawn from the city, had limits, and those limits could be worn down. If Cato hid in the squats until someone else had solved the problem, there was a very decent chance that the problem would be 'solved' by the Terens defeating Beckett and extinguishing Marek magic for good. After which they'd most likely start rampaging through the streets looking for Marek sorcerers to extinguish. And, of course, they'd know Tait – they already had it in for Tait – and Cato absolutely wasn't having that.

This was still a fucking stupid idea.

They reached the barricade without anyone developing any surprise extra holes in them, which was a relief, whatever the captain had said about that not having happened since the first day. This was only day three, by that reckoning; it might feel like a bloody long time, but 'hasn't happened since a bit less than forty-eight hours ago!' didn't sound like a ringing endorsement of anyone's safety to him. Bracken jerked a thumb at the current three soldiers and exchanged a few brief soldier-y words before they headed back to the inn. Cato looked longingly after them, then sighed, and turned back to apply himself to one of the spy-holes in the barricade.

The 'barricade' was constructed out of some carts and a bunch of wood roped and nailed across them. It clearly wouldn't stop any determined advance, but equally clearly, right now the Terens were settled across the yard, tents and all, and not about imminently to start a determined – or indeed a half-hearted – advance.

Not on the physical plane, at least. Cato, out here at the edge of Beckett's power over the city, could feel the Teren spirits push-push-pushing inwards. Not forcefully, not all at once, just there, constant, like a drunk repeatedly poking you in the shoulder until you snapped and punched them. It made his teeth itch. It must feel far worse to Beckett.

"Uh," Bracken said, awkwardly, from behind him.

"What?"

"If you need anything, you'll tell us, right?"

Given that these people might be in charge of rescuing him if something unpleasant happened, Cato bit back his initial impulse to tell Bracken that the only thing he needed was to be *left alone* to concentrate, and instead agreed mostly-politely that yes, he would. Even more irritable than before, he returned his attention to the sorcerers, and the spirits, outside.

The irritation faded as he concentrated. Now that Tait had shown him what he was looking for, he could see how the sorcerers, even those without visible spirits near them, faded away slightly. It wasn't exactly around the edges. It was more that they weren't quite there throughout. As if it was something in the binding that moved them *away* from here, as well as the spirit *towards* here.

What he couldn't see was anything like a link that he might be able to get a grasp on.

But the binding existed. Obviously. So there must be a way he could see it, or feel it, or *something*. There had to be. Because if there wasn't, if it was something that only existed from the inside, he was screwed. He bit his lip, and corrected himself. He *would* solve this problem, whatever it took. But if the binding had no external handles, he would have to *think again*, and that would be a time-consuming nuisance. Because he *was* going to fix this, and get back to sitting around doing as much or as little as he felt like at any given moment, the way he'd very deliberately arranged his life.

He looked over to the right of the Teren camp, eye attracted by movement. The sorcerer Tait had pointed out to him stood up and took a few steps away from where she'd been sitting with a couple of soldiers. She gestured, and a demon blossomed into the air beside her. He *saw* – or sensed? It felt like vision but he wasn't sure it was, like the aura he saw around Reb or even Jonas – the moment when the sorcerer pulled at the link, and the link opened up, the spirit emerging into this plane. He was vaguely aware of the soldiers near the sorcerer shying away, but his focus was on the spirit. It was vibrating, and he could sense even from here its deep unhappiness. Distress. The sorcerer spoke to it, her body language commanding and impatient, though he couldn't hear her words, and it turned and, reluctantly, moving slowly, shot great holes into the earth around the edge of that part of the barge-yard. The sorcerer said something to the soldiers, who laughed, still looking a little nervous, and then gestured and the spirit disappeared again.

But now, Cato could still see the link. Or, not *see* it exactly; it was more that he'd got his mental eye in, and he could sense the nature of the binding. It was like – but not *enough* like, not *quite* identical to – what he did when he enclosed a consenting spirit in an object, and from here he couldn't quite identify the differences. It looked more slippery, somehow, or perhaps differently anchored? But he daren't try to reach out and affect it from here, in case the sorcerers noticed something amiss. He'd notice if someone messed with one of his workings, after all.

He chewed at his lip as he switched his gaze from sorcerer to sorcerer, and after a little practice, was able to see the dip in the atmosphere, the faint purple tinge, more in his mind than in his vision, marking the link to the binding. Tait had said, when they'd talked about it once, that the binding trapped the spirit between dimensions, which was indeed very much like what Cato did. But Tait hated talking about it; and in any case, Tait wasn't great at the sort of detail Cato needed.

What Cato needed was *more information*. Such as, for example, someone constructing the spell for him. Which Tait wouldn't be willing to do, even without trapping a spirit in it. Well, they might, but Cato didn't want to ask, because they would hate doing it, and Cato would hate making them unhappy.

Except there wasn't anyone else, was there? And Cato had to get more information about this. He couldn't just barge in and start hacking at sorcerers' links. He had to know how to break them; what happened when they broke. He had to work out how to do it successfully but also how to release the spirits back into their own plane, not into this. Some of them would probably take themselves back home even if they were released here. Some of them might take the opportunity to help themselves to a bit of life-force, if they could, and there were definitely circumstances under which a released demon could do exactly that. And they might have it in for their former binders, but that didn't mean they'd *limit* themselves to that. There were spirits out there who were just…not very nice. Cato shuddered, remembering one or two of his own more hair-raising experiences. And if Beckett was already weakened…

So he would have to ask Tait, wouldn't he, and Tait would just have to lump it. Ugh.

"Right," Cato said briskly, wriggling backwards. "I'm done. Let's go back."

Bracken and Pill looked blankly at him.

"Back to the inn?" Cato tried again.

"Shift changes in another three hours," Bracken told him. "We're here 'til then."

Cato looked incredulously between them, before realising that they were not, in any way, joking.

"*Shit*," he muttered, and settled down grumpily to wait.

TEN

Waiting for Cato to return to the inn started out tense, and became, over the next three hours, boring. Tait couldn't see properly from the common room; there was only one corner window where you had line of sight out to the centre of the yard. There was one soldier there watching, and Tait insisted on squeezing in to sit next to her, despite the lack of room. After the first while, where Cato was obviously observing and thinking hard, he turned and sat with his back against the barricade. Finished? Tait wished they could *tell* Cato not to waste this time; even if he thought he knew what was happening, surely more observation couldn't go amiss. Not that Tait really knew what Cato was looking for; they might have learnt to do Teren demon-sorcery themself, but they'd only actually done it once, and they'd never really understood the principles or the underlying theory in the way that Cato did despite never having done that sort of magic. Though he did have his own dealings with spirits; perhaps that helped. Blood-magic, now, that Tait was good at. Better, they reflected, than Marek magic, which was... something to worry about another time.

Cato did, in the end, turn around and spend more time watching. And more time waiting. He was too far away for Tait to see his expression properly, especially under the too-large helmet that fell over his brow, but his body language screamed 'irritated boredom'. Tait just hoped he was thinking at the same time. At one point he leant over and began sketching on the ground with a splinter of wood tugged from the edge of the cart he was leaning against. Eventually, shift change came, and Cato, one soldier either side of him, slouched back across the yard. Tait's heart was in their mouth again while the three were out in the open; then, finally, they were in the inn. Back

141

inside. Safe. Tait took three swift steps across the room and put their arms around Cato, not caring who was looking. Cato, after the first startled moment, hugged them back.

"I'm fine," he said, into Tait's shoulder, then let go, and stepped back, eyes bright and focussed, suddenly full of energy. "And I think I know – not what to do, not quite yet. Wish I'd had a notebook with me, might have been able to get a bit further. But I probably can't now without trying something." He grimaced. "And asking you some more questions, sorry. But I know what I need to know, and I know what to do next. What we need…"

He broke off as a soldier came running into the room. "Where's the captain?" they demanded. "There's some Marekhill type in the hallway! Says that woman out there *summoned* her here? Did the captain know?"

"What the…" Cato's eyes went suddenly wide. "Oh shit. Tell me it's not…"

The soldier ducked out again, across the hall. There were footsteps in the corridor, and Tait heard Captain Anna's calm voice, then…

"It's *Marcia*," Cato said, and ducked down onto the dilapidated armchair that had its back to the door, dragging Tait down with him, effectively hiding them from sight. "For *fuck's* sake."

There wasn't quite room for both of them, really, but Tait was hardly going to complain about sitting on Cato's lap, even if it was in the middle of a roomful of soldiers. And they understood Cato not wanting to encounter Marcia, here and now, if it could possibly be avoided, given how things had been between them the last time. Whatever was happening must be political stuff, and they just needed to wait it out; then Cato could get on with the magic stuff. And Tait had every confidence – well, nearly every confidence – that he could fix it.

They couldn't hear voices any more – had Captain Anna taken Marcia into the other room? A door banged open.

"Either way, Captain, I will be going out there." Yes,

that was Marcia, in full Marekhill mode. "With or without an escort. Or your *permission*."

Cato was swearing under his breath. From their corner they could see a slice of the yard; they both saw Marcia emerge from the door at the corner of the inn and walk across their field of view into the bargeyard. She was wearing a grubby white tabard which didn't fit properly over her bump, and a soldier, visibly reluctant, shoulders slightly hunched, trailed after her.

"What the fuck is she *doing*?" Cato demanded, as she crossed out of view. "Come on. Off, off." He pushed at Tait, then once Tait had stood up, scrambled out of the armchair and towards the corner window which had the view of the yard and the barricade. He barged in front of the soldier stationed there, who gulped – Tait could almost see the thought 'sorcerer' forming over their head – and didn't try to prevent him. Tait did their best to squeeze in to Cato's side, against the whitewashed wall and out of the soldier's way, and peered over Cato's head. The benefits of height.

"Is this some kind of attempt at a parley?" Tait asked doubtfully. "Political stuff? That soldier said *summoned*."

Cato scowled, without looking round. Tait wondered if they should suggest taking advantage of the moment to leave quietly, but that didn't seem to be in Cato's mind right now. "Unlikely. That would involve – more people, for starters. Unless Marcia's taking things into her own hands again, but one has to hope the Council situation hasn't deteriorated quite that far."

"Who's that?" Tait asked, pointing. "Coming out on the other side?" Whoever it was didn't look like Tait remembered Selene, but admittedly the last time Tait had seen Selene they hadn't been quite in the best frame of mind for reliable identification and memory.

"What the *fuck*." Cato's hand had clenched on the windowsill. "It's – Madeleine. Our – Marcia's mother. What is she *doing*."

"Are you sure we shouldn't just…go?" Tait asked tentatively, but Cato didn't appear to hear them.

Marcia had stopped in the middle of the yard. Madeleine was still walking towards her, then stopped with a few yards, and the barricade, between them. Someone was shouting – the voice officious-sounding, not alarmed – but neither Marcia nor Madeleine were paying any apparent attention.

Cautiously, Tait reached over and opened the window in front of them, enough to let more sound in. Cato didn't react, or look round.

They couldn't hear the low-voiced conversation between Marcia and Madeleine; but they saw when someone else stepped forward to stand by Madeleine – wasn't that Selene? – and they could hear her well enough.

"So, Fereno-Heir? Will you agree to our conditions?"

"No," Marcia said, clearly and loudly. "I will not, and the Council will not."

"Ridiculous to expect that the Council will lift a finger just because one of the Heads is threatened," Cato muttered. "Even if all of them were, because then the Heirs would just be rubbing their hands with glee." That was, Tait felt, slightly unfair, but they agreed that what Selene was trying didn't make sense to them either. Was she hoping Marcia would do something? But surely Selene knew the limits of what a single House could do.

Selene gestured sharply and demandingly, and a pale-green smoke began to boil around the sorcerer standing a few feet behind her. It didn't coalesce into a demon-figure. Instead, it began to stream towards Madeleine.

Marcia swayed slightly towards Madeleine, but didn't move. Madeleine turned, calmly, to look over her shoulder, then turned back again.

"Are you absolutely certain, Fereno-Heir?" Selene asked. "Be warned, this is only the first. Any of the Council who stand against me will face the same fate."

Marcia's hand shifted, as if about to go to her belly, and then she dropped it again, and her head went up.

She was going to stand there, and watch her mother taken by a demon.

Tait realised, suddenly, what the point of this was. It wasn't that Selene expected the threat to Madeleine to make the Council change their minds. Of course, if that *had* happened, doubtless she'd have been pleased enough to take the victory. But what she wanted was to use Madeleine as a very public example of what awaited anyone else who stood against her. She wanted to scare them; that was the point. And perhaps, given what little Tait knew of the history between Selene and Marcia, she also wanted to hurt Marcia, specifically and personally.

And they were about to see that happen, right in front of them. "Cato, are you sure..." Surely there was something they could do. Surely Cato wasn't just going to *watch*...

Cato shrugged. "Not my problem." But he swallowed convulsively, and Tait saw his hand clench on the windowsill.

Tait looked out at the scene, at the smoke that had nearly reached Madeleine, at Marcia just *watching*, chin high, refusing to look away...

Madeleine was going to die. She was really going to die.

What they didn't know was whether Cato really believed that. Cato hadn't been in Teren. Cato hadn't run from Teren rather than carry out the sort of orders that the Archion and the Academy had been issuing. Was Cato really ready to watch his mother die, to watch her eaten by a demon, right in front of him?

More to the point, was Tait ready – willing – to watch anyone die in front of them, if they could prevent it?

And they could prevent it. They'd brought a knife. Just in case, when Cato was out there, they'd need the translocation spell. Their hand went to their belt.

They couldn't just let this happen. Never mind Cato and what he thought; never mind who Madeleine was to him. This was someone who Tait could save, and that decision wasn't Cato's, was it? It was Tait's own.

They didn't wait for Selene to warn again. They grabbed the knife from their belt, sliced it across their forearm, and *pulled*.

A bare fraction of a breath later, they felt Madeleine appear a few feet to their right, in the middle of the inn common room. Tait turned, their own head spinning, in time to see her sway and fall to the floor.

Outside, Selene was shouting. Marcia was being hustled back to the inn, as fast as she could go, by the shouting, visibly terrified soldier. The smoke was still swirling around the barricade, trying to move after Marcia and the soldier, but Beckett's power was still there, stopping it. Tait hoped there wasn't time to get the sniper set up.

Cato spun round and stared at Madeleine, in a heap on the floor, before his eyes went unerringly to Tait.

"What the *fuck* did you do?"

☺ ☺

Tait and Cato stared at one another. There was a lot of commotion around them; Tait ignored it all. Their stomach felt cold and uncomfortable. Cato's eyes flicked down to their arm, and Tait, belatedly, scrabbled in a pocket for a handkerchief to clap over the shallow cut.

"We will talk about this *elsewhere*," Cato began, eyes skating round the room, obviously looking for a way out that didn't go through the inn corridor, which, presumably, Marcia was already in; and then the door to the common room slammed open.

"*Mother*." Marcia rushed in and knelt next to Madeleine, a couple of guards rushing in after her with an overset look. Tait heard Cato's sharp inhale. She'd be able to see the two of them, if she looked up, but all her attention was on Madeleine.

"Mother?" Marcia was shaking her gently by the shoulder. She turned to one of the guards. "She's still breathing, but…"

"Shock, probably," the guard said, sounding authoritative. "Give her a little time."

"What are you doing here?" the other guard demanded. It took Tait a moment to realise that the question was

146

addressed to them and to Cato.

"Captain Anna..." Tait began. "We were..." They weren't feeling all that well themself, come to think of it.

Marcia, at the sound of Tait's voice, sat back on her heels and looked up.

"*Cato*," she said, her voice catching. "You changed your mind." Her hand rested on Madeleine's shoulder.

Cato's shoulders stiffened. "I bloody did not. For all I care that demon could have dragged her straight off this plane and I wouldn't have given the smallest of shits." His voice was arctic-cold, and more Marekhill than Tait had ever heard him. "Tait did it." He flicked his fingers at Tait without looking at them. "And if I'd known what they were doing I'd have stopped them."

"*What*?" Marcia got to her feet.

"You keep *failing* to *listen*. She didn't care about me. I don't care about her."

"She was a hostage! She was innocent!"

"Innocent my arse. She's never been innocent in her life. She never lifted a finger to help me. I wouldn't have so much as spat on the floor to help her. Fuck the both of you." He met Tait's eyes for a brief moment, and Tait was horrified by the despair and anger in Cato's gaze. "And fuck you too."

He strode past Marcia and out, without looking back. Tait realised, distantly, that they were shaking.

Marcia looked at Tait. "Thank you," she said, sincerity evident in her voice even as she shifted her weight awkwardly. "I don't know exactly what you did, but...Thank you. I'm sure Cato..." Her voice trailed off. She obviously wasn't any more *sure* that Cato would anything in particular than Tait was.

They hadn't done it for Marcia. Or even for the baby. It didn't seem like the moment to explain that. They shrugged awkwardly themself. "I hope she's...well," they said, eventually, and skirted round Marcia, giving her a shallow bow, to go after Cato. They ought to fix their arm up properly, but that could wait. For now, they just held onto the handkerchief, now damp and red-blotched. It wasn't much of a cut, in any case; it would close up soon. Wasn't like they hadn't done this before.

Cato was already a fair way down the road; but Cato never ran, not even under the grip of strong emotion. Tait caught them up after a few minutes, close to where the city proper began, simply by dint of having longer legs. They still didn't know what they were going to say.

"Cato?"

"As I said already," Cato said, glancing briefly sideways at Tait then looking away again. He sped up a little, but it wasn't hard for Tait to keep up. "Fuck you too. How dare you. You knew how I felt."

Very suddenly, without expecting it, Tait was furious. "And what about how I felt?" they demanded. They dropped the cloth from their arm to grab at Cato's shoulder, swinging him round to a stop. "What about how I felt? You wanted me to leave someone to die right there in front of me when I could have saved them? I had the knife right there. It was *right there*. And I *know* that spell. I had it *ready*. I had everything ready to pull *you* out, you idiot."

Cato blinked at them, seeming not to understand.

"You're going on about people making their decisions," Tait said. They felt blood trickle down the inside of their arm. "What about my decision? You wouldn't save her. That's up to you. You didn't want to – pull her out of there, when Marcia asked. If you even could. Fine. That's your decision. That doesn't mean you had the right to stop me from doing it."

"She made her choice," Cato said. His shoulders were hunched.

"What choice? She was a *hostage*, Cato."

"She chose to remain Head. She chose to go to bloody Teren, and to Ameten even. She chose to stand around doing what Selene told her to. This is what happens."

"And what should she have done instead? When Selene was doubtless holding that demon over her anyway?"

"She didn't lift a finger to save me," Cato said. His voice cracked. "Not when I was starving in the squats, not when I had the plague. Not a finger. She'd have let me die and never even shed a tear."

"No. She didn't. And of course she should have done. I'm not suggesting you forgive her for that. Marcia helped you. I would have done, if I'd been here then."

"You'd have died too," Cato said through white lips. "Sorcerer."

"That's not the *point*. You're my partner. I love you. Of course I hold what she did to you – what she didn't do for you – against her. Just not enough to let her die right there in front of me when I had the means of stopping it. That wouldn't make anything *right*, would it? And while I'm at it," Tait suspected they might regret this, but they were on a roll now, "I don't believe that you were really ready for that to happen either, regardless of whether you were willing to stop it."

"I don't care." Cato's gaze skated away from Tait.

"Cato…"

"Fuck off and mind your own business," Cato spat. "This wasn't yours to do."

"Yes, it was," Tait said. "Just like it would be if I hadn't known her from, from the statue on the Ameten Bridge. And you don't get to take this out on me, either." Their patience suddenly stretched thin, and snapped. "I love you, but that doesn't mean I do what you tell me to. Fuck off yourself."

They turned, and walked towards the city as fast as they could, their arm aching under their fingers. They didn't look back; and Cato didn't call them back.

☉ ☉

Jonas strode into the Dog's Tail and looked around; no sign down here of Tam or Asa. He bought himself an ale at the bar – considered and discarded the idea of getting a round in, not knowing how long the others would be – and went up to the upper room. The balcony was shut, far too cold to be outside at this time of year – even if the sun had been out today, the air was still cold, and any warmth didn't last past late afternoon never mind early evening. Tam and Asa weren't up here either, nor were many other people – the city was oddly, or perhaps not so oddly, quiet – so at least it was easy enough to find a table.

He slumped down on the bench, leaning back against the wall, and brooded irritably on the discussion he'd had with Cato earlier. He'd done his best to run his irritation off with work, and he'd had a successful day, but it hadn't worked as a distraction.

It wasn't *fair* for Cato to exclude Jonas from his attempts to solve the whole demon problem. Fine, Jonas had been suspicious of spirits in the past, but he'd been there when they all scared off Selene's last sorcerer-summoned demon, and he'd seen Cato summon that spirit Yorick. And he was *interested*, curse it, especially after what he'd heard about elementals out on the ocean from some of the Salinas sailors he'd spoken to lately. Surely the rise in elemental activity – and those weird storms – had to be linked with what Teren was doing.

He could contribute! Usefully!

It was totally unreasonable for Cato to tell him to get lost, even if he *claimed* he was only doing it for Jonas' own benefit.

A part of his mind pointed out that this probably was in fact true; it wasn't like the situation was *safe*, was it? But then, sitting and whittling wood while Cato did all the work, that wasn't going to be *safe*, either, because no one in Marek was going to be *safe* if Cato didn't find a solution to this.

He didn't have to be in Marek. He could get on a ship, any time he liked. There'd always be a berth for a Salina far from home. He could get on a ship, keep quiet about the flickers and all the rest. Sail away and abandon all his Marek friends to whatever happened here.

Yeah. As if.

"Hey! Jonas!"

He glanced over to see Tam coming up the stairs, mug in one hand and a folded news-sheet in the other, with Asa just behind.

Asa slid onto the bench next to him and gave him a one-armed hug, then rested their shoulder companionably against him. He smiled over at them; he always felt calmer when Asa was next to him. Of course he wasn't going to up and leave Asa and Tam – or even Cato, or Reb, or Tait. He just wanted to *help*.

Tam sat down opposite him and spread the news-sheet out on the table. "Did y'see this? We've taken over the warehouses!"

Jonas blinked down at the news-sheet. "Which we is this?"

"Tam's taken up with the political types," Asa said. Their voice was gently teasing, and Jonas looked over to see the roll of their eyes.

"Well, and seems sensible to me, that *everyone* should get a say in how Marek's run," Tam said. "Doesn't it?"

Asa shrugged. "Can't say as how I've ever thought all that much about it."

"Anyway," Jonas interrupted. "What's this about warehouses?"

"Before the shortages really start to bite," Tam said. "What with the fact that there's nothing coming down the river, just at the moment. There's grain and that stocked in Guild and House warehouses, is the thing. So why not take it over, make sure it's distributed fairly? And that's exactly what happened." He tapped the news-sheet proudly.

"The Marekhill types aren't at *all* happy," Asa said.

"Messages?" Tam asked. "I wasn't working today."

"I've been up and down the Hill all afternoon," Asa agreed. It would be against the messenger code to discuss anything one might have gathered about the *content* of the messages one carried, but a certain amount of speculation based on reactions was fair game. And it wasn't like this wasn't public news, apparently, even if Jonas hadn't known. He'd been over in the south-west all day, dealing with a set of small merchant deals, and he rarely bothered with news-sheets.

"Anyway," Tam said. "I know there's stuff comes in

from ships, too, so it's not like I'm worried or anything. About food and that, you know. Just, I don't mind saying, I'd rather it was folk from our side of the city were looking after what we do have."

"There won't be, though," Jonas said slowly, realising slightly too late that he was speaking aloud.

The other two looked at him, both frowning. "Won't what?"

"The ships. They bring stuff in, right? And then load up and take other stuff away. Why would they keep coming if there's nothing to go out?"

"It's all Guilded stuff, though," Tam argued. "Right? That don't come in on barges down the river."

"Some of what comes down the river ends up on Salinas ships, bound for Exuria or the Crescent," Jonas said. He'd learnt to read from ship manifests; he knew this stuff without even thinking about it. "And yeah, there's the Guilded stuff too, for sure, but where do the raw materials for that come from?" Lots of places, as it happened, but a good sight of it from Teren.

"Oh, well," Tam said comfortably, taking a draught from his mug. "It'll all be sorted before *that* becomes a problem, right? You sorcerer types will fix up the demons, or the cityangel will, and the political types will send Teren away with a flea in their ears, and the barges will be coming down again before anything can go that badly wrong." He stood up. "Another one?"

"Have you seen anything," Asa asked Jonas quietly, once Tam had gone to the bar. "You know." They made a gesture that indicated *his flickers*.

Jonas shook his head. He hadn't, and he hadn't tried, either, which he felt… *uncertain* about.

"I don't need to predict the future," he said, "to know that Salinas captains all have their eye on their profit."

Profit; and risk. And sitting around in a city this close to an army of Teren demons, especially given the way Salinas felt about spirits of any sort, was a pretty big risk. What if Teren did break the city boundaries? What if Beckett couldn't keep them out? Jonas had seen Beckett fight one single demon. He didn't want to find out whether the cityangel could take on a dozen.

(They couldn't. He was trying not to think that thought, but it was there anyway. Beckett could last only so long once the Terens began to push, the way they hadn't yet. And 'so long' wouldn't be long at all. Jonas had been out to the bargeyard. He'd seen the demons beyond the barricade. Beckett was only one, albeit with all the power of Marek. Only one.)

But he didn't want to mention that to Tam and Asa. No point in scaring them. And maybe Cato would fix it, after all, and maybe the Salinas captains would be happy to wait for Marek to sort itself out, and maybe Jonas would have the moon on a stick as a name-day gift and all, while he was wishing.

ELEVEN

Marcia paced up and down House Fereno's main reception room, unable to bring herself to sit down. Andreas, perched on the edge of one of the couches, watched her anxiously. Which only made her more irritable.

"What are they *thinking*?" she demanded for the fourth or fifth time since the end of that morning's emergency Council meeting.

"That it isn't a problem," Andreas said, also for the fourth or fifth time.

"But it is! How can it not be?"

Andreas shrugged. "Most of the Houses are sitting on plenty of their own supplies. Not to mention their own trade warehouses. The fact that the Guilds are having problems doesn't affect them."

"*Yet*," Marcia said darkly.

"I know, I know. I'm not disagreeing with you. But the Houses being self-centred, or even short-sighted, is hardly news, is it, now? Marcia, please, won't you sit down and...I don't know, have a nice calming infusion or something."

"I don't *want* a nice calming infusion," Marcia said through her teeth. The baby chose that moment to kick, hard, and she winced. *Not now, thank you.* "The Guild warehouses have been taken. Why do they think that our own are inviolable?"

"Are you worried that whoever you've got on the doors of your warehouses will be suborned?" Andreas asked.

"There's nothing in them right now," Marcia admitted. "We just loaded up a ship last week, and we were expecting more in from the barges for our next contracts. Which is a problem in itself, and the Council aren't thinking about that either."

"The Salinas are still bringing in loads from the Crescent

and Exuria. Fine, we'll be short on barley for a while, until we sort this out, but rice, vegetables…Exurian wheat is more expensive, to be sure, but…"

"But what?"

"Well, it's not the end of the world if bread is a little dearer for a few days, is it?"

A few days. And what if it were more than that? Beckett couldn't hold out longer than that, maybe, but the Council – even Andreas – weren't thinking that way, were they? They weren't expecting to be overrun; they just couldn't envisage this *not* being resolved soon. It was hard to take Selene seriously if you weren't willing to take magic seriously, because it *looked* like she didn't have the resources to be a threat. If you didn't believe in the demons – or even if you accepted that they existed but didn't emotionally engage with what that meant – she looked like a weak fool, who would surely give up and go away if you were patient.

"Dearer bread might not be the end of the world for you, maybe," Marcia said, teeth clenched, returning to the matter at hand. "But what happens if the Salinas decide that they don't want to be offloading cargo here when we can't reload anything?"

"Well," Andreas said, then stopped. "But. We have *contracts*."

"Which we're breaching. Why shouldn't they?"

"I didn't see you mentioning that in the Council."

"Yes, well, I didn't think anyone was listening." Marcia pulled a face. "And I need to sort my own House out before I start warning everyone else, come to that. Consider this advance warning of your own, though." Not that she was quite sure *how* to sort things out. But speaking quietly to Kia might be a good start; and getting the factor to speak to some of the captains currently in dock. They might have cargo they were carrying on their own cognisance that could fit the routes for the upcoming ships…it was going to be a challenging puzzle if it was possible at all, and it wouldn't help if everyone was scrabbling around to do the same.

"My thanks," Andreas said, somewhat doubtfully.

"But what are we going to do about the warehouses?"

"Leave them to it? It's the Guilds are inconvenienced, and if the lower city are solving their own problems, why not let them? I wouldn't have people going hungry, for certain, but they're not, are they? Isn't that the whole point of what they're doing?"

"Well, indeed, but then what is the point of us claiming we manage the city? We're painting ourselves *out*, Andreas, don't you get it? Athitol-Head might not be capable of believing she might become unimportant, but I know you're quicker than that."

Andreas scowled at her. "Marcia. I know you're irritable, but there's no need to be this obnoxious."

He had a point. Marcia forced her shoulders down, took a deep breath – then another one which didn't help any more – and went to sit next to him. "I'm sorry. You're right, that's not fair. I'm frustrated, and my stomach hurts, and I can't *eat* anything half the time, and I'm still worried about Mother."

Madeleine had returned to House Fereno the previous afternoon, taken directly to her bed, and refused to see Marcia or to let her in the room 'until she felt better'. Fine, it hadn't even been a day yet, but it was still tremendously unlike her. Cousin Cara was looking after her and assured Marcia that Madeleine was just overwrought, and would be perfectly fine after a little rest. It didn't entirely help.

Andreas sighed, and patted her knee. "That's understandable. It's all...a bit much, right now, I suppose." Marcia tried not to hear that as patronising. Andreas wasn't, usually; and he was wound up too.

A footman tapped on the door. "Excuse me, Ser, but Kilzan-Heir is here to see you."

Nisha? Marcia hadn't been expecting her. But then, Nisha was making something of a habit of turning up unexpectedly, wasn't she? "Do bring her in."

"Marcia, darling." Nisha swept in, a box in her hand. "My mother insisted I bring you these biscuits. Terribly

157

good for the stomach at your stage, she says. My sister says they taste awful but eased her heartburn enough that it was worth it. Mother wouldn't brook the slightest delay, sent down to Cook and upset all the lunch plans the moment I mentioned you were feeling unwell."

"I'm not *unwell*," Marcia insisted, but took the box. "Give your mother my regards."

Nisha sat back in the armchair, then glanced over her shoulder as the door shut. "And whilst all of that is perfectly true, why I'm really here is; have you – and it's good to see you here too, Andreas, because you know the wretched man better – have you any idea what Daril is up to?"

Marcia and Andreas both stared at her.

"What do you mean?" Marcia asked cautiously.

"I'm *told* that he's down in Marek Square announcing that the Leandra warehouses will be distributed tomorrow among the lower city – fairly, he says, whatever that might mean – in order to relieve the obvious concern there, and so on and so forth. So. What is he up to?"

"He's giving *away* his goods?" Andreas echoed.

"Says he has a load of Teren barley and so forth. Giving it to Marekers instead of sending it off to the Crescent."

"He's pre-empting it being confiscated," Marcia said. "We all heard the rest of the Houses this morning trying to pretend it isn't happening. But if the radicals have the Guild warehouses already, ours must be at risk." Trickier, because it was House staff minded them, not Guildfolk, but Marcia wasn't inclined to count on that. "But he must have more in mind than that."

"Maybe he's just concerned about people?"

Marcia and Nisha both turned and stared at Andreas, whose cheeks darkened a little.

"Daril?" Marcia said incredulously.

"Andreas, sweetie, I know he's your friend, but the man isn't exactly renowned for his open-handed, uncalculating compassion, is he now?"

Once again Marcia really wished she could tell Andreas

and Nisha about the full detail of Daril's attempted coup, back when he'd temporarily removed Beckett. She confined herself to nodding meaningfully. "He's planning something," she agreed.

"Man of the People," Nisha said thoughtfully. "But where do you go with that?"

"That depends," Marcia said, "on where you think the people are going. Doesn't it?" She didn't believe that Daril wanted a revolution any more than anyone else on Marekhill did – not the sort of revolution that did away with the Houses, anyway. Daril liked his comforts as much as anyone else, and he had power now. Why would he undermine himself?

But if his goal was not to support their revolution, but to bring them to supporting him... Daril Leandra-Head, the people's voice. Just as Nisha had suggested, but – perhaps – one stage further. He'd wanted to be *in charge* before. Now he had power – Head, even, not just Heir, of his House – but shared, one of thirteen, or more if you counted in the Guilds. Did he see this as an opportunity to be the one on top, rather than one of many?

And if that *was* his goal...what could she do about it? She didn't share the vision of the most radical of the radicals, but she did think that Markhill needed reform. And she didn't think funnelling that through Daril would be good for Marek overall. It certainly wouldn't be good for her, or her House. She didn't even think it would be good for the lower city, in the end. She didn't believe Daril really had anyone's interests in mind other than his own, and eventually, the two would cease to coincide.

"There's a difference," she said aloud, "between being seen to do something, and actually doing it."

Nisha nodded thoughtfully.

"On the other hand," Andreas said, "does it matter? Really? Don't we have bigger things to worry about? We've spent all morning fretting over warehouses when we still have Selene to deal with. And aren't Reb and Gil due here soon?"

"*Are* they?" Nisha asked with interest.

"To discuss magic again," Marcia agreed, glancing over at the clock against the wall. "Oh goodness, very soon indeed. *Yes*, Nisha, you can stay. I didn't think you needed convincing over magic."

"I don't, but I'm nosy." She beamed at Marcia.

Well. Nisha too then would – hopefully – get to meet Beckett. Which was what Marcia was counting on to finally convince Gil about the reality of their *situation*, as Gil insisted on putting it.

She heard Reb's voice in the hallway and went out to meet her, to get a moment alone.

"You realise," Marcia began, carefully, after giving Reb a welcoming kiss, "that you are going to have to go back to the Council again."

"*Have to*, you say," Reb said, but there was a note of resignation to her tone. "I suspected you were going to say that, when you invited me round."

"The trial group," Marcia said. "Yes. I considered inviting Daril as well – at least he recognises the existence of magic – but I thought Beckett might get a little. Uh. Irritated." And apparently Daril was off dishing out grain, anyway.

Reb made an agreeing noise, then sighed. "I understand why you're saying this. And if you can promise me that there'll be *slightly* more in the way of people willing to listen to me."

"Well. That's the point of this morning, isn't it. Gil, in particular. But Nisha, too – she can't be publicly on my side, but she's good at shifting opinion." Which did mean it was just as well she was here. Marcia only realised she was chewing her thumbnail – a habit she'd *almost* entirely shaken as a teenager – when Reb gently took it out of her mouth. There was so much that needed to fall into place, and half of it wasn't even slightly there yet, and...

"Come on," she said. "Let's get started." She still needed to tell Reb about Cato, too. Not just yet, though. After. One problem at a time.

Andreas still looked slightly uncomfortable around Reb, but the two of them, aided by Nisha and the refreshments the servants had brought in as soon as Reb arrived, managed to make conversation until Gil arrived, precisely on time.

"Sorcerer Reb," Gil said – Marcia hadn't been wholly sure they would recognise her, but Gil was good at that sort of thing. There was a line between their brows; Marcia had been coy about the specific purpose of this meeting.

"So," Marcia began. "I believe, after the other day, you all know Sorcerer Reb?"

Murmurs of agreement. Andreas looked anxious; Gil wary; Nisha like she expected entertainment.

"Sorcerer Reb is here on behalf of the Group, the body which as you may recall, governs Marek's sorcerers." Skipping lightly over the fact that of Marek's five sorcerers, three were still apprentices, and the other full sorcerer refused to set foot past the bottom of Marekhill even when he was on speaking terms with her.

Marcia took a breath. "Ser Reb will ask the cityangel to come and speak to us."

Gil nearly choked. Nisha stopped, pastry halfway to her mouth, eyes wide. Andreas looked like he was trying not to shut his eyes altogether.

No point in delaying. Marcia nodded to Reb.

She was hoping very hard that this would actually work. Historically, it wouldn't have; historically, no one *summoned* the cityangel, even politely. But lately, Beckett – since they'd inadvertently spent time as a human, sort of, and become Beckett – had been making more appearances on this plane. So maybe, perhaps, they'd show up when Reb requested. Otherwise this was going to be a significant setback.

"Marcia, darling…" Nisha began.

But Reb was already gesturing with a pinch of something. Marcia thought she smelt ginger, and a black-purple light crackled across her field of vision. When it cleared, Beckett stood in front of them. She tried to see them with the eyes of someone who hadn't before. Tall. Human-like – more so, Cato said, than other spirits – but obviously – surely? – *not* human. Their head was devoid of hair, their face pale and their expression distant; something draped around them that wasn't quite *like* cloth. There was nothing that Marcia could point to, exactly, but... They had just appeared out of the air, of course, but would the others expect something more dramatic from Marek's cityangel? Beckett never made much of their appearances and disappearances; truth be told, Marcia found it more alarming than if they had gone in for flair. The idea that they could just *appear* like that.

She should say something. "Beckett. Hello. Uh..."

"I do not engage with the political," Beckett said, flatly. Of course Beckett knew who was here, who they were. This was Beckett's city. "That is the arrangement."

"I know. But. There's other things going on. And this isn't the Council, this is just...people."

Beckett looked faintly unconvinced, but... "Demons," they said.

"Demons right outside the city," Marcia agreed. "We need...we need to speak to you." Really, they needed *Beckett* to speak to *them*, more than anything else, but Marcia wasn't sure how Beckett would take 'some people don't believe you exist'. "Please."

Reb was standing quietly with her arms folded, just watching. Her calm presence steadied Marcia.

"Excuse me," Gil said, clearing their throat. "You are...the cityangel?"

"Marek's cityangel. You may call me Beckett."

Gil's eyes were wide with curiosity, and borderline awe, but Marcia could see their determination not to be rolled over. That was very Gil. "You...defend the city?"

"I made an arrangement," Beckett said. "The city is mine, and I look after it. The city and I are together."

It was, Marcia was vaguely aware, more complicated than that.

"And demons aren't allowed in." That was from Reb.

"No." The word, from Beckett, rang in the room longer than it ought to. "No other spirits may come into *my* city."

"Are they trying?" Nisha asked. Her eyes were wide

too, fixed on Beckett. Nisha might have believed already that the cityangel existed, but seeing them in person was another experience altogether. "They're there, right?"

Not that anyone in this room was seriously challenging that, not any more – that was one reason to start here, and without inviting, say, Athitol-Head. Baby steps. She'd made a mistake, trying to just bring Reb straight into the Council; and she wouldn't be *able* to bring Beckett into the Chamber.

Beckett's eyes narrowed. "Yes. They do not yet…push. Not hard. But they are there."

"You're keeping them out."

"Yes." Beckett turned round, as though hearing something, scowled, and disappeared.

"They do that sometimes," Reb said, dryly. "Well. That was the cityangel."

"Is that enough for you?" Marcia asked Gil.

Gil looked pale and shaken. "I…I do not know, in all honesty. That it was a spirit, I suppose I must accept that. But the cityangel, *Marek*'s cityangel. Well –"

There was another purple-black crackle, and Beckett stood in front of Gil. They bent over – they were several inches taller than Gil – and came nearly nose-to-nose with them.

"I am the cityangel," they said. "Do you doubt that?"

Gil, to their credit, swallowed hard, put their chin up, and said, "I do not wish to be insulting. But the mere appearance of someone – spirit or otherwise – claiming to be such a thing is hardly proof, is it?"

Beckett scowled. Gil's shoulders tensed, but they didn't step back.

"What would you see as proof?" Marcia cut in.

Beckett scowled at her instead now. At least she'd been here before; but Beckett's scowl wasn't human, that was the thing, and right now it was fucking terrifying. She caught Reb's eye, and her breath steadied.

Gil was giving the matter visible thought. "What is it that makes Marek's cityangel unique? What is it that makes the cityangel what it is?"

"So you are accepting there is such a thing," Nisha said dryly.

Gil shrugged. "If there is something that defines the cityangel, and this spirit has it," they bowed slightly to Beckett, which, somewhat to Marcia's surprise, reduced the scowl, "then they are, by definition, the cityangel."

"Another spirit might have the same power," Andreas objected. "It might not be unique."

"True," Gil allowed, "but in the circumstances, since one of the claims being made here is that other spirits cannot enter Marek, and the fact that the former Lieutenant is still sat out in the barge-yard with a collection of sorcerers does incline me now to believe *that*, I'll accept it."

"Beckett enables our magic," Reb said, "but I understand that without knowing what other forms of magic look like, that may not be particularly helpful."

Beckett had looked less and less irritated as the conversation progressed; perhaps Gil's dedication to ideas like *proof* and *truth*, and their willingness to engage with discussion, was having the same impact on Beckett that it often did on recalcitrant members of the Council. Gil had a gift for calming hotheads and moving debates into a place where something useful might come of them. Because Marcia would not have said, prior to this moment, that Beckett was likely to take kindly to any request that they prove themself.

Beckett's expression went remote for a couple of seconds, before they brought their hands together, then pulled them apart, to show within them a small, softly glowing globe. Gil, frowning, seemed about to speak, until Beckett pulled their hands further apart, and Marcia saw the gleam of a river, specks of buildings tumbling up a hillside...

It was Marek. Marek, within Beckett's hands.

Gil's mouth fell open, then closed, and they bent in, glancing up at Beckett for permission, to look more closely. Beckett, obligingly, made the globe larger still, and now Marcia could see a little ferry-boat moving across the river, pulling away from the foot of Marekhill towards the dock at the Old Market; tiny specks moving over Old Bridge, and there was the still-ruined New Bridge further down. There was a dizzying moment as Beckett twisted their hands, and suddenly the globe was the same size but what they all saw was larger, rushing up Marekhill, past the door of Petrior's, seen from above, through a cloud of steam rising from the roof of the Third Street bathhouse, and now a roof of a House...

Of this House. That was House Fereno, on the edge of the cliff, close enough to see someone bent over and working in the kitchen garden. She glanced automatically towards a window, but you couldn't see the useful gardens from this room. She could see the ferry, though, now most of the way across the river to Old Market.

"My goodness," Gil breathed.

"You can see yourselves, if you wish," Beckett said, and shifted the globe again towards the windows of the building.

"No," Marcia said hurriedly. "Unless Gil..." She wasn't sure she could handle seeing herself seeing herself. Also it didn't, somehow, sound entirely *safe*.

Gil shook their head. "I am satisfied. More than satisfied." They stood up, as Beckett brought their hands back together and the globe vanished. Gil's eyes were alight with something that looked like...hope? Joy? "Yes. This is the cityangel. And to think, all this time...Well. Well."

Beckett, very slightly, bowed to Gil; and then disappeared.

"Well," Andreas said. "Now you're satisfied...we need to decide how we're going to get the Council to engage. Because I, personally, am very keen to get Selene and everyone she brought with her out of our bloody bargeyard. And I can't see how we can do that without magic."

Gil sucked at their teeth. "The cityangel – Beckett? – said, they can keep the demons off."

"Not forever," Reb said, reluctantly. "Not that, I

suspect, they would like to admit that. But – I have dealt with this before, with a single demon, and whilst Beckett did see that one off, it was closer than I would have liked."

"And there are a dozen of them with Selene," Andreas said. He looked sick.

"So they are not a danger just yet, while they are not – pushing hard, Beckett said? But they will be in due course," Gil said. "And Beckett cannot simply get rid of them?"

"Beckett's influence ends at the city boundary," Marcia said. "About halfway across the barge-yard. Any demon outside there is in Teren and nothing to do with Beckett."

"Right. Right. We need another solution to get rid of them." Gil's eyes were distant. "Diplomatic?" They grimaced slightly. "Magical?"

"We're working on that," Reb said.

"And *we* need to work on the diplomatic," Andreas said. "And on supporting the magical. Which – to return to my earlier point – means we must work out how to bring this to the Council, before things get any worse. Never mind Beckett's strength, there's the blockade as well…"

"And after all," Nisha put in, "the first Teren asparagus is due *very soon*, and missing the season would be a tragedy, darlings. Let's get on with it."

☺ ☺

Reb could have wished that Marcia had told her about what went down with Cato and Madeleine in the bargeyard rather sooner. Immediately after it happened might have been good. She'd quite like to have known about their initial falling-out, as well. But she knew now; and she could try to do something about it.

However twitchy she felt – they didn't have *time* for this shit, they had much more important things to do – she didn't challenge Cato the moment he was through the door, because that would only lead to him turning round and going straight back out of it again. She was surprised enough that he'd come when she sent the message. Instead she offered him a chair, a mug of rosemary and liquorice infusion from the seller that worked on her street, and a basket of plain rolls. Cato tended to forget to eat at the best of times.

He looked absolutely terrible; not just that he clearly hadn't slept enough lately, but he was haggard, almost distraught-looking. And he smelt like he'd been drinking to an extent that he hadn't for a while. That, she suspected, was about the business with Madeleine, and possibly with Tait, but first things first. Marcia was worried about Cato's emotional state, fine; but Reb had other priorities.

"What," she demanded, "were you doing down at the barge-yard yesterday?"

For a moment, Cato looked as if he were about to get up out of the chair and leave, infusion and all notwithstanding; then he slumped, very slightly.

"Trying to find out how to solve this little problem we have, if you remember it?" His tone was sarcastic, but there was barely any life in it.

"Yes. The problem *we* have. We're supposed to be working *together*, did you remember that?" He shrugged, and Reb gritted her teeth. "What if you'd gotten shot? I'd know nothing about what you've been up to, or if you'd had an idea you were trying out, or anything. I'd be starting from scratch, except I'm not the one with the knowledge, so basically, I'd be screwed. We'd all be screwed."

"Nice to have my expertise acknowledged," Cato drawled, but there was a flicker of something that might have been guilt in his eyes. And surprise? He'd been expecting her to be talking about Marcia and Madeleine, she'd bet. Time for that in a moment.

"Look. I know – we both know – that you're the one who's most likely to be able to come up with something. And we both know that we *need* a solution, before…" Her voice died away. Before Beckett gets overwhelmed, before they try to overwhelm Beckett – because they both knew that Beckett couldn't hold out against this many. It was peculiar enough that Selene hadn't been pushing already. Politics, maybe; Marcia had theories.

"Yeah. All right." Cato scrubbed at his face with a hand.

"So you can't just wander off without *telling* me anything. You can't just put yourself at risk like that. You –"

"I *get* it, all right? It won't happen again."

Reb wasn't sure she believed him. "So you're going to tell me what you've got so far? And you're not going to go wandering off within reach of Selene's demons without at least consulting me?"

"The demons couldn't have got me. I was on our side of the line."

"Yes, and I'm sure bullets respect that too."

Cato grimaced and squirmed slightly in the armchair. "The barricade's pretty robust. And Captain Whatsit said the sniper hadn't been up to anything lately." He didn't sound wholly convinced. Perhaps he'd at least *think*, another time.

"So what have you got?" Reb asked.

"Not enough, not yet. But…half an idea." He stopped. Stared into space for a moment, then absently snagged a roll and began to eat it. That was a good sign. And at least it sounded like he was had something to work on, whatever else had happened yesterday to throw him so badly off himself.

Reb waited, doing her best to be patient, but he didn't say any more. "Half an idea?" she prompted, eventually.

"I don't think I can explain it just yet," Cato said, but he sounded ever so slightly apologetic. "It doesn't…" He gestured in the air, as if describing something with his hands. "I can feel the edges of it, but I can't describe it yet."

"Yet?" Reb didn't dare let herself hope.

"I need to know more about Teren magic, though. I have questions. But I'm not sure how to get the answers."

"Can't Tait answer them?"

For a fraction of a moment, Cato's face was anguished, before it shuttered down. "No. They can't."

Reb hesitated, wondering if she should ask. "Are you....Is Tait..." She'd hoped that Cato might volunteer this of his own accord, but apparently not. Time to move on to the trickier part of the conversation. "Marcia told me that Tait saved Madeleine."

"Oh, of course, Marcia. That's why you're on my case about this." Cato's voice was flat, exhausted.

"If you mean, that's how I knew you were out there, yes. But as we've just agreed that another time you'll *tell* me first, let's leave that. My question is about Tait." She did need to know this part. And it kept them on slightly safer territory for just a few moments longer. "How did Tait do it? Because – look. They're my apprentice. And as far as I know, they're just not capable of anything that big."

"Because Marek magic isn't working for them. Yeah." Cato sighed. "They did it the same way they rescued Bracken at the flood, of course. Blood magic."

Reb cursed. "I *told* them..."

"Don't think Tait's the type to pay attention to that if they can save a life." The bitterness in Cato's tone cut at Reb. That wasn't about blood magic; Cato didn't care about that. Time to get to the properly difficult part. Which was none of her business, except that she needed Cato functioning. They all did. And maybe she was about to fuck things up worse, but she had to try.

"Right. So now, you're not talking to Tait because they saved your –"

"That woman is no relative of mine," Cato cut sharply across her. "And Tait's decisions are their own and none of my business. You want to know, you ask them."

"Oh, I will," Reb said grimly. And she didn't know how she was going to deal with that, either. She'd left it alone after the flood, the last time Tait had pulled this stunt, and now she was regretting that. The Group was supposed to enforce the rules of magic in Marek, and one of those was – always had been – no blood magic. Because inevitably, sooner or later, someone went beyond the acceptable use of their own resources, and moved onto others. Zero tolerance, that was the only way. Regardless of the goal.

And she, of course, had always obeyed the rules, under all circumstances. The hypocrisy tasted bad in her mouth. And she'd just been giving Cato a lecture about the Group, about working together. Tait might be her apprentice, but blood magic was Group business.

"Cato – it is your business, too, you know. If Tait's using blood magic, it's the Group has to deal with that."

"Oh for *fuck's* sake," Cato burst out. "I'm trying to save the sodding city from being ripped apart by demons. Can we perhaps leave Tait's fondness for ripping their arms up at the drop of a hat for another time?"

Reb bit her lip. On the one hand – fine, not the priority. On the other hand – they surely couldn't, *she* couldn't, just let this slide *again*. And on a third hand…

"You're not talking to Tait," she said, again. "Because you're upset with them about what they did."

"Fuck off."

"You're right that that part isn't my business," Reb forged on, "even if the blood magic is. Now or another time." Maybe not right now, the way Cato looked. "But – look." Her insides were curling in on themselves, but if she didn't at least try to say this, she thought she'd regret it. Not that she wasn't already regretting trying to say it. "After the floods. You told me – some things that I needed to hear. So. This is me, returning the favour, and you can shut up and listen. I've known you for a long time. You and Tait – you work well together, the pair of you. And maybe what's just happened means that's no longer true, but Cato, you've been happier the last months than I've ever known you."

"Fuck off," Cato said again, but he wouldn't look Reb in the eye. He was ripping tiny pieces off the remaining half of his roll.

"Maybe this really is the end of your relationship."

Cato winced. "That's your call. But – expecting Tait to watch someone die when they could avoid it…"

"By using blood magic," Cato interrupted sententiously.

"Oh, goatshit. You don't care about that and we both know it. Just – *talk* to them, all right?"

Cato didn't say anything for a moment. Then he pushed himself up out of the chair, dropping the roll onto the floor with a flick of his wrist. Reb refrained from comment. She wasn't going to rise to this. "Are we done?" he asked, with excessive politeness, the Marekhill in his accent foremost. "Because if you'll *kindly* excuse me, I have a city to save. Rest assured I will inform you once I have any more information."

He stalked out without waiting for an answer. Reb watched him go, and then slumped back in her chair and rubbed at her face.

So. That went well.

☹ ☺

Alyssa glared at Marcia. "This is crap. You just don't like us pointing out the *problems* with the current situation."

They were in a slightly down-at-heel, blue-walled infusion-salon out towards the barge-yard; Alyssa's choice. Marcia had suggested Irin's. She suspected that Alyssa just wanted to be in charge.

Marcia had suggested the meeting for several reasons. One, she uncomfortably suspected, was the sheer need to be doing *something*, while Andreas and Gil and Nisha where trying to shift some ideas on the matter of magic – which they'd all agreed she would be ill-suited to. The other was that – on the matter of both warehouses and representation – if the Council as a whole wasn't going to deal with the lower city, someone had to. And perhaps that someone should be her, given that, at least in theory, she had some level of connection with Alyssa.

It wasn't going as well as she'd hoped.

"The problems with the current situation," Marcia said

tightly, "are that Teren is trying to reclaim Marek. Take it back over. With a bunch of demons that are *right there* waiting to get in. Not only have you been writing pamphlets about what they've been using demons to do to radicals in Ameten, but you're a *sorcerer*, for pity's sake. You know what that means."

"That's not the point!" Alyssa was right up in her face. Marcia didn't move.

"What is the point, then?"

"The point is that when you say, 'Marek is declaring its independence, and Teren is trying to prevent that', what you mean is, 'the Council are declining to pay *taxes* to Teren, so they're changing the wording about who gets to be at the top'. It doesn't make a blind bit of difference to the rest of us." It was more that Teren had been trying not to pay port fees to Marek, but Marcia was aware that was not really the point.

"It will do if Selene gets back into the city," Marcia said grimly.

"Fine, yes, and I don't want that any more than anyone else does. But you're saying, back off, let the Guilds have their food back, sit tight, because right now there's too much else going on. You're saying, we just need to trust you and wait patiently for your scraps once it's all settled. That's what you people always say. Another time. Not right now. Wait patiently. And *another time* never bloody happens. *Right now* is when we need to be heard. Because once the Council has settled its differences with Teren, absolutely nothing will have changed for anyone who isn't on Marekhill. *Now* is when we might actually make a difference."

"*Now* is when half of the Council want to use the fact that we're under siege to smack you down over the warehouses far harder than they ever could any other time," Marcia pointed out. It was an overstatement; it hadn't been as much as half the Council. It was most of the Guilds, though; and Athitol, who was happy with any reason to suggest a crackdown on the radicals.

Alyssa snorted. "Yeah, right, like they wouldn't find

another reason if the situation was different. I'd be charmed by your naivety, except that you're one of the people *running* this shitshow and you still don't know – or claim you don't know – what the rest of them are capable of. That's inexcusable." She sat back in the soft armchair, the angles of her elbows at odds with the way she sank into its plush if slightly threadbare cushions. "You haven't brought me here because you're worried about me, or anyone else down here. You've brought me here because you think Daril is going to get something out of this, after his performance of generosity, and you don't want that."

"Don't you think Daril is going to get something out of this?" Marcia challenged her.

"Of course. I'm not stupid, and I'm not unobservant, and I don't trust any of you Marekhill lot at all." She rolled her eyes. "Unlike some of my compatriots, I admit, who might talk a lot about equality of persons but who have internalised a bit too much of the idea of Marekhill superiority, in the backs of their minds. They *say* they're just happy we have support from someone on the other side, but they're way too willing to believe him, because they want it to be true. Of course he's in this for himself. What I care about is whether that's going to give *us* leverage, or not."

"He's playing you," Marcia said.

"And again, I say, so what? If I – we – can play him too."

"He's not supporting you, though. In Council discussions, all the rest of it. He's sitting back, making the odd comment when it's not too controversial, keeping his mouth shut. And that's what he's going to keep doing. He's not speaking against you, but he's not putting his reputation on the table in your favour, either." He wasn't calling for forcible retaking of the warehouses, but he wasn't saying anything else.

"Playing both sides," Alyssa said, shrugging. "Colour me surprised. And what about you?"

Marcia shrugged. "I'm not telling you any lies. Nor

them either. As you'd know if you knew what my current reputation is in the Council. I think the Council is out of touch, and I want to fix that. I don't think getting rid of it altogether, or replacing it with your People's Parliament, is the way forward. Right now, Marek is prosperous. Everyone here has enough to eat, and somewhere to live."

"Yes," Alyssa's tone was one of forced patience. "Marek is prosperous, its people are largely in a reasonable state, and yes, if you talk to anyone from Ameten, for example, they'd agree that they'd rather be poor here than there. But that's not all that matters. Are you seriously telling me that you see no difference between your situation and mine?"

Marcia felt her cheeks flush.

"That my daughter has the same chances as your child will?" Alyssa pressed, refusing to let her gaze drop.

"Well. No," Marcia replied reluctantly. "Not that my child will necessarily be Head, or even Heir, of the House, of course…"

"But they'll be brought up to that, and if for some reason they don't become Heir, they'll still be looked after." Alyssa's mouth twitched sideways, sardonic. "Unless they go the way your brother did, I suppose."

"I would never cut my child off," Marcia snapped. "I am not my mother."

"Tell your kid that, once they're old enough to understand Cato's situation, don't flap your lips at me," Alyssa recommended. "My point is that things aren't balanced, are they?"

"And my point is that Marek's a complicated system. You can't just take it all apart and assume everything will keep running. And we've got the money, which is most of the driver of it anyway."

Alyssa's eyebrows were up. "Honest," she remarked.

"Well, yes. I didn't think this was a conversation in which we were skating awkwardly around difficult subjects. Is it?"

"No, indeed, let's put all our pieces on the table." She

tipped her chin up. "So. You lot have the money, so you have the power?"

"Regardless of the formalities of the Council, yes."

"What if we took the money?"

"Came in with swords and took over House Fereno, you mean? It wouldn't be easy."

"No, indeed, but there's more of us than there are of you, and we're not a warlike city, are we, now? You lot don't have much defence." Alyssa's eyes were narrowed, watching Marcia.

"I suppose you could do that," Marcia said. She fought down images of people taking over her House, her home. Alyssa wasn't actually threatening that, she didn't think; not here and now. If Alyssa were seriously considering that, she wouldn't let Marcia know. "You could, but it's the Guilds and the Houses control Marek's trade, and it's the trade that keeps us prosperous."

"Pretty sure the Salinas would be happy to negotiate with whoever had control of the stuff."

Marcia shrugged. "If you think you'd do a better job of negotiation, there's nothing stopping you from trying it."

"We don't have the goods."

"So you're not just taking over the Houses, you're taking over the Guilds and the goods too? Who makes more goods?"

Alyssa laughed, although there wasn't much humour in it. "Well. You've made your point. And it's not like I didn't know it anyway, to be fair. We're not there yet, are we? Doesn't mean we couldn't be."

"Marek's a system," Marcia argued. "We have our role to play too."

"So you're saying, everyone has their role? But right now yours is the only role that's taken seriously. It's all very well saying we can't prosper without you. We're not prospering *with* you. Not all of us. If some people's *role* is to eat shit, that's not a system you can fucking defend."

"I know," Marcia said. "You're right. I don't want to defend that. I want to change it. I just don't know *how* to fix it as quickly as, I think, both of us would like. And what I don't think will work is to pull the whole thing down and start over."

"You want a halfway house." Alyssa didn't look impressed. "Because you're too afraid, and you want too much to keep hold of your own power."

Marcia opened her mouth, automatically, to deny it, then shut it again and made herself stop, and think.

Because – it was true, wasn't it. She kept tiptoeing around the difficult stuff, because she didn't think she had the political capital to deal with it. And it wasn't like that was entirely untrue. She *had* spoken up for unpopular views, and she'd certainly blown a lot of respect on magic and on Reb, but maybe that wasn't the point. She was Fereno-Head, now, in all but name, Madeleine's return notwithstanding. They couldn't kick her out. There were a number of reasons why the rest of the Council didn't necessarily trust her, but none of those were going to go away any time soon, were they? She could sit around fiddling at the edges and waiting for something to happen, or, she could stand up and actually do something, even if it didn't get anywhere. If she didn't have the capital now, it could hardly get her into more trouble, could it?

There was a sort of freedom in that.

"I'll support your demands," she said, abruptly.

Alyssa narrowed her eyes. "What do you want in exchange?"

Marcia shook her head. "I don't. What I *want* is for Marek to be successful. And as Cato has spent some quality time pointing out to me lately," when he was still speaking to her, and at that thought there was a sudden clench in her chest which she ignored, "that can't just mean successful for those at the top. The way the Council dealt with the floods. All this business with food and the warehouse – the lack of *trust*, too. So many things over the last few months…it's just not true that if the Houses prosper, Marek prospers. Maybe the Houses do need to prosper, some, for the city to prosper, because as has been coming very clear in the last day or two, it's trade that runs this city. Which includes running it in the sense of 'what its citizens need'. But the Houses most certainly can – and often do – prosper without that passing on to anyone else. That's no good. That's not what Marek needs."

"You sound like you're talking about charity," Alyssa said.

Marcia shook her head. "No. Charity goes from powerful to powerless. I want power shared. I'm talking about everyone in the city having more of a say in what happens, in what decisions are made. I don't know if the way you're suggesting is the best way to achieve that, and I'm going to be honest, the fact that I'm pushing it doesn't mean for a second that it's actually going to happen. But – I believe that it does need to happen, and at least in theory, I ought to be able to do something about that. We might have to wait for some people to die before anything really moves," brutal but true, "but I want change. I want more of the city involved in making decisions, in what the Council does. I'm willing to support you. And I'm more trustworthy than Daril Leandra-Heir."

"Maybe," Alyssa said. She stared at Marcia narrow-eyed, arms folded over her broad chest. "I don't trust any of you."

"That's fair. Because you can't," Marcia said, bluntly. "Or at least, there's nothing we can do that'll mean that I couldn't turn around and change my mind. That's what the sort of power I have means." She snorted. "Of course, you could tell Reb on me."

"If you think I have the smallest intention of getting between you and Reb, you have another think coming," Alyssa said, mouth comically twisted to one side, and Marcia grinned, tension releasing.

"The point is, I think you're right. But I also think that the last thing we need is conflict within the city. Because it's not out of the question that the whole city will be needed to sort this out, if my brother doesn't manage whatever he's plotting. You think the Houses and the

177

Council are no good. The Archion and the rest are definitely worse. We've both spoken to people about what's coming out of Teren. We both know it's true." She met Alyssa's eyes. "Are you willing to work with me to get what you want?"

"I won't *get* what I want, working with you. You've just said as much."

"You won't get it any other way, either. You sure as demons won't get it working with Daril."

"Yeah. That's right enough." Alyssa sighed, and raked her hands through her hair. "You reckon we can do anything if Cato can't manage it? If Teren do come in with their sorcerers?"

"No. To be honest. But I reckon we can try."

"Fuck." Alyssa rubbed a hand over her mouth.

"And right now," Marcia pressed, "it's on a knife-edge about whether something is about to go horribly wrong right now. Athitol-Head wanted to send the guard in to reclaim the wretched warehouses – as if we can spare them right now – and I don't think she's about to win that argument even with most of the Guilds supporting, but..." Piath had been trying to talk her down, last Marcia heard, or at least make sure she didn't talk anyone else round.

"Athitol-Head is an arse," Alyssa said, and Marcia was shocked into laughing.

"You're not wrong," she conceded. "But that's not the point. The point..."

"Yeah. Yes. I hear you." Alyssa took a long breath. "All right. Co-operation. Let's give it a go."

TWELVE

Marcia had been unreasonably exhausted after meeting Alyssa.

Or possibly she'd started off reasonably exhausted – apparently broken sleep was completely normal for this stage of pregnancy, and that was before someone showed up to invade her city – and it was trying to keep up with Alyssa, and create some kind of plan for moving forwards, that had moved things into the realm of the unreasonable. Either way, once she got back to House Fereno, having taken a litter as soon as she'd reached Marek Square rather than struggle up the Hill on foot, her maid Griya had arrived in the hallway clucking and insisted she lie down for an hour. Marcia had been too tired to resist.

But it was late afternoon now, and Andreas was due shortly to report back about his afternoon of Council-member wrangling. Griya had woken her with a ginger infusion that steamed gently on the table by the window.

Marcia dressed slowly, looking out of the window as she did it. At least it was only Andreas she'd be seeing, so tunic and trousers sufficed, no need for anything more complicated. Griya had put extension panels in the front of her trousers a few months back, but it was still increasingly awkward to get them done up under the bump. She sat down on the window seat to pull on her soft boots – anything with laces she needed help with, now – and stopped to sip at the infusion. The baby was moving again, and she rubbed at her stomach. *In this together, you and me.*

She glanced to the window again. She kept looking down to the barge-yard, despite knowing that it wouldn't be useful or informative. Nothing was moving down there; if it did, she wouldn't know until it was too late anyway. She made herself turn her gaze the other way, towards the sea. The sun was lowering itself in that direction, but there were still a couple of hours of daylight left. This felt like it had been a very long day already. Down in the mouth of the river, a ship was making its way out to sea. A ship, not a fisher-boat; so Salinas, even if she couldn't make out the flags. Idly, she wondered if there were any House Fereno goods aboard. She knew they'd just loaded out that warehouse; she needed to check in with the factor about other deals and incoming goods. The woman was reliable, but Marcia really did ought to check her work. And discuss how to handle the absence of Teren imports. *Temporary absence.* Another thing to add to the list; or maybe Madeleine could do it, when she was recovered. Which surely she would be soon?

Marcia ran a hand over her face; then broke off her train of thought, squinting down out of the window. There was another Salinas ship, following the first one. And another. Ships often went at similar times, something to do with the tides, but it was rare for more than two ships to be leaving on the same day, outside of Mid-Year and their departure for the storm season.

Four ships. And...there was a fifth, now, tagging after them. From this window, the curve of Marekhill got in the way of her seeing right down into the docks, to count the ships remaining, but she was getting a nasty cold feeling in her stomach.

Five ships leaving, all at once. It could be coincidence, of course, but...well. If she'd been a Salinas captain, would she want to sit around in a semi-besieged city, waiting for Teren to come in and take it? Teren would be fools to do anything to the Salinas ships of course, but arguably they were fools already, doing any of this instead of just renegotiating their existing deals with Marek. They'd been given a *very* generous offer, after all. Instead they were sitting in the barge-yard with a bunch of demons, and...

And the Salinas hated magic, didn't they? Really

hated it. None of the captains would want to risk being in a city which might be about to be overrun with demons. Anything could happen. It wasn't *going* to, because Marcia believed – had to believe – that Reb and Cato were going to solve this problem, but the ship-captains didn't know that. And who knew what sort of rumours were circulating in the lower city around the docks.

Shit. If she was right...She had to speak to Kia. As soon as possible. Kia must, surely, know what was going on. Unless the Salinas had pulled out altogether, embassy and all...surely not. Marcia gnawed at her thumbnail. Embassies. If the ships were leaving, Marcia didn't believe for a second that they wouldn't be taking steps to prevent their sister-ships from coming in.

Which meant – oh, shit. Which meant that they wouldn't hear back from Exuria, or the Crescent, about the results of their diplomatic endeavours, would they? Both of the ambassadors *could* act on their own, but neither of them had been willing to so far; and the current situation wasn't making that any more likely.

Kia. Kia had to be her first stop. And someone – Andreas? – must speak again with the Exurian and Crescent ambassadors. Maybe there was a way around all of this. Maybe, in the circumstances, the ambassadors would be willing to make an interim commitment that the Council could work with. They *had* to have allies. It was no use just getting rid of the demons without being able to support themselves politically. Teren would just find another way to attack. And of course, the ambassadors knew that. Marek had to show its own strength to be worthy of allying with.

Or maybe she could persuade Kia to bring the ships back...

Griya tapped at the door, and Marcia jumped. "Ser Andreas is here. I left the biscuits in the small reception room."

Marcia pulled on her second boot, and followed Griya down the stairs. Two heads better than one, and all that.

Maybe Andreas would have some bright ideas.

She found him in the small reception room, which looked over the gardens, and took him through to the larger one instead, where they could see out to the river-mouth.

"The Salinas ships have gone," Andreas repeated flatly. He sat down heavily on the couch, then got up to go back to the window and peer out again. "*All* of them? Are you absolutely sure? I can't see the docks from here."

"Not absolutely sure," Marcia said. She made herself take one of the biscuits Griya had fetched through. No value in letting herself get faint with hunger. "But five ships, leaving all at the same time. That's not normal, outside of Mid-Year. Look. You can still see the sails out there."

Andreas squinted. "Five ships? I'm counting six."

Marcia scowled. "Another one, too, then. I saw five sailing out before." There couldn't be that many left in the dock now. "Assuming I'm right, what I don't know is whether they're actually left, to go to their next stop –"

"Surely they can't," Andreas interrupted. "If you're right, I mean. They wouldn't be loaded. Would they? If they are, after all, well, they're just leaving as planned."

"Well, that's one of the open questions. Because the other option is that they've just decided to sit outside for a few days and see what happens."

"Do they know what the food situation is?" Andreas wondered aloud. "Because if they think this is all likely to be resolved one way or another in no more than a couple of weeks..."

"Then they'd be more likely to sit tight, out of reach of any marauding demons," Marcia agreed, "and hope they can finish loading in a few days and catch up. It's not like they care who's running the place as long as their contracts are met."

"And if the Houses fall, who are their contracts with?"

Most of the Houses would fold, if it came to it. Marcia didn't say that; they both knew it.

"It's not like we're genuinely besieged," Andreas said

irritably. "They could have left at any moment."

Marcia nibbled at another biscuit. She felt sick, and she was hoping it was just hunger. "At any moment subject to the business of collecting their crew from on-shore, and not having demons rampaging all over wrecking bits of their ships. In their shoes I'd be tempted to remove myself from the situation too." If only she could.

"What does that mean for the ships we're expecting?" Andreas asked, horror writing itself across his face as he thought things through.

"The messages for the ambassadors, you mean? Yes. That was my first thought too." Although the likelihood that no more food would be coming in from Exuria was hardly good news either. "I assume they'll leave someone, stationed out there to warn other ships off. But as for the rest of the ships..." She shifted restlessly. "I was thinking of speaking to the ambassador. Or maybe even the dock master."

"You are *not* walking all the way down to the docks," Andreas said firmly. "I will go. You can speak to Kia. You've got a good relationship with her."

Marcia shifted irritably – her pelvis was aching again, and the baby had been very active today – and conceded the point. "Ask her to come here, or go down there?"

"Ask her to come here," Andreas said. "And not because of you walking, either, before you say anything. Because we don't want to be going cap in hand. And because you might be wrong." He squinted out of the window again. "I really hope you're wrong." He stood, running his fingers through his hair in worry. "I'll go to the docks. See what I can get out of the dockmaster."

"Someone needs to speak to the other ambassadors, but not until we're more certain of what's happening. If the dockmaster and Kia aren't forthcoming..." Marcia looked at him doubtfully. "I'd say you could try a couple of pubs, too, but...being blunt about it, you don't exactly blend in with the average dock worker."

"True," Andreas allowed. "Not like you could do much better on that one."

True enough. Marcia nibbled again at her thumbnail. She could, however, send a message to Jonas. Who might or might not be willing to help, but... it was worth trying. "I might be able to do something on that," she said. "Without needing to leave this room," at least for the moment, "so there's no need to fuss."

"I'll stop by and speak to Daril, too." He caught Marcia's expression and interpreted it correctly. "I know you don't like him, but he's smart, and he's on our side."

"On your side, maybe," Marcia muttered.

"He's involved in this, whether or not you like it."

"I know. It's not like I haven't worked with him recently, remember? I just reserve the right not to like it."

Andreas crossed the room, caught Marcia's hand up and pressed it to his lips. "Take care, see what you can do with your Salinas contacts, and I'll come back later to confer." He pulled a face. "I was, after all, supposed to be reporting back on the other conversations I had today. First things first. I assume the sorcerers aren't yet ready to move?" Marcia shook her head. "So that can wait for a couple of hours. Until then."

As the door shut behind him, Marcia was already at the writing desk, pulling pen and paper towards her for a message to Kia, then one to Jonas. Surely building a bridge between Marek and Salina, in these complicated times, was exactly the sort of thing he'd be good at.

☺ ☺

Jonas was working when Marcia's message caught up with him. Cato was busy doing his demon-related research, which he wasn't willing to involve Jonas in (not that Jonas was still bitter about that), and it turned out that lots of people in Marek right now were keen to send lots of urgent messages to one another. All the messengers were making the most of the windfall.

It was Tam who told him Katelyn was looking for him. "Message from up Marekhill," he said, his eyes widening in comically exaggerated horror. "What've you been up to, then, eh? Or have you some fancy admirer I should be telling Asa about?" Jonas swiped half-heartedly at the back of Tam's head as he grinned.

Marekhill. Pretty much had to be from Marcia, didn't it? Which almost certainly meant trouble. Jonas contemplated ignoring it and deliberately dodging Katelyn; then further contemplated the likelihood of that making both Cato and Reb irritable with him. Cato's relationship with Marcia might be complex but that didn't mean he was happy for other people to mess her around. Besides. Maybe it was important trouble. He sighed. "Where's Katelyn, then?"

"Hanging out in Marek Square. When I told her you were working today she figured you'd haveta pass through there eventually." Tam nodded at him cheerfully, and was on his way again, bare feet quiet against the paving stones.

Jonas finished his current run, and detoured through Marek Square on his way back. Katelyn was sitting on the stone surround of the fountain, dabbling her fingers in the water and chatting to the lass selling infusions, who had put her padded kettle down so she could do a better job of pretending not to be posing for Katelyn's benefit.

"Jonas!" Katelyn's cheerful face brightened. "Message for you!"

"Tam said," Jonas agreed, collecting the thick, expensive-feeling paper from her. He bought a lemon verbena infusion in its little clay cup – Marek Square was nearly empty, so while he might be having a good day's work, he would bet the infusion lass wasn't – and left her and Katelyn to their flirting. He sat down around the other side of the fountain and opened the message.

Jonas – I believe the Salinas ships have all left. Most certainly many of them have, as I saw them go. I presume due to concern about the current situation. But I need to know how far they've gone and what the expectations / plans are. I need to know if we are still in contact with the rest of the Oval Sea. Andreas (Tigero-Head) has gone to speak to the dockmaster, but he can't go to the dock pubs and expect to get anywhere, and I don't know how forthcoming the dockmaster will be. Will you go? I realise I will owe you a favour – but also, Marek needs everything, every bit of help, she can get.

– Marcia

☺ ☺

Politics. Of a sort, anyway, and he hated politics. But it was also about Teren and their demons and everything that was coming of that, and as a sorcerer – or a sorcerer's apprentice – he doubtless would be involved anyway whenever Cato deigned to include him or needed his help. And in any case, he was a kind-of semi-adopted resident of Marek, and he couldn't just ignore the city's need.

Well. He could. Plenty of folk did. But – he didn't fancy telling his mother the story, after, if he stood aside. She'd say that wasn't how she'd raised him, and she'd be right.

The flicker that came when he glanced back down at the message didn't help. Or rather, it did, in one way. It showed him himself, in a pub he thought he recognised, talking to a woman with short dark curly hair and a grubby vest over broad shoulders and thoroughly-tattooed bare arms – a dock porter, he'd bet. At least now he knew who he was looking for, and he knew he'd find her, even if he didn't know what would happen after that.

"Go safe, Jonas!" Katelyn called as he passed her, and he raised a hand in greeting to her and called back "Go safe!" in return.

At least the flicker hadn't shown him danger. Not there and then.

The dark-haired woman was in the second dockside pub he got to, the Anchor, which was one of the least imaginative names going. There was an Anchor, or sometimes a Something-and-Anchor, in every port Jonas had ever been to, including one dry port far away to the north that served the highly spiced local hot drink rather than booze. This Anchor was well enough: decent beer, stocked a reasonable brand of berith, not that Jonas could afford berith often, and he could usually find someone shipboard to talk to when he was missing home.

Not today. Today, the Anchor, like the previous pub, was halfway-empty, and not only that, but it *looked* wrong. There were no sailors with their blonde braids; and despite it being daylight, the porters were all in here drinking instead of out there working. The empty docks outside were even more peculiar – Marcia had been right, not that he'd seriously doubted her. For sure, he'd seen them empty for a whole eight weeks the year before, during the storm season when everyone went back to Salinas to wait it out, and celebrate, and do all the things that had to be done on the islands. But this felt different.

It made him feel the same way he had in the storm-season though – like he truly wasn't a sailor any more, not even truly Salinas, because he was *here* when no one else was. He shook it off, and went up to the bar, leaning on it next to the dark-haired woman.

"Pint, please," he asked Lavall behind the bar.

"Aha! You've not *all* gone, then?" the woman said, sounding hopeful. And drunk; definitely a little drunk.

"I'm not shipboard," he said, apologetically.

"Jonas here left the Lion t'Riseri to come live in Marek," Lavall said cheerily, handing Jonas his beer and collecting his coppers. Jonas wasn't quite a regular here, not exactly, but he was here often enough to be on friendly terms with Lavall.

"The Lion? Did you now? What on earth for?"

Jonas shrugged. "You know. See the world a bit. Different from just visiting, eh?"

"Me, I'd love to go shipboard," the woman said wistfully. (Never happen. The Salinas didn't take crew from elsewhere.) "But it's not that another ship's come in, then."

"Docks looked empty to me," Jonas said. "What's that about?"

"Bloody Teren," the woman said. "Fuckers. They come in, and all the ships up anchor and off they go. Say they're not waiting around to be ripped at by demons. I said, I said, rubbish, ain't no demons bothering us, we're under the cityangel's protection. Teren can sit on the doorstep as long as they like, right? We're independent now, with the cityangel to mind us. Off they went anyway. Cowardly fuckers."

Yes, she was definitely drunk, and Jonas had best step careful if he didn't want to get into a fight.

"Ships coming in all the time, though," he said, playing up his confusion.

"Aye, well," said Lavall, leaning on the bar to join in the conversation. "I reckon, they'll sit out and warn people off, won't they? Wouldn't be like a Salinas ship not to look after their own."

"They can't have been *full*, though." Jonas, slowly working through the implications of what had happened, found himself almost more shaken by that than by anything else. "They can't go on to the next port, can they?"

"Certainly they're not full!" the woman said, sharply indignant. "I was halfway through loading the *Heartsease*, I was, when they said, off you hop, all of you, shove the rest back in the warehouse, we're off. I was fucking *counting* on that work, I was."

"You're all laid off?" Dockers were paid by the hour, or sometimes by weight for heavy stuff, so laid off wasn't quite the word.

"Yeah, that's right. Fuckers." It wasn't quite clear this time whether she meant the port management or the ships; technically it was the management who paid the dockers but it was the ships that kept them busy, so the difference wasn't much remarked upon unless and until there was a disturbance.

"You got a bit extra, Meg," Lavall said, trying to sound consoling.

"Yeah," Meg snorted, "an extra half-day and now what?" She spat on the floor. "No ships is no work, and it's not like we're all saved up like at storm-season, eh? Another one, Lavall." She slammed another couple of coppers down on the bar, which didn't seem to Jonas like the smartest move if she was that broke, but that was hardly his business.

"Well," he said. "Hopefully it'll all be over soon, eh? Cityangel'll scare Teren off," they wouldn't, but Jonas wasn't about to get into the intricacies of sorcery, and he did believe that Cato would find a solution, "and ships'll come back in."

"Or they'll find better sources for everything," Meg said morosely, "and never trade here again."

"Yeah, that definitely won't happen," Jonas said with conviction. Because one way or another, he was pretty confident that Selene wasn't going to sit out there for all that long. And the Salinas would be just as happy trading with Teren-Marek as with Marek-Marek or half-Teren-Marek like before. But he wasn't going to get into that, either.

"Yeah, well, let's hope," Meg said. Lavall slid her another beer, and she downed half of it, then turned more fully towards Jonas, and gave him a once-over. "Say, though, pretty Salinas boy, given that I'm at a loose end…"

"Ah, thanks," Jonas said hurriedly, "but I'd better be on my way. Hope you're all doing better soon." He made his way out onto the street, then stopped to take stock. What now? He didn't have that much more information than he'd started with: the ships gone, and fine, he knew now definitely because of Teren. But they might not be all the way gone. Perhaps they were just…hedging their odds a bit. No skin off anyone's nose to be anchored out over the horizon for a few days, waiting to see how things shook out.

Or, they might have gone altogether, cutting Marek out of their trade routes at least for now. Or they might have left one ship to warn the others off. And that was the sort of thing Marcia wanted to know, wasn't it? For a moment he considered sailing out there himself to find out – Asa would have access to a dinghy if he couldn't borrow one elsewhere – but whilst that might be more fun, it wasn't the most sensible option, was it? What he needed was to talk to Kia.

☺ ☺

"Oh good, it's you," Kia said ungraciously as Xera showed Jonas into her office. It had taken a combination of heavy reference to his and Kia's history as shipmates, and outright begging, to get Xera to let him in at all.

Kia looked exhausted. Her sleeves were pushed up to her elbows, she had inkstains on her fingers, and there was a patch of smeared blue-black at her hairline where she'd obviously pushed her hair back off her forehead with inky fingers. A set of papers were stacked at one side of her desk – Jonas could tell just from a glance at the layout that they were shipping contracts – and a much older-looking document was at her other side.

"You look… busy," Jonas said hesitantly.

"Of course I'm busy, you idiot," Kia snapped. "Every

ship in the place just left, *if* you weren't aware, and before they did, they handed me their contracts to see just how much this landbound nonsense is going to cost us and if I can find a way out of it. And I've been getting a series of variously distraught and irate letters from all thirteen bloody Houses, culminating in a request from Fereno to meet and a threat from Athitol to seriously rethink our treaty now that Marek is *independent*."

Jonas squinted at her. "Can Marek do that?"

Kia held a hand out and tilted it from side to side. "On the one hand – is an independent Marek bound by a treaty signed by Teren? Assuming they actually remain independent for more than another day or two. On the other hand, if we boycott them, they're screwed. On the other other hand, in reality, neither Marek nor we actually want to do anything other than reaffirm the perfectly good current treaty. We hadn't got around to it yet because we didn't want to be the first to recognise them. Athitol's just trying to get me to bring the ships back in. Which I don't have the authority to do even if I wanted to." She sank her head in her hands, smearing more ink over her forehead. "Sometimes I really hate this fucking job. Anyway, I've been writing messages grandstanding about the independence of Salinas and telling them that moving the ships back in would be an untenable risk and I don't have oversight of the captains anyway. The latter's true, the former might be, with this demons business, though I think the captains are overreacting. Fereno, though, asking to meet, that's a bit bloody excessive, and she should know better. I presume she's panicking about money, though I didn't know Fereno was that much worse off than the rest."

Jonas tapped his fingers on the desk, thinking. "I don't think it's just money," he said, slowly. "Something else is going on. Something more urgent than that. She got in touch with me as well."

"Oh, that's why you're here, is it?" Kia gave him a jaundiced look. "Anyway. Something more urgent than money, to the Marek Houses?" She snorted. "Haven't met it yet."

"Something about independence. And the demons."

"The demons are real, then." Kia eyed him sideways.

"Oh yes," Jonas agreed. He really wished he could say otherwise.

"But Marek's safe from them, right? No external spirits here, isn't that part of the deal with their...cityangel?" She pulled a face.

"There's a lot of them," Jonas said, reluctantly. "I wouldn't...I mean, the sorcerers are trying to find a solution. But." But, the last time, it had been hard.

"Shit." Kia put her head down on the desk. "I should have got them to take me with them," she said, muffled, into the desk, then sat up and fixed him with a hard look. "A solution – you're involved with that, then?"

"Me? No," Jonas said. "Cato won't let me." He hadn't quite meant to sound like a sulky kid.

"I thought the whole point of Marek was the bloody cityangel. Well, the cityangel and the fact that it's Teren's only outlet to the Oval Sea, which will be why Selene out there is spitting nails about this independence thing. Anyway. *Can* your cityangel hold them off?"

"Yes," Jonas said, then was compelled to add, honestly, "for a while."

"But not indefinitely. Right, well, that's what all those captains thought, too, except I figured they were exaggerating, which they're not, fine. So what's the alternative?"

Jonas shrugged. "Send 'em all back where they came from some other way."

"Make the sorcerers release them?" Kia sucked at her teeth. "Well, I can see the attraction. What I want to know is, is it going to happen? Or should I be packing up my own bags and hailing a fisher-boat to get me out to where I can have a nice reliable deck under my feet again? Come back once it's all over."

Jonas badly wanted to say that yes, of course it would happen. But the last time he'd seen Cato, Cato had been swearing and chewing his fingernails down to the quick. "Cato's working on it," he temporised.

"So I should be leaving," Kia translated. "Fuck."

"He'll find a solution," Jonas said. "I'm sure he will. He's very good, and he's very motivated, and…"

The flicker hit with sudden, overwhelming, intensity. It was a patchwork of pieces, this time, rather than a clear image: *Cato, Beckett, Tait looking scared with some other spirit Jonas didn't recognise. And then the barge-yard, just after dawn, flashes of multiple colours, someone screaming…*

"Jonas? Jonas!"

He was crouched on the floor, arms over his head. He hadn't reacted like that to a flicker in a while.

"I'm all right," he managed. He forced his eyes open again. Kia was kneeling next to him, face worried.

"You sure? Because that didn't look like all right."

There was no way on this plane or the other that he was going to explain his flickers to Kia. It was bad enough that she knew about the sorcery. "I'm fine. I get…headaches, sometimes. Just very briefly. It's gone now."

He began to lever himself upright. Kia stood up faster, and tried to help with a hand under his elbow.

"Have you seen a doctor?" she asked. "Or asked anyone about it?"

"Yes," Jonas said, with some relief, able to answer the second question honestly at least, and if Kia thought he was answering the first, so much the better. "It's fine. There's nothing wrong with me." That rather depended on how you looked at it. "I haven't had one that bad in a while. It's probably stress or something, I don't know." He tried a smile, even though his head was still clanging with the aftermath of the flicker. He needed to go and see Cato; except more urgently, he needed Kia to talk to Marcia.

"Look," Kia said, sitting on the edge of the desk. "I'd like to go, but we both know I have to stay. You, on the other hand…your mother would skin me if I let you get stomped over by Teren soldiers, never mind demons. How about you get a nice friendly fisher-boat to take *you* out to the ships? That friend of yours, Asa, that came to dinner, aren't they from the fishing village?"

"I can't," Jonas said. "I can't just leave. Look. You said Marcia wanted to talk to you. And she wanted to talk to me, too. And I think it's about – all of this."

"I'm not being summoned by Fereno-Heir..." Kia began hotly.

"Not formally, fine. But can't you come along with me, like, informally?"

Kia chewed at her lip, then stood up abruptly. "Right. That works. Come on then. No time like the present."

Which was a turnaround from five minutes ago, but that was Kia all over, wasn't it?

When the two of them reached House Fereno, they were shown into a reception room, where Marcia was ensconced on a beautiful pale-blue couch, a pile of papers and a couple of pens sitting on a table next to her, and a writing-desk propped on her lap. There were rugs tucked around her, and cushions propping her up. She looked exhausted, bags under her eyes, but despite that still managed to give the impression that she was fully in control of the room.

As ever, being around Marcia made Jonas feel as if he had too many limbs. It was worse, on this occasion, because he was still wearing messenger-clothes, and he'd just realised that when he'd taken a message to the Smiths in the morning and cut through the yard of their Guildhouse on the way out, he'd evidently run too close to their big pile of charcoal. The bottom of his trousers was still thick with black dust, despite all the running around he'd done since.

"Sit down," Marcia said, tiredly, gesturing at the chair that sat at right-angles to her couch. "Please excuse me not getting up; I've been told I need to rest more. Very tedious."

"No, indeed, you're best exactly where you are. Reef now, rather than having sails to mend later," Kia said.

"And this is only an informal visit, after all." She crossed to Marcia's couch, and took her hands in the Salinas double-handshake, before sitting down.

Jonas shifted, still on his feet, and gestured uncomfortably at his trousers.

Marcia huffed a quiet laugh. "Hah. Last year I'd have said, oh, don't worry about it, but Reb would give me into trouble for not considering who'll have to clean it up. If you wait for a moment, I'll ring for a sheet that'll be easier to clean."

"So," Marcia said crisply, once Jonas was seated. "If you two are here, I assume it's to update me on the Salinas ships. And, perhaps, to see if we can find an agreement?"

"Well now," Kia said, cautiously, "Salina would always prefer relationships both with and between all of our clients to run smoothly. But we must protect our ships, you understand, not to mention the goods of our other clients."

"Indeed," Marcia said. "And I can of course understand your concern about the unfortunate situation with the Teren forces at the river. I deeply appreciate you taking the time to come up here and visit when you must be very busy keeping in touch with your ships."

"Of course," Kia said, "it is a little difficult to keep in touch when they're all a few miles out at sea."

"But not gone altogether?" Marcia asked, her tone far too offhand to be truly unbothered.

"They're a bit offshore," Jonas said. "For the moment. They're not fully loaded." He wanted to be careful about what he said; he'd best not cause more problems for the ships than he solved. But if Marcia was this bothered...it had to be something to do with Teren, and he was sure that Teren taking over Marek would be bad news for everyone.

"It would be our preference," Kia said, "if, one way or another, the ships could return and load up before their deadlines. But you understand, of course, that we have a trading relationship with both Marek and Teren."

This was true in the strict sense, but only just. Very nearly everything that Teren traded came via the Houses and the Guilds. There were a few single-loads of barley in the autumn, and occasionally of meat and fleece in the summer, which individual Teren merchants negotiated directly with the Salinas, but the profit on those was low – which was why the Houses didn't get involved. What Kia meant, and all three of them knew it, was that the Salinas wanted to be able to negotiate with Teren if Marek were to become subsumed entirely back into Teren.

"Yes, indeed. The barley crop..." Marcia murmured into her cup.

Kia flicked an eyebrow at her. "Our reputation relies on our not taking sides in this or any other dispute."

"And at this time of year," Marcia said, tapping her thumbs against one another, "it'll be gifting season by the time they reach the Crescent, won't it? That won't go down well. Right. So surely the solution that's quickest and best for all is for us to get rid of Selene and her soldiers, and everyone can come back and load up."

"Can you do that?" Kia asked bluntly.

"The sorcerers are working on a solution," Marcia said, her mouth pulling sideways.

Kia eyed her thoughtfully, rubbing at her chin. "There's another problem," she said, abruptly. "What is it?"

"What, apart from the fact that we've got a bunch of demons trying to break into the city and all that's in front of them is a grouchy cityangel and a barricade made out of carts and a couple of pub tables?"

Kia waved a dismissive hand. "You're not fretting about the Salinas ships because the Crescent won't have jewellery for the Festival of Candles. Or because the Houses and the Guilds will lose a few demmers. What is it?"

"I find myself wondering," Marcia said delicately, "if preventing the passage of information in and out of Marek *is*, accidentally of course, I would never suggest otherwise, taking sides?"

Kia shrugged. "There won't be any information going

into Teren either, then, will there? If your mail is held up, so is theirs. That's even."

Jonas saw the moment when Marcia decided to be honest. "Because neither the Crescent nor the Exurian ambassadors will support us until they hear back from home," she said, bluntly. "*You* won't take sides either way, I know that, which is why I'm not insulting you by asking you not to pass that to Selene."

Kia snorted. "I'll not be insulted, then, since you're not asking."

"What do you mean by *support*?" Jonas asked. "You want Exurian soldiers coming in against Teren?" Surely that could only end badly.

"Goodness, no. That's not the issue." She shook her head. "Diplomacy. Strongly worded missives. All that sort of thing."

"But. Demons," Jonas said. "Isn't that a bigger issue?"

"It's all an issue at the same time," Marcia said, with a sigh. "Yes, we need rid of the demons, or support from around the Oval Sea won't make a blind bit of difference. But if we can – if the *sorcerers* can remove that threat, we're still at risk from Teren insisting that we stay part of them by force. There aren't that many soldiers out there, because they're counting on the demons, you see? But they could bring more, if they wanted. And that would be a shitshow for everyone."

"I still don't get it," Jonas confessed.

"Teren won't do that if they'll see consequences from Exuria and the Crescent," Kia explained, obviously thinking hard herself. "But Exuria and the Crescent won't move unless and until they think it's possible to scare Teren off, and that means taking the demons out of the equation. If it's just a matter of soldiers…it becomes, most likely, not worth it."

"And the Archion's dying," Marcia agreed. "So…we may have other avenues. In due course."

This was well beyond the sort of thing that Jonas had ever managed to grasp, much to the despair of his mother. Kia, though, was evidently following, nodding along slowly. Jonas went back to the one point that he had fully understood.

"But the ambassadors, they're waiting for word from home. On Salinas ships."

"Exactly. So if no one's coming in…"

"None of the ships that just left harbour have any new mail, messengers, or anything else," Kia pointed out.

"The ships that they'll be intercepting will," Marcia said, baldly. "And we both know that if your ships are out there waiting, at least for now, then they'll be intercepting other ships. That's more or less the purpose of a blockade."

"It's not a blockade," Kia said, chidingly. "We are just keeping ourselves safe."

"That's as maybe, but the effect is the same," Marcia said. "Happily, I believe there is a straightforward answer to this problem, whereby we can at least keep information and mail flowing, even if we cannot yet promise safety enough to load your ships."

"Someone could go out there," Jonas said.

"Indeed," Marcia said. "And that someone, perhaps, might be able to carry messages. In, perhaps, both directions?"

"Diplomats," Kia said thoughtfully, "such as myself, most likely couldn't do such a thing. But Marek messengers. That's literally their job, isn't it?"

"Is the sea Marek?" Marcia asked, with a sideways half-grin at Kia.

"Oh, indeed not," Kia said, "but if you're within fishing-boat range, let's say, I'm sure we could come to some arrangement."

"So," Jonas said, "if a messenger had a message *for* one of the ships, and then the ships happened to have…"

"…a diplomatic pouch, let's say," Kia put in, rubbing at her chin again.

"Then they might feel it best to allow the messenger to take the mail in," Marcia finished.

Both of them were looking, bright-eyed, at Jonas, who was developing an uncomfortable feeling.

"Civil unrest is bad for business," Kia said. "For us, as well."

"M'mother always hated it when we went out to the western islands and they were fighting again," Jonas agreed, slowly. It was obvious what they wanted, and he didn't want to say yes too soon. But – Kia was right. Civil unrest was bad for the Salinas just as much as for Marek. And he lived in Marek, now, didn't he? He didn't want it run over by Selene and her demons. "Had to turn around and come back," he added, "and you can only get out there once a year."

"The western islands?" Marcia's eyes suddenly lit up. "Have you really been there? I always read…" She stopped herself, mouth wry. "Not now. Another time. Right now, I think I need to write a message to…" She raised an eyebrow at Kia.

"The *Heart's Dragon*," Jonas suggested. He'd get to say hello to Xanthe, at least.

"And then, if there's someone around with a messenger's armband," Marcia said, "I think I would give them a demmer for this one."

"That's above rate," Jonas protested. "*Well* above rate."

"It's a lot further than average. Needs someone who can handle a boat," Marcia said. "And arguably, it's about the right rate for negotiating between nations. Or, at least, facilitating that. Diplomatic messenger."

"Fine," Jonas said, giving in, and fishing his armband out of his pocket.

"Wonderful," Marcia said, pulling the writing desk back towards her, then paused and looked at him. "And – Jonas?" Her tone was suddenly sombre. "This really does matter. For Marek, but…I think it matters for a lot of people, as well. I don't think Teren is a good place, right now. I don't think we want them to get more of a foothold here than they have already. Marek's been independent, really, for a good few decades now. This is just us codifying that. Because, well. I don't think we want to go the way that Ameten has been, do we?"

Slowly, Jonas nodded, and next to him, Kia too.

"Salina can't support, not directly," Kia said, but her tone said something different; and as they left House Fereno, message tucked into Jonas' pocket, the clap on the shoulder she gave him said something different too.

THIRTEEN

Immediately after leaving the bargeyard and the row with Tait, Cato had stormed back to his room by a slightly roundabout route, half-hoping Tait would be there, ready to apologise, by the time he got back. When they weren't, he'd spent the afternoon into evening lying on his bed drinking his way through half a bottle of Salinas berith he'd found in a corner. Foul stuff, but he couldn't go out to get something better, because firstly, Tait would be round to apologise at any moment, and secondly, he was doing important thinking about the Teren sorcerers and he was doubtless about to have a breakthrough.

He'd awoken the next morning when the sun blazed through the curtains and straight through his eyelids – or so it felt, anyway – because he hadn't thought to draw the drapes the night before. Back in the day, he'd never bothered to undraw them – or, no, that was drawing too, wasn't it, in both directions? Shit, his head hurt. He'd never let the sun *in*, was the point, because he'd never felt the need. Tait was a horrible influence. The arrival of Reb's messenger had been a welcome distraction from trying not to think about Tait, or his headache.

On his return, furious at Reb's *interference*, the wards had indicated Tait still wasn't in their own room, not that Cato would have been about to lower himself to go and knock anyway. Not that he cared. Bruised, despite himself, by Reb's comments – and he really did want to solve the demon problem, for a whole host of reasons – he spent the day alternating between sketching theory in his notebook, fruitless experiments with the space between planes, and, increasingly as time passed, staring out of the window, going over his grievances and polishing them up to a high shine. Where *was* Tait, anyway? Cato needed to ask them about Teren sorcery. It was fucking irresponsible of them to just disappear.

After a while, Cato gave up and went to the Purple Heart. It was much quieter than normal; people were worried, Cato supposed, about the whole *demons on the doorstep* business, which yes, was quite worrying, but really not nearly as worrying as the fact that he was sober and he didn't want to be. Happily, this was a solvable problem, unlike the demons, or the fact that Tait had saved M– *her* life, or the expression on Tait's face when they told him to fuck off. Cato dedicated himself, with some conviction, to solving it, until he'd reached the point where Set-from-the-bar escorted him home to his room and told him firmly *not* to bother Tait that night. Cato hadn't *intended* to pay that any attention, but he hadn't been able to manage to get himself off the bed, either.

The sun woke him up again, because the fucking curtains were *still* open, and as his eyes opened, he was hit all at the same time by a series of realisations he'd been trying to avoid since leaving Reb's front door.

Tait had been in the right. That was the first one.

He was never going to forgive Madeleine – well, that one wasn't new – and he didn't regret not trying to save her himself. She didn't deserve it. That was the second.

But – and Reb hadn't *said* this exactly, because she didn't know enough about it, but Cato was dismally sure that she would have done if she had known – that didn't justify anything he'd said to Tait, or his attempting to make his decision be Tait's decision.

Tait might not come *back*, given how Cato had been to them, and – this was horrible to admit, but he couldn't escape it – that would be perfectly reasonable of them.

The final realisation, which hit as he leapt out of bed just in time to throw up out of the window, was that he knew how he might – *might* – be able to handle the demon problem.

He slumped down on the edge of his bed, legs shaking, and buried his face in his hands. One thing at a time. He needed to find Tait – the wards still indicated that they weren't here, and now he really was beginning to worry about that – and then he needed to apologise, which was a problem, because he was shit at apologising.

Tait would come back, surely, at some point? Wouldn't they? If only to collect their stuff?

Footsteps on the stairs. Tait's footsteps. Tait's feel in the wards.

Cato stumbled to the door and yanked it open. Tait, on the landing, startled badly and took a step backwards, eyeing Cato warily.

"Thank fuck you're back. I'm sorry," Cato said, getting the main thing out before he could think better of it, or stumble over his words, or over his stupid pride.

"You stink like a pub after midnight," Tait said, voice cool.

"Well, that's not surprising," Cato admitted. He waited. Nothing more seemed to be forthcoming. "I said, I'm sorry."

"I heard you," Tait said. "What I'm wondering is, what you're sorry for, exactly?" They were holding themself tightly, shoulders tense, eyes wary.

"Everything?" Cato tried. "Oh, shit, can I sit down before I go through it all?"

Tait raised one shoulder in the smallest of shrugs. Cato gave up and slid himself down the doorframe to end up on the floor.

"I'm sorry for telling you to fuck off," he said to his knees. "I'm sorry for telling you I wish you didn't do it – no, actually, I'm not sorry about that. I do wish you hadn't done it." Tait took an audible breath in, but Cato barrelled on. "I'm sorry for telling you you *shouldn't* have done it, because that's not my decision. You were right. I'm sorry for trying to, to impose that on you. And I'm really sorry for – saying everything the way I said it. Taking it out on you. You're right. I did. I shouldn't have. Oh fuck, can I stop talking now?"

Tait knelt down in front of Cato, and Cato steeled himself to look up. "I love you," he said in a rush, meeting Tait's eyes, "but that doesn't, it isn't…"

"It's not an excuse for being horrible to me?" Tait asked, quietly.

"That. Yeah. Did I say sorry, already?"

Tait sighed. "I don't much care about sorry, exactly, unless you actually mean you're not going to do it again."

"I won't," Cato said, instantly.

"How do I know that?"

Cato shut his eyes. "I have no idea. I'm not – I haven't. Before. I've never tried to –"

"You've no experience in changing your behaviour?" Tait suggested.

"Yeah. That."

"And I haven't exactly asked you to. But you – expect me to go along with you. Don't you? And," Tait sighed, "I've rather gone along with that myself, so there's that, too. But I can't keep doing that. We can't keep doing that."

"I don't know what to say," Cato said, clinging onto the possible implications of that *we*. "I...suppose I just want you to give me another chance. But I don't know why on earth you should."

"Well, mostly, because I love you too," Tait said, with a rueful half-smile, and Cato's heart soared with hope. "And..." They sat back on their heels, and rubbed their face with their hands. "Look. Things were a bit tense, day before yesterday. With one thing and another. That's why – I wanted to be somewhere else. For a bit."

"Where were you?" Cato asked, briefly derailed.

"Stayed with a friend. Don't get off the topic. The point is, all right, that happened, and you've said sorry, and all the rest of it. It's – it's not *fine*, but I accept your apology."

"Oh, thank fuck." Cato sagged sideways against the doorframe.

"But..."

"But not again. I get it." He did. Not that it was going to be *easy*, exactly, but – Tait was worth it, weren't they. Cato would just have to take the more horrible bits of his personality out on other people.

Tait sighed, and reached out to clasp his shoulder. "I would, like, hug you or something, but honestly, I'm not joking, you *smell*."

"I'll go to the baths," Cato said. "Will you hug me after that?" He meant it to sound jokey, but it came out pathetic, which to be fair, was roughly how he felt. At least he hadn't been sick again. Yet. Then he remembered. "Oh, shit. But I can't."

"Can't what?" Tait looked suddenly alarmed.

"Can't waste time at the baths. I had an idea. The demons. Spirits." He gestured irritably, trying to make his words catch up with himself.

"You can't do sorcery with a hangover," Tait objected.

"Oh, I absolutely can. Otherwise I wouldn't have been able to do anything at all for about three years in my early twenties."

"You might still be drunk, even. Surely…"

"Referring you to my previous answer." Cato pushed himself to his feet and turned to go back into his room. He needed to look through his jars.

"No," Tait said, very firmly, grabbing him by the shoulder, which Cato should hate, but didn't, because it was Tait. "Stop. Even if you have got the right idea. It can wait for a couple of hours for you to drink something that isn't alcoholic, get yourself *clean*, and have something to eat. I'll come with you, and you can explain it on the way, and while we're there, make sure it's all straight in your head. All right?"

"People will hear," Cato said, doubtfully.

Tait rolled their eyes. "Trust me, no one is going to be able to understand you once you're off on magical theory. We're in a hurry, yes, but apparently not so much of a hurry that you didn't have time for a bender, so I'm sure you've time to sort out the aftermath of the bender."

"Sorry," Cato said again. Tait waved it away. "Oh fuck, and I ought to tell Reb."

"Reb?"

"She dragged me in yesterday. She was – irritated, that I'd been out there, wandering around with soldiers and all, when she didn't know anything about what I was doing. I said, I had half an answer, but I didn't *know* yet, but I think…"

"Cato. *Cato*. Slow down. Look. You'll think better once you're fed. If you go back to Reb's now you won't make any sense to her either. And I'll feel more like working with you when you're clean…" Tait hesitated. "Uh. Assuming you want me to…"

"Fuck yes," Cato said, fervently. "Absolutely I do. Two heads and all that. And Teren stuff. Questions. I need you." He made himself look up and catch Tait's gaze. "I do need you, you know." Tait smiled, and Cato's breath caught. He jumped up, desperate suddenly to get moving. "Yes. All right. Let's go."

"Open the windows properly before you go. The room's as bad as you are."

Halfway along the road to the baths, Tait said, quietly but without any of their customary hesitancy, "You might need to talk to Marcia, you know."

Cato's stomach clenched. "Don't think she's talking to me."

"Mmm," Tait said, noncommittal.

"And I'm not going to apologise to her for not helping, because I don't regret that." That, he was still certain of.

"Maybe," Tait took his hand, and Cato's eyes prickled at the feeling of their hand against his, "you should talk to her about that."

"Fuck that noise," Cato said, shoulders hunching; but he didn't let go of Tait's hand. He might never let go of Tait's hand again. Invent one-handed sorcery. "She should never have asked me, and she knows it. She can apologise first."

Tait sighed. "Well, if both of you are too stiff-necked to invite the other one to try to resolve the issue, I suppose it never will get resolved."

"Fine by me." Cato scowled down at the road.

"As you prefer." They squeezed Cato's hand. "I'm sorry to bring it up."

Cato shook his head. Tait's presence, there next to him,

was warming him more than seemed feasible. "It's fine."
He turned to smile at Tait. "You're like that. That's part
of what I love about you. How much kinder and more
thoughtful you are than me."

Tait was smiling at him. Thank fuck he hadn't screwed
this up, after all. "I suppose I love you for who you are,
too," they agreed.

"Horrible and unpleasant?" Cato suggested.

"Committed and stubborn, I was thinking of," Tait said,
still smiling.

Well. That would do.

☺ ☺

It was a gloriously sunny morning. Jonas, messenger
armband on, pulled strongly on the oars of the little
rowing boat he'd borrowed from one of the fishermen
after Asa vouched for him. He'd hoped to go the night
before, but tide and wind had been against him. He was
timing this for the turn of the tide; easy both ways. He
hoped. Even if it had meant a very early start.

Xan was on deck when he hailed the *Heart's Dragon*,
which he took as a good omen.

"Hey there Jonas! Wasn't expecting you here. Coming
aboard?"

"If I may."

He threw the boat's rope up to Xan and scrambled up
the side. Once he was over the rail, Captain Dirin was
there already, looking quizzical.

"Jonas t'Riseri," he said. So Xan'd told him who it was
coming. That was – probably for the best "And with a
messenger's armband, no less. What is it I can do for
you?"

"I've a request from Kia t'Riseri, the Ambassador,
regarding any messages that have come into the fleet."
He'd noticed on the way in that the ships were up to
seven, now. There should have been a couple more, by
his count; he wondered if there had been some swapping
around of cargo. The *Heart's Dragon* was riding a little

higher in the water than it had been; perhaps someone had taken on any goods that were going directly to the Crescent or to Exuria.

"Have you now," the captain said thoughtfully. "Well. How about you come on down to my cabin, and we'll have a chat."

This – wasn't going to be as smooth as he'd hoped, was it? Well. He was here now. He'd manage something.

Down in the cabin, the captain poured him a coca. "And I've breakfast coming in a moment – egg wraps. You're welcome to join me."

Well, Jonas wasn't about to turn down free food. And especially not food from home. And even more not a cup of coca, which Marekers didn't drink at all.

"So," Dirin said. "Messages."

Jonas tapped his armband. "I've been sent out to fetch anything you were bringing in. Sent out by the ambassador."

"Your former shipmate," Dirin noted. "With your mother."

Jonas really hated how everyone knew his mother. The *Heart's Dragon* wasn't t'Dirin yet; its shipmates would be, at least any of them who'd stayed long enough. If Dirin did well enough, in the next years, he'd get the honour of the shipname. Jonas guessed he was going for it; he had the feel of an ambitious man.

"Indeed," he agreed instead. "So, if you or the other ships have got anything – maybe you could send over to the other ships?"

The door to the cabin opened, and one of the crew came in with a tray piled high with wraps – not just the promised egg, but a couple of sweet ones as well, from the smell. Dirin waited until the door was closed again before he took a wrap and said, "The trouble is, we're not in Marek, are we? So that armband of yours doesn't, in fact, say much."

"The ambassador wanted you to send the messages," Jonas said, after a moment of indecision, then hurriedly took a sweet wrap.

"The ambassador is in Marek," Dirin pointed out. "And might potentially be said to be affected by that. Decision-making-wise. We, on the other hand, as I mentioned, are not in Marek."

Jonas considered a number of options, but really, he hadn't the skill for this kind of thing. He opted for blunt. "The Marekers are waiting for diplomatic mail. Kia's struck a deal with them. She sent me because I'm a messenger. And I have a letter from her, even." He produced it from his jacket. He, Kia, and Marcia had decided to rest on Kia's authority, not mentioning Marcia or anyone else of Marek.

Captain Dirin read it carefully, then rolled it back up and tapped it on the table. "You live there, now? In Marek?"

The abrupt change of subject startled Jonas. "Yes. A couple of years now."

"So you understand the situation over there?"

"Um. Perhaps. A bit."

He ended up trying to explain both the political situation, and the Teren demon situation. Captain Dirin listened to him carefully.

"You seem to know a lot about demons," he observed.

Jonas shrugged, managing not to twitch in panic. "Well," he said. "Marekers, you know. Talk about it a bit more, don't they? Than what we do."

"City of magic," Dirin agreed. He was eyeing Jonas curiously. "They say they've their own special spirit, don't they? What do they call it, now?"

"The cityangel," Jonas said.

He really wanted to get off this subject. He was hunting for something to move them back onto the matter of letters, and ambassadors, when the ship began to rock. Dirin and he both looked up, sea-instincts flaring. Jonas hadn't *seen* bad weather on the horizon, coming in. Clear blue skies, calm seas. What...?

"Captain!" Someone was banging on the door, and Dirin was on his feet already, flinging it open. "Captain, there's an elemental! Right there in the bay! Right by the ship!"

Jonas followed on Dirin's tail at a dead run, up to the deck, the ship shifting more and more alarmingly underneath him. And yes, there, right enough, he could see out to starboard a sea-elemental, unmistakable, whirling the sea up into a whirlpool. But you never *saw* them as close as this – a bare few tens of yards away from the bunched Salinas ships. They never came up – came into this plane, Jonas supposed, but 'came up' was the Salinas expression, like for mermaids– next to ships, not even when they seemed to be friendly, or at least weren't actively creating bad sea or weather. And, of course, if you saw one from a distance you went right the other way and sharpish.

Jonas peered over the rail at it. The whirling made it hard to see what it looked like, exactly – there was red and sea-green and gold in there, forming something almost like a pillar, with perhaps something faintly humanoid spinning there in the centre. Foam wave-tips spurted up and down the whirling pillar, their edges whipping around the elemental, and it was *glowing* the same way Beckett did.

Why was it right here? Why so close?

Dirin was cursing, visibly unsure what to do, before he turned to bark orders at his crew – get the sails up, get them away from the elemental. Jonas could see similar movement on the other ships. Except if it had chosen to be this close – would it stay where it was? Or was it trying to cause them trouble? Would it chase them?

The sails were up, the sea-anchor lifted, and they were already moving.

The elemental followed them.

One of the other ships, smaller than the *Heart's Dragon*, was visibly in trouble. Jonas swallowed. The way the sea was behaving now – and the elemental was still going; it would get worse yet – they wouldn't be able to get back to Marek before at least one ship was overset. Clouds were rolling in too where minutes ago the sky had been clear, a completely unseasonal, *abnormal*, storm. Jonas thought of the last storm, the land-storm, he'd been involved with. He couldn't just let this happen. He had to do something.

There had to be a reason it had chosen to be this near to the ships. It had to know what it was doing. And if it was doing this deliberately – maybe it could be persuaded otherwise.

"Where's my boat?" he demanded of the nearest crew-member.

"Jonas, either help or get below," Dirin bawled at him over the noise of the rising wind.

"If you find me my boat, I'll help!"

Dirin was not looking impressed.

"I'm a sorcerer!" There was no more time to work around this, or try to find a way not to admit it. "I'll go out. Talk to it. See…"

"*Talk* to it? Are you insane? You can't *talk* to an elemental!"

"You only say that because no one ever has." Tait had mentioned a sorcerer that had tried to research them, and hadn't been able to get a Salinas ship to go close enough. Because you didn't go that close to an elemental, and you only ever – until today – found them out in deep ocean, beyond the reach of any ships that weren't Salinas. "No one's *tried*," Jonas said. "Because no one thinks it's possible. It's circular, right? What have we got to lose, right now?"

"You could die."

"People are going to die if I don't!" Including, maybe, himself.

Jonas could see on Dirin's face that the man didn't believe it could work. But water was coming in over the rails now, and the elemental was coming closer, and…

Dirin's jaw set, decision made. "Get that rowing-boat back over the side!" he shouted, then, to Jonas, "Good luck." He didn't say, *or we'll all be drowned.* He didn't have to.

Jonas didn't give any thought to what he was planning to do until he was already over the side and rowing hard towards the elemental. Towards the whirlpool that was

211

accelerating towards *him*. This was *stupid*, he knew it was, no one had ever done this before because it *wouldn't work*. But he couldn't think of anything else to do, and he couldn't do nothing.

He must be within hailing distance now. He was certainly having to fight with everything he had for the little boat not to just get pulled down into the sea.

"Hey! Hey! I want to talk to you!"

To his immense surprise – and even more immense gratitude – the whirlpool began to slow. Not stopping altogether, but slowing to the point that he could see the being within. The wind was dying too. He couldn't spare a moment to look back over his shoulder and see how the ships were doing.

He'd been right: the being was faintly humanoid, but not human (human-ish) the way Beckett was. There were no lower limbs as such, just a single pillar-like shape pointing downwards into the water, but it had long flexible upper limbs, flowing around it like water, and the suggestion of something like a head at the top. The sea-green colour was more prominent now, the red and gold sparking through the film of water that surrounded the being, and the glow was more pronounced.

They'd stopped; but they weren't speaking. The elemental had no mouth nor eyes in that head-like space, but surely that needn't limit them?

"I want to talk," Jonas tried again, and the water rippled and shifted, but nothing else happened.

Elementals were spirits; did he need magic to talk to them? Automatically, he reached for that space where he found Beckett – and Beckett's power – and lurched mentally downwards with a jerk into emptiness, like stepping onto a stair that wasn't there. Of course; this was outside Marek. Beckett didn't reach out here.

The elemental was getting restless; the water beginning to froth and churn around them again. He had to think of something.

His flickers were magic, too, weren't they? Or so Cato maintained. At least, there was some kind of link between

212

them and magic. And he'd had his flickers long before arriving in Marek. That was, after all, *why* he'd come to Marek in the first place.

Once upon a time, that wouldn't have helped. Once upon a time, his main interactions with his flickers were avoiding them, ignoring them, and hoping they went away. But he'd spent time thinking about them, now; he'd tried to make one happen, even. It was the same sort of feeling as finding Beckett, the same sort of space in his head, just…inside, not outside. Sort of.

He stared at the elemental, and concentrated.

…hurt steal gone gone GONE…

It felt rather like a blow to the head, if a wholly internal one; he found himself sprawling on his back in the dinghy. But…but he'd heard something. He'd understood something, for a value of 'understood' that didn't yet include much actual understanding.

He tried again.

…an image he couldn't understand of a place he couldn't be in, but the beings that he sensed there did belong there, they were together, and then there was space, empty space, empty missing space…

It was marginally less painful this time. And the elemental was calmer; that sea-green pillar leaning perhaps slightly towards him, and the red-gold sparking in what might even be a pattern.

He carefully formed an idea in his head that consisted approximately of a great many question marks, and extended it into that mental space in the hope that might work for his side of the communication.

…hurt HURT stop HURT stop GONE come BACK…

"Spirits are going missing," Jonas said aloud, understanding the wave of emotion more than the image. His head thumped in time with it, his stomach churning in sympathy. "To Teren." That had to be it.

Which meant that what he needed to do now was to convince the elemental that he – and by extension the Salinas ships he could hear behind him sailing further away, which was at least a relief – was on their side, and most definitely not responsible for any of their people going missing.

It took a while. Jonas wasn't at all sure that the elemental really got the difference between different parts of the human world. But they did – Jonas thought, anyway – get the idea that if they drowned the only person they'd managed to explain anything to, then he wouldn't be able to *fix* it. He sincerely hoped that this was going to extend to the Salinas ships, too; he'd done his best to convey the idea that they were essential to fixing this.

From the elemental's side of things, Jonas still wasn't wholly sure he had the entire right of it, but it seemed that spirits were disappearing, pulled away, and were coming back damaged or not at all. It had the flavour of – he couldn't quite put it into words, but something that wasn't entirely new but had never been quite like this. Perhaps, knowing what little he knew of non-Marek magic, it was to do with there always having been the odd Teren-style sorcerer, but only recently that the Academy really started trying to produce so many of them, or using so much demon-power? Jonas, like everyone else, had read the reports from Teren refugees in the news-sheets and pamphlets.

Eventually, he persuaded the elemental to go away for now, though their final blast of communication gave him the strong impression that there was a time limit on this tolerance.

The Salinas, Jonas reflected as he pulled his way back towards the ships, exhausted beyond belief and his head still throbbing, might have to start taking sides after all. If the alternative was their ships all going down to the bottom.

It took him some time to explain it all to Dirin once he got back.

"So, you're telling me that it's all down to what these Teren sorcerers are up to," Dirin said, rubbing at his chin. "You realise, that's your word on it?"

"Talk to Kia," Jonas said, wet and fed up. "She'll tell you."

"And if I let you take these letters back, that'll help Marek against Teren," Dirin said. "Which is convenient for you."

"I'm out here on Kia's behalf," Jonas said. "You're accusing her of being biased?"

Dirin shrugged. "She's been in Marek a while. But. You're right, I'm not saying I don't believe her."

Just as well; since Kia was one of Jonas' former shipmates, he'd have to challenge Dirin if he had been.

"And you *spoke* to the thing? You're a sorcerer?"

Jonas sighed. "Apprenticed to one, more accurately. But the sorcerer I'm apprenticed to deals, sometimes, with spirits. It's him reckons he has a way to deal with the Teren ones. I don't understand it – not quite – but I know a bit, now, about spirits."

He was completely screwed now, of course. This was going to be all over every Salinas ship who'd seen it, and every ship they spoke to. His mother would be furious. And Dirin was likely about to throw him straight off the ship, even if he *had* kept them all from drowning.

"Huh," was all the captain said. "Interesting. That's why you stayed in Marek, then." He sounded like he had the solution to a problem. "People did wonder. With your mother."

Jonas felt a pull of panic. His mother might know about his magic, but it wasn't, it couldn't be, *public*. "I don't want to talk about it. With others," he said, stiffly, searching for the words to say 'keep it secret' without giving the captain that much power.

"I won't say anything, don't worry," Captain Dirin said. "To be blunt with you, I want this ship to be t'Dirin someday. Someday soon. And antagonising your mother won't help."

"Undercutting her might," Jonas said, looking the captain straight in the eye. "By telling everyone about her abnormal son." He was distantly proud of himself, that his voice didn't shake as he said it.

The captain shrugged. "Honestly? I think we worry too much about that. I've always found elementals

215

interesting, myself, though," he laughed ruefully, "I admit, always before now from a very safe distance. But…I'm not going to claim it's not an alarming thought, but I begin to think now – what if one could partner with them, somehow? Have we been missing something, all this time, avoiding them so assiduously? Maybe…" His voice trailed off.

"Really," Jonas breathed. A sudden stab of unlooked for hope rose in his chest, and he remembered that flicker, him on shipdeck, Asa beside him…

"In any case," the captain said, dismissing the subject for now. "I accept your letter, and I accept the reasoning of the Ambassador, and I'll send you back with your letters. But," he looked at Jonas, "I'd also be grateful to hear a little more of magic, perhaps another time, once you and your sorcerer have sorted Marek's little Teren problem out."

As Jonas sailed back towards Marek – at least the wind was still in his favour, because he wasn't sure he'd have been able to row all that way, given how he felt after dealing with the elemental – with a sack of mail nestled safely under the thwart of the fishing boat, he tried not to wonder too hard whether he might, finally, have found what he was looking for. What that flicker had – maybe – promised him. A way to be Salinas, and magical, at one and the same time. To have both sorcery and the sea, together.

But for now, he was still part of Marek; and he had messages to deliver.

FOURTEEN

Working with Madeleine to talk to the Council about magic was…not an experience Marcia ever thought she would have. Her mother, as they had discussed beforehand, entered the Council leaning on a stick and wrapped in shawls, Marcia supportively at her elbow; though Madeleine's stumble as she went to sit down might have been overplaying the role. Meanwhile, Marcia gave her mother her best concerned-filial looks while Madeleine was looking in her direction, then let herself appear grim and frustrated – not hard, in the circumstances – behind Madeleine's back. They'd come in last, after a protracted fussing at the door whilst extracting Madeleine from her litter, in order to be as well-observed as possible. From the smirk Marcia caught on Athitol-Head's face, the conclusions they wanted were being drawn.

Madeleine had finally summoned her the night before, a couple of hours after Marcia's conversation with Kia. She'd given Marcia a certain amount of information about Selene, and rather less about Teren and what she'd been up to in Ameten, then – requested, rather than demanded, which was unusual in itself – an update on the situation within Marek. Marcia had seen her lips compress when Marcia mentioned magic, even though she'd avoided Cato's name. But Marcia wasn't going to avoid facing up to magic any longer, with Madeleine any more than with the rest of the Council. And to her surprise, once she was done, her mother had nodded crisply and said, "Well then. We need the Council to see sense with regard to working with the sorcerers during this crisis. I believe I can handle that."

And now here they were, the two of them. Everyone finally settled, the Reader banged their staff on the floor and announced that Fereno-Heir wished to bring in the Sorcerer Reb, to contribute to discussion of the matters facing the city. There was a murmuring around the room, but no audible surprise. Andreas, in front of her, visibly set his shoulders; he'd been casting anxious glances over his shoulder at Madeleine as Marcia and she came in. Marcia hadn't brought him in on the discussions she and Madeleine had been having, on the grounds that, in her experience, he wasn't all that good of an actor. His reaction could only be helping.

Marcia went to rise, slowly enough to let Madeleine brush her aside as she too rose, glaring across at her daughter. Marcia herself made an abortive movement then sat slowly back down again. Athitol-Head, she was pleased to notice, sat back with an air of expectation. Waiting, at a guess, for Madeleine to disavow her errant daughter.

Bad luck.

"As I am sure you are all aware," Madeleine said, her voice clear, "I have recently spent time in Teren, and in Ameten. And then, against my wishes, in the custody of the former Teren Lieutenant, on the edges of the city. I was, of course, not present in the city when Marek declared our independence, and as such, there may be aspects of that of which I am still unaware. But," her voice solidified into steel, "what I do know all about is the threat currently poised on our border. And I am *horrified* by the abject failure of this Council to agree any approach to it. Do you all intend to cower here talking endlessly, until Selene simply walks into the city, unopposed?"

"We intend to *negotiate*," Athitol-Head said impatiently, without bothering to raise her hand.

Madeleine made an irritable noise. "Negotiate. As if that woman will engage honestly in *negotiation*. Have none of you learnt anything? Do you even know what she wants? What she *truly* wants? Because, conveniently, I am in a position to tell you."

Tabriol-Heir politely gestured to the Reader, and Madeleine indicated she was willing to give way.

"With all due respect, Fereno-Head. You say you are in a

position to tell us what the former Lieutenant wants. Due, I presume, to your recent unfortunate captivity. But I must ask, why so? Why would she risk letting you know?"

"She didn't tell me, I observed," Madeleine said scornfully. "Although perhaps more pertinently, she did not anticipate me leaving her custody. Or, rather, she intended to kill me, if she could not engage to trade my own personal safety for the wellbeing of the city. A trade which both you as a body, and my daughter, quite correctly turned down. I was saved, instead, by magic. As may too the city be."

There was a hubbub around the room. Athitol-Head's mouth was open in shock.

Madeleine raised her voice and spoke over the noise, voice ringing out across the Chamber. Marcia was suddenly, fiercely, proud of her. The baby kicked, and she found herself hoping, absurdly, that they could hear their grandmother. "Magic is being used against us. It is foolish to deny that. Therefore it is just as foolish to turn down whatever options we have for countering it. Such as, for example, the magic of our own. Which we, here, know nothing about; and yet you ignore the sorcerers who might be able to save the city?"

She let it hang there for a moment. Marcia was looking around the room. Some faces – Athitol, unsurprisingly, among them – spoke of unmoving resistance. Others, fear. Others still were more thoughtful.

"In any case," Madeleine continued. "In case it informs your opinion," a certain amount of scorn, "I can tell you that Selene will not *negotiate*. She will accept nothing less than total surrender to Teren's overlordship, and to everything she proposed last year, with doubtless a little more on the top. Her goal is to be named as the new Archion, and to do that she *must* take Marek back with her as a prize, wrapped whole and entire. Any less and the Archion will simply continue his deathbed dithering. If she is forced to go back, tail between her legs, her political career will be over altogether. I can tell you that she cannot – will not – abide that. She will do anything in her power, however apparently foolish, to avoid it. At present, she is considering two possibilities, and she is willing to wait for her preferred outcome – which, as you all already know, would be for the Council to bow before the threat and let her in." She paused. "I would expect that few of the Houses would survive the immediate aftermath of her entry to the city. Those that might beg her indulgence would struggle to maintain their wealth given what Teren would like to pull *out* of Marek. I do not imagine that many of our current systems would survive. Guild independence, too; Teren would prefer our Guilds merged into theirs, and Teren goods coming through Marek at a far higher number – and far higher rate."

No one looked happy now. Even Athitol-Head – who was surely a good bet for initial survival – wasn't a fool when it came to business. Her lips were bloodless where she was pressing them together.

"I am willing to admit," Madeleine went on, "that I myself did not foresee this outcome, during Selene's previous visits here. It seemed to me perfectly reasonable to rebuild, to strengthen, our decaying links with Teren. Indeed, with the Teren I was imagining – which might yet exist with a new Archion – who is to say that an independent Marek cannot still rebuild those links, under our own terms? But Selene is not that potential Archion, and if she ever might have been, her desperation has overtaken her."

Marcia wondered whether Madeleine's stay in Teren had given her any ideas about who *might* be that potential Archion; it had nearly come up in discussion but Madeleine had avoided the question, and it wasn't important right now. She'd been there for weeks, though. She'd surely been dabbling her fingers in the relevant pies; Marcia couldn't believe she would have stayed out of it.

"We must," Madeleine concluded, "use everything at our disposal. And that brings me to Selene's second option. That of pushing her way into the city with her sorcerers and their demons. And let me assure you, my friends, that there *are* demons. I have seen them. I have been threatened, personally, by them. At present, the cityangel," Marcia was impressed she managed to say that without hesitating, "prevents them from entering. Selene seems certain that, when she chooses to abandon her waiting game, this protection cannot last. We cannot continue to cower passively, waiting for her to see sense and give up. She will not give up. But. Magic saved me, at the very last moment, from the demon Selene's pet sorcerer set on me. Magic could yet save all of us. I move to introduce the Sorcerer Reb." With great care, she sat back down again.

Marcia saw Nisha whispering urgently to Kilzan-Head. A number of other Heads and Heirs were having whispered consultations. It was almost an anticlimax when, this time, the Council voted – albeit not overwhelmingly – to let Reb in.

Reb kept to the point. The Group, she said, had a possible solution. Marcia scrutinised her expression as she was speaking. Reb wouldn't *lie*, but she might put the best face on the truth – but she looked more hopeful than the last time they spoke. Maybe Cato really had come up with something.

They were, Reb said, still working out the details. But they would not move without Council agreement, and they would likely need support from the guard and the mercenaries.

"It seems likely," she said, carefully, obviously unhappy about what she was about to say, "that we will have to let Selene into the city before we can overwhelm her."

"Let her *in*?" someone demanded from the Guild seats at the back.

"The cityangel," Reb said, obviously aware that many of the people in the room doubted the existence of the cityangel, "is the underpinning of Marek magic. The cityangel cannot operate outside the city. Which is part of why Teren has remained outside so far. But that also means that if we are to draw on their power, we must be inside the city boundaries."

Cityangel, a few people muttered, mouths twisting.

Even Madeleine was tensing, though she didn't say anything.

"A trap," Andreas called out. "We must create a trap."

"Perhaps," Haran-Heir suggested, blinking in a way that suggested he was constructing street-plans in his head, "we could use the streets themselves…create a bottleneck. Would that help?"

"It might do," Reb agreed. "Certainly, the Group may be able to handle the magic, but we need help to find the solution as a whole. Overall."

"Tactics," Haran-Head agreed, and subsided with a low thoughtful murmur.

For the first time, Marcia began to believe this might work. Next to her, under the cover of her shawls, her mother grasped her hand and squeezed it.

☺ ☺

Cato had reached an impasse, which was awkward, given that in his message to Reb he'd assured her that he was pretty sure he had the solution. And he did, he really thought he did, it was just…turning theory into practice, was the issue. And picking Tait's brains wasn't working out. Which would have been a real fucking problem, except that Cato had just remembered who else was kicking around Marek and who might be *persuadable* into helping.

"There must be another way," Tait said, again, following Cato down his stairs. "That doesn't involve you finding," 'getting screwed over by', their tone said, "that *toad* Hira."

Toad Hira might be, but Teren sorcerer he definitely was – well, had been, before Marcia blackmailed him into betraying Selene, and thus having to remain in Marek for fear of her wrath. Which was convenient, for Cato's purposes.

Cato shook his head. "Look. I know you've been trying, but what you're saying doesn't make sense. I accept it's what you were told," or at least what Tait remembered of what they'd been told, which wasn't quite the same thing, "but either they've changed stuff, or…I don't know. It doesn't make sense, and it doesn't fit properly with anything I know. And you can't try it here to check, and it seems like you going outside of Marek right now is a shockingly poor idea."

"Still…" Tait argued.

"Also you're a Marek sorcerer now, and still an apprentice even, so best not to confuse yourself by doing something different. Even just to show me. Especially given that you're not *my* apprentice. Reb knows what I'm trying to do, but I doubt she wants you dragged into it. And finally," Cato stopped in the street to face Tait, "you don't want to do it. Do you."

Tait's mouth was set in a stubborn line. "Define *want*. I want to help you. And Marek. This isn't really a situation in which it's reasonable to be all…squeamish."

"Yes," Cato said patiently, "which does you credit and so on, but conveniently, you don't have to, so how about let's not? Instead, I can just find Hira and ask him." And he'd actually done things with a demon – granted, one of those things was 'set it on Tait', which Cato wasn't all that thrilled about – but it implied that, even if he was a shit, he knew his stuff. And Tait, cityangel bless their gentle heart, did not.

"Will you be able to find him?" Tait asked. "Where did he go, after Beckett wouldn't talk to him?"

"Reb said, back when it happened, Marcia paid him off. Set him up with housing in the new bit, out in the south-west. But then I heard the other day that he's back in the squats. So either he's run out of rent money, or he spent it on booze instead. From what I gather was the state of him, probably the latter."

"What do you do, if you're not a sorcerer any more?" Tait wondered.

"Earn your living the way everyone else does?" Cato said with a shrug. Beckett had threatened, once, to take Cato's access to power away. The idea sent a shiver down his spine. Still; Hira had attacked Marek directly, hadn't he? Attacked *Tait* directly. It was fair enough.

You tried to put another cityangel in Beckett's place, a small voice inside his head reminded him. Cato scowled down at his feet. It hadn't been him had taken Beckett out in the first place, though, had it? And he'd screwed Daril over, in the end, and got Beckett back. So...

Not the same thing at all.

"You all right?" Tait asked, putting a hand on his shoulder.

"Yeah," Cato said, shaking it off and smiling at his lover. "Just...never mind. It was the Fish Hira was seen in, so I'll start there. No point in both of us going, though. You stay here. Rest up a bit, eh?"

Tait wasn't entirely convinced, but Cato was insistent. He didn't want to be limited in how he spoke to Hira by knowing Tait was listening.

The bartender at the Fish was quite happy to answer a few questions, especially once Cato put a few nice shiny coins on the bar.

"I know the one," she said, flipping her dark hair out of her eyes. "Didn't much like him, truth be told, but that wasn't your question."

"No," Cato agreed. "My question was, where is he?"

"Haven't seen him in a couple of days."

"He fell out wi' Johnny," someone else put in from along the bar.

"Ohh," the bartender said, sounding enlightened.

"And this prevents him from coming here?" Cato demanded, then went on without waiting for an answer, "Which is all very well, but I don't want to know where he isn't. I want to know where he is. Such as, for example, if either of you know where he lives."

"I'd guess, somewhere 'tween here and the Keys, 'cos I saw him in the Keys the other day, and the thing is, Johnny's barred from the Keys."

"Is he?" the bartender demanded with interest.

"On account of he got caught cheating at cards..."

"Thank you for your time," Cato interrupted. "Please do buy yourself a drink."

He slammed the cost of another pint on the table and took off for the Keys, where he didn't need to ask the bartender anything because there was Hira, tucked into a corner with a drink. It didn't, in Cato's professional opinion, look like the sort of place where one might be barred for cheating at cards, but there you go; perhaps appearances deceived.

"Hira," Cato said, cheerfully, sitting down on the stool opposite him.

"What...? Oh. It's you. Fuck off."

"What a charming greeting."

Hira raised a shoulder. "Don't have anything to say to fucking *sorcerers*."

"It's not my fault Beckett won't have anything to do with you. Would another pint help you feel more warmly towards me?"

Hira just grunted, so Cato got him the pint anyway, and one for himself. It had been a long morning.

"So," Cato said, chattily. "What I need to know is, how do sorcerers in your part of the world do their demon-binding."

"Fuck off," Hira said again.

"Because," Cato persisted, "there are a whole bunch of them camped on Marek's doorstep, and I'd rather like to get rid of them. And what Tait's telling me doesn't fit with what I saw out there, nor yet with any of my theory."

"Well of course not," Hira said irritably. "Firstly, Tait was shit at it, and secondly, they never got beyond student level."

Aha, Cato thought, but Hira caught himself and stopped. "Don't see why I should care," he said instead, truculently.

"Because Selene is with them, and I am fairly sure that Selene doesn't like you much," Cato said. "If they get in here, and they find you, I think there will be consequences."

Hira shrugged again. "Lots of people in Marek. Not going to find me in particular."

"Oh, they will," Cato said. "I promise you they will,

because if you keep pissing me off like you're doing right now, I'm going to write Selene a nice message telling her to look out for you."

Hira looked up and glared at him. "What makes you think I'll give two shits?"

"Not wanting to be eaten by a demon?" Cato suggested. "Gotta admit, it's a big motivation for me personally. I mean, you can count on them not being able to find you if you *like*. Or you could give me a little bit of help and I'll be able to keep you safe while everyone else is also being kept safe. And if I'm *not* safe, I will do my very best to make sure you're not either."

Hira stared at him for a long moment. "I want to do magic," he said, abruptly.

Cato winced. "I really wish I could offer you that. It's not my decision, is the thing. If Beckett won't work with you…that's where our power comes from. That's it." He paused. "I'm sorry," he said, with genuine sincerity. The idea of losing your magic was a horrible one. "And I'm happy to try to talk Beckett into it again, if you like. I just can't guarantee an outcome. And I can certainly tell you that it is not going to be something Beckett goes for right now, because of the whole thing where they're pretty pissed off about demons camped out there poking at the boundary." He paused. "Of course, helping out with that *might* make them feel more positive about you."

Hira scowled. "Thirty demmers."

Cato didn't, right now, *have* thirty demmers, even if he had been inclined to give it to Hira, which he wasn't. "Thirty demmers? You can fuck *right* off." He threw the pinch of bindweed-and-sand he'd had tucked in his palm into the air, yanked power, and Hira was suddenly plastered against the wall behind his table, pulled bodily from his seat. His eyes went wide with panic.

"No fighting indoors," the bartender called over, sounding bored. "Take it outside."

"This isn't fighting," he called back, without taking his eyes off Hira. "Fighting is a two-player sport. This is me about to kick the shit out of someone."

Hira began wriggling even harder to get free. He wasn't having any noticeable success.

"You can take that outside too," the bartender said. "Messy."

"If you don't shut up," Cato said pleasantly, "I will curse this place underwater and you will never so much as sniff the shadow of the cityangel ever again." He hoisted Hira higher up the wall, to add further clarity to his point. The bartender shut up.

"Now," Cato said to Hira. "I refer you to my previous request. Otherwise, in about three seconds I am going to start trying to extract your intestines through your nose, by magic. I'm told that it's all quite complicated in there, and I'm not great with body-magic, truth be told, so it may take me a while to find them. Alternatively, we can skip directly to you coming with me and I will put the intestine-extraction part of events on hold. If you're co-operative enough, even on hold permanently."

Hira glared at him for a moment longer, then sagged against the wall. "*Fine*," he hissed. "Fine! I'll come quietly."

"Excellent news," Cato said, and dropped Hira onto the floor. "And just so's we're all good friends here, I'll buy you a beer to take with you, how about that?" He probably shouldn't be tiring himself out this way but, well, it got the frustrations out. And Cato was feeling very, very frustrated right now. (Not scared. He didn't get scared. He was going to fix this. There was no need to be scared.)

Hira, open beer jug in hand, trailed sulkily after Cato back to his room.

"Right," Cato said, once they were in there and the door closed. "Tell me about Teren demon-binding."

Hira was looking around curiously; he seemed most interested in Cato's worktable, with its neatly arrayed rows of jars on the shelves above it, and a jar of feathers and bits of stick and bone sitting on one side of the table. "You need all that stuff, for Marek magic?"

"No, I just collect street-sweepings for fun. Yes. Or sometimes, anyway. You don't for Teren?"

Cato did some small things without a focus, and it was something he practised deliberately, unlike Reb, but more complex magics definitely needed one. When he made a consent-binding for a spirit, he used a carved ball, deliberately more ornate than anything he'd do for a magic limited to this plane, but the same idea. It hadn't occurred to him that you could do it without.

"It's anchored in yourself," Hira said, tapping himself on the breastbone.

"Ugh," Cato said, frankly, though it matched what he'd seen with the Teren sorcerers, and partly explained why what Tait had been saying didn't work. "Why not use an object? Tait said they used animal blood, which was grim enough."

"Student-level, that is. You start with that, then your blood, then your bone-and-soul. They say, at the Academy, that's strongest. Makes it harder for the demon to break away from you. And less messy than blood."

Cato sucked air in thoughtfully through his teeth. "Yes, I suppose that's right. When I'm doing it I'm not trying to compel them by force, after all."

Hira looked honestly startled. "How else would you do it?"

"By *asking*," Cato said, testily. "And paying them," he admitted.

Hira blinked at him a couple of times. "Really? Well. I guess Marek really is different."

"Most Marek sorcerers don't work with spirits at all," Cato said. "Except for the whole Beckett thing, obviously. Owing as how Beckett is a bit precious about spirits in their city, as you knew already. Anyway. So, you anchor it in yourself, lovely. Then what?"

"You create a loop, out between the planes. And then you do a summoning – that part still uses blood, mostly, yours or someone else's – and whichever demon answers, you cut them off with the loop, and there they are, tied to you."

"So the loop is attached to the sorcerer, and the demon's inside the loop, and there's no exit from there." When Cato did it, he made a loop, but it lived with the focus, and it could be accessed from either plane at will. He was beginning to see the model, and it fit with his theory, though he didn't like it. If it was anchored in *you*, it made sense that it wasn't accessible; it was protected by your whole self and essence.

Hira shook his head. "No exit, no."

"What I need is to punch holes in those loops," Cato said. And what that would do to the sorcerer, he didn't know. "For which, I need to see them nice and close-up. Can you make one for me?"

"You want me to summon a demon right in the middle of Marek?" Hira said incredulously.

"No, no," Cato assured him. "If I wanted you to summon a spirit we'd go outside the city. But actually I don't want you to trap any poor spirit, thanks all the same. I just want you to form the loop. You said it's anchored in you, so it's not like it needs any other source of power, right?"

"No-o," Hira agreed, with some hesitation. "I haven't…"

"Just try," Cato said, impatiently. "I need to know what it looks like."

"And then you punch a hole in it? And what does that do to me? No fucking thanks."

The first problem they ran into, once Cato had convinced Hira – with, in the end, ten demmers, which did not make him happy, as well as a solemn promise not to touch the loop – was that Hira did in fact need power to create the thing, and he didn't have any. Because this was Marek, and Beckett controlled sorcery here, and Beckett wasn't going to help Hira. Cato felt like this might imply something for Teren sorcery, and how they bootstrapped themselves into creating this link, if Hira couldn't do it here, but in the immediate term, it meant that Cato had to lend some power to Hira, which he liked doing only slightly less than he liked not getting to see the wretched loop.

Once he'd handed Hira enough power to do it, the loop was exactly like the not-purple ends of what he'd seen in the bargeyard. With a kind of tug away, making Hira very slightly absent from this plane; the binding was in him, the loop was out into the other plane, and that shifted Hira with it, just a little. Hira's was less pronounced than those of the other sorcerers, possibly because there was no demon in there pulling at it.

"Right," Cato said thoughtfully, and cast his own. It took a few goes until he was satisfied that it was the same as Hira's – Hira was unhelpful, saying that the instructors at the Academy had mostly just shouted at you until you got it right – and once he was done, he carefully transferred it to a small oak box. Boxes were good, because of the symbolism of opening and shutting lids. It felt fucking horrible though, pulling at his breastbone.

"That'll do," he said, with satisfaction. "I've got something to try it with, now."

"Can I go, then?" Hira demanded.

"Sure, sure," Cato said absently. "Unless you've got any comments on my loop-making."

Hira shrugged. "No. Looks pretty much right to me. Just hasn't got a demon in it."

"Indeed," Cato said. Which was the next problem. He wasn't about to bind some unfortunate spirit by force, but...The first problem, though, was trying to make a hole in it without damaging himself.

He barely noticed Hira leave.

☺ ☺

Madeleine, Andreas noticed as he helped her out of the litter in front of the Crescent Embassy, had apparently become much more frail between House Fereno and here. She leant heavily on his arm and went slowly up the steps. By the time they reached the front door, it was already open, and Berdian was standing in the hall, eyeing the two of them with a wariness that was somewhat at odds with the cordiality of his voice.

"Fereno-Head! Tigero-Head! How delightful to see you both. Please, do come in."

This time they were seated in a small parlour, instead of in Berdian's office as Andreas had been on previous visits; deference perhaps to Madeleine's age or apparent state of debility? Painted silk banners hung on the walls – more of Berdian's silk imports, no doubt – and the tiled floor was small delicately-executed mosaic rather than the plainer large tiles in Berdian's office. It was beautiful; Andreas might have to consider something similar for his next round of improvements at House Tigero, though he feared it might be cold in the winter, Marek's climate being cooler than the Crescent.

"An infusion would be lovely, thank you," Madeleine said, as soon as she was seated, just as if Berdian had offered already, which in fact he had not.

Berdian flickered a diplomatic smile, said a few words to the servant who had opened the door, and came to sit with them.

"I was so pleased," Madeleine said, "that at least some of the mails from the Salinas ships were able to reach us here in Marek. I heard from a dear friend over in Rigal. I trust you too have been able to hear from your friends and colleagues?"

Within two minutes of arriving, Madeleine had taken charge of the interaction, directed the conversation, and told Berdian that she knew the diplomatic bag had been delivered. (A real coup on Marcia's part.) Honestly, there was little point in Andreas being here other than to watch and learn, which he was absolutely going to do. And to create the impression that Madeleine was frail and in need of support, though Andreas suspected Berdian might already be revisiting any initial thoughts on that matter.

"It is always good to hear from loved ones," Berdian deflected, as the servant reappeared and set infusion-pots and tiny almond-cakes on the table. "I in turn am delighted by your escape from what I gather was a very unfortunate situation."

"It was a harrowing experience," Madeleine agreed, coughing a little stagily behind her hand, then helping herself to a cake. "Especially given that, as you may be aware, I was away from Marek in the first place for the sake of my health. I was very fortunate in my rescue. Of course, I would not have wished for that at the cost of my city's wellbeing."

"But if both are achievable?" Berdian suggested.

"Well, one has apparently been achieved, indeed. But my unfortunate city is as yet still balanced, as you know, on a knife-edge."

Berdian nodded, eyes watchful.

"My dear arianet, Andreas Tigero-Head," *arianet*, that was archaic – it meant 'contracted parent of my grandchild', but Andreas hadn't heard it since he was studying old texts in the schoolroom, and he wasn't sure Berdian would know it at all, "has of course updated the Council with regards to the potential agreement he and you came to."

"Indeed," Berdian said.

"Obviously, we understand the desire of the Crescent to maintain good relationships with Teren as well as with ourselves," Andreas added. Teren didn't have much of a direct trading relationship with the Crescent, but the Archion, not to mention various other Ameten institutions, absolutely did have relationships with the Crescent banks. Although in the absence of any significant alternative, that wasn't something the Crescent banks needed to worry about all that much; the Archion, however irritable he might get, was hardly going to start keeping his gold under his mattress.

"And I know that our dear friends in the Crescent – our dear, much-valued, friends – would not wish to contribute to any *insult* to Marek." Madeleine's eyes were sharp on Berdian.

The day Selene arrived, Andreas had finally managed to convince Berdian – who, himself, wasn't terribly keen on the idea of demons threatening the city he lived in – to agree, in theory, to send a diplomatic missive from the Crescent to Ameten, conveying their concern for Marek's safety and inviolability. That was in exchange for a generous five-year discount on trading between Marek and the Crescent, banks and independent traders both; plus the completely co-incidental purchase by Andreas of a significant quantity of heavy upholstery silk that Berdian happened to have available after the market for it in the Crescent plummeted.

What Berdian hadn't been willing to commit to doing was to sending it without having had confirmation from home that they were, in theory, willing to support an independent Marek. The same problem he'd been citing since the very start of negotiations, before Selene and her demons were involved at all. Andreas knew that things moved slowly sometimes in the Crescent, but *really*.

"If it were possible to confirm that arrangement today," Madeleine went on, "we are authorised to do so, and to offer," this had been strenuously argued in the Council, but Madeleine had prevailed, "a further point on the already agreed discount. And I personally would be delighted to be able to confirm the long and important links between our two countries."

Berdian's eyes had brightened at the further discount, which brought the agreement from 'generous' to 'extremely generous', but he didn't look entirely convinced. "The situation," he said carefully, "remains somewhat uncertain, to my eyes."

Madeleine smiled at him. "Of course, one must always remember that one's knowledge may be outdated." She paused to sip her infusion. "The offer, as I say, stands for today only."

Berdian's eyelid twitched, and Andreas watched him search for a diplomatic way to find out whether the Council had a plan to get rid of Selene.

"For example," Madeleine continued, "one of my messages was from my dear niece Sophia, who is currently in Darem. I was deeply perturbed to learn from her that one of the factors some of the other Houses work with – not, I am relieved, someone *we* have ever used – was under the impression that the current negotiations meant that they did not need to pay duty at all."

Berdian twitched again as Madeleine shook her head.

"Indeed. Shocking," he agreed after a moment's silence.

The factor in question banked with Berdian's conglomerate. Berdian would be under significant pressure, as soon as the conglomerate found out – that might even have been one of the messages in his own mailbag – to make the problem go away quietly.

"Obviously I am sure that was merely a misunderstanding," Madeleine said, "which will be easy to resolve with our much-appreciated trading partners once our new arrangements are finalised. I would hate to have to make anything *significant* of it."

Madeleine ate another cake. After a few more moments of silence, she nodded to Andreas, who rose and offered her his arm.

"It was delightful to spend time with you. But if you'll excuse me, we also have an appointment with the Exurian ambassador."

"Surely you have time for another infusion," Berdian said, and Andreas' ears pricked up. The threat of the Exurians recognising them first – which would invalidate the existing agreement-in-potentia – might have worked after all. Andreas, in all honesty, hadn't expected it to.

"Oh, perhaps just a single cup," Madeleine agreed graciously, gesturing Andreas down again.

Berdian summoned the servant; just after that, a clerk hurried into the room, bowing apologetically, and handed Berdian a folded document. "If you please, sir, my apologies for the interruption, but…"

Berdian read the document soberly, folded it back again, and handed it back. "No need to apologise. You were right to bring this straight to me." He turned back to Madeleine. "I am deeply gratified to be able to let you know that I have heard from home. I would be delighted to sign the new trading terms with you today."

"Oh, that is good news. What fortunate timing." Madeleine smiled warmly at Berdian, and Andreas joined in with congratulatory agreement. It was entirely clear that Berdian had signalled for the 'sudden interruption', but appearances mattered in these things, didn't they?

The signing of the contract went off smoothly. Afterwards, Berdian said, "Of course, I would usually write immediately to my counterpart in Ameten to pass this information onto them, but unfortunately, in the current circumstances…"

"As it happens," Madeleine said sunnily, "We have a courier about to leave for Ameten. I would be delighted to take your correspondence."

Berdian looked genuinely taken aback for the first time. "A courier…"

"We have found someone able to navigate the swamps," Madeleine said. "It will take a little longer than usual, of course, but perhaps worth your sending word, in any case?"

What Madeleine hadn't mentioned – it would, after all, have made her ostentatious hobbling a little too obvious – was that she was going back to Ameten as well. Much against Marcia's very strongly expressed wishes; but it wasn't like anyone could stop Madeleine doing exactly as she pleased. And for Andreas' money, it was a good idea. Madeleine's political acumen was excellent; she had contacts in Ameten; if anyone could navigate those waters to Marek's benefit, it was her.

Litters took them both from the embassy to a somewhat down-at-heel boatyard on the edge of the south-western side of the city. Marcia was already there, with the mercenary captain, and a short man and slightly taller woman, both dressed in nondescript brown and grey heavy linens.

"Mother," Marcia greeted Madeleine. "Are you really sure…"

Madeleine, getting out of the litter by herself this time, scowled at her, and Andreas cut in before they could argue in public. "Hasn't this already been decided?" he asked peaceably, and went to take Marcia's hand. She sighed, and subsided.

"Bracken and Lenia will, I am sure, look after me perfectly well," Madeleine said. Both the man and woman gave her firm nods.

"Just – oh, Mother, just be careful, please?"

They'd had this discussion several times already in Andreas' hearing, and, he suspected, a few more times out of it. Madeleine had to be the one who went back to Ameten, to speak to the Archion. No one else had the same personal connections. No one else would have the smallest chance of getting past the doorstep, if the Archion didn't feel inclined to see them. Madeleine had strings she could pull.

And Madeleine, Andreas was sure, although she hadn't quite put it this way, very badly wanted to do *something* to contribute.

"We'll be up the river in two shakes of a goat's tail," Bracken said cheerfully. "But we'd best get on, begging your pardon. Boat's packed already, so, if you please, Ser."

Madeleine allowed herself to be handed down into the boat. The captain had a few quiet but emphatic words with Bracken and Lenia, before stepping back so they could join Madeleine in the boat: Bracken at the prow, with a short stick for fending off bits of swampland, and Lenia standing in the stern with a pole.

Marcia and Andreas watched as the boat slid off into the swampland.

"They're two of my best people," the captain offered. "Your mother couldn't be in safer hands, Ser."

"I'm sure they are," Marcia turned to smile at the captain. "My thanks for sparing them."

If Madeleine could pull this off – that, plus the diplomatic pressure, plus whatever Marcia's wretched brother was cooking up...

It all had to pull together, that was the problem. And quickly, too – and it would take time for Madeleine to reach Ameten. Time they might not have, if Selene decided to make her move. But maybe, just maybe...

Andreas sighed, and turned for home.

FIFTEEN

Tait squeezed their eyes shut against the morning light streaming through their window. Generally they were happy to have no curtains and rise with the sun, but they'd been up late the night before, sitting with Cato while he muttered and experimented. When they'd finally taken themself off to their own room sometime after midnight, Cato had still been going.

Dragging themself out of bed and going next door to investigate, they discovered that Cato was, in fact, still going.

"Tait? Didn't you just...?" He pulled aside one of his own thick curtains and recoiled backwards. "Oh fuck, it's morning. Wonderful."

There was, at least, no sign of booze; at some point during the previous evening Cato had said wistfully that he was *sure* a drink would help him think more creatively, and Tait had dissuaded him.

"Can I get you some water?" Tait offered. "Or breakfast, maybe?"

"*Fuck* breakfast," Cato said. "I've got it. I think I've actually got it."

Tait almost didn't dare hope. "You really mean it? How to deal with the spirits?"

"I think. I just need – one last test."

"Right," Tait said. "You haven't slept, I'm guessing. I am going to go downstairs, and get you a fried wrap and a ginger infusion, and while I'm gone, you are going to drink the rest of that jug of water. *Then* you can try your last test."

Cato squinted at them, rubbed his forehead, and sat down on the edge of the bed. "Fine. *Fine.* I'm not going to out-argue you, am I?"

Most of the time Cato was the stubborn one, but once in a while Tait did find it in themself to insist.

"Take some money, though," Cato added, a pathetic note in his voice. "Don't want you wasting your coin feeding me."

"I was going to," Tait assured him.

When they came back upstairs, Cato was staring thoughtfully at a row of jars with one eye mostly shut, muttering under his breath. The water jug was at least empty. Tait shoved wrap and infusion into his hand, took the water jug downstairs to refill, and came back to eat their own wrap.

"Do you need help? Or do you need to be left alone to make sure you've got what you're doing?"

Cato sucked thoughtfully at his teeth. "If you don't mind me talking at you for a bit, that would be good. Just to make sure I have it."

"So you're saying I was right to stop you," Tait said, straight-faced.

Cato bumped them with his hip. "I said that once already. Don't think you're going to trick me into saying it again. If you could see your way clear to fetching us both another couple of infusions, though…"

"Liquorice?" Tait asked, with resignation, and Cato nodded enthusiastically. He swore that liquorice was the best option for sorcery, which Tait could only hope was either untrue or Cato-specific, because Tait absolutely loathed liquorice.

When they returned, Cato was sitting on the edge of the bed, staring at his line of jars, and tapping his teeth thoughtfully.

"Right," he said. "So, all the demons out there – or spirits or whatever they are, yes, but let's use the shorthand for now, because I don't want to start thinking of them as potentially helpful types. Let's assume they're all the ones who don't much care for human morals, and are going to be even less inclined to after what the Academy sorcerers have been up to. The demons. They're all linked to a specific sorcerer. Formally bound, by force."

"Yes," Tait said.

"So if I just break the link –if I can just break the link – they'll all be on this plane and free to do whatever they want. Because the loops would still be there, in the sorcerers, unless we killed all the sorcerers as well. Which – I am assuming we would rather not do, all things being equal, and also, might be tricky. So I need to *both* break the link, *and* shove them all back through again. Like we did with Hira. But Beckett isn't strong enough to do it all at once, and it has to be all at once, so they haven't time to pull it together and start hitting back. They can't get a warning. We haven't got force of numbers – we *really* haven't got force of numbers – so we need force of surprise." Cato scrubbed at his face. "And I'm saying, like we did with Hira, but as well as that only being one lousy demon, even then we only managed that using the extra link through you, and a lot of power, because of the strong link to Marek through," he paused, minutely, "my sister."

"Right." Tait nodded.

"Which is, it has turned out, the central problem. Apart from the numbers issue, this time around, we have only one of those things – the link to Marek. Lots of ways to get that. Last time we were trying to keep it all secret, but this time everyone knows. Lots of volunteers."

"But no link to the demons."

"Exactly. And perhaps not enough power, but that's a problem for further down the line. If I could find a way to tap into the link of just one demon, that would be a good start." He took a breath. "But that still leaves the problem of, what happens once the link is broken? Where do they go? Because, right, I've been thinking about it from the wrong angle. The spirits are bound, and I was thinking, bound to the person, so that they can always be summoned. A bit like how Beckett is bound to Marek – Beckett can come and go as they please, between the planes, but they're always tied to Marek, in this plane. And in their case they've made a particular commitment to magic here, but that's not relevant right now. The point is, these spirits, they're bound to the sorcerer right enough, but it's not for a repeated summoning – it's like when I bind a spirit to an object that then exists in-between. *So* part of the sorcerer then exists in-between too, which is the weird bit. But the spirits can't go anywhere, in either plane, while the binding is active, without permission. It actually works a lot like the trick I do except that they weren't given a choice, and they can't extract themselves from it."

"Your spirits could extract themselves?" Tait asked.

"Yes, but only to go back into their own plane, not to come into this one. For obvious reasons, and not only the Beckett-related one."

"So how can we change these bindings to that sort?"

"Is exactly the question I have been asking," Cato agreed. "Because given the choice, I reckon they'll all scarper straight off, but we don't want them to have the option to come over here and wreak some havoc. Spirits are quite keen on life-force, after all. Obviously, I wouldn't care much if they did the havoc-wreaking entirely on the idiots who summoned and bound them, but I really don't think we want to count on that, plus it would upset Beckett."

"And you think you've found a way of doing that?" Tait asked. "Changing the bindings?"

"Maybe. I hope. The problem is…right. We need to," Cato gestured, sliding one hand inside his other fist, "get inside the bindings and install a back door. An escape route."

"How?" Tait didn't understand how you could possibly get into someone else's magic that way.

"By stepping into the space in-between," Cato said. "Things look different there. I've been experimenting and I can – I think – open up the weave of it, kind of, and put in the piece of magic I use to give a spirit an exit route. But I'm going to need to test it properly."

Tait was sure they could see, now, where this was going, and they badly wanted to say no. "Cato…"

Cato blinked at them. "What? No, I don't want you to do it, don't worry."

The relief almost took Tait out at the knees, and Cato took their hand comfortingly.

"I'm sorry. I should have been clearer. I just want you to – spot me, I guess. In case I manage to tangle myself up and I can't get free."

"Of course," Tait said immediately. "I mean, you'll have to explain how I'd break you out."

"You'd get Reb and get her to talk to Beckett," Cato said promptly. "Because honestly, I'm not sure *I* know, if I can't do it the way I'm planning. I wouldn't want you to handle it on your own. Just, I need someone to get help if I'm stuck. All right?" He looked anxiously up at Tait.

"Of course," Tait said again. They really hoped Cato didn't get stuck.

"I can't wait until I've worked it out further, or more incrementally, or whatever," Cato said, grimacing, "which is what I would *like* to do, because I don't know if you've really realised this, and for the love of fuck, don't tell Beckett, but if that lot out there get bored of sitting around with their thumbs up their arses and actually attack, we're screwed. You remember what happened with just one. This is *lots*. There's no way Beckett can hold out against a concerted push. Honestly, I don't know why they haven't gone for it already."

"Reb said Marcia thinks Selene would rather everything was resolved peacefully."

"Right. And she thinks that'll *happen*?" Cato sounded incredulous.

"She's been making approaches to some of the Houses and the Guilds." Tait shrugged. "Apparently Marcia thought it wouldn't work, but Reb thought some of the others – she mentioned Andreas, I think, and Daril – are less certain."

"Daril's probably right." Cato sounded absent. "He's always out for the main chance, that one, and he understands how other people are. Marcia's too starry-eyed, still, despite everything. Right, well, that makes sense. Selene thinks she can do it all nicely, avoid ructions, hand the city back all gift-wrapped to the Archion on his deathbed, get the nod to take over. In which case, sending in the demons to take everything apart wouldn't be ideal. Bad for business."

There was a tightness in his shoulders when he mentioned Marcia that wasn't just about having been up all night. Tait themself still wasn't feeling all that happy with Marcia. Fine, Marcia was pregnant, she was under a lot of pressure, of course she wanted to save her mother. But it was hard to think kindly of Madeleine, given what she'd done to Cato. And Marcia must have known how he would feel about her request.

And yet – weren't they all doing things they didn't want to, right now? Because they were necessary? And it was Tait, in the end, had saved Madeleine. They just – hadn't asked Cato to do anything about it.

"It's already bad for business," they said. "All the Salinas ships leaving."

Cato flapped a hand. "Not our problem. Demons are our problem. And my point is, whatever Selene's very sensible strategy is, if they know we're trying to get rid of their alternative strategy, the hammer they've got waiting in the wings, then she is going to react. Badly. If I go in and do this, it has to work, and it has to work first time. Which means…"

"Which means you need to test it," Tait said. "I get it, honestly." They smiled at Cato. "Stop explaining, and get on with it."

It wasn't the most interesting thing to watch, except that Tait knew more, now, about Marek magic, and could see in what ways what Cato was doing diverged from what was usual.

"I can't ask Beckett to help with any of this," Cato said in explanation, frowning down at the way he was twisting things together. "Other than the kick to get it started. It all needs to be outside this plane altogether, once I'm done, and that means outside the city, and that means, not something Beckett can – hmm. Access. Power. Both of those, maybe."

Apparently it had taken Cato a while to work out how to create the loop without also attracting spirits to come and investigate – "Usually that's a feature, not a failure," – but eventually he was holding a small wooden box just above his hand, passing his fingers through it. "Here but not here," he said with satisfaction. "Now, then." He concentrated, and stepped back into the circle he'd created. From where Tait was, he looked translucent, and left a shimmer behind when he moved, as thought Tait was seeing a trail, the way a bright torch left a trail of light behind it, relics of your eye's vision.

Cato had a piece of string in one hand, wrapped around his fingers, and the box in another. Slowly, leaving those trails as he moved, he brought the two of them together. There was a flash of light, and the string vanished. Cato seemed to be shaking his hand; but he stepped backwards, out of the circle, and when Tait could see his face again, his expression was victorious.

"Snapped my hand like nobody's business," he said, "but it worked."

"Now do you want me to..." Tait asked, reluctantly.

"No. Now I want to know if it works with a spirit in it." Cato grimaced. "I'm really not at all sure Yorick's going to go for it. But all I can do is ask."

Yorick, when they showed up, looked, as far as Tait could tell, deeply unimpressed with the idea. Both Cato and Yorick were back within the circle, and Tait couldn't hear anything; could just see Cato gesturing, almost pleading, and Yorick standing well back. At one point, Cato turned to look at Tait, then turned back again, saying something fiercely to Yorick; Tait could tell by Cato's body language.

Eventually, however, Cato stepped out of the circle; but Yorick was still in there.

"Will they do it?" Tait asked.

"Not without surety of some sort." Cato looked like he'd bitten into sourfruit.

"That seems not unreasonable," Tait said. "I mean, trapping themself, based on only your word..."

"Well. Maybe. The problem is, the only surety they'll accept is you."

Tait blinked at him. "Me?"

"They want you to go in there with them. That way, they say, they'll know I'll let them out."

"Oh." Tait considered the matter. "Well, that's all right, isn't it? You were in that in-between space yourself just now, so it's safe."

"But what if I can't do it? What if I can't put the back-door in?"

"Then you'll let us out again?" Tait didn't understand what Cato was worried about.

"What if I can't?"

Tait smiled at him. "I trust you."

"You shouldn't."

"I believe in your abilities," Tait said, with a shrug. "If you hadn't been able to get rid of that demon last year, I'd have been dead anyway. You got me out of that, and that wasn't even your magic. You'll get me out of this." It seemed obvious to Tait. They didn't understand why Cato was balking.

"Shit." Cato looked down, then back up at them. "You are far better than I deserve, you know that? Right. Let's do it."

The amazing thing was, it worked. Not that Tait had had a particularly enjoyable time, trapped in there with Yorick. Yorick was pleasant enough, but it was a small space, and really, Tait didn't have *any* positive associations with being that close to a spirit. But it was only a brief moment before Cato successfully broke the bond.

"That's it, then," Cato said, once it was all untangled again. "I just need to do that. Twelve times. Very fast."

"Cato," Tait said, "Not half a chime ago you were telling me how we needed to have the element of surprise, because we haven't got the numbers. If you're going one at a time, they are definitely going to notice."

Cato looked stubborn. "I can do it. I told Reb already, she needed to get the Council to sort out some kind of tactical – something. An ambush, a trap, I don't know. Get those soldiers to do something useful."

"Or," Tait suggested, "you could show the rest of us how to do it. You, me, Reb, Jonas, Alyssa. That's five. You said Hira offered to help, didn't you? Six. That's two each." It was still going to be difficult for the second round, even if the first worked. But there was no way Cato could do this twelve times. He looked tired already.

"Oh, fine," Cato conceded, more easily than Tait would have guessed.

"If I can help further?" Yorick offered. "I would rather my compatriots were free than otherwise."

"They'll all need to practice," Cato said apologetically, "so, if you don't mind, later today, once I've explained?"

"Of course," Yorick said graciously, and winked out.

Cato shut the circle down. "Well then. Let's go talk to Reb and get this show on the road."

Marcia was on her way down the main stairs when the messenger arrived at the door, panting hard like they'd been running – enough that she could hear it in their voice all the way from the first-floor landing. She heard *urgent*, and came round the turn of the staircase to see a piece of paper being handed over and the footman reaching for the box of coins kept in the hallway; deliveries came to the kitchen door, messengers to the front.

"A message?" she demanded, navigating the last step awkwardly, one foot at a time, as her pelvis gave a threatening twinge.

"One for Fereno-Heir personal, one for the House," the messenger said. He had a round cheerful face, and she had the vague sense she recognised him. She took the folded papers from the footman, nodded thanks to the messenger, and took the messages into the small parlour.

Both in the same hand, and scrawled rapidly. Captain Anna's writing, if she wasn't mistaken. Her stomach lurched. She opened the one to the House first.

> *Heads, Heirs, Guildwardens, Council members all,*

it began.

Not the best of starts.

> *It is my duty to inform you that Teren appears to be preparing to move against us. As yet I cannot estimate when, or whether something specific is informing their decision. We will hold as long as we can.*
>
> *Captain Anna Barcola*

'As long as we can' wouldn't be all that long, Marcia knew. Not against demons. Reb had said they had a plan, or the start of one. Was that ready yet? And why was Selene moving now? What could have happened? Was Beckett…weakening, perhaps? Already? And yet, it had been days, hadn't it? Maybe it was of more note that this hadn't happened sooner.

She ripped at the second message, tearing the paper under the seal, the charcoal of the messenger's mark coming off on her fingers.

> Fereno-Heir – I think something magic is happening. They are pushing across the yard, beyond what I was told was the city boundary in the magical sense. Not far as yet, but they have not done that before. I have sent to Sorcerer Reb, but wanted you to know too. Cpt Anna.

The boundary was moving. Chills ran up Marcia's spine. That had to mean that Beckett was weakening, the way Reb had said would have to happen, eventually, if Selene's sorcerers began to push.

And whilst Captain Anna wasn't wrong that putting the word 'magic' in the one directed to the whole Council wouldn't have helped, the Council had to know what was happening. This couldn't wait.

There was a knock on the door, before the footman, looking harried, reappeared. He was halfway through "Ser, apologies…" when he was pushed aside, and Reb, with Alyssa just on her heels, barrelled past him.

"It's fine," Marcia assured him, before Reb shut the door almost in his face. Which wasn't like her.

"We've got a problem," Reb said.

"Selene's moving. I know."

"That's not the problem. Well, it is, but it's not the crucial point." She swallowed, setting her jaw. "Beckett's failing."

Marcia sat down heavily. "Shit." She realised she'd been desperately hoping that Captain Anna had been wrong, somehow. "Captain Anna says the boundary's moving."

"Yes, well…" Reb looked tired; almost overwhelmed.

"You want to know *why* Beckett's failing?" Alyssa

247

interrupted. "I worked it out, because the rest of you can't see beyond your own bloody noses." She sounded incensed. More than incensed.

"Alyssa," Reb said, wearily, but not as strenuously as she might once have done.

"The city, Beckett says, is divided. And Reb here was all about, hmm, the river? Some people wanting to fight, some not? Nah. Beckett doesn't care about the river, and the other's too complicated, too recent. What Beckett cares about is that there's us, down there distributing food and looking after each other, and you, up here, refusing to listen to us, refusing to let us take part in decisions. Ignoring us. Splitting the city apart. And it's splitting Beckett apart too."

It made more sense than she wanted to accept, and Marcia hated that it hadn't occurred to her before now. Except...

"But it's always been like that," she said. "Isn't that your point?"

Alyssa shrugged. "I'm guessing, it hasn't always been like that in the face of a threat like this. Or when Beckett is pulling as much power as this."

Marcia looked over at Reb.

"She's right," Reb said, wearily. "I don't entirely understand it, but Beckett was pretty clear, once we managed to ask the right questions. And we've got, by my reckoning, a couple of hours left at the most. Selene must know, too, that things are weakening; you can feel it. Well. We can feel it. I'm guessing there's a fair chance Selene's sorcerers can, or if not them themselves, their demons."

"Can you move against them? Right now?" Marcia demanded.

Reb shook her head. "I sent to Cato again, before I came over here, but haven't heard. He said *nearly*, last time we spoke, but – nearly's not enough."

"We need more time." Marcia yanked at the ends of her hair. "If we can do something to unite the city – will that work? To give Cato," saying his name made her stomach hurt that they were still at odds, "more time?"

"Maybe," Reb said. She didn't sound all that hopeful. "But if we don't, then…"

"We're all definitely fucked," Alyssa finished when Reb trailed off. "But either way – isn't this exactly what you claimed you wanted?" She stared, challenging, at Marcia. "All this softly-softly we-can-change-things stuff you were saying just *yesterday*."

"I haven't had *time*!" Marcia protested. "Don't tell me you're having a go at me because I'm trying to prioritise getting rid of the bloody *invasion* that's about to happen."

"Fine, whatever. Good news! It isn't an either-or. Time to put your money where your mouth is."

"Enough," Reb cut in. "We don't have time for you two to argue. Beckett said: you need to call a Council meeting. Up at the top of Marekhill, at the statue. That's where Beckett's strongest. Because Alyssa's right. Your Council need to talk to her lot. And Beckett needs to talk to everyone. Right now."

"Oh *shit*," Marcia said, and grabbed for paper.

SIXTEEN

The air felt strange as Marcia walked up the Hill towards Marekhill Park. It felt like there was a storm coming, except that the sky was a cloudless spring blue; it felt oppressive like a humid summer day, except that it was still only early spring and the sun wasn't warm enough to go without a shawl. The servants had seemed ill-at-ease as they brought breakfast; and half of the usual things were missing. There were rolls, but no pastries; only one sort of infusion. *Hard to get things*, had been the word passed up from the – apparently very unhappy – cook. And yet somehow it felt worse than only ('only') limited supplies.

She passed the Council Chamber, and kept going, up the loop of the road that led to Marekhill Park itself, on the top of Marekhill above all Thirteen Houses. Some of the trees were beginning to show the fuzz of their first spring foliage; others were still bare. Crocuses and the first daffodils showed in the grass to either side of the path. It should have been a beautiful spring day, but the air was entirely still, and that oppressive sense of something *wrong* was getting steadily stronger as she climbed.

A couple of people wrapped in shawls hurried past her, and Marcia overheard their conversation.

"No one in Marek Square at all, not even one infusion-seller, and maybe that you'd understand, but the fountain? Full of feathers."

"I found my good luck charm on the floor this morning," the other replied, "shredded into pieces."

The air felt thicker by the minute, harder to breathe. She wasn't imagining this. This was what it felt like when Marek's cityangel was failing.

Right at the top of the Hill was the statue where Beckett had wanted people to meet. The bronze figures of the founders of the city, Rufus Marek and Eli Beckett (after whom Beckett had chosen to name themself, when they decided they wanted a human name), looked out towards the sea, more purple and yellow crocuses blooming around their feet. According to Beckett, this was where they had made the covenant, agreeing to trade power for power. Marcia, more out of breath than she was happy with, her ears ringing slightly, looked around. She was early, but a few folk were here already – mostly lower city, although Gil was deep in conversation with Daril and Piath on the other side of the statue. Daril looked drawn and shaky, as though he hadn't slept.

With a surge of grateful relief, Marcia saw Reb leaning against a tree, and went over to her.

"Can you feel it?" she asked.

Reb nodded grimly. "Been feeling it for a while. More worrying that you can too now." She meant, because Marcia had no magical power at all. She looked over to the other side of the Hill, and her eyebrows went up. "Huh."

Marcia looked in the same direction, and saw Tait arriving. She hadn't expected them – and as they spotted Reb and made their way across the grass, Reb leaving Marcia to walk swiftly towards them, Marcia realised with a sudden lurch in her guts that this might be a message from Cato. Good news or bad? She was too far away to hear the conversation, and couldn't go over to join in. Reb was frowning deeply as she listened, then nodded sharply and turned away, making her way back to Marcia with Tait following.

"Cato's found a solution," she said, and Marcia's heart, and hope, soared, then settled again. There was relief in Reb's expression, but also concern. "We all need to learn it, though, and then we need to power it, and it's going to mean some kind of trap…"

"Haran-Head has been thinking about that," Marcia assured her. "But – you need time, you mean."

"Cato can explain it," Tait broke in, "but not immediately, and Reb says she needs to be here right now, she can't come straight down…"

"And you can feel it," Reb said. It wasn't a question. Tait's shoulders hunched. "This is good, and it's a way out, but it's not enough, we can't move quickly enough, to make this," she gestured around the Hill, "any less necessary. Not from what Beckett said. And even if we could move right now, we'll need power…"

"And that means a united city," Marcia finished. "But if we can pull this together…"

"Then we can get rid of the demons," Reb said. "Or – we have a plan, anyway. The best hope we can get, I think."

"Well then." Marcia turned to look at the people arriving up into the park, people from all across Marek, eyeing one another suspiciously. "I suppose we'd better hope this works."

She was almost surprised that everyone was willing to move this quickly; maybe she did have more pull, still than she thought. Or maybe the sense of *wrong* that was settling over the city was enough to drive everyone else, too. It helped that the Houses, who were the slowest moving, didn't have that far to come to the park on the top of Marekhill; evidently Alyssa had been effective in rallying the radicals and giving them to understand how urgent the situation was. (Plus, the lower city didn't need to be convinced about the magical aspect). The Guildwardens in the end were the last to arrive; and then they all stood, around the statue, eyeing one another. Marcia turned to look down the Hill; there was Marek Square at the bottom, and the curve of the river, and the square of the barge-yard. Too distant to see what was happening down there. She had to hope that they were still in time; that Beckett's strength held. For now.

"I've brought you here," she said, then stopped. Her voice sounded thin in her own ears despite the fact that the air was entirely still; no wind to carry her words away. She tried again, louder. "I've brought you here because Marek is at imminent risk. I've heard people talking about strange things this morning – the fountain in Marek Square full of feathers," several people muttered agreement, "charms falling apart. And you must all feel the –" she hesitated, unsure what to say, but she couldn't allow herself to pause for long. "The wrong. It feels *wrong*. The cityangel has been holding the demons off, but they are losing power. They will fail, soon. The covenant," she gestured at the statue which symbolised the founding of the city and the covenant made with the then-nameless cityangel, "should protect us. But our own distrust of one another, our fighting –"

"Nonsense," Athitol-Head interrupted at full volume. "Cityangel – nonsense. The weather is strange today, I'll give you that, but it's nothing to do with the *cityangel*. And the *threat* that Teren poses – ridiculous. All we need to do is to go and tell the former Lieutenant that we are willing to engage in discussion, and…"

Loud and heated expressions of disagreement broke out across the park; not only, Marcia was pleased to see, from the lower city group.

"And if you believe that," Daril snapped at Athitol-Head, "I've half a ship of Crescent rubies you might be interested in."

Athitol-Head, cheeks flushing dark, was about to answer, when Marcia cut in more loudly. "The sorcerers have a solution," she shouted, projecting as forcefully as she could with the baby pushing into the bottom of her lungs, and was relieved when the hubbub died down. "The sorcerers have a solution. They can get rid of Selene, and her demons. But they need time, and they need power. Right now we have neither. The cityangel is struggling, because the city is divided." She gestured to one side of her, where the Houses stood, and to the other, where the lower city groups stood; the Guilds filling the space between them on the other side of the statue. "The city is divided, and the cityangel's power fails. That's what we're all feeling. And to get rid of Teren, that's what we need to fix." She paused. "So. We are all here, and we *can* fix this. I suggest that we begin by talking over the Petition presented at New Year…"

"Well," Pedeli-Head cut in. "Isn't it *most* peculiar that

the 'cityangel' just happens to be in favour of *your* radical ideas about the lower city, and your ridiculous arguments against those who should be your closest collaborators." An unusual view of the relationship between the Houses. "You are taking advantage once again of your mother's absence…"

There was a rising hubbub among the lower city radicals – Marcia recognised one of them as Jeres Arianden who'd been responsible for managing the Teren refugee influx – and some of the Guildmembers.

"Excuse me," Andreas cut in, "but it is hardly only Marcia…"

There was a sudden sense of immense pressure. Andreas stopped with his mouth half-open. The air felt soup-thick, and Marcia's heartbeat pounded in her ears. Around them, all the trees were bending inwards, towards this space at the top of the park, towards the statue right at its peak. A hard silence descended across the park; even the birds suddenly quiet.

The statue shimmered, rainbow colours that hurt Marcia's eyes. And then Beckett was there. They didn't look the way Marcia usually saw them; they were far less human-seeming than usual, shimmering the same way the statue had, larger than the statue, somehow occupying the same space as it. Reb had spoken of Beckett seeming to *glow* in a certain way, but Marcia couldn't usually see that. Right now, she could.

Everyone swayed backwards at the same time; some people even retreated a couple of rapid steps, then seemed to stop against their will.

Well. This was one way to resolve the 'magic is a superstition' issue.

"I cannot hold the city if the city does not hold itself," Beckett said, and the force of their words was enough to make Marcia hunch her shoulders, one hand going protectively to her belly. "Resolve your problems, or I will be gone, and the demons will be here, and you will all most deeply regret it."

Blunt and to the point; backed by more power and more

sense of *something else* than Marcia had ever felt in her life. And yet – would anyone listen?

But, looking around, she realised that they were. They were all listening, and they were all taking it seriously. Possibly only because they were all freaked out about the same amount, and that, in itself, linked them.

Possibly because of Beckett's influence. She decided not to think too hard about that; whatever was happening, it was needed, right now, and that would just have to do.

"How long?" Warden Zeril of the Woodworkers demanded. He was uncle to Jeres, Marcia remembered. She looked at the Guildwardens again, and noticed, this time, a shift in how they were grouped. Hagadath was there, but towards the back, not standing forward and speaking on their behalf. It was Zeril, and Ilana, who were to the front. She clutched that to herself as a positive sign.

Beckett did something that wasn't quite a shrug. Their form rippled in a way that had nothing to do with the wind that wasn't blowing. "An hour. Perhaps."

"There isn't time to negotiate properly," Alyssa said, bitterly; she'd come round to stand with Reb, and the two of them were close enough for Marcia to overhear. "We're going to get rolled right over."

"We will have to make enough arrangements to feel bound to one another, then," Jeres said, evidently having overheard as well. She stepped forward. "Let us begin with the Petition."

☺ ☺

In Alyssa's opinion, this was still all raging goatshit. She sat on a bench a little away from where the negotiations were – somewhat heatedly, from the look of it – going on by the statue, and scowled impartially around. It wasn't like the Council were going to offer them anything like what they should be getting. It wasn't, for example, like the Council were about to quit their positions, open up their ridiculously sized houses – having walked right past them on the way up here, the utter waste of space was very fresh in her mind – to the rest of the city and share their income, built on the back of the city as a whole, *with* the city as a whole.

But, she supposed, they might get something. In this specific moment, with this specific set of pressures, they might get something that would otherwise take years of sweat. And she'd decided already, however reluctantly, that she wasn't quite prepared to turn down 'something' on the grounds that it wasn't 'everything'.

Unlike, say, Simeon, who was making his way over to her right now, around the edge of the crowd that had gathered about a centre of the Council, Jeres, and a couple of people from the Parliament. Tey, on crutches still, had needed help getting up here – and Alyssa would be critical about the location, except that it was Beckett's call and she wasn't about to argue with Beckett about their needs – but was facilitating the discussion together with the Council's Reader. That did at least show a willingness to co-operate on the part of the Reader.

"It's crap," Simeon said, and Alyssa made an agreeing noise. "It's arrant crap, and we should walk out right now."

"And the cityangel can't keep the demons out any more and we all die," Alyssa said. "Good plan. I like it. Let's go."

Simeon scowled at her. "The cityangel's exaggerating." He didn't sound all that sure. "Or, like, on their side."

"No," Alyssa said. "I mean, I'd like to believe that too, because it would be much more comfortable. But unfortunately, I am in a position to tell you – you do remember I'm a sorcerer? – that the cityangel is not exaggerating, that the demons are not exaggerated, and that we have to find some way of coming to some form of agreement with those Marekhill shitheads, before we all get ripped apart. Or maybe we survive – plenty of folk will, for sure – to be taken over by Teren. You've printed enough about what's been happening in Ameten. Do you fancy that? Can't imagine it'll be good news for either of us, my friend."

Simeon looked over at her. Whatever he saw in her face must have convinced him, because he made a harrumphing noise, and settled next to her, arms folded, on the bench.

"Which," she added after a moment's silence, "is why I'm staying out of it."

"You don't want to shift things to our side?"

"I'm not capable of doing all the compromising that I know for a fact is going on over there, and I'm not willing to go in and put my point of view and steer it off course because, as previously mentioned, I don't want lots of people to die." She sighed. "I'll be pulled in for some kind of magic bullshit in the near future too, so I might as well save my energy for that."

Whatever Cato had come up with, assuming Tait had the right of it; it sounded like it was going to be tough on all of them. *If* they could buy enough time, here and now, to be able to implement it.

Simeon, who wasn't entirely comfortable with magic, shifted awkwardly in his seat, but didn't contradict her about her ability to compromise. "They've secured agreement that the Parliament can exist, and all the prosecutions are to be dropped," he offered.

Which had been high on everyone's list – including, to be fair, the Petitioners who hadn't even taken part – but it was still a pleasant surprise to Alyssa.

"That was fairly easy," Simeon continued. "The business with the warehouses took a bit longer. There's some Guild types were very arsey about it. Eventually Jeres got them to agree that we can look after them for now, and there'll be a managed return once the Terens are gone. And no prosecutions there either."

"Right. So what're they on now?"

"Participation, of course. The Petition, basically."

"So, I'm guessing that 'the Council get disbanded and the Parliament take over' isn't part of the terms of negotiation?" Alyssa said dryly.

Simeon snorted. "Yeah, well, agreeing Jeres to front it, what did we expect?" He muttered something about 'abandoning the whole thing', which Alyssa chose to ignore. She'd made her point already.

"Something's better than nothing," she said, eventually. "I suppose. Don't have to like it, mind." She looked over at him and sighed. "We'll keep fighting, eh? Once we're all safe again. No point in securing political power over a pile of rubble and a lot of corpses. And – like I said. Isn't like Teren would be keen to share."

That was one of the really uncomfortable things Alyssa had had to think about lately. The Council shouldn't be where they were. Marek wasn't set up fairly. None of this was how she wanted it to be.

But. She'd listened to the refugees. If she were in Teren, she'd likely be dead by now. Or run downriver, maybe, if she were lucky. And from here, there wouldn't be many options for her to run again. Nor the folks who'd come here, to Marek, for safety. Whatever else happened, they couldn't let Teren in. And that meant the Council had the power in these negotiations, when it came right down to it. She was certain they knew it, too.

"Come on," she said to Simeon. "Let's go find out how they're getting on."

She levered herself up off the bench, and went close enough to the crowd to hear.

The wretched Daril Leandra-Head – she wondered how many other people recognised him from his 'secret, only not' appearances at the Bucket – was speaking.

"We have to find an agreement, here and now," he was saying, and Alyssa rolled her eyes. Yes, fine, the lower city needed to know their place, roll over and agree to do what the Council wanted. "We, the Council," he went on, "must listen to the rest of the city. We have imposed ourselves on them for too long. Now, if ever, we must make a change."

Her eyebrows went up. That wasn't quite what she'd expected. Maybe his visits to the Bucket hadn't been entirely insincere. She saw Marcia, somewhere on the Council side of the crowd behind him, listening with a cynical twist to her mouth. Then again, perhaps there was some kind of internal Marekhill politics going on here that wasn't obvious to Alyssa. Marcia had certainly suggested as much when they spoke, and it wasn't like Alyssa was particularly inclined to trust anyone from the Hill. On the one hand, perhaps she didn't care, if Daril was arguing for their side. On the other hand, perhaps he had a long game that wasn't in the lower city's interests.

On the other other hand – they were on a deadline here.

"We have a deadline," Daril said, and there was a murmur of agreement through the crowd.

"We cannot possibly," another House-Head spoke up, sounding querulous, "agree the detail of a total reorganisation of Marek's politics, here on Marekhill at the drop of a hat."

"No," someone else, quiet-voiced, another Marekhill accent, said, "but we can agree some kind of premise, can we not?"

"A commitment to involving voices from the lower city in the Council," Jeres jumped in. "In what way? That alone would hardly be sufficient to create the unity the cityangel told us they need."

At least Jeres was making *some* effort to pin things down.

Beckett reappeared next to Jeres, who nearly jumped out of her skin.

"The boundary will fall soon," they announced. They looked, to Alyssa, pale somehow beyond the fact of their customarily pale skin; drawn, perhaps, their shape odd on the eyes too and that glow of magic only a flicker.

"We must have an agreement," Daril said, urgently. He was staring at the cityangel. Could Daril too see that glow? Marekhill types weren't supposed to have magic. "We must find *something* to settle on, here and now."

"The Council agrees," the quiet-voiced one said, "to involve voices from the lower city in our deliberations in future. The details to be arranged once the city is safe."

"Jyrithi-Head, with respect, it is not enough," Jeres repeated, stubborn, and Alyssa was caught between applauding her and horror at the possible consequences.

"Not specific enough. At least one person from the lower city to have voting rights in Council."

"I cannot countenance voting rights!" someone from the Council burst out. Ah. Athitol-Head. Of course.

"Speaking rights," Jyrithi-Head countered.

Athitol-Head subsided, due partly, it seemed, to Andreas speaking urgently and quietly to her.

Jeres hesitated. "That as a *minimum*. Details to be agreed."

Jyrithi-Head turned to the Reader and requested a vote. It would pass, then; Jyrithi-Head clearly wasn't the sort to move to a vote they didn't think they'd win. Alyssa was concentrating instead on Jeres and Tey, who'd turned to those on their side of the crowd.

It wasn't the way to make a decision that affected the whole of Marek; Alyssa was horribly aware of that. But time was pressing; she could feel it now even absent Beckett, something pulling at her magic-sense. And – this was a minimum. They could push for more, get more people involved, once Beckett was safe and the Terens gone. This wasn't the end.

From the faces around her, Alyssa knew that everyone was thinking much the same. It wasn't enough; and yet, here and now, it had to be.

Tey was speaking. "I know this isn't ideal. But. Can we have an agreement? Does anyone wish to prevent it?"

"Bearing in mind," Jeres put in, "that there are demons on the move."

Tey scowled at her. "Does anyone," he said more loudly, "wish to prevent it?"

There was a lot of muttering, but no one moved. Tey turned back to the Reader. "I believe we can agree to that. Can the Council?"

The Reader was already halfway through conducting their vote. A couple of the Heads actually voted against, which was some kind of tremendous goatshit, but apparently wasn't enough to prevent agreement.

"We are agreed," Tey and the Reader announced, at the same time, and Alyssa *felt* something slamming together.

She saw the same shock on Reb's face as she moved around the crowd towards Alyssa, and Tait, in Reb's wake, blinking wide-eyed.

Beckett had reappeared again, looking – to Alyssa's enormous relief – more solid than they had. "It will do," they announced. "For now." They disappeared, the same instantaneous way they'd arrived. (They always arrived. Possibly at some point Alyssa would get used to it.)

"I guess it's time, then," Reb said. "Alyssa, Tait, come with me. We need to find Cato, and Jonas. Haran-Head is going to speak to Captain Anna about setting up a trap. First thing tomorrow, he suggested, so we have time to learn this trick of Cato's." She cast a glance up at the sun, now past its noon zenith. "I'm going to find him. Someone else needs to speak to Captain Anna. And you," she pinned Marcia, who had come up to their group from the other side of the crowd, with a hard glare, "are going to stay right here – or even better, at home – and wait."

Marcia looked like she wanted to argue, but she pressed her lips together and nodded.

Better hope all of this would be good enough. Or they were all fucked anyway.

SEVENTEEN

Jonas reached the bottom of Cato's steps at a run. He'd been resting in Marek Square, waiting for a message to be needed, when he'd felt a weird kind of *something* from Beckett; then the flicker hit. It had been – intense. Well, right now, everything seemed intense. Like the fact that if Cato couldn't fix all of this, the seas wouldn't be safe for shipping any more, from what the water-elemental had said. He'd *told* Cato and Reb that, even, yesterday after he'd delivered the mail to Kia, but it didn't seem to bother them as much as it did him. It ought to; Marek was only the way it was because it was a trading city. They needed the Salinas just as much as the Salinas needed their ships.

That was true for Teren as well, of course, but he doubted Selene would be open to that argument even if he could reach her.

In any case. He didn't even know if Cato would be in, but it seemed like the best place to start. He wasn't about to try to fix this by himself. He'd learnt *that* lesson, for certain.

He reached the top of the stairs at almost exactly the moment Cato's door opened. Cato was dressed for going out, mouth grim; Tait, at his shoulder, looked properly scared.

"Jonas? Good. We need to get moving. I've done it. Got a solution. You all need to learn it, it's going to be tricky, but, Reb just sent Tait –" He stopped and stared at Jonas. "What is it? What's wrong?"

"I had a flicker," Jonas said, heart sinking even more than it already had. But surely that Teren sorcerer wouldn't *know* Cato's solution? "That sorcerer. The Teren one. With the demon, and Tait, you remember? I saw him with Selene. Outside. At the barge-yard. It seemed important."

"Hira?" Cato demanded. "Are you sure?"

Jonas nodded. "I guess he came down from Teren?"

"No," Cato said, grimly. "He did not. What he did was, he screwed Selene over after my sister screwed him over, claimed sanctuary here a couple of months back. Then just this week he helped me work out what we're about to do. And I just had him over here, showing him what I'd planned so he could *help*. He did it, even, right in front of me. I thought...Stupid. *Stupid*. Because your flicker is quite obviously him going to tell Selene all about it. *Fuck*." He hit the wall with his hand, hard, and both Tait and Jonas flinched at the bang.

"Flicker?" Tait said. "What?"

Jonas realised he'd just given his secret away, again, assuming Tait hadn't worked it out during everything with the floods. He hadn't time to worry about it. Or to explain to Tait, just now. "I came as fast as I could," he said to Cato. "The time lag isn't – sometimes it's further away than others. So maybe..."

"Maybe there's still time," Cato finished. "Right. Let's go. Wait."

He went back into the room and scrabbled under the bed, pulling out a chest. He crouched over it with his back to Jonas, so Jonas couldn't quite see what he was fetching, but from Cato's body language as he stowed whatever-it-was about his person, Jonas was willing to bet that it was weapons of some sort. Seemed excessive, if you could apply magic, but on the other hand, in Jonas' experience, a sharp blade at the right moment could really focus someone's attention.

"Flickers?" Tait said again. "What are we doing?"

"Jonas sees the future sometimes," Cato said, slamming the door behind him and gesturing the wards up. "On this occasion, he's seeing Hira screwing us over. But if we move fast, we might be able to stop him." He was already halfway down the stairs.

"Huh," Tait said, but they seemed accepting enough. Just as well; Jonas didn't have time or energy to go into detailed explanations right now.

"I don't usually have as long as that," Jonas said, miserably, following Cato.

"But sometimes you do, and it's worth a go. And then I can kick the shit out of him for even thinking about it, and then kick the shit out of him some more just for fucking fun."

Right at this precise moment, Jonas didn't have any doubt at all that Cato would manage exactly what he was threatening.

"How could I have trusted him?"

"You weren't to know," Tait said quietly, miserably. "I thought he wanted to help, too, when you told me about it. He's in Marek now. Why would he…?"

"You're the trusting one. I should know better." Cato shook his head.

They made it to the Keys, where apparently Cato had found Hira before, in record time; Cato was moving faster than Jonas would have believed him capable of. The bartender said she hadn't seen him that day. "He's staying over the road, though, I think. The one with the wooden fish on the door."

Cato took the easy approach to locating the correct room in a squats walk-up, and banged on the first door he came to. The woman who opened it looked initially irritated, then saw Cato's expression and became immediately more co-operative. She'd seen Hira pass the window, just a few minutes ago.

"With a bag," she added. "Could have been all his stuff, could not. *I'm* not one to spy on my neighbours." She sniffed and shut her door with a bang.

Tait had already gone upstairs to look at the room she'd said was Hira's; they came back down shaking their head. "Door was open. Nothing there save some empty bottles."

"*Fuck*," Cato said. "Do we run for the barge-yard, then?"

"It'll be too late," Jonas said. He could feel the certainty of it. If there had been a window to change this, he'd missed it.

"Unless he took a detour?" Tait asked, doubtfully.

"That would be pretty stupid," Jonas said. "But I'd have thought so was ratting us out to Selene, from everything you've said of her." Jonas remembered Selene's face when Hira's demon failed. And apparently Hira had betrayed her again since then.

"He thinks she's going to win," Tait said quietly. "And he thinks he can get on her side this way. He's probably right about that part, at least."

"He's in Marek without magic," Cato said. "And I should have fucking *seen* that. *Fuck*. We need to know. But I need to tell Reb too, immediately, and we need to work out if everything he told *me* is still reliable, never mind that he knows, I showed him exactly...And now he's there spilling his guts. Fuck, fuck, fuck. We don't have *time*."

"I'll go," Jonas volunteered. "Ask the captain if anyone went out there."

"If by some miracle he hasn't been seen yet, put them on alert to stop anyone who tries. Though you'd have thought...Anyway. Right. Good call. Go. I'll go to Reb."

Jonas was off immediately, as Cato and Tait turned towards Reb's place. Once he reached the bargeyard, chest burning with effort, only just able to gasp out the message, the soldiers and guards there confirmed that yes, someone had gone out and over the barricade to the Teren troops.

"Tried to shoot 'em," a small, slight woman said gloomily. "Missed every time. I never bloody miss." She looked doubtfully at her hands.

"He was a sorcerer," Jonas said, briefly, and watched her cheer up. Not that Hira could have done his own sorcery, not right there and then, but there was no value in her doubting her abilities. And there was a fair chance one of the other sorcerers had protected him, so it might even be true.

He sighed, accepted the offer of a pastry and a draught of water – no point in running himself sick, not when there was certainly more to be done – and took off back to Reb's to report back. None of this was good, not in the slightest. What now?

☺ ☺

When Jonas showed up on Reb's doorstep, Cato had just explained the flicker, and Hira's disappearance, to Reb and Alyssa. Jonas had made bloody good time, Cato could say that; but one look at his face confirmed that Hira had, indeed, gone.

"He's out at the bargeyard," Jonas said anyway, unnecessarily.

"Well, shit," Reb said. "Come on in."

"I don't know if he was planning this all along. So I can't rely on anything I heard from him. And," Cato grimaced; he hadn't got to this part yet, "he knows exactly what we're planning, because after I'd sent Tait to find you, I went looking for him to see if he'd help. Since we needed people so badly. And I could have funnelled power to him, to get past the Beckett problem." And he'd thought, maybe he could repay Hira for his help by convincing Beckett he was worth keeping around after all. More fool him. "He said he would. I can only assume he didn't think it'd work, and he's running for the winning side. Shit. *Shit.*"

They all stood around staring at each other. Cato felt sick, worse than he ever had. It had *worked*, it would have worked, but Hira didn't think it would, so he must have done something wrong. "Or it was just going to be too slow, maybe," he said aloud.

"You tried it," Reb said, briefly, seeming to follow his train of thought. "I believe you that it would have worked. But – yes, it was going to be slow. That was the main thing you were worried about, right? Why we were all going to do it?"

"It would have been bloody close anyway. What now?" He could hear the bleakness in his own voice; could feel it in the room.

Jonas, tentatively, raised a hand. "What if – I could see it."

Cato blinked at him. "See what?"

Jonas' shoulders had hunched slightly. "I could try. To see what we do."

"Maybe we don't do anything," Cato said.

"But maybe we do." Jonas' jaw had firmed. "And if I *try*, maybe…"

"Maybe you can see a future in which we do something, and it works?" Cato asked. "I didn't think your flickers worked that way."

Jonas shrugged. "They don't. But – I've seen stuff, haven't I, and tried to stop it, or not to stop it. Maybe I can see something useful."

"You can bring them on?" Reb asked, obviously at least partly following the conversation. Alyssa on the other hand looked completely confused. Tait leant over and whispered to her, and her expression cleared, but as she looked back at Jonas, her eyebrows went up and stayed up.

"When I do magic. Sometimes." Jonas' chin went up. "May I borrow your workroom, Ser Reb?"

Reb shrugged. "By all means. Do you need anything specific?"

"Something – some kind of magic related to Marek, would be best, I think," Jonas said. He sounded more certain than Cato had expected.

"Scrying?" Reb asked.

"Scry the barge-yard," Tait suggested.

They all crowded into Reb's tiny workroom to watch. Jonas, at least, was reasonably good at scrying. All of them could see the little image of the barge-yard. Cato squinted at it, trying to look for that *rat* Hira…

…and then Jonas dropped to one knee on the floor, clutching at his head. *Flicker*, Cato diagnosed immediately, even as he crossed the room to hold Jonas up. It must have only lasted a second or two; it seemed longer.

"Fuck," Jonas said hoarsely, sitting down on the floor. "Demons. Demons rampaging through the city, except, I saw, there were all of them, close together, they were in a square, an empty square, and there was something about the light, and the sorcerers, close to them were Teren sorcerers, it wasn't any of us, and they were all – half-flickery." Jonas was shaking.

"Half-flickery," Cato said softly. "Like with the binding…And all of them at once…" Something was ringing a bell in his head, a very faint and distant one. Something about a demon in the city, a larger bubble, and…

"Oh," he said. "Oh, fuck me. Reb, you are not going to like this."

"Like what?" Reb demanded.

"We need to talk to Daril Leandra. Right now."

The next five minutes contained a lot of shouting. Reb, as predicted, didn't like it one bit.

"Shut up!" It was a roar, louder than either Cato or Reb, and the shock of realising it came from *Tait* was enough to have Cato stop, mouth open mid-sentence. Reb at least looked equally surprised.

"Please tell me and Jonas and Alyssa," Tait said more quietly, "what on earth you are on about." Alyssa nodded in firm agreement.

"Right. Daril – now Leandra-Head, but at the time, b'Leandra – and M– my sister, when she and I were sixteen and he was a bit older," Cato said. "Summoned a demon right here in the middle of the city."

"But Beckett…" That was Jonas.

"They – wasn't just the two of them, there were a whole batch of 'em – made a space in the city which wasn't the city," Reb said grimly. "Big one. Took quite a lot to send the demon away again." She didn't, Cato noticed, mention Zareth's death. Fine, he wouldn't either.

"I hadn't thought about it in years," Cato said. "I knew about it at the time, because of Marcia, and because Daril tried to recruit me and I told him to knob off. But I was busy," busy learning magic, proper Marek magic, not Daril's half-arsed dicking around; and also busy being disowned and everything that came after that, "and, well, yeah, hadn't thought about it in a while. But there was a *big* space there, and it must have been something like I do, with the box and all that. But can't be the same, because mine doesn't go that big."

"How big?" Alyssa asked.

"About the size of a square," Reb said.

Cato hear Jonas' intake of breath. "*Which* I couldn't do on my own," he said, "so it didn't occur to me. But if we can find out from Daril how he did it…"

Cato looked round. Jonas might have worked it out, and he could see Reb thinking, now she'd stopped yelling; the others were all just staring at him in a puzzled way. And it was a fucking long shot, he knew that, but…

"It's a trap," he clarified. "If we can make something that big, if we can get them *into* that square Jonas saw, we can trap the lot of them. All at once. And Hira isn't here, is he? They won't see it coming."

EIGHTEEN

Getting Daril Leandra-Head in to help rescue the city wasn't even slightly Reb's idea of a good time; still less was the idea of Marcia's likely reaction. It wasn't like Marcia wasn't *right* about the wretched man, and the things he'd gotten away with in the past.

But if Cato was right...

They didn't have time to be squeamish, was what it came down to. If Daril's terrible past decisions meant something they could use right now – well, they were just going to have to do that. It did give Reb some satisfaction that he'd never be able to publicly trade on it. Magic and Marekhill: still not a good mix.

Reb would strongly have preferred to keep Marcia out of this altogether, but it seemed unlikely Daril would be willing to be summoned by a sorcerer, even after the negotiations on the Hill. And there wasn't time to mess around. Using Marcia as a go-between was sensible, even if Marcia was going to have opinions about it. Like a coward, Reb sent Jonas up the Hill to pass the message on – verbally – and give any needed explanations. Marcia'd be less likely to shout at him. Alyssa had to see to her daughter; Reb would call her when she was needed. Tait, offered the opportunity to go and rest before the morning, just shook their head, glancing over at Cato.

Jonas arrived, panting, at Irin's teahouse, which they'd commandeered for the extra space. "She wasn't thrilled," he reported, "but she's gone to talk to him."

"It was a *long time ago*," was the first thing Daril said as he walked in to the teahouse. Marcia was just behind him, jaw set and shoulders tense, one hand protectively on her belly.

"We're not here to shout at you about your past misdeeds, Leandra," Cato said impatiently. He wasn't looking at Marcia; his shoulders were up too. Reb suspected neither of them would thank her for noticing just how alike they looked right now.

"Do you remember anything about it yourself?" Reb asked Marcia quietly, stepping over to stand beside her. They'd only ever discussed that particular bit of history once, and very briefly. It hadn't been Marcia's idea, she'd only been sixteen and besotted by Daril, and she'd regretted it afterwards – which was more, Reb suspected, than Daril had done – but Reb's mentor Zareth had died, fixing what had happened, and she knew Marcia still felt the guilt.

Marcia shook her head. "I just," she winced minutely, "did what I was told."

"No magical power," Daril said with a shrug. Not that he had any himself; he'd just – more than once – managed to pay, convince, or manipulate other people into using theirs on his behalf.

"Well then, no need for you to be here," Cato said, eyes still sliding past Marcia. He made a flipping gesture with one hand. "Run along."

Daril glanced curiously between the two of them, visibly scenting trouble.

Marcia took in a breath, and Reb headed her off before she could speak. The last thing they needed right now was Cato and Marcia having a stand-up row, much though it might help the two of them clear the air. There wasn't *time*. "The fewer people there are in here messing around with this the better," she said. "What we need you to do, Marcia, is to tell the Council what's going on."

"What do you mean?" It was, thankfully, enough of a distraction for Marcia to stop glaring at Cato.

"Cato's original plan won't work – Jonas told you that?"

Marcia nodded. "That shit Hira."

"Exactly. So this is – we hope – an alternative." *If* they could get enough information out of Daril. *If* Cato could replicate it. If, if, if. "But something will happen soon, whatever we do." Whether or not they could counter it.

"Because Selene knows you'll miss Hira, and she won't want to give you time to regroup." Marcia got it immediately. "When, though?" She glanced out of the windows, where the red light of the sunset was glinting off the windows of the house opposite. "You think she'll move tonight?"

"Night attacks are messy," Daril said, "and she doesn't need the advantage if she thinks the demons are enough of one."

"We have reason to believe," Reb said, not looking at Jonas, "that it'll be morning."

"Dawn," Jonas put in.

"Reason to believe..." Daril sounded sceptical.

"I'll tell the Council," Marcia said. "Talk to Haran-Head and Captain Anna."

"We still need a trap," Cato said to the wall next to Marcia, "but this – if it works, it *must* all be in the same place at the same time. Area of effect."

"The previous plan, I said to Haran that we'd be going one-by-one, but we needed some kind of element of surprise," Reb explained. "Or to keep latecomers from seeing what was going on. That won't work, with this."

Marcia was nodding. "All at once. Right. I'll make sure everyone's ready for dawn."

Reb pulled her in for a quick kiss. "Thank you."

When she turned round, Cato's shoulders were hunched even further up to his ears, his jaw tense, and Tait was looking unhappy, glancing after Marcia and back to Cato. Daril – of course, he hadn't got to where he was by not being able to read a room – had visibly drawn his own conclusions.

"Fallen out, have we?" he asked, smirking. "How's your mother, Cato?"

Cato spun round, and Reb intervened again. "Shut up, both of you. We haven't got time."

For a wonder, it worked. But then, Daril – architect of Marek's independence – hardly wanted Selene and Co breaking in either, did he?

273

"Let's get on with this," Cato said instead. "If we've only got 'til dawn. Daril. Back when you raised that demon. What did you do?"

"Not the one you helped me with?" Daril asked, mock-innocent.

Cato rolled his eyes. "Obviously not, Beckett wasn't *here* then, that was the whole point. Back before then. You did something. I don't think it's what I do."

"What you do?" Daril, obviously surprised that his second barb had missed, was on the back foot now.

"When I work with spirits. Keep *up*. It's not like you don't know about that, that's why you hired me that time. You didn't do that. So. You must have done something different. What?"

"You're not going to hold this against me?" Daril looked doubtfully between Cato and Reb.

"If we don't work out how to solve the current problem," Reb said, "there won't be any of us left to hold anything against anyone. I can't imagine Selene will forgive you for the independence thing, and neither is she likely to leave sorcerers who aren't under her control wandering around. We need this, and we need it right now." Assuming it worked. "No one is picking this up just to get you into trouble." She didn't bother to rein in the scathing edge to her tone.

Daril gave a tiny shrug, and began to talk.

The biggest surprise was that he remembered, and could explain, what he'd done back then. At least, well enough for Cato to follow it, although Reb herself was lost almost immediately. She wasn't about to regret that; she'd chosen not to work with spirits other than Beckett, not to bend the rules the way Cato did, or break them altogether the way Daril had. But she wished, a little, that she at least had more of the theory.

Still. Cato knew what he was doing; right now that was what mattered.

"Right," Cato said, scratching at his chin. "The candles and the chanting, clearly bullshit. It's the circle that matters. Stand round then, come on."

Daril stared at the rest of them doubtfully.

"*Yes*, you as well, you're here, aren't you? Come on," Cato said impatiently.

It took them more than a few tries; it was well past midnight when they finally got it to work. After Alyssa had shown up again, so perhaps it was a matter of sheer power as much as technique. But it did work. And when they tried again with Cato's spirit acquaintance Yorick, it worked that way too.

"Bound *by* all of us, but not *to* any of us," Cato said. "To the space itself. Huh."

"What happens if we drop the circle?" Reb asked.

"They get out," Cato said briefly. Which, now Reb thought back on it, matched what had happened that time with Daril.

"And Beckett will struggle to limit them," she finished, thinking back to it, and to what Zareth had had to do, "because they're already inside. Right."

"So let's not drop it!" Cato said brightly.

"I fear, however," Yorick was still standing, looking interested, within the circle, "that if many spirits worked together, they might be able to break it even without your dropping it." They cocked their head slightly, and Reb felt the pressure. "Strong. Too strong for one, indeed. But many…" Yorick hemmed. "If you have more power," they said, "I would advise calling on it."

"Right," Cato said. "Thank you. We'll let you go back, now, shall we?"

"I wish you all the best of luck," Yorick said. "I do not like what is being done to my compatriots. If I can help again, please call on me." They nodded, and Cato closed the circle, sending them back.

"Well," Cato said. "So, that works, and I think I can cast it big enough to take all the spirits, if we can get them in."

"That's Haran and the captain's job," Reb said.

"Setting a trap," Cato agreed. "I'll need to talk to them, find out what the setup is. Somewhere we can corral them, I guess. That square Jonas described…"

275

"But Yorick said, perhaps they might break out," Tait put in.

"So," Cato said. "We've got a couple of options there. The first one, is to hope that they're too keen on breaking free of the sorcerers that have bound them."

"You're going to trap the sorcerers too?" Reb asked.

Cato shrugged. "Not deliberately, exactly, because I think we can all see how that might go. But I'm not going to go out of my way *not* to, put it that way."

Reb saw Daril shudder.

"It's hardly enough, though," Tait objected. "Just relying on that…"

"Yes, well," Cato said. "The other thing is, like Yorick said, to make it stronger. Find more power."

"We don't have any more sorcerers," Reb said, heart sinking.

"I wasn't thinking of sorcerers. They're not the only source of power we have, not for something like this." He glanced towards Daril, who had begun edging towards the door.

"Yes, well," Daril echoed, "if you don't mind, I think now I've given you the information you need…"

"Oh no you don't," Cato contradicted him. "We need this as strong as we can make it. That means you, and any of the other Heads you can pull in." Reb noticed, again, that he didn't mention Marcia.

In Marcia's current condition, Reb wasn't sure she wanted to mention her either.

"None of them," Daril said, looking horrified. "That's how many I can *pull in*. None. Do you *realise* what you're asking?"

"Fine, just you then, if you prefer," Cato said. "We need Guildmembers, too, if we can get them."

"The city," Reb said, suddenly understanding what he was getting at.

"Exactly. We've sorcerers. Houses." He rolled his eyes. "One House. Honestly, even after Beckett's performance, *none* of them?"

"Ugh. Andreas, maybe." Daril looked like he'd bitten

into something unpleasant. "And Marcia? She's not a Head, of course. And there's the baby…"

"We want Guilds," Cato said tightly, "and lower city folks, and messengers, and…"

"And anyone else who isn't going to need too much explaining," Jonas finished. "I'll fetch Asa and Tam. Where?"

"Near the bargeyard, I assume," Cato said. "I suggest we meet at that inn they're using as a guard-post. The idea will be to pull them further into the city, but we can start from there. I'll go now, see what the plan is. Make sure they're planning for the right square."

"I should come," Daril said, though he didn't look happy. "The captain won't jump when you tell her."

"Wanna bet?" Cato muttered, but he nodded.

"And apparently you're not on terms with your sister just now," Daril added slyly. Cato didn't rise to it, but Reb saw his lips tighten. She hoped the two of them would manage to get to the barge-yard without bloodshed.

"Guilds," Alyssa said. "There's Jeres, I suppose."

"And any of your radical friends that'll show up and do what they're told," Cato said. "Which I'm guessing is *none*, but never say never."

"I'll find someone," Alyssa said.

Daril was already scribbling notes, bent over one of the tables Reb had pushed to the side hours ago, folding them and scrawling across them.

"I'll take them," Jonas said, tying his armband on. "Then meet you at the inn."

"Right then," Cato said. He rubbed his hands over his face. "Time to set a trap."

☺ ☺

Two Emergency Council meetings in one day was definitely overkill as far as Marcia was concerned, especially given that the second one had to be after dinner, and arguably didn't need to decide anything as such. But the alternative had been Marcia going round all the Houses and Guilds individually and answering the same questions over and again, which didn't appeal either. They'd been bad enough taken all at once: yes the sorcerers had an answer; yes, they'd been betrayed; no, the solution probably wouldn't work any more; yes, they were working on an alternative; no, Selene might not take advantage immediately, but...Haran-Head had broken in at that point to explain how unlikely *that* was.

"I thought this *cityangel* that you were all making much of this morning would handle such things," Athitol-Head had broken in querulously. "Or what was the point of all that?"

"Buying time," Haran-Head had replied briefly, saving Marcia the trouble. "Won't last forever. Can't count on it, either. If there is another solution...no point in waiting around, is there now? Let's control what we can."

Daril's wide-eyed younger cousin, the prospective Heir, looked extremely anxious at representing her House alone, but managed quite adeptly to turn aside the various queries about where Daril might be. Marcia didn't comment; not her problem.

Once the meeting was done, she'd gone home, and let Cousin Cara put food in front of her, and tried restlessly to sleep...until the sky began its very first lightening, and she couldn't bear to wait any longer. She was already out of bed and dressed when a sleepy maid knocked on the door, rubbing her tired eyes, to hand her a note.

We think we have it, but we need all the help we can get. Come to the inn by the bargeyard as soon as you get this _ Reb.

☺ ☺

Reb wasn't there when she arrived. Captain Anna and Haran-Head were, both obviously having been up all night.

"We're ready," Haran-Head said, over Captain Anna's attempts to insist that Marcia shouldn't be there. "Where's your sorcerers?"

"On their way." It was a relief to hear the door, and to turn to see Cato, Daril, and Reb arriving. Running footsteps outside, and Jonas came in behind them, breathing hard and untying his armband.

Assuming Reb was right that they had a solution, Marcia supposed Daril must have been able to explain what he'd done when they were all much younger. She hated being beholden to Daril at all, never mind being beholden to something she regretted so badly being involved with. But however much she'd tried to find other solutions, however much they'd talked to ambassadors and whatever Madeleine was doing in Ameten – if she was even there yet – in the final analysis, if they couldn't deal with the demons here and now, none of that would matter in the slightest. And if Daril's idiocy back in the day helped resolve that…She *hated* this.

Reb's sage-green tunic looked fresh, but as Reb came closer, Marcia could see that her eyes were tired. Cato still wouldn't look at her. Daril inclined his head to her politely.

"Everything ready?" Marcia asked, trying not to sound as anxious as she felt.

Reb sighed, and Marcia's stomach flipped. "There are – complications. But – yes."

Cato muttered something under his breath that Marcia couldn't hear. She didn't ask him to repeat it. She took Reb's arm, needing the comfort.

"Right," Haran-Head said briskly. He glanced over them, then fixed his gaze on Cato. "I gather you're the one in the lead here. It's been a while. Good to see you. Come, we need to get this nailed down."

Cato, looking surprised, let himself be taken to a table with Haran-Head and Captain Anna, where a collection of papers and little lumps of clay were scattered, then turned to beckon Jonas over to join them.

"Tell me what's happening," Marcia demanded of Reb. "And what these complications are."

"You remember when we sent the last demon away?" Reb asked. "We needed a connection to the city."

A connection which Marcia had herself provided. "Yes," she agreed.

"Well. This time, we need more than that."

"More...?"

"More people," Reb clarified.

"Me, for example," Daril added. He didn't look comfortable. "And I've sent to Andreas."

"Andreas isn't going to get involved with magic," Marcia said in disbelief.

"Honestly, I suspect not, but we'll see. It was worth trying. From what Cato and that spirit of his said." There was clearly a lot Marcia was missing, but now wasn't the time to get caught up.

"Jonas and Alyssa have sent for people too," Reb said.

"It'll be a whole circle," Daril said flippantly. "A bit like last time."

Marcia glared at him, but he didn't seem to notice.

"So once they get here..."

"We're ready. As ready as we're going to be."

Captain Anna was peering out of the window again. She turned round. "Fereno-Heir! With the greatest respect, they are about to try to move out there, and I need you *not to be here*."

"I'll be where Ser Reb and," she tried not to pause, "my brother tell me to be."

"They won't move 'til they think the sorcerers can get through," Cato said, straightening up from the table. He folded his arms and leaned against the wall, the picture of laziness, unless you noticed the tightness of his shoulders, the pinched look of his face. Light was seeping into the world outside. Dawn.

"It looks like they do think exactly that, then," Captain Anna said bluntly.

Cato and Reb exchanged glances.

"Then they think Beckett's about to collapse," Reb said. Marcia saw her swallow. "Which is good, because that's what we need them to think."

It was good, as long as it wasn't actually true. Whatever Cato had planned, presumably he'd need *some* of Beckett's power.

"We have a trap." Captain Anna nodded. "Which – we have to assume that someone out there understands tactics."

"And Selene's not stupid," Marcia added.

"But. She is desperate, we know that, and if they have reason to think this might be what they anticipate happening, for real…" Captain Anna sucked at her teeth. "Well. We assume they'll lead with the sorcerers, that's their main strength. So. There's three alleyways come towards the city from the barge-yard. Two of them meet in the next square along. We've brought up a wagon of supplies to block the other one."

"So we're hoping that doesn't look too obvious, and that they haven't got anyone who knows the territory," Marcia said.

"Hira's just been hanging around drinking since he got stuck here, not wandering around making maps. Selene certainly won't know this side of the city well," Cato said.

"But even so – they're going to suspect something. Surely." Marcia chewed her thumbnail.

Reb's mouth was thin. "I was thinking about that on the way over. How about – I try the trick Cato thought up, the one Hira knows about. Just me. They'll break that – we assume – then Beckett drops the city's protection in that one area, and we fall back in apparent confusion, to the next square."

"The sorcerers will think Beckett's gone," Marcia concluded, then forgot herself, and grasped at Reb's arm again. She saw Daril's smirk out of the corner of her eye, and ignored it. "Is that safe for you?"

Reb shrugged. "Define 'safe'. I was going to do it from on top of the inn, so physically I ought to be safe."

"You won't be much good at it," Cato noted clinically.

"All the better," Reb said. "And in any case. We don't know what'll happen when it breaks, and you can't do it. We need you for the next bit. So." She half-smiled at Marcia. "Let's hope for the best, eh? I'll come down to join the rest of you if I can."

"So once that happens – it'll be obvious?" Captain Anna was watching her intently.

"You'll have sorcerers running towards you," Cato said. "Should be fairly obvious."

"Then we'll fall back to the next square."

"And keep going after that," Reb said. "You want to stay well out of the way of this."

"Back to the wholesale market," Captain Anna said, almost to herself. "Well, it's as good a place as any, I suppose, if we have to…" She didn't finish her sentence.

"Then Cato'll spring his trap as soon as enough of the Teren sorcerers are in it," Reb continued.

Cato gave them all a little wave. Marcia could tell how nervous he was, and her chest clenched.

"All of them, surely?" she said. "All of the sorcerers."

"That would be nice, but we can't afford to lose any at the front, can we?" Reb shrugged. She was more than nervous, too. "Better to try to mop them up at the back, where the others are getting in their way. If we have to."

Marcia shut her eyes for a moment. "It's thin."

"They're coming in anyway, very soon now. Beckett

hasn't got much longer left. Cato and I spoke to them earlier to get them to agree to this, and, well. This is our best chance." She took a long breath.

"Very well," Captain Anna said briskly. "What else do you need?"

"You and me, back at the next square back," Cato said to Daril. "We'll likely catch Jonas or whoever there, but," he turned back to Captain Anna, "if anyone shows up here looking for me, send them back there."

"I need to get up on the roof," Reb said.

"There's a ladder." Captain Anna pointed it out. "We've had a sniper up there."

"What about me?" Marcia asked. "You wanted me here."

"You stay out of it," Reb said bluntly. "You can't be channeling power through the baby. I called you in to manage the Council. If this works, someone will need to deal with Selene."

"If we don't manage to flatten her too," Cato put in. "Can but hope."

"She's not daft," Marcia said. "She'll be back out of the way."

Cato ignored her, but Reb nodded. "I think so too. So we'll need someone to represent the city."

"Better me than Athitol-Head," Marcia agreed.

Daril had an irritated expression, but he didn't disagree. Doubtless he'd prefer to be the one representing the Council, but he didn't say anything. Maybe he'd actually realised where he was genuinely needed, for once. Marcia remembered providing that link to the city, when they'd faced Selene's sorcerer. Daril's turn, this time.

"Oh, there's Andreas," Daril said, voice lightening in surprise, gesturing up the road as they all came out of the inn's back door.

"Come on then," Cato said. "We'll update him on the way." He strode off briskly, followed by Daril, towards the advancing Andreas. Who Marcia wouldn't have minded speaking to as well, before they all got flattened by demons; but there wasn't really time for that.

Captain Anna had disappeared back into the inn. Marcia turned to Reb, and took her hand.

"Are you all right?"

Reb shrugged, and smiled bleakly. "Well. We have to try, I suppose. Anything that works."

"Anything at all that works?" Marcia asked curiously.

"No. Not – anything. But yes, fine, there are things I would usually disapprove of that I'm willing to accept right now. For example, the whole business of Cato working with spirits isn't my favourite thing, but we'd be completely screwed right now if it weren't for that." She pulled a face. "I met one of them, last night. That was – interesting."

Marcia's eyebrows went up. "And Beckett didn't mind?"

"Complicated. They weren't exactly here, so..." Reb waved her free hand. "A discussion for another time, perhaps. It's all about this thing that Cato and Daril have worked out. Anyway. Your brother can be very...focused, sometimes."

"He cares much more about outcomes than methods," Marcia said, bluntly. "I am fully aware of that, believe me."

"In any case," Reb said. "I need to get up on this roof. Not much time now. I'll come to help afterwards if I can, but otherwise, I'll have to leave Cato to it, and trust that he knows what he's doing, in all the relevant directions."

"I could wish I'd heard back from my mother, but – we can't wait any longer, can we?" Marcia took both of Reb's hands, turning to face her. "Take care. I love you. See you on the other side."

Reb smiled at her crookedly. "I love you, too. And – I'll keep an eye out for your brother. All right?"

"I want you to keep an eye out for *yourself*," Marcia said, but she leant in to place a grateful kiss on the corner of Reb's mouth. "But – yes. Thank you. I would appreciate it." She sighed. "Very well. Let's go."

NINETEEN

Cato had spent some time trying to work out a version of this that *didn't* involve them letting the Teren sorcerers into the city, but there wasn't any help for it. Out in the barge-yard, it would be too obvious what was happening, and no chance of getting all of them close enough for the trap.

This wasn't a *good* option, but it was better than any other. Or at least, than any other they could think of with the time they had to hand.

The good part was that at least they were all high up; on roofs around the square one back from the barge-yard, with the hope of making the trap as large as possible before they sprung it. In an ideal world it would be small enough to get physical contact, but there was no way for that to work with a dozen Teren sorcerers and their demons to get into one place before they realised what was happening. Instead, Cato had scattered the sorcerers in between the others – himself, Daril, Tait, Andreas, Alyssa's Guild friend, Alyssa, Jonas' partner, Jonas, Jonas' messenger friend, and back to himself. It should be enough. He hoped it would be enough. And being up high meant that they were somewhat shielded from retaliation, although of course if this didn't work they were all screwed anyway.

It had taken a bit of persuading Beckett, who would far rather just hold the city boundary until they collapsed. (And died? How did spirits dying even work?) It was Reb who'd talked them into it. They'd pushed back again, just now, when Cato explained the detail to them after his discussion with Haran-Head – and hadn't *that* been quite the surprise; a House Head just treating him, Cato the House-exiled sorcerer, normally – and his maps. Cato was fairly sure Beckett had understood the idea in the end. He bloody well hoped so, or they were all screwed. But *if* this went as planned, once the circle was created, and the sorcerers trapped, Beckett ought to be able to extend their power out again into this space to reinforce the circle. Even though it would be created without them. There was some very interesting theory in there, which Cato did not have time to think through just now.

So here he was, up on a sodding *roof*, which did not feel anything like as secure as Jonas had insisted it was. Jonas was used to masts and things. Cato was used to being on solid ground. He shifted restlessly, then sat still again to avoid the risk of falling off. Surely the Terens would realise it was a trap, that they were being funnelled in a particular direction. The hope was that if they did realise, they'd discount it; they believed their demons couldn't be overpowered by ordinary soldiers, and they would think that was all was left. Beckett had agreed – reluctantly – to drop the boundary as if they were collapsing, so the sorcerers would – hopefully – believe Marek was unprotected.

Hopefully.

He glanced back towards the barge-yard, and heard a volley of shots. That was it, then. Reb doing her thing; it collapsing; Beckett going.

He felt it, sudden and unexpected in exactly how awful it felt. Beckett's power not just gone, the way it had once, absent when you reached for it, but ripped away. And maybe that *absence* showed in itself how much power Beckett had been pouring into holding the boundary. It felt like something tearing, breaking.

Maybe it really was. Maybe this wasn't a fake-out. Maybe Beckett really was…

But Cato, even as he retched, dry-heaving, at the *feel* of that separation, pushed that fear firmly aside. He had a job to do, here. This was a fucking good fake, and it fucking well ought to pull the Terens in. As long as it pulled them in *here*.

He straightened up, looking around to check everyone was still in place. Their own soldiers would fall back now

– and there they were, right on time, pouring into the square and disappearing down the alleyways around it. And stopping, presumably, because they were the fallback if this failed altogether, not that it would be much use.

A gap; then another soldier, in Teren green, looking around them warily. Cato let them pass, and the next soldier too. Through the square, one to each corner. Then – his stomach turned over like falling – the first sorcerer, their demon fully visible now. It reached out and grabbed a chunk of the building over the road, ripping it out. At least there was no one in there – Captain Anna had evacuated them all in the night. There was only Jonas, on the top, and the roof of the building was sagging a bit, but it wasn't falling.

Fuck, none of this was good. Cato very very badly wanted to turn and run. This wasn't his sort of thing at all. He wanted to be at home. Glass of something in hand. Hiding under the quilts. Whatever. He wanted this to be *someone else's* problem. But Tait was across the square from him, and if he turned and ran Tait would be screwed, and in fact Cato himself, in due course, would be screwed too. He gritted his teeth.

Wait.

Wait.

The sorcerer. The demon moving across the square. Shit, were they going to leave this much gap between them? Because if they only got *one*…

Another couple of sorcerers, another couple of demons, and Cato let out a breath of relief. Another handful more. Safety in numbers, maybe, they thought, except they were wrong.

He hoped.

The first one was nearly across the square. It had to be now.

He threw up his hands, the signal to the others to be ready, and cast. Beckett's power *thank fuck* still there after all when he needed it.

The circle snapped into place, almost thrumming

287

between them. He couldn't quite believe it had worked first time, even if they had practised half a dozen times in that tearoom; even the newest recruits, who admittedly didn't have to *do* anything but be there, had been pulled cleanly into it. He felt a moment of sheer proud overwhelming satisfaction. He'd pulled it off.

This part. There needed to be more, though.

He was beginning to pant. It was fine. This wasn't hard. It wasn't.

They'd realised what had happened, down there. Some sorcerers had been caught in the circle; some hadn't. The ones that hadn't – Cato felt the pressure as their bindings snapped, broken in two by the strength of the circle. He'd half-hoped their spirits would shift planes after that, but they didn't. Yorick had been able to get out; Cato had kept recasting the wretched thing until he'd worked out how to get his back door into it. There – a couple of pops, each nearly knocking him off his feet, and the pressure eased slightly. Some had gone. The others – either their sorcerers were still holding them. Or they wanted revenge. Which he totally understood. But. He'd just hoped – something else would happen.

He was going to have to break them out. And that bit – that bit they hadn't fucking practised.

Sweat ran down his back. He pulled hard from the circle around him, which at least was holding firm, Beckett's power thrumming in there strong enough to taste.

It was agonising. Still six or eight of them in there, at least, all pulling and pushing in different directions. He had no idea how long he could hold this, but he had to, didn't he? He hadn't worked out what the next step was, and he couldn't just let them all go again.

His breath was coming in ever shorter pants. Behind him, someone said something he couldn't quite parse; it was Reb, but he didn't know what she was saying. She put a hand on his shoulder and he felt the influx of power, which helped, but not *enough*. He didn't have a solution. He couldn't just let them out again.

Then Reb swore, and her hand was gone, and Cato almost cried.

He hung on. Tried, at the same time, to think through – how could he stop this? There must be something, some way, but if he just let it go, they might just…

Zareth had *died* when that idiot Daril did his thing, and that was just one demon.

Something shifted, in the circle, and Cato's eyes snapped open. Tait. Where was Tait? But he could feel Reb in it now, and that…He squinted, eyes burning, across the square, and saw Reb where Tait ought to be.

Tait had to be all right. Reb wouldn't just leave them. If Cato let go now, to go and look, he'd – that might be worse. For everyone.

And then he heard something behind him, and felt Tait's presence, and Tait's hand on his shoulder, and even if he couldn't let go, still couldn't let go, that was in itself a relief, something to hold onto until he expired altogether…

"You *have* to let me," Tait said, urgently.

Let them what?

And then Tait gripped both of Cato's shoulders, and a hurricane ran through the two of them, the rest of the circle suddenly popping out of existence, but the demons weren't running rampant, the trap hadn't disappeared…There was an iron-smell in the air – *blood*, Cato thought at the back of his mind, *blood magic* – but it was working. Tait was doing it, sending each of the demons – spirits, they were spirits – winking out of this plane, one at a time, the agonising pull of the trap lessening with each one. One by one, the sorcerers collapsed as they lost their bindings, and Cato could let go, could pull his self back into his self.

They were gone.

"What do you know," he croaked. "It worked."

Everything went black.

It was clear as soon as the circle started that Tait wasn't doing it right. They couldn't – they couldn't find the magic. They could feel something, that they were held in something, could feel the taste of Cato's magic. And then the thrum of Beckett's power back again but only dimly, like through a thick wool blanket. Worse than ever before. Worse than when they'd all practised, and that hadn't been great but Tait had been *trying*, so hard…

They held on, held on as hard as they could, and it seemed like the circle was holding, the spirits below trapped.

They were shaking so much with the effort they nearly lost their footing on the roof when Reb said their name from behind.

"I'll take over." Her voice was neutral, but Tait felt the sting of failure as they dropped their hands and fell back out of the circle.

They couldn't do this. Couldn't *help*.

Across the square, they saw Cato's head come up, and he looked over in their direction. Even from this distance Tait could see that his eyes were wide, almost blank. This was harder than he'd been expecting, Tait was almost certain – and yes, the trap had worked, but *something else* needed to happen now, didn't it? They couldn't just keep a bunch of spirits right here forever.

This was the bit no one had worked out. This was the part that Cato had said, oh well, we'll work it out when we get there, something will happen, we haven't time to nail it all down. *It'll be fine*, Cato had said.

And now – it wasn't fine. It wasn't working. The power was pulsing around the square, the spirits couldn't get *out*; some of the binds, Tait was fairly certain, had broken, and some of them maybe had even gone – but not all of them. Cato had hoped they'd all choose to leave, or that their sorcerers might release them from within the trap, but that didn't seem to be happening either.

Tait began to clamber across the roof, towards the ladder at the edge. They weren't sure what they were going to do, other than that they wanted to get over to

Cato, to...help him somehow, even if they didn't know how.

To sit with him while he did this until he passed out, and they both got ripped apart by released spirits? Or maybe the spirits would all meekly go home.

And maybe Tait would get a dancing unicorn for their next birthday.

They glanced over again. Cato was visibly swaying, face screwed up. The soldiers – the Teren soldiers – more of them had come into the square and been stopped; now they fanned out behind the edge of the trap, obviously working out that something had happened. Tait looked down and saw one of them pointing upwards, shouting to their comrades.

And someone had a pistol, pointed up at them...

Tait flung themselves along the ridge of the roof, towards where Tam was perched, and down behind the ridge. There was a bang, and something pinged off a slate.

Tam, on the roof-ridge above them, unable to dodge, shouted and looked down, face pale and shocked, hand clutching at his arm. Blood was already seeping through his fingers. Tait scrambled upwards to catch him, automatically cataloguing the injury – they'd helped the healer, sometimes, back in their village, as a child. Blood, yes, but it was down from the shoulder joint; it was in the arm itself, which was a relief. Joints were complicated. Looked like only a flesh wound, through the meat of the arm, missing the bone. Was the bullet still in there? Tait couldn't dig it out sitting up on top of a roof, but they could bind the wound for now, stem the bleeding, if they could find a cloth... Who knew how long Tam might need to stay here. Part of this, the way Tait wasn't.

"Tam," they said, urgently. "I can help, if you'll let me."

Tam's face was white, and he was biting his lip, breath coming fast, but Tait could tell that he was still holding his place in the circle. Despite not even really understanding what was going on. Another wash of shame pinged through Tait. *They* hadn't been able to hold their own place, and them a sorcerer too. Allegedly. Not much of one, that was for sure.

"Yeah," Tam gasped. "All right. Yeah."

Tait moved Tam's arm, trying to be as gentle as possible, looking for an exit wound, and let their breath out in relief when they found one. The bleeding wasn't slowing, though; not fast enough for one of the really important blood vessels, but bullets could do a lot of damage. "Are they...?" Tam tried to look down at the square below them.

"They're fine," Tait soothed automatically, lowering Tam downwards so the two of them were a harder target – they couldn't see the square from here, past the guttering of the house, and that presumably meant they couldn't be seen. The bullet had gone through Tam's sleeve, which meant fragments might be in the wound, and that was a problem too. They gently peeled Tam's sleeve away, looking for missing fabric, and gripped Tam's arm again with their other hand to slow the bleeding.

Their fingers tingled, and they looked down at their hand in surprise.

Blood. But someone else's blood. That wasn't – Tait couldn't use that. Not for power. Never. That was a bad road to start down.

But no. This wasn't blood magic. It didn't feel the same. The blood had started it, yes, they could tell that, but it was *Beckett* they could feel now, Beckett's power almost a living bond between them and Tam. And it was the simplest thing in the world just to reach out and touch Tam's arm again, and to watch as it healed up, inside to out, to a pink shiny scar and all that was left was a smear of blood across Tam's arm and a tiny bloody scrap of linen clinging to Tait's fingers.

"Aw, thanks!" Tam said, eyes wide. "I didn't think you meant *that* much help! That's better than the sorcerer round the corner ever did." He was already sitting back up, the circle steadying. Tait glanced over towards Reb, looking more and more worried; and Cato, across the square, shaking hard enough that Tait could see it all the way over here.

Blood. But healing! And through Beckett, not the blood magic they'd learnt in Teren. Tait didn't know what to think, how to process this – but there was Tam, whole and well again, and even if Tam's blood had been the conduit, wasn't that a fair trade for the wound healed and healed clean? Surgeons cut, and sewed again. Sometimes you had to hurt to make whole.

Cato had bitten straight through his lip, a streak of blood running down his chin that Tait could see from here, and Tait thought, *maybe I can help after all*. Because if Cato was holding all of those spirits, all that power, didn't he need healing?

Tait scrambled over to the ladder and down it, fast as they could. Maybe they could be useful after all. Maybe it wasn't too late.

⊙ ⊙

In the end, from where Marcia waited by the wholesale market – inside a building, where she just about had a clear view of the space, after a stand-up row with Captain Anna about safety – it was almost anti-climatic. A handful of soldiers came through cautiously as far as the edge of the open square, pausing just by the end of the street into it, flattening themselves against walls. Waiting for the sorcerers to come.

The sorcerers didn't come.

One of the soldiers went back to look, after an urgent debate across the mouth of the street. Marcia could see gestures, but not hear anything.

They came back on the run. There was another furious gestured debate, and this time half the group went back.

Captain Anna was waiting with her own soldiers, scattered around the edges of the square. Marcia had sent messages to others of the Council to pass on about what was going on; somewhat to her surprise, several of the Heads – including Athitol-Head, of all people – and

Guildwardens had come to join her. They were all
peering out of the same couple of windows, in breathless
silence.

Captain Anna must be tempted to move now, but the
hope was to do this entirely bloodlessly – well, apart
from whatever happened to the sorcerers, which Marcia
wasn't keen to think about – and if she tried to take the
soldiers now, it wouldn't be bloodless. They had to know
they were defeated.

If they were defeated.

Everyone waited.

There was a lot of banging from up the way, and
Marcia wanted desperately to know what was happening.
Had Cato managed it? Were they trying to break in to get
at him? What was going *on*?

Then Jonas appeared over the rooftops, and gestured
wildly down at Captain Anna.

He'd done it. Cato had done it.

After that, mopping up the soldiers took hardly any
time at all. It wasn't like they didn't know that they
couldn't do this without the sorcerers. The sorcerers,
shaking and miserable, were even easier to round up. It
seemed to Marcia that there were slightly fewer of them
now, which was something she wasn't going to think
about.

What had happened to *their* sorcerers? Jonas was fine,
she'd seen that, but where was Reb? And the rest of them
– what about Andreas?

Where was Cato?

More waiting.

"The former Lieutenant is in the bargeyard," Captain
Anna reported, after another long, tense wait. "She
refuses to surrender."

"I will go and speak to her," Athitol-Head said briskly,
and somewhat to Marcia's surprise.

"Ser, with all due respect, I cannot guarantee your
safety…"

"Nonsense." Athitol-Head began marching towards the
door.

"Wait!" Marcia turned to Captain Anna. "Can we at least safely return to the inn? Assess the situation?"

Captain Anna reluctantly allowed that the rest of the city was once again secure, though she insisted on her soldiers escorting the little group of Heads and Heirs – Nisha had shown up now too – and Guildwardens there.

Halfway across the market square, Marcia saw Reb coming towards her, and stopped abruptly, knees weak with relief. Reb opened her arms and Marcia fell into them without worrying about who was watching.

"Everyone's fine," Reb said. "Exhausted, but fine. Andreas is at the inn. So's Cato – knocked himself out, stupid bugger, but Tait's looking after him. Jonas' friend took a bullet to the shoulder, but Tait healed it."

"They did?"

"Long story. For later. You lot off to talk sense into Selene, then?"

"That's the hope," Marcia said, then realised she was being left behind – Athitol-Head was setting quite the pace – and had to hurry to catch up, still firmly holding Reb's hand.

Selene's handful of soldiers, out in the bargeyard, looked pretty miserable.

"*They* know the score," Captain Anna said irritably, glaring out at them.

Athitol-Head, after a frank discussion with Captain Anna – "If she shoots me, you can get on and shoot her," – insisted on going out to speak to Selene. There was an exchange of glances behind her back – everyone remembered that Athitol-Head had voted against independence. But she'd also made oath to hold the decision of the Council. And she surely had to be the one that Selene was most likely to listen to.

Everyone crowded forward to the edge of the bargeyard, though Captain Anna insisted on the Heads and Guildwardens staying behind the soldiers, pointing out that they *did* still have weapons out there, and if Selene wasn't surrendering, then she might yet try to attack, however foolishly.

Even from this distance, Marcia could hear Selene's refusal of Athitol-Head's offer. She didn't understand it, though. Selene had lost. It was clear to everyone that she'd lost. Surely?

"She's desperate," Nisha remarked, standing next to Marcia. Reb was on her other side. Marcia still didn't intend to let go of her hand just yet. "What's waiting for her back in Teren?"

"Well," Marcia said slowly, aware that several of the other Heads and Heirs around her were listening in. "She won't be Archion, not now. But – she can't change that anyway."

"How prone is the current Archion to fits of displeasure?" Nisha asked. "Might it, for example, be better to be sent back under arrest than to voluntarily surrender? Looks better?" She pursed her lips. "Might she prefer it if we shoot her?"

"She might if she thinks she'll be demon-food," Andreas said. He looked exhausted, but healthy. Marcia badly wanted to give him a hug.

"Surely not," Marcia said, horrified.

"There's been plenty of others," Andreas pointed out.

"But not – no one of Selene's stature, surely," Pedeli-Head said, sounding baffled.

"Madeleine would know," Marcia said.

But she wasn't here, and Marcia didn't know where she was, or when she'd be back, or whether she'd drowned in the swamps somewhere. Her stomach muscles twinged sharply, and she put a hand on her bump, rubbing it to soothe it. Athitol-Head, arms folded, was holding a quieter discussion with Selene now. Marcia, having been on the wrong end of a 'discussion' with Athitol-Head before, felt almost sympathetic.

Which was when a messenger, red armband on, came running full pelt from the centre of the city, from beyond the evacuation area. "Message!" they cried as they got closer. "From Teren! From the Archion!"

Behind them, covered in mud and moving rather more slowly, was – Bracken? But where was Madeleine?

Bracken, as he approached them, didn't look like someone who'd lost his charge. "Afternoon, Sers," he said, only a little out of breath. "Ser Fereno, your mother's fine."

Marcia let her breath out.

"Sers," Bracken carried on, as the Heads and Heirs quietened to listen. "Excuse me comin' here in all my travel-dirt, but well, I think it's urgent. I'd have been sooner at that, but they wasn't allowing us through here, not even with a messenger." He looked faintly disapproving. "I'm not come official from Ameten – there's an official messenger on the way, we encountered them on the road, Sers, on the way to Ameten. They'll be taking longer, getting through the blocks on the river and all, and not knowing the back ways like what I do. And I thought speed was needful, because – Sers. The Archion in Ameten is dead."

Noise rose all around them. Marcia glanced over to Selene, who was close enough to hear. Bracken had pitched his voice loudly. She had slumped, defeat beginning to overtake her.

Marcia's mind was racing. The Archion dead...but who, then, would be the new Archion, and what would their policy be to Marek? Selene had been hoping to return Marek to the fold as part of her campaign to become Archion, but if she were here, now, had she missed her moment? Or would this encourage her to attempt the city even without her sorcerers? Given that she hadn't been willing to back down when surely she couldn't achieve her goals...

"Sers, I bring a message from the *new* Archion." He pulled an envelope out of his jacket and held it out. Gil took it, glancing around at all the rest of them.

"Greetings from Grainne, the Archion of Teren, may she guide us well. Who is pleased to recognise Marek as an independent city, and – Madeleine Fereno as its ambassador."

So *that* was what her mother was up to. And it was her friend who'd made it to Archion. Well. Wasn't that interesting, now. And how on *earth* had Madeleine managed that in the last two days? She couldn't even have reached Ameten yet – Bracken had said *met on the way*. Then – Marcia hadn't had time to ask her mother what she'd been up to in Ameten, had she? Well. No wonder Madeleine had insisted on being the one to go.

"And would also like to apologise for the behaviour of the former Teren Lieutenant, which was not undertaken with the Archion's blessing."

Or at least, the new Archion wasn't willing to stand behind it. It didn't much matter. This was good enough. Selene crumpled, visibly, and Athitol-Head leant forward to speak to her again. She really had lost, now.

They'd won.

They'd really, actually won. And with barely a shot fired.

TWENTY

Alyssa sat in the near-empty Bucket, nursing a mug of ale, and waited for the return of the first representatives of the Lower Council to the Council. Which to her mind really should be renamed itself – not like the Marekhill one was *the* Council and the other an afterthought – but no one else had felt that to be a hill worth dying on.

The eventual agreement between the Marekhill types and the radicals, reached over two full days of wrangling once the aftermath of the attempted invasion had been cleared away, had two parts. The Council continued as it was; the lower city got its own Council, which could make representations to the Marekhill Council. No *votes* for the Lower Council representatives, mind; they had speaking rights only. Alyssa had fought hard for voting rights, but it had always been a lost cause. For now.

Several of the Houses and a few of the Guildwardens quite clearly thought this would be a technicality that they could ignore at will. Alyssa, of course, had no intention of letting that be the case. And to be fair, there were folk on the Marekhill Council – Marcia, the untrustworthy Daril Leandra, Gil Jythri, and Andreas Tigero, though for her money he wasn't as convinced as Marcia or even Daril were – who meant to insist on the Lower Council being properly recognised.

The Lower Council itself wasn't formed of representatives or any of that; it was open to all, the way their People's Parliament had been. That was the compromise that Jeres and the Petitioners had eventually made. Well, to be fair, it wasn't like the Petitioners were *against* that system, not exactly – although Jeres might have preferred things a little tidier. Alyssa reckoned the very untidiness of the Lower Council was part of its strength. Many views; no one left out. That was how you made better decisions, even if it was a bloody exhausting and, fine, often deeply annoying process. Their representatives up to the Marekhill Council, though, those were elected. Alyssa hadn't stood; she didn't much fancy traipsing up the hill to talk gently to Marekhill folk once a week.

The door of the Bucket banged open and Simeon strode in, dark hair up on end as usual. He had stood as a representative, but hadn't been voted in; in all honesty, while an excellent rabble-rouser, Simeon wouldn't have been a great choice for the softly-softly that Alyssa – reluctantly – had to admit was needed for the job. But he'd gone up in the procession that accompanied the representatives to their first meeting. Alyssa hadn't. Her hip had been aching lately, and she felt she'd done enough trekking up and down to bloody Marekhill for a while.

"It went *excellently*," Simeon proclaimed, as others streamed in around him to the bar. "We won both of the votes we wanted."

Well, that was good news, even if it wasn't quite how she'd have put it. 'They happened to vote the way we wanted' was maybe more like it. Still. It was good, either way.

The place was filling up with cheerful people. Jeres came up to her table.

"Hey there, Alyssa. You doing all right?"

"Hey there, Representative." She grinned up at Jeres. Cynical or no, she couldn't help but be pleased things had got this far, even if she and Jeres had their disagreements. "Come, have a seat. How was it then? Once they managed to find you some chairs, I mean."

Jeres rolled her eyes as she sat down. There had been a ridiculous amount of hassle over where the Lower Council representatives should sit in the Chamber. The Houses – or some of them, at any rate – refused to move, on the grounds that they had their colours behind their traditional seats. Marcia had been scathing about the whole business when Alyssa had encountered her at

Reb's and thrown it up to her, but had nevertheless maintained that given that the Houses *were* kicking up about it, it would be better to find a different solution than to antagonise them all right at the start. Which, Alyssa acknowledged with reluctance, might even be right. More practically, the Guildwardens, who occupied pews at the back of the circular Chamber, were already crowded enough after the addition of the extra three seats the previous year. What there was, though, was a seat for the Teren Lieutenant, who no longer existed. (Well, as far as Alyssa knew, Selene herself still existed, although who knew what was happening to her now she was presumably back in Ameten. Not Alyssa's problem. The job was gone, either way.)

"They've fitted three chairs in where the Teren Lieutenant used to sit," Jeres said. "Comfortable enough. Very fancy carving up the wall." She smirked slightly. "We did get a few glares from Athitol when we made a point of admiring it before we sat down."

Gossip had it – Marcia had refused to comment – that Athitol-Head had resisted this *strenuously* due to the fact that it was a fancier pew than anyone else's, but had also resisted the idea of taking it out and building something plainer in the space, because it would be historic vandalism. Evidently she'd been overruled.

Alyssa clinked mugs with Jeres. Annoying Athitol was always worthy of celebration. "So," she said after taking another swig of beer. "You got the apprenticeships resolved?"

Jeres nodded. "Hagadath was anti, of course. Shame it wasn't next week; scuttlebutt is they're going to lose their election. About bloody time. Didn't matter this time though. Ilana – of the Jewellers – spoke in our favour." She nodded approvingly. "And Cerit-Head said he thought it wasn't the Houses' business and they should vote with whatever the Guilds thought."

"Not what you lot thought, then?" Alyssa sniped.

Jeres shrugged. "Well, there we go; we won anyway."

"Not missing having a vote yet, then?"

Jeres glowered at her, but it was friendly. "I'd like us to be voting just as much as you would, and you know it."

"You say that now, before you find yourself pulled into defending the Council and how it operates."

"That why you didn't stand?"

Alyssa shrugged. "You know fine well why I didn't stand. I don't want to be boxed into a corner."

"You don't want to have to represent people you disagree with," Jeres said, her tone mostly light.

"Eh, if you want to put it that way. I think the job's important, of course it is, and yeah, right enough, the *job* is, representing what the Lower Council thinks. I want to be able to push the Lower Council harder than that." She grinned sideways at Jeres. "Don't worry, I'll most certainly be participating *there*."

"You know," Jeres said, mouth quirking, "that is not, in fact, something I was worrying about."

It was all true enough; but as well as that, there was the matter of being a sorcerer. She agreed with Marcia that in the long run, that needed not to be an issue, but she agreed with Reb too that it was unwise to push it right now. One of the reasons she rarely reminded Jeres or Simeon or any of the rest of them about it. Wasn't like she was that strong of a sorcerer, anyway; and she was fine with that. Reb was the official magical representative, and only in that she could be called upon if needed, rather than that she had any intention of showing up at the Marekhill Council regularly. That all seemed well enough to Alyssa.

But in the long run…if Jeres could be Guilded and a Lower Council representative at one and the same time, why couldn't she be a sorcerer and the same?

For now, she'd take the rabble-rousing.

"Simeon said you got the business with the warehouses through, but only just." Barges were coming in from Teren again, but fewer than there had been before; there was still concern about supplies and who got to control them. Hopefully it would adjust with time. The refugees had more or less stopped coming, with the new Archion, and messages coming downriver suggested that it wasn't due to folk being stopped more effectively. For now at least, Ameten sounded to be a less dangerous place to live. "And with Daril Leandra voting with us, very ostentatiously too?" she added.

Jeres pulled a face which mirrored Alyssa's own eye-roll. "Don't worry, I don't trust Leandra any more than you do."

"You trust Marcia Fereno though, and I wouldn't trust any of them."

"Marcia wants to deal with us fairly."

"Marcia will do what she thinks is best for her House, and for the city. Which might not be what I, or even what you, think is best for the city. But," Alyssa allowed, "she isn't driven by what's best for her personally, the way Leandra is, I'll give you that."

"She'll twist an advantage, for sure, but she deals fairly," Jeres said. She grinned. "She is very pregnant right now, poor woman. I remember that stage well."

"The 'oh well it could be tomorrow or it could be in a fortnight' bit?" Alyssa asked. "I remember my midwife saying that to me, all cheerful-like. Angels and demons, I was so ready to be done by then." They grinned at one another companionably.

"Right, well, talking of children, I'd best be off, I suppose." Alyssa levered herself out of her chair. "Promised my daughter we'd have dinner together, and she tells me I owe her a whole bargeload of bedtime stories."

"All the best." Jeres raised her glass in salute, and turned to answer someone who was coming towards the table, looking perturbed. Another reason Alyssa was just as glad not to be a representative.

She made her way out of the pub, pausing at the door to cast a glance backwards over her shoulder at the celebrating.

Well. They might not be there just yet, but this was something, wasn't it? This was moving forwards.

And about time too.

TWENTY-ONE

The good news was, the midwife had been right. Half an hour after the first twinge had started, Marcia certainly did know that this was different. The bad news was, she was in the middle of a Council meeting.

Athitol-Head had commented on her belly, with fake concern, when she walked in, and she'd been dismissive; she *really* wasn't keen to walk out in the middle telling everyone that it had started. And the contractions – they were definitely contractions – were a good fifteen minutes apart. She wasn't about to birth right now in the middle of the Chamber floor. She could just stay put, and pretend it wasn't happening.

Admittedly, she didn't pay a huge amount of attention. Thankfully there wasn't anything all that important or controversial today, just more of the interminable wrangling with the builders in the south-west; Piath was quite capable of dealing with that by themself. She got through the meeting without anyone commenting on how she looked, then walked slowly out of the Chamber, contemplating whether to walk home or get a litter. The midwife had told her it was good to stay on her feet, and she felt weirdly restless in between contractions.

The foyer was busy as she made her way through it, trying to avoid catching anyone's eye without being obvious about it. The Council was one member down at present; Hagadath had, to Marcia's surprise, lost their Guild election to a moderate, which in turn meant a by-election for their Council seat. It was hotly contested, and one of the candidates was on the more radical side; but even if Marcia did have an opinion (which she did) it wasn't something she could have anything official to do with as a House Heir-nearly-Head. The Guildwarden Council members were, of course, politicking busily; if she'd been less distracted she'd have tried to eavesdrop on some of the conversations she passed. Andreas wasn't here today; he'd sent his Heir, who was polite enough to her but – thankfully – not likely to hang around asking awkward questions or noticing that she looked odd. If Andreas were here he would *fuss*, which she very much didn't want.

"Marcia."

Fuck. Daril. Another thing she didn't need. She turned as he came up behind her.

"Marcia. I wanted a word."

The contraction hit just as he spoke – they were down to ten minutes apart now – and she wasn't as successful, this time, in hiding it. Daril's eyes widened, then dropped, inevitably, to her belly. "Marcia? Are you…"

"Shut up," she said through gritted teeth.

Daril, for a wonder, shut up. He did not, unfortunately, go away.

"Would you like me to arrange a litter?" he asked, thankfully quietly.

"I'm fine. The midwife said walking is good, when it starts," though Marcia, restless or not, was beginning to wonder if the midwife had ever done this herself. "What did you want to say?"

"Uh. In the circumstances, it can wait. I really think a litter…"

"Are you an expert in this, now?" Marcia asked, nastily, as she got through the doors and into the outside world. The fresh air was a huge relief. Walking was definitely the thing, the midwife had been right after all. "I am walking back to my House. Either say what you wanted to say, quickly, or leave me alone." Thank goodness it wasn't far. She ought to get home, now, before the next one hit; and they weren't *that* bad now she was getting used to them.

"I'll walk with you," Daril said.

Marcia rolled her eyes. "I'm fine. Since when have you given a shit about my welfare?"

Daril looked uncomfortable. "We might disagree, but

I'd rather see you safe home, in the circumstances."

This seemed unusual, from where Marcia was standing – or possibly just a reflection of the way people got very peculiar about pregnancy and babies – but she wasn't about to stand around arguing with him. "Fine. Come on, then. What did you want to talk about?"

"It can wait."

"If you're going to insist on walking with me, you can make yourself useful and distract me."

She set off down the road, and Daril lengthened his stride for a moment to catch her up. "Very well. If you insist. Honestly, Marcia, you are ridiculous sometimes."

"Not the *best* of starts."

"Fine. If you really want to talk about trade rates with Teren and whether your mother is a reliable negotiator, we can do."

It was surprisingly successful as a distraction for the few minutes it took to reach House Fereno. They didn't come to a conclusion, but she hadn't expected to; Daril wasn't exactly arguing at his most forcefully. Perhaps she should have pushed harder to get a concession out of him while she had the advantage.

"Here. I'll, uh." He hesitated. "Should I send a messenger for someone? Your midwife? Andreas? Your sorcerer?"

"I'll send myself," Marcia said. "I can manage, I assure you. But –" she sighed. "Thank you. I appreciate the thought."

"Good luck," Daril said, bowing, and stood aside for her to go in through the House gates.

Slowly, a step at a time, she got herself up to her own front door, and reached the hall as the next contraction hit. The footman looked at her and his eyes went wide.

"Paper," Marcia demanded once it had subsided, and leant over the hall table, scrawling a note to the midwife, to Reb, and finally, a slightly different one to Andreas; to tell him things were happening, but *not* to request his attendance.

She handed the notes to the footman, then hesitated,

and sighed. She wouldn't have admitted it to Daril for all the world, but she did in fact feel like she needed some support right now. Halfway through requesting the footman find Griya to help her up to her room, the front door opened and...

"Reb?" Marcia, foolishly, glanced down at the notes still in the footman's hand.

Reb scrubbed a hand over her face. "Beckett told me the baby was coming and I should get up here. But I can leave again if they were wrong."

"*Beckett* told you?"

"Yes, well, I was quite surprised too. I can leave."

"No! No. Definitely not. I was just going to message you...but if you don't want to be here..."

"I am happy to be here," Reb said, firmly. "You're my partner. I love you, and I'm here for you. Whatever you want." A little tentatively, she took Marcia's hand. "I don't want to run away again."

Marcia leant in and kissed her, very gently; and then another contraction took over – they were definitely coming faster now – and Reb's offering hand became support and lifeline all at once.

"You're sure," Reb said, after the contraction ended. "That you don't want...?"

"Please don't ask me again." She couldn't accept magical assistance, however much she might wish that she could, and she really didn't want to have to refuse it again. Reb nodded, and held her hand tighter.

Some time later the midwife arrived – forcing Marcia, very much against her will, to climb out of the bath Griya had filled – and agreed that yes, this was labour, and yes, it was likely to be a good while more, and did Marcia want to be on her own just now, or did she want someone with her? She eyed Reb, slightly suspiciously.

"I'll stay on hand, of course," she added. "But some people like to have me hold their hand and so on, even in the very early stages like this, and some want a partner or a friend, and some just like to be left alone. It's up to you."

"Reb's here," Marcia said, firmly. "I want her to stay."

It took a long time, and afterwards, all Marcia ever remembered was snapshots. The midwife coming and going at intervals, making encouraging noises. Pacing the room, infuriated that things were going so *slowly*. Throwing up. What felt like hours where she alternated between crouching over the chamber-pot with her insides cramping, and standing with her hands against the wall, head hanging down, regretting that she'd ever started this. Reb talked her through things, and held her, and sometimes was just there – and at one point fell asleep, which Marcia was extremely envious of but couldn't bring herself to wake her up. Also that was the point when she was spending a lot of time on the chamber-pot, and she didn't feel she needed Reb's assistance.

The midwife came back again and stayed. Everything became blurry. Marcia expressed the deep wish to stop all of this and come back to it in a couple of days time, which everyone in the room did her the courtesy of ignoring. Her body took over in unstoppable overwhelming convulsions that she assumed, in the moments of quiet in between them, must be what people talked about when they mentioned 'pushing'. Except that implied some kind of agency, which at that moment Marcia did not feel that she particularly had. She had a feeling that she might be shouting. She didn't really care. She just wanted it to be over.

And then, there was a baby. Small, and red, and covered in white flecks, which surprised Marcia, but the midwife didn't seem to think anything of it. She was crying, perhaps at the indignity of emerging into the world.

"Hush now, hush now," Marcia whispered, holding the baby to her breast, looking at the tiny open mouth, and the strange-coloured eyes. "Hush now, little one. Hello. Hello."

She became aware that there was a lot of blood around, but apparently this too was normal; or at least, neither Reb nor the midwife seemed disturbed.

"You'd need a lot more than this to worry about it," the midwife said comfortably, and wrapped Marcia and the baby in more blankets, before engaging in the slightly undignified process of dealing with the afterbirth, and then confirming that Marcia hadn't damaged herself in the process of getting the baby out.

Marcia, once cleaned up and transferred into bed, leant against Reb, and looked down at the baby. She'd had some milk, and now she'd fallen asleep, or at least her eyes were closed.

There were a great many things Marcia needed to think about. Teren trade. Independence. The Lower Council, and how to make it work better with the Marekhill Council. Magic, and Reb, and how Marek worked.

But right now she was here, and she had a baby, and she was safe.

"Congratulations," Reb said, softly, and kissed the top of her head.

☺ ☺

It was Tait who set the meeting up; booked a private room in the usual infusion-salon near the Old Bridge, told both Marcia and Cato to be there. Marcia hadn't pushed back all that hard. She didn't know how much effort Tait was putting in to get Cato there. Assuming he did, in fact, show up. It wasn't normally that much effort for *her* to get there, but she wasn't exactly walking far just yet, a bare week after Ada's birth; getting down the stairs left her uncomfortable enough. But this was worth it. She'd taken a litter down, leaving Ada at home with the child-nurse. She was surprised at how odd it felt to know she was this far away from her. She wouldn't be able to stay too long; Ada would need feeding.

Cato was late, of course. She'd expected that. Habits of a lifetime, and so on. She couldn't quite settle into a book, this time, even though she'd brought one with her.

"Hello." Cato stepped through the door, shoulders tense. His red-brown hair was longer than he usually wore it, falling into his eyes. They looked awkwardly at one another, and then he jerked his chin up slightly, and slouched himself into the other chair. "Congratulations. On the baby."

Marcia nodded. "Thank you. Her name's Ada, though we haven't had the ceremony yet. She's back at home." She gestured, Hillwards. And then regretted it. Obviously the baby was at home. She wasn't *here*, was she?

There was another silence. "Uh. Infusion?"

"Is it too early for wine?" Cato sighed, and reached to pour himself a cup of the liquorice. He liked liquorice. They both did.

"You..." Marcia was not going to be the more awkward one here. She was not. "You did a good job. With the demons."

"Thanks. You did a good job. With the... politicking."

"Yes, well. Recognition we might have," though she wasn't about to mention Madeleine's part in that, not here and now, "but all the internal stuff, the lower city and that...I don't know where we go from here."

Cato shrugged. "Sometimes shaking things up a bit is all you can do. That's something, for now. And they've got those representatives. Even if they don't have votes." His eyebrow flicked upwards. "Not really my thing," he added, overly casual.

Neither of them spoke for a few excruciating moments. Cato was flipping a silver spoon over his knuckles and back, staring intently down at it.

"They were *demons*, Cato," Marcia burst out. "I thought you were going to die."

"Right." Cato shifted warily, still staring down at his hands. "And you'd have missed me?" He was trying for his don't-care tone, but hadn't quite hit it. She could hear the fragile note.

"Of course I would, you idiot. You're my *brother*."

Cato looked up, and met her eyes, and then she leant over towards him, and he towards her, and they met in the middle for an awkward but heartfelt hug.

"I shouldn't have asked you," Marcia said, into Cato's

neck. "I'm sorry." It felt easier to say that, now, than it had done a few days ago.

"I'm not sorry I said no," Cato said. "But I shouldn't have had such a go at you about it. Or at Tait." He sat back a bit and winced. "I apologised to them already."

"I thought you probably had, what with them making all the effort to set this up."

Cato's eyes widened. "They did? They told me *you* did. The scheming arse." His voice was appreciative.

Marcia laughed, and the next thing felt easier to say. "I understand now. I think. Why you wouldn't help."

Cato sighed, and looked back down at the spoon, flipping it more slowly now. "I always wanted you to choose me, you know. Over her. When I left." His voice was soft, and his shoulders were up around his ears again.

"I always wanted you to choose me," Marcia said; the thing she'd never said before. The thing neither of them had ever talked about. "Me, the Hill, us. Over magic. I wanted you to *stay*. You'd have been better than me, at all of this. I used to think we'd do it together, whichever of us was officially Heir or Head. Or even – do you remember when we were small and we used to plan being the first House to have a shared Headship?" There was a lump in her throat that she wished wasn't there. It was such a long time ago, now, and she'd given that up, she had, but...

But.

"I couldn't stay," Cato said. His voice ached, but she understood it was for her, not for anything else he missed.

Marcia sighed. "I understand that now. I mean, not just now. I understood it not that long after. I just – I missed you. I miss you, always, even after I realised eventually you'd made the right decision for you, even if I didn't like it. Even if you sometimes didn't seem that happy with it." She looked at him. "You're happier now, you know. Than a few years ago."

"Yeah," Cato said. "I suppose I am." He looked up and held her gaze. "What about you, though? You stayed. And I understand why. But. Are you happy? Really?"

Marcia sighed. "Yes. I've made my decisions, and I'm happy with them."

Cato made a sucking noise through his teeth. "That's not actually quite the same thing, you know."

"Yes, well. I suppose – I don't always know," Marcia said, letting herself be brutally honest for once. "But I've made all those decisions. They're done. And there's Ada now, and...well. I'm Heir." Head soon; she and Madeleine had discussed it by letter, now Madeleine would definitely be staying in Ameten. "So. It is what it is, and I am where I am. Ada is wonderful." Hard work, even with the child-nurse to help, and Andreas there regularly, and Marcia could already wish babies understood *sleep*, and she was ruefully aware she had a good long while of that, and then *another* baby she was contracted to, which she was not thinking of just now; but still wonderful. "The House is doing well. I'm comfortable. I'm making Marek better than it was before. I'm content here, Cato. I didn't want to break out." She never had. That was Cato, not her. She wanted change, had done even when she was sixteen and making bad decisions with Daril; but she didn't want out.

"Fair enough," Cato said after a long moment. "I suppose we both are where we are. Where we've chosen to be. Fair enough. Just – if you ever change your mind. I'll break you out, no bother." He smiled at her, half-joking. Half not.

"Thanks," Marcia said drily, and meant it. Even if she'd never take him up on it.

Maybe Cato was her get-out clause. Maybe he always had been.

The one of them who got to break out.

"Oh, though I should tell you, I don't care what arrangements you've made with the Council and magic and all, I'm still never coming up on the Hill," Cato added. He made it sound amusing, like a jest or a personality quirk. Marcia knew he meant it, right down to the bone.

"Then I guess I'll have to bring Ada down here to see

you," she said cheerfully. "But possibly not to your horrible rooms."

They smiled at one another, and affection bubbled up, overwhelming, inside her, threatening tears. She'd been emotional, this week.

"I suppose," Cato said thoughtfully. "I am well able to carry off the role of the disreputable uncle." He glanced sideways at her under his lashes. "Make her aware that there's other options than Marekhill." There was a challenge there.

"Yes," Marcia agreed. "You should do that. But I rather hope Marekhill might not be quite how it is, by the time she's grown up enough to think about that."

"Yeah, well, aren't you the optimist." Cato rolled his eyes.

"But it's good to have options."

"And talking of options, I really don't think it's too early for a glass of wine, now I come to think about the matter seriously. I know you can't *much*, and I'm guessing you can't stay away from Ada all that long, but perhaps, a small one?"

"Oh, go on," she said, and it was Cato's turn, this time, to lean across and give her a hug, slightly awkward, but heartfelt.

"All right then. I'm sure there's a whole lot of gossip to catch up on."

"Did Reb tell you," Marcia began, grinning slyly over at him, "that she received her first official Marekhill evening invite yesterday?"

"She did *not*. So? Is she going?"

Marcia pulled a comical face. "I didn't know she even *knew* words that bad! Not this time, no. But we'll see." If Marekhill was accepting magic – sort of – then it was going to end up being social currency in some way. It might even get as far as Cato himself, come to that, although she wasn't going to mention that. Nor the fact that Madeleine might have spoken in favour of allowing Reb into the Chamber, but she'd neatly avoided the issue of having to be in the same room socially as her daughter's sorcerer lover by going to Ameten.

She'd be back to meet Ada, soon, though. She'd promised; and she had to hand over the Headship. And Marcia would have to find some sort of solution then, she supposed. Not something to discuss with Cato; nor indeed the fact that Madeleine seemed quite happy to give up the House now she had something else to do – and somewhere else to be. She did seem really quite close to Grainne, the new Archion, from her letters. "How's Tait?" she asked, instead.

Cato looked triumphant. "Well, we've finally worked out what their best magic is. Healing. Which is right and proper for someone as kind as them, though it took them a while to come to terms with the idea that it's effectively a way of using their affinity with blood."

"Affinity with blood?" Marcia said, wrinkling her nose.

"Oh, don't you start. Surgeons cut into people and we think that's perfectly fine. It makes Tait the strongest healer Marek's known in decades, and that seems like a fair enough trade."

"Fine, fine!" Marcia said, raising her hands in surrender. "I can't imagine Tait doing anything unpleasant with it, after all."

"Let me tell you, healing is *deeply* unpleasant in many ways. But no. You're not wrong." Cato's face was soft and fond, in a way that made Marcia's heart feel good. Then he leant forward, taking a slug of his wine. "Now. *Do* tell me how Athitol-Head has been taking things."

"Oh, you'll enjoy this," Marcia said with relish, and settled in, with a sigh of relief, to catch up with her brother.

TWENTY-TWO

Dawn would have been uncomfortably early to get up, except that Ada was two weeks old and so all times were much of a muchness to Marcia.

What did bother her was that Madeleine wasn't here – although she'd known that was likely when Madeleine went back to Ameten, and certainly when she chose to stay there and become ambassador. She'd be back to meet Ada and invest Marcia as Head in another two weeks, but they couldn't just wait the naming ceremony until then.

And Cato wasn't here. Cousin Cara was the only representative from House Fereno other than Marcia herself, and fond though Marcia was of her, in a habitual sort of way, she wasn't the relative Marcia would have chosen to carry the candle.

She had invited Cato. He'd declined. She hadn't expected otherwise – he'd been very clear on the matter, that day in the infusion-salon – but...well. She wished he was here. Even if it would have scandalised the House Tigero contingent. She'd very briefly considered moving the ceremony down to somewhere in Marek Square (would they let her use one of the Guildhall rooms?) but had given up when she realised how much effort it would take to find somewhere suitable, the level of explaining she'd need to do, and the fact that there was a fighting chance that Cato still wouldn't be willing to set foot in a room full of Marekhill types. It was what it was, and she'd been living with the consequences of Cato's ability and Madeleine's decision about it for long enough now to be used to it.

Half an hour before dawn, she made her way downstairs, wincing slightly at the still-present dragging soreness between her legs (Eveline, the child-nurse,

317

assured her that was perfectly normal and it was all healing up fine). Eveline followed with the baby, swaddled in miles of the Broderers' best lace, worn by Marcia and Cato – they'd had to make it into two, and now back into one for Ada – and Madeleine, and generations of babies before. She wasn't surprised to see Reb waiting in the hallway. She was a lot more surprised to see Tait standing next to Reb, looking awkward.

"Couldn't convince Cato," Reb said, coming forward to give Marcia a hug. "Thought I'd try again, this morning."

"This morning? Bet he loved that." Marcia hugged Reb back, and kissed her cheek.

"I couldn't either," Tait said. "But he…well. I said I'd come, and he didn't stop me. I thought. On his behalf. Sort of." Tait looked deeply uncomfortable.

"They mean, 'there was a flaming row'," Reb said into her ear. "But I think Cato was pleased, in the end, that Tait insisted."

"Thank you for coming," Marcia said, gratefully, giving Tait a half-bow. "And please tell Cato that…that I understand." She did. And she was glad to hear that Tait was willing to give as good as they got, flaming-row-wise. Cato needed someone who stood up to him.

She glanced up at the clock. "Andreas and the Tigero people will be here soon. And I would quite like to sit down…"

The ceremony would be conducted outside, but they were gathering first in the main reception room. Marcia, gratefully, made her way to the blue couch and sat down with a sigh of relief. She was doing better than last week, and she *felt* better in herself, but walking or standing up for very long was still uncomfortable.

"If there's anything I need to do…" Tait said, shifting anxiously from foot to foot.

Marcia shook her head. "You're just observing. Don't worry."

A clatter in the hallway, and a murmur of voices; a moment later Andreas, his grandmother Leanne, and his cousin Jamara, currently Tigero-Heir, came into the room, all as formally dressed as Marcia was. Marcia greeted them all, then gestured to Reb and Tait.

"Ser Reb, and Ser Tait. Ser Reb is of the Sorcerer's Group, and Tait her apprentice." After that wretched trial, of course, everyone knew that Marcia and Reb were involved. She wasn't about to go any further into the matter, but Reb was her partner; the Council had decided there was no case to answer, and Marcia was no longer willing to hide her. Andreas knew that Reb would be there, and he knew what she'd asked Reb to do.

Jamara's eyebrows went up, but she didn't say anything, just gave a polite half-bow. Leanne smiled, polite and cold, as Reb nodded to her and Tait, after an anxious look, copied the nod.

"Delighted to meet you, Ser Reb, Ser Tait," Leanne said, in tones that suggested that she wasn't the slightest bit delighted. Ruefully, Marcia wondered just how much she had been marked down by, now, as a mother to House Tigero's future Heir – assuming a second baby came along in due course – compared to how Leanne had considered her when the child-contract was first signed. Still, there wasn't much Leanne could do about it now, was there? And Jamara, presumably, cared much less either way. Cousin Cara, at least, they both knew, and Cousin Cara was good at managing social situations; she moved over to Leanne to start the polite chit-chat.

Gil and Nisha arrived shortly after that; the naming-ceremony wasn't a large gathering, traditionally, but one could invite allies as well as family, and Marcia had wanted them there.

"Greetings, and congratulations," Gil said, bowing to her, to Ada, and to Andreas.

"She's adorable, Marcia," Nisha said warmly, putting out a finger to stroke the baby's head. "Congratulations to all of you."

The light outside was increasing as dawn grew closer, and Marcia glanced at the clock, levered herself up, and led them all out into the garden at the back of the house, where you could see out to the east. The sun still wasn't quite up, but there was a glow on the horizon over the sea. The candles were arranged on a little table, with two tapers next to them and a glowing brazier by the table. A chair was placed behind the table, for Marcia; once she'd sat and Eveline had handed her the baby and stood back, everyone else grouped themselves around her. Tait, looking solemn, stood just behind Reb's shoulder.

The horizon was unclouded; that was a good omen. They could get the moment exactly right. Andreas came to stand next to her, and handed out the tapers and the candles, one each to Leanne and to Cara.

The sun emerged above the horizon, blazing out over the swamps, shining off the ribbon of the river.

"Welcome the light," Andreas said.

Leanne and Cara both lit their tapers from the brazier, carefully lit a candle each, then passed them to Andreas and Marcia; Cara to Marcia, Leanne to Andreas.

"Welcome to the light, Ada," Marcia said, to the baby in her arms.

"Welcome to the light, Ada," Andreas echoed, laying a hand on Ada's head.

Marcia set her candle down on the table, and Andreas set his down next to it. His shoulders twitched slightly. He knew what was happening next, and he'd agreed, but that didn't mean he was entirely *happy* about it.

Reb stepped forward, and there was a murmur from the spectators, but no one else moved. Marcia had counted on that; the ceremony wasn't over yet.

"The cityangel welcomes you to the light," Reb said, and held out a hand. The two candles blazed high for a long moment, higher than could be explained by a simple gust of wind. Ada, not even looking at them – not that she could see much further than a couple of feet at her age – made a cooing noise. The candles died down; Reb nodded to Marcia and stepped back.

Andreas, lips pressed slightly tight, put his hand back on Ada's head. "We all welcome you, Ada, to the light, to your families, to the city," he said.

"To the light, to your families, to the city," everyone else echoed, and Marcia leant forwards to blow the candles out. Andreas looked over at her and smiled. Slightly rueful, but a smile.

That was that, then, done. Cousin Cara began to lead Leanne and Jamara back into the house.

"Thank you," Andreas said to Reb. "On my daughter's behalf." He paused. "I think."

"I did wonder if Beckett would show up," Marcia said.

Andreas looked horrified.

Reb shrugged. "I asked them not to. I didn't think…"

"Probably for the best, yes," Marcia agreed, voice dry. Reb put a hand under her elbow and helped her up.

Andreas gestured Eveline back as he came forwards to take Ada. "It's fine, I'll carry her."

"We both know," Marcia said, as she'd said to him the day before, "the way the Council thinks about magic and sorcerers and all the rest of it needs to change. We need to act, not just to talk about it."

"And one House-spawn's naming-ceremony is acting?" He lifted Ada up to rest her head on his shoulder.

Marcia shrugged. "It's a start."

Leaning slightly on Reb, she made her way across the grass. "There'll be infusions, now, and pastries. Half an hour more before you can leave," she said to Reb and Tait. "Apologies in advance for anything Leanne says."

"I'm sure I'll cope," Reb said.

"I'll tell Cato about it all," Tait said, softly, smiling tentatively at her.

"Take him a pastry," Marcia recommended. She still wanted to have had her brother here. And her mother. She wanted a lot of things. But Ada had a name, and she had the blessing of the cityangel, and Marcia was bringing Marekhill kicking and screaming towards modernity. And there was an infusion and a pastry waiting for her. It could be worse.

"Are you sure about this?" Cato asked, looking intently at Jonas.

The two of them, with Tait, were standing on the docks, surrounded by people shifting bales onto the *Heart's Dragon*. Jonas could tell just by looking that the ship was nearly full. Which was just as well, as the tide was all the way in and about to turn. Time to go.

"I'm sure," Jonas said. He shifted the bag on his shoulder. "I know I'm not done apprenticing here."

"Indeed you are not," Cato agreed, eyebrow twitching, but his tone was fond.

"But – I think I need to find out a bit more about magic, different sorts of magic. Sea-magic, maybe." He glanced over his shoulder at the *Heart's Dragon*.

"I'm amazed they're willing to take you." Cato shifted his weight to look up at the ship behind Jonas. "Didn't think your lot liked magic."

"They don't," Jonas agreed. "But Captain Dirin is – interested, in lots of things. And the crew liked the idea of not going down in the next sea-spout or unseasonal storm that comes along. Which hopefully there'll be less of now, of course, now Teren has stopped what they were doing. But still, it happens sometimes. So they're willing to take the risk in exchange for maybe getting the elementals to consider us."

It helped that he was t'Riseri, there was no denying that. And he had the strong feeling that Captain Dirin had done a certain amount of fast talking to convince the crew. He'd need to pull his weight to be accepted. But he could do that; he knew he could.

The elementals were still likely to be more troublesome than before, even though Cato and Reb had been communicating with the Archion and the Academy about Teren magic and its impact on the other plane. Jonas wasn't sure how well that was going. From what he'd gathered from Cato, the current Archion seemed less enthusiastic about demon-magic than the previous one had been, but the Academy were pushing back. For now, Yorick had informed Cato that the return of the demons

Cato had freed had been greatly appreciated, and that there had been no new disappearances in recent days. But that was Reb and Cato's problem to pursue, not Jonas'.

To be back on a *ship*, finally, without having to hide his magic...It felt like his lungs were expanding properly for the first time in years.

"Well," Cato said. "Good luck. And, you know, you're always welcome back here. Should you wish to learn a bit more Marek magic, *which* I would highly recommend. Learning is always useful. On which note, I'm counting on you reporting in about what you learn of the elementals, next time the ship's through here."

"Of course," Jonas agreed. He held out both hands, for a double handshake, and Cato reciprocated. "Thank you. For everything."

"Good luck," Tait said, quietly, stepping forward to offer, slightly tentatively, the same handshake.

Jonas was glad Tait had finally found a way of working Marek-magic, even if it was slightly unusual. Reb had been initially uncertain, given that it was blood magic of a *sort*, after all. But Cato had argued strongly for Tait – Jonas had been there, and there had been a *lot* of swearing – and Beckett had approved, when asked directly. Reb had finally thrown her hands in the air and said *fine, but with extensive supervision*, which worked for everyone. Tait was working now with both Reb and a non-magical healer, and seemed very happy, if still nervous.

Asa came running barefoot up the dock, bag banging against their back. "Sorry! Sorry. I got caught by Tam. He wants to come say goodbye, but his message is running long...anyway, he's sent word via me, but I'll tell you on the ship." They nodded shyly at Cato and Tait.

"Amazed you're getting them to let someone not Salinas on board," Cato said.

"I'm a passenger," Asa said. "Not crew. The captain was very clear about that." They pulled a face. "On the one hand, I quite like the idea of just sitting around. On the other hand, might be tough to keep my hands off the ropes in a storm."

"Time to board!" Xanthe called from the rail.

"Good luck to you both, then," Cato said. "I won't wait to wave you off. Can't bear hanging around." He turned and walked away; Tait nodded at Jonas then followed.

It would have been rude – it was rude, a bit – but it was also Cato, and Jonas understood Cato now, the way he hadn't when they first met.

He looked at Asa. "Are you sure?"

"I'm sure," Asa said. "It'll be fun, to see out to the north. All the way to the Northern Isles!" They grinned. "Come on. Let's go."

The two of them went up the gangplank. "About time," Xanthe said, mock-sternly, and hauled the plank in after them. "Go see the captain, then I'll show you where to stow your things. Cabin to yourselves, you two get! Very fancy!"

Which was partly an honour, and partly a reflection of the fact that no one wanted to share a berth with the sorcerer. Well. He was doing as much as he could, just being aboard. That was enough.

Captain Dirin was on the quarter-deck, towards the stern, leaning on the rail and watching everything that was going on to prepare the ship for sail. Everyone was moving neatly and without waste; this was a good crew, Jonas could tell.

"Afternoon," he said, nodding at them. "Welcome aboard."

"Thank you," Jonas said, meaning a lot of things with it.

"Well," Dirin said, hearing all the things he wasn't quite saying. "It'll be interesting, won't it?" He nodded towards the back rail. "You can stay there, if you like, while we get underway."

He leaned over the rail and called something down to one of the crew.

Jonas and Asa crowded back against the rail, and watched the last preparations for departure. Then, all of a sudden, the ropes were off, front and aft, and the sails caught the breeze, and the ship was on the move.

Away from Marek. Out into the sea.

"Jonas! Asa!" They turned to see Tam on the dock, jumping and waving at them. "Good luck! Go safe!"

"Go safe!" they called back, waving back to him. "See you when we're next in!"

Marek slid past them, the docks to port, the rise of Marekhill to starboard. Jonas saw House Fereno, at the turn of the top street, and the tiny upright figure of the statue on the top of Marekhill Park. Then they were past that, too, the fishing village sliding by to port, and out into the Oval Sea proper. Another sail was pulled into place, the wind caught it, and the ship surged forwards. Asa's hand found Jonas' hand.

"It'll be interesting," Jonas said, smiling across at them.

"It will that," Asa agreed; and they both looked forward, out to sea, and let Marek drop away behind them.

* * *

THE END

* * *

AUTHOR'S NOTE

Writing a book is at various times a great deal of fun and also a great deal of flailing, self-doubt, and swearing. Writing a series means all of the above repeatedly, whilst you attempt to remember which corners you already wrote yourself into. I encourage you to see any apparent continuity errors as a reflection of the fact that the real world is a strange and occasionally discontinuous place, so why shouldn't fictional worlds be as well?

Thank you to my delightful beta readers for this final book, Laura Shapiro, Phoenix Alexander, maia, and doop, all of whom were encouraging and helpful (even when telling me things I sort of knew already but didn't want to hear like "you need to rewrite this part"). Thank you too (so much!) to anyone who has ever said that they enjoyed reading one of the books, or that they were looking forward to the next one. Virginia Preston in particular made enthusiastic noises at me at a point when I was feeling particularly low about editing, which was incredibly cheering. Kaytie, Eden, Sara, Rae, and the rest of the 8am Zoom crew kept me going through the final line edit stages; and folks on the writer-Slack and -Discord always have great insights.

It has been an absolute pleasure to work with Pete and Alison at Elsewhen, and with Sofia who does outstanding editing work and has been hugely helpful with the whole series. Tony Alcock has created wonderful covers for all four of the Marek books, for which I feel both lucky and grateful.

Thank you to my parents for being supportive (especially to my Dad who doesn't read much but does read my books!).

Thank you to Pete, doop, and Leon for letting me grumble at them from time to time; especially Leon for excellent hugs and many encouraging words like "You can do it, Juliet!". Our dog Sidney also helpfully supervised a certain amount of the writing process by lying flat out on the floor of my room and snoring at me; irreplacable skills right there.

Juliet Kemp
London, 2022

Elsewhen Press

delivering outstanding new talents in speculative fiction

Visit the Elsewhen Press website at elsewhen.press for the latest information on all of our titles, authors and events; to read our blog; find out where to buy our books and ebooks; or to place an order.

Sign up for the Elsewhen Press InFlight Newsletter at elsewhen.press/newsletter

BY JULIET KEMP

THE MAREK SERIES BY JULIET KEMP

1: THE DEEP AND SHINING DARK

A Locus Recommended Read in 2018

"A rich and memorable tale of political ambition, family and magic, set in an imagined city that feels as vibrant as the characters inhabiting it."   **Aliette de Bodard**
Nebula-award winning author of *The Tea Master and the Detective*

You know something's wrong when the cityangel turns up at your door
An agreement 300 years ago, between an angel and Marek's founding fathers, protects magic and political stability within the city. A recent plague wiped out most of the city's sorcerers. Reb, one of the survivors, realises that someone has deposed the cityangel without replacing it. Marcia, Heir to House Fereno, stumbles across that same truth. But it is just one part of a much more ambitious plan to seize control of Marek.

Meanwhile, city Council members connive and conspire, manipulated in a dangerous political game that threatens the peace and security of all the states around the Oval Sea. Reb, Marcia, the deposed cityangel, and Jonas, a Salina messenger, must work together to stop the impending disaster. They must discover who is behind it, and whom they can really trust.

ISBN: 9781911409342 (epub, kindle) / 9781911409243 (272pp paperback)
Visit bit.ly/DeepShiningDark

2: SHADOW AND STORM

"never short on adventure and intrigue... the characters are real, full of depth, and richly drawn, and you'll wish you had even more time with them by book's end. A fantastic read."   **Rivers Solomon**
Author of *An Unkindness of Ghosts*, Lambda, Tiptree and Locus finalist
Never trust a demon... or a Teren politician
The new Teren Lord Lieutenant has an agenda. A young Teren magician being sought by an unleashed demon, believes their only hope may be to escape to Marek where the cityangel can keep the demon at bay. Once again Reb, Cato, Jonas and Beckett must deal with a magical problem, while Marcia tackles a serious political challenge to Marek's future.

ISBN: 9781911409595 (epub, kindle) / 9781911409496 (336pp paperback)
Visit bit.ly/ShadowAndStorm

3: THE RISING FLOOD

"Fantasy politics with real nuance ... a fantastic read"   **Malka Older**
Author of the *Centenal Cycle* trilogy, Hugo Award Finalist
Hope alone cannot withstand a rising flood
A darkness writhes in the heart of Teren, unleashing demons on dissenters. Marek's five sorcerers with the cityangel can expel a single demon, but Teren has many. Storms rampage across the Oval Sea. Menaced by the distant capital, dissension from within, and even nature itself – will the rising flood lift all boats? Or will they be capsized?

ISBN: 9781911409984 (epub, kindle) / 9781911409885 (392pp paperback)
Visit bit.ly/TheRisingFlood

The Vanished Mage

Penelope Hill and J. A. Mortimore

A vanished mage…
A missing diamond…
The game is afoot.

"From Broderick, Prince of Asconar, Earl of Carlshore and Thorn, Duke of Wicksborough, Baron of Highbury and Warden of Dershanmoor, to My Lady Parisan, King's Investigator, greetings. It has been brought to my attention that a certain Reinwald, Master Historian, noted Archmagus and tutor to our court in this city of Nemithia, has this day failed to report to the duties awaiting him. I do ask you, as my father's most loyal servant, to seek the cause of this laxity and bring word of the mage to me, so that my concerns as to his safety be allayed."

The herald delivered the message word-perfect to The Lady Parisan, Baroness of Orandy, Knight of the Diamond Circle and Sworn Paladin to Our Lady of the Sighs. Parisan's companion, Foorourow Miar Raar Ramoura, Prince of Ilsfacar, (Foo to his friends) thought it a rather mundane assignment, but nevertheless together they ventured to the Archmagus' imposing home to seek him. It turned out to be the start of an adventure to solve a mystery wrapped in an enigma bound by a conundrum and secured by a puzzle. All because of a missing diamond with a solar system at its core.

Authors Penelope Hill and J. A. Mortimore have effortlessly melded a Holmesian investigative duo, a richly detailed city where they encounter both nobility and seedier denizens, swashbuckling action, and magic that is palpable and, at times, awesome.

ISBN: 9781915304186 (epub, kindle) / 97819153041087 (212pp paperback)

Visit bit.ly/TheVanishedMage

The Avatars of Ruin
Tej Turner

Book 1: Bloodsworn

"Classic epic fantasy. I enjoyed it enormously"
– Anna Smith Spark
"a stunning introduction to a new fantasy world"
– Christopher G Nuttall

It has been twelve years since the war between the nations of Sharma and Gavendara. The villagers of Jalard live a bucolic existence, nestled within the hills of western Sharma, far from the warzone. They have little contact with the outside world, apart from once a year when Academy representatives choose two of them to be taken away to the institute in the capital. To be Chosen is considered a great honour… of which most of Jalard's children dream. But this year, their announcement is so shocking it causes friction between villagers, and some begin to suspect that all is not what it seems. Where are they taking the Chosen, and why? Some intend to find out, but what they discover will change their lives forever and set them on a long and bloody path to seek vengeance…

ISBN: 9781911409779 (epub, kindle) / 9781911409670 (432pp paperback)
Visit bit.ly/Bloodsworn

Book 2: Blood Legacy

The ragtag group from Jalard have finally reached Shemet, Sharma's capital city. Scarred and bereft, they bring a grim tale of what happened to their village, and a warning about the threat to all humanity. Some expect sanctuary within the Synod to mean an end to their hardships, but their hopes are soon dashed. Sharma's ruling class are caught within their own inner turmoil. Jaedin senses moles within their ranks, but his call to crisis falls mostly on deaf ears, and some seek to thwart him when he tries to hunt the infiltrators down.

Meanwhile, Gavendara is mustering its forces. With ritualistically augmented soldiers, their mutant army is like nothing the world has ever seen.

The Zakaras are coming. And Sharma's only hope of stopping them is if it can unite its people in time.

ISBN: 9781911409991 (epub, kindle) / 9781911409892 (474pp paperback)
Visit bit.ly/Blood-Legacy

HARPAN'S WORLDS:
WORLDS APART

TERRY JACKMAN

If Harp could wish, he'd be invisible.

Orphaned as a child, failed by a broken system and raised on a struggling colony world, Harp's isolated existence turns upside down when his rancher boss hands him into military service in lieu of the taxes he cannot pay. Since Harp has spent his whole life being regarded with suspicion, and treated as less, why would he expect his latest environment to be any different? Except it is, so is it any wonder he decides to hide the 'quirks' that set him even more apart?

Space opera with a paranormal twist, Terry Jackman's novel explores prejudice, corruption, and the value of true friendship.

Terry Jackman is a mild-mannered married lady who lives in a quiet corner of the northwest of England, a little south of Manchester. Well, that's one version.

The other one may be a surprise to those who only know the first. [She doesn't necessarily tell everything.] Apart from once being the most qualified professional picture framer in the world, which accounted for over ten years of articles, guest appearances, seminars, study guides and exam papers both written and marked, she chaired a national committee for the Fine Art Trade Guild, and read 'slush' for the *Albedo One* SF magazine in Ireland. Currently she is the coordinator of all the British Science Fiction Association's writers' groups, called Orbits, and a freelance editor.

ISBN: 9781915304179 (epub, kindle) / 97819153041070 (320pp paperback)

Visit bit.ly/HarpansWorldsWorldsApart

ABOUT JULIET KEMP

Juliet Kemp lives by the river in London, with their partners, child, dog, and too many fountain pens. They have had stories published in several anthologies and online magazines. Their employment history variously includes working as a cycle instructor, sysadmin, life model, researcher, permaculture designer, and journalist. When not writing or parenting, Juliet goes climbing, knits, reads way too much, and drinks a lot of tea.